"This is the Fre

*"We are the tool of [...]
Senate. We are our [...]
now take that sky back to ourselves, in arms with those who
know what freedom is worth, and who will help us be slaves
no more. Live or die, we have nothing more to say to you,
tools in the hands of tyrants!"*

The announcement from the Grand Fleet ships persisted
only a few moments longer, then simply broke off, in mid-
playback, as if whoever had been playing the recording
simply could not believe the response. Behind Ael, Aidoann
listened to the silence that followed, and let go a soft hiss of
anguish. *"Khre'Riov,"* she said. "If this doesn't work, all
those cities, all those many people—"

Ael sat silent and watched the curves of the starships'
courses become more acute as they neared the planet.

"Khre'Riov, can we not stop it? Let us stop it!" Aidoann
whispered. "If we move quickly enough, we could seed the
star—or have tr'Mahan give the order."

Ael shook her head. "I will not," she said, her voice terribly steady, far more so than her heart. "You heard Courhig.
You heard our kinswoman down there. The Art3eleirhin
have made their preparations. They know how this battle
must unfold, for their freedom's sake. Their choice is made.
Now we must honor their intention, or condemn them to the
loss of their own honor, forever."

"But Ael—!"

She would not answer.

STAR TREK®

THE EMPTY CHAIR

A *RIHANNSU* NOVEL BY

DIANE DUANE

**BASED ON *STAR TREK*
CREATED BY GENE RODDENBERRY**

POCKET BOOKS
New York London Toronto Sydney ch'Havran

The sale of this book without its cover is unauthorized. If you purcha
this book without a cover, you should be aware that it was reported
the publisher as "unsold and destroyed." Neither the author nor th
publisher has received payment for the sale of this "stripped book."

This book is a work of fiction. Names, characters, places, and incidents
are products of the author's imagination or are used fictitiously. Any
resemblance to actual events or locales or persons, living or dead,
is entirely coincidental.

An *Original* Publication of POCKET BOOKS

POCKET BOOKS, a division of Simon & Schuster, Inc.
1230 Avenue of the Americas, New York, NY 10020

Copyright © 2006 by CBS Studios Inc. All Rights Reserved.
STAR TREK and related marks are trademarks of CBS Studios Inc.

CBS and the CBS EYE logo are
trademarks of CBS Broadcasting Inc.
All Rights Reserved.

This book is published by Pocket Books, a division of Simon & Schuster,
Inc., under exclusive license from CBS Studios Inc.

All rights reserved, including the right to reproduce this book or portions
thereof in any form whatsoever. For information address Pocket Books,
1230 Avenue of the Americas, New York, NY 10020

ISBN-13: 978-1-4165-0891-5
ISBN-10:   1-4165-0891-0

This Pocket Books paperback edition December 2006

10 9 8 7 6 5 4 3 2 1

POCKET and colophon are registered trademarks of Simon & Schuster, Inc.

Cover art by Tom Hallman

Manufactured in the United States of America

For information regarding special discounts for bulk purchases,
please contact Simon & Schuster Special Sales at 1-800-456-6798
or business@simonandschuster.com.

In memory of DeForest Kelley
. . . now immortal in the realm of archetype,
remembering that long-ago sore throat

of James Doohan
. . . revealed during an Everglades boat ride
as a possible relative

and of Mark Lenard
. . . first of all the Romulans,
recalling a long train journey down to London
and a masterful analysis of the politics of rebellion

ACKNOWLEDGMENTS

A work that stretches over such a long period of time always carries in its train a great number of people who need to be thanked for their help. Some of them would be:

The noble and excellent Dorothy (D.C.) Fontana, without whom there would be no Romulans.

The staff of the Fels Planetarium in Philadelphia, who helped me sort out where (at that point) it seemed most likely that the Romulan Star Empire might lie.

My former housemates at "SMOF Central" (or as it was called by some, "The House of Dangerously Single Women") in Bala Cynwyd, Pennsylvania: Sara (then) Paul, Wilma (then) Fisher, and Teresa (then) Renner, all of whom watched the first installment of this series being written, and didn't pull me away from the work to make me shovel the driveway more often than absolutely necessary.

My long-suffering agent, Don Maass, who—knowing that his client has a long-term and incorrigible soft spot for this particular patch of the genre—simply rolls his eyes in a genteel and forgiving kind of way every time he hears me say the words "Star Trek."

All my *Star Trek* novel editors, all of them endlessly patient with me—from Dave Stern and Kevin Ryan, on through John Ordover, right on down to Marco Palmieri and Keith DeCandido, not forgetting, of course, the memorable Mimi Panitch, the original inspiration for Ael.

And last but never, ever least, Peter, who "hot-bunked" the work on *The Romulan Way* with me on what was supposed to be our honeymoon—a whole book written "chapter about" in a shade more than two weeks—and thereby proved in his own person the truth of the Rihannsu saying that the Ruling Passion is truly and gloriously unreasonable.

Thank you all!

Wage a clean war.

> —Balthasar Gracian, *The Art of Worldly Wisdom*

Was none who would be foremost
    To lead such dire attack;
But those behind cried, "Forward!"
    And those before cried, "Back!"
And backward now and forward
    Wavers the deep array;
And on the tossing sea of steel
To and fro the standards reel;
And the victorious trumpet-peal
    Dies fitfully away.

> —Macaulay, *Lays of Ancient Rome*, L

The Elements lead those who will . . .
    And those who won't, They drag.

> —tr'Hmaellieh, *Contemplations*

ONE

WHEN *ENTERPRISE* AND *BLOODWING* dropped out of warp together in the Artaleirh system, the tension on *Enterprise*'s bridge was considerable. The ship was on red alert for safety's sake, though Jim had told Uhura to kill the siren, which was no longer doing any good as regarding alertness, but only getting on people's nerves. Spock was bent over his scanner, intent, and as the warp drive's hum faded down into silence, Jim said, "Report."

"Long range scan shows no other vessels incoming at this time," Spock said.

McCoy, standing behind the center seat, gave Jim a thoughtful look. " 'What if they gave a war and nobody came?' "

"Fat chance," Jim said. "We're just early. Now we have to see what use we can make of whatever extra time we have."

He looked at the schematic of the system that the front viewscreen was now displaying, courtesy of Spock. Artaleirh was a big star, an F0 "demigiant," with a big solar system: twelve planets, mostly sunbroiled rocks or gas giants of various sizes and types, along with the asteroid belt that was the system's main source of wealth, in the third orbit out from the sun. The planet in the fourth orbit, also called Artaleirh, hung small and bright and faintly green in the distance—just visible from here, maybe a hundred million miles out, as a small, very bright disc with the same kind of morning-star albedo that Earth showed from about the same distance.

"I'm receiving a hail from Artaleirhin system control," Uhura said. "They know who we are, but all the same they're welcoming us to 'Free Rihannsu' space. . . ."

Uh-oh, Jim thought. *The first salute.* He remembered how much trouble the poor Dutch governor had gotten into, six centuries or so ago, when first the flag of a country three weeks old had been dipped to his fort in San Juan harbor— and how dipping his fort's flag back, thus officially recognizing the salute as that of another independent nation, had plunged the Netherlands into a diplomatic broil that led, however eventually, to war. *Well, this is the reverse of that situation,* Jim thought. *But they will know what an answer, or the lack of one, means.*

Then again, if we haven't caused a diplomatic incident yet, probably this is the time. This was one of the things the Federation had been waiting for: to give the enemy of an enemy a chance to prove that it was a friend. "Thank them, Commander," Jim said, "and tell them I hope to have time to talk to them more about their new name for themselves and their space later on." Asking questions like, *And how are you planning to defend yourselves after this initial engagement is over?* For one battle was no war; if the Romulans really wanted to take this system back, they had the resources to do it.

"*Bloodwing* is hailing us, Captain," Uhura said.

"Put her on."

The screen shimmered into a view of *Bloodwing*'s little bridge. Ael was standing there; behind her, Jim caught a glimpse of something on her command chair that surprised him. He shot a glance at Spock, then said, "The locals seem surprisingly friendly, Commander."

"They have reason to be, Captain. They see you as part of their salvation—though it comes in an unexpected shape."

"And how do they see *you?*"

Ael's look was fairly wry. *"Oh, some of the epithets being bandied about right now are embarrassing enough. Not to mention premature. For my own part, I refuse to be hailed as 'savior' of anything until it has actually been saved. Especially since I am, at best, a convenient excuse. Meanwhile, we have other business. Maintaining so high a speed on the way here has given us some slight advantage that we must now quickly determine how to use, for those nine Imperial ships are incoming."*

This was an update which Jim had very much been wanting. "When?"

"The Artaleirhin local-space command and control center estimates four hours until the cruisers arrive. This is not based on any direct sensing yet; the range is still too great. But messages have been passed on via subspace communications from other star systems friendly to Artaleirh, indicating that the subfleet has passed their way at speed."

"I would have thought those ships would be coming in cloaked," McCoy said.

"Indeed they will be, Doctor, but as you know, there are ways to defeat cloaking protocols," Ael said. *"At least enough to read some insufficiently shielded signal through them. Such defeat measures are wasteful of energy and betray one's own position. But when the facility is planet-based, why not? For not even we know how to hide a whole planet—not yet."*

"A cloak's main strategic usefulness is out in open space, Bones," Jim said. "Where your opponent either can't spare the energy to defeat your cloak, if he knows how, or grudges the energy because it's needed more for propulsion or weapons. Ael, we need to confer right away with the Artaleirhin; I need to know more about the strategic possibilities of this system so that we can decide where to make our stand."

"Captain, I will arrange it," Ael said. *"I will call you again in twenty minutes."* The screen flicked back to the view of the Artaleirhin primary as *Enterprise* coasted in past it, toward the colony planet.

Jim gazed at the screen. "Spock, I want you to do an in-depth survey of the system. Let's see what our best tactical options are, depending on which way the attacking force comes in. Engineering."

"Scott here. Captain, I hope you're not expectin' us to go anywhere sudden after that run! We've got to swap a new dilithium crystal into the warp engine array; the old one's developed a stress fracture due to all that time at high warp, and it's no longer dependable."

Jim frowned. "How long's that going to take you, Scotty? Looks like there's about to be a battle here in four hours."

Scotty made one of those sucking-in-your-breath sounds that Jim knew all too well meant there was trouble that not even Scotty could finesse his way out of. *"It's only an hour or so to do the actual swap, Captain. But then there's the matter of testing and calibrating the new crystal. No two are ever really alike, no matter what the cutters say, and tryin' to use standard calibrations for a new crystal is a sure way to damage other parts of the engine, or even to blow the crystal itself if it's stressed too much before it's run in. Which it would be in battle, no way around it."*

"How long is the test cycle going to take you, Scotty?"

"I'd hate to spend less than three hours on it, sir."

"You may have to, if things heat up."

"Then I'd best get started now."

"Scotty, one thing first! Sunseed—"

"Aye," Scotty said, *"we were considering the option of seeding this star if worse came to worst. And it's a good candidate for induction. But Captain, there's a question as well of what other friendly forces will be in the area—or may turn up suddenly and get blown to bits for their pains because*

*they didn't have the right screen tunings beforehand. And
there's the question of the planet's atmosphere: will it be
able to stop the worst of what's going to come out of the star
if we do seed it? K's't'lk's working on the atmospheric propagation predictions, and on the shield-tuning algorithms;
she'll be passing them to Mr. Spock shortly, for dissemination as you see fit. But the tuning algorithms'll need fine-
tuning when the process actually starts, and we may be a
wee bit busy then."*

Jim sighed. "We'll have to see how it goes. Do what you
can, Scotty."

He turned to Spock, who had come down from his station
to stand by the center seat, gazing at the tactical view of the
system that he had restored to the viewscreen. Jim glanced at
the asteroid belt and said, "Mr. Spock, are you thinking what
I'm thinking?"

"Yes, Captain, and without the benefit of extraneous in-
strumentalities." Jim threw Spock a look at what sounded
like a joke, but his first officer didn't glance away from the
screen. "In any case, the venue is certainly suited to the classic planetary defense strategies of Orondley and Indawal as
developed for Starfleet during the so-called 'early coloniza-
tion engagements' of the late 2100s, and implemented at the
battle of Donatu V, among others. And the Artaleirhin have
the advantage in that they have forced the Empire to respond
from a considerable distance, so that any move they make,
even cloaked, is quickly telegraphed, and any major commitment of forces would leave the Empire stretched thin in
other areas."

"So you're saying the situation looks favorable?"

"There are the usual imponderables associated with a
large engagement, Captain," Spock said. "Much can go
wrong, or right, in a surprisingly short time, and the skill, or
lack of it, of the commanders is also an issue. But there are
also factors with which I think the Imperium may not have

reckoned." He glanced back at the monitor over his science station. "That asteroid belt, even to a cursory scan, betrays multiple energy sources that do not match well with a mining operation, even a large and well-established one; there are too many of those sources, too widely distributed. While the attack seems to have been hastily contrived, I would suspect the defense has been some time in preparation."

"Yes," Jim said. "Well, all right, continue your analysis and see if you can get a sense of exactly what's going on out there in the belt besides what's being openly advertised. Meanwhile, in fifteen minutes, you and I should meet in my quarters for that transmission from Ael." Jim got up, glanced over at Uhura. "All stations to remain at yellow alert, Commander. I don't want to wear anybody down, but the idea that there might be some gate-crashers at this party has been giving me indigestion."

He headed out.

Many light-years away, in the neighborhood of Eisn, a conference was taking place in a small, bare, snoop-proofed room overlooking the Senate dome. Three men stood there—or rather two of them looked out the window, and behind them, one paced, restless, furious, waiting for the single small telltale light in the wall to turn blue.

Finally it did. "Did it get away safely?" were the first words out of Urellh's mouth.

"As far as we can tell."

"What do you mean 'as far as we can tell'? Who do we have to ask to find out for sure?"

"Urellh," said Armh'n, "our people in the field dare not query the device at the moment. It is still too close to where numerous Federation forces are operating. If they get even a hint of its presence at the moment, they might well be able to hunt it down. Let it proceed quietly for a few days at least, until its signal will be so swamped in larger amounts of code traffic and other routine signaling that no one will notice it. Then we can find out what we need to know. A few more days makes no odds."

"I want to know," the Praetor muttered. But for the moment he seemed to decide to let the subject rest. "What about Artaleirh?"

"The Fleet will be there in a matter of hours," tr'Anierh said.

"They are to chastise the planet immediately, and then turn their attention to finding that woman," Urellh said. "She must be destroyed without delay. Word of what happened to end the negotiations will certainly leak out—damn those treacherous *neirrh* who stole Farmer Gurri out of *Gorget*'s very infirmary! But we can at least slow it down."

"Once the Fleet handles Artaleirh—"

"Assuming they can," Urellh snarled. "The under-commanders are so divided among themselves at the moment, the Fleet Master Admiral tells me, that they can hardly even fly in the same direction. This blasted infection is spreading, and I don't doubt some of it has been spread by you two." He glared at tr'Anierh.

"This seed's of *your* sowing, Urellh," tr'Anierh said, more mildly than he needed to. "A couple of years ago you were all for 'strengthening personal ties with the Fleet,' as you called it. Of course what you meant was, 'wresting its individual commanders' loyalties to oneself so as to render the Grand Fleet Admirals largely powerless in any crisis.' And as you did so, then so did we all; for what one of the Three does, we all do, in self-defense if not out of policy. Why should it be any news to you now that the commanders are now studying to dance to their masters' harps—that is to say, ours? And why has this outcome surprised you?"

"If we were unified in our opinions," Urellh said softly, "it would not matter."

Even Armh'n looked amused at that. "We're not one mind

in three bodies yet, Urellh. Nor will be, at the rate things are going. Each of us has his own power bloc to manage in the Senate, and each of them is trying to go in its own direction, like wayward *hlai* before the dinner pail's heard clanking. Soon enough they'll all be lined up at the gate again. But for the time being we must let them think what they're doing is their idea. And we must not lose our nerve. Artaleirh's outcome will settle them down."

"It had better," Urellh said. "How long now?"

"Three hours, give or take a little time."

"We must meet at the Grand Fleet command center in five hours, then. The signal will be delayed coming back, but not too much."

The other two nodded, and Urellh slapped the blue light to kill the antiscan devices. A moment later the door swung open, and the Three came out again.

Their small suites of attendants were waiting for them, all of the Three having come from a morning session of the Senate, one of the last before the sessions could move back to their proper place under the Dome. Urellh rounded immediately on one of his attendants. "You are to get in contact with the heads of the news and broadcast services," he said, "and let them know that *their* heads, not their reporters', will answer for any escape of the news about the . . . difficulties . . . at the talks. Not a breath of it is to come out on ch'Rihan and ch'Havran; they may say that *Gorget* has come back for instructions, if they like, while the other ships remain engaged elsewhere. Control of the information may be more difficult farther out, but we can still make our presence felt. Tell Intelligence to get out there and offer swords to a few of the most outspoken of the reporters. And help them along a little bit if they don't understand the gesture. That kind of thing is what Intelligence is best at, anyway."

Off Urellh went, growling orders to the four directions and the five winds as he went, while his sweating attendants hurried to keep up with him; and tr'Anierh watched him go. Beside him, Armh'n did not move.

Both their own groups of attendants hung back for the moment. There in the momentary quiet, tr'Anierh said softly to Armh'n, "I am sorry to hear of your loss at the talks."

"That idiot," Armh'n said. "Plainly he got caught in the middle of someone else's game, or in one of his own, as if I thought him capable of playing any game with the slightest degree of subtlety. Well, something may come of this anyway. Once I finish overseeing the interrogation of the pertinent crew on *Gorget,* we may be able to accuse the Federation of old Uncle Gurri's death, if nothing else."

"We have accused them of a great many other things, but nothing has come of it," tr'Anierh said. "This, I think, will not trouble their sleep."

"Other things soon will," Armh'n said, more softly still. "Especially if they like sleeping with the lights on."

Jim and Spock were down in Jim's quarters when the desk monitor whistled for attention. Jim swung around behind his desk, hit the button. "Kirk here."

Ael's image, from *Bloodwing's* bridge, appeared. *"Captain, I would like to make known to you Courhig tr'Mahan stai-Norrik, who leads the local defense fleet. I believe his title, if the locals were much for titles, would translate as 'commodore,' if by that you mean the most senior-ranked of a nonmilitary captain-group."*

The image on the screen divided. Standing on a bridge that was, if anything, even more cramped-looking than Ael's, was a short, round Romulan with close-cropped bristly gray hair, wearing what looked more like a businessman's dark one-piece suit than any kind of uniform. His round face, wrinkled like that of someone who spent a lot of time outdoors, made Jim think of a bulldog—one that wasn't angry yet, but was looking forward to becoming so. *"Captain,"* he said, *"whatever relations between the Federation and the Empire have been until now, please believe me when I say that you are very welcome here."*

"Sir, I thank you," Jim said, "but one thing I'd very much like to clear up is exactly where the local government stands on what is about to happen here."

Tr'Mahan smiled slightly. *"Captain, both from the Imperial point of view and from that of my cohabitants here, I am the local government. As much of it as the Imperium routinely paid any attention to, at least. 'Planetary governor' would probably be a good rendering. I am native to Artaleirh, involved in politics here for a long while before I was chosen by the Imperium, they thought, as a good candidate to get the taxes in and keep the locals in line. But I do not have that much power anymore—not after the way we have been treated over the last decade. So I have taken this opportunity to change jobs."*

There was a wicked look in his eye, but his expression also looked a little tentative, as if he were wondering how Jim would take this. "The job security," Jim said, "might not be much like that of your earlier position."

"True," tr'Mahan said. *"But it seems increasingly preferable. We have had many years during which the rulership of the Imperium over our system has become increasingly irksome—our resources depleted and wasted on military adventurism, our rights curtailed. For perhaps the last decade and a half, as you reckon time, the great families here and other political activists have been investigating other options. Finally, having made ourselves sure of how many other worlds around the Imperium share our way of thinking, we chose this time to move. We informed the Imperium ten days ago that we would no longer deal with them except as an independent entity. The dispatch of a cruiser task force to enforce our 'loyalty' and collect hostages was the result. They have given us no choice: we must fight."*

"With what?" Jim said.

"We have five small vessels, which I believe you would rank as 'light cruisers,' " tr'Mahan said. *"I speak to you from one of them, Sithesh. These vessels have been . . . attached? commandeered? . . . from the first Imperial forces to visit us in an attempt to enforce their demands."*

"Not, I would take it, with their cooperation," Spock said.

"Indeed not, sir. We were fortunately able to keep the Grand Fleet from discovering what had happened to the captured ships for some days, but no more—this being part of the reason those nine much more heavily armed ships are now on their way here."

"I take it you've re-ID'd all the captured vessels by now."

"We have, Captain. We will be passing that data on to your communications officer when I finish here. Now, the light cruisers are by themselves too few to engage the biggest of the incoming ships effectively. However, we also have nearly three hundred smaller vessels, formerly in civilian service, now all fitted with phasers or single-shot photon torpedoes. Singly and scattered, they would not be worth much in a major engagement, but as a whole coordinated microfleet, they will be of value."

"If not deployed too soon," Spock said. "There is great danger if they are brought into play before the most powerful of the Imperial vessels are disabled or destroyed."

"Which brings us to the coronal injection protocol you have been calling Sunseed," tr'Mahan said. *"We would ask you not to use this instrumentality unless you absolutely must. Doubtless you would prefer not to anyway. But first of all, we would rather not recklessly endanger the planet— some of us still desire to live there after all this is over. And secondly, your description makes it sound as if the effect would almost infallibly destroy any ship that hits it with its screens incorrectly tuned, and we do not want to destroy those ships."*

Jim nodded, though he had been afraid of this. "You want more prizes."

Tr'Mahan looked slightly bemused. *"Your translator may have a fault, for it is using a word indicating what one receives on winning a game."* He grinned. *"If this is a game, we play for the greatest stakes: our lives and our world's freedom—or at the very least, the right of its people to seek their freedom elsewhere. But yes, Captain. It is difficult for powerful ships like yours to disable one another without doing massive damage that will take very prolonged repair at a space-dock facility. And destruction is all too likely if someone misses, or misjudges the status of another's screens. Small ships, however, are more nimble than the big ships in a combat like this, far more maneuverable at the lower speeds that intersystem combat mandates."*

"As long as you can enforce those low speeds," Jim said.

"That," said tr'Mahan, *"is what our asteroid belt is for."*

Spock was already nodding, for this was a part of the classic tactics-set he had mentioned to Jim. "It is a useful strategy, Captain, one that has proven its effectiveness elsewhere. The crucial factor, of course, is forcing an opponent to engage you there."

"And once we have forced such an engagement," tr'Mahan said, *"we can concentrate our efforts on disabling the attacking vessels. Once taken, they will be valuable additions to our fleet."*

"Just how are you planning to make this fight happen where you want it?" Jim said.

"The incoming fleet will almost certainly initially attack the planet," said tr'Mahan, *"to try to make the battle happen there instead. But there will be no response to that attack. If they wish to engage us, they will do it where we please."*

Jim nodded again, very slowly, thinking that these people must have nerves of steel, or an extremely angry planetary population, to willingly take such a stance. "All right. If you're thinking along these lines, there are doubtless sites in the asteroid belt that the Imperium feels you're more likely to defend even than the planet. That would probably be the best place for us to position ourselves."

"The central dilithium processing facility is as important to them as to us. They will attempt to secure it, or if they cannot do so, to destroy it so that it will be no use to us either."

"Or to the Klingons," Jim said, "should they turn up."

"Yes, Captain. Though there has been no sign of them as yet, we are still alert to that possibility."

"All right." Jim thought for a moment. "If you'll pass the coordinates you suggest via my communications officer, I'll have a look at them and give you my thoughts within a few minutes. Ael?"

"I have seen them, and knowing this system from previous visits, I find the suggestion a good one," Ael said. *"I await your opinion."*

"Right. Meanwhile—" He looked hard at tr'Mahan. "In a 'surgical' operation like this, as regards attempting to take the ships of the incoming fleet, first of all, they're likely to try to self-destruct."

"We have protocols by which we hope to keep that from happening," tr'Mahan said.

Do you indeed? Another interesting new development. "But the other matter is potentially more painful. You're likely to lose a significant number of your little ships to both firepower and confusion."

"Our pilots understand that," tr'Mahan said. *"They are willing to take the risk, and to pay the price, or they would not all still be out there in the belt, waiting, as they have been for several days. Such long waits out in the dark and the cold give plenty of opportunity for second thoughts, but we have had very few defections."*

Jim glanced at Spock, now understanding the source of

some of those extra "energy sources" in the asteroid belt that he had mentioned. "But, Commodore—"

"*Please, Captain. Tr'Mahan is good enough; I haven't yet done the service to earn me such a title, and taking names to oneself without justification is only tempting the Elements.*" The man eased his bulk down into his command chair. "*I understand your concerns. Courage and luck are not enough: skill is needed too. I can say only this: before I was a planetary governor, when I was just starting to be a politician, I was also a dilithium miner. I am used to working out in that belt. Some reflexes don't get lost over time, and are quickly recovered in life-or-death situations like this. The rocks are not close together, of course, but working at substantial fractions of lightspeed can make them seem so, and in such circumstances, my pilots and I may show you a thing or three about rock-dodging that you didn't previously know.*"

"I hope so." Jim let out a breath. "You also have to understand that as far as saving those big ships for you goes, I'll do what I can within reason. But as for myself, if things get too hot for *Enterprise*, I'll blow up just as many of them as I have to."

"*Feel free,*" said tr'Mahan, and he grinned. "*In the aftermath, we will simply tell the Empire that we have* all *their ships, and are keeping some in reserve. By the time they find out the truth, they will have many other things to worry about. But in any case, if we cannot have those ships, they are better destroyed. They'll not then make trouble for us later, when we move on ch'Rihan.*"

Jim had to smile slightly himself. He was beginning to like this man.

Ael said, "*A number of other systems, Captain, are watching to see what happens here. If we can make a success of this engagement, they will come out into the open and join us.*"

"We get to be the pebbles that start the landslide," Jim said. "Better than being at the bottom of the slope watching it come down, I guess." He pushed his chair back. "I'm going to go look at your schematics now."

"Your communications officer has them," tr'Mahan said. He paused and added, *"My own ops officer tells me that a subspace message just in from the monitoring buoys associated with a nearby system confirms the approach of those nine ships. They are coming in together, from the galactic north-polar direction. For us, that is a dive straight into the system, most likely toward the planet, at an angle nearly perpendicular to our local ecliptic. My ship is presently in orbit around Artaleirh. If you'll follow me out on impulse, I'll show you where we will make our stand."*

"We'll be right along. A pleasure to talk to you, tr'Mahan. Let's meet again after this is over."

"Preferably while still breathing," tr'Mahan said, grinning again.

His image flicked away. "Ael," Jim said, "give me a few minutes."

She nodded; the screen went dark. Jim got up and headed for the door, Spock right behind him.

TWO

A FEW MINUTES LATER Jim came up into the bridge with Spock. "I have a lock on *Sithesh,* Captain," Sulu said as they entered. "Following them into the belt."

"Very good, Mr. Sulu. Spock, let's have the detailed schematic of the belt."

Spock brought it up on the main screen. It was not a dangerous place for small ships working at small fractions of impulse, nor was there any reason that it should be, with the average distance between even the smaller bodies a matter of hundreds or thousands of kilometers. Nonetheless there were places where gravitational "knotting" and other minor perturbational drifts brought the asteroids clumping closer together than usual, sometimes only ten or twenty or fifty kilometers apart. For little ships, again, the situation was manageable. But for starships . . .

Sulu was looking at that schematic as closely as Jim and Spock were. "It's the briar patch, Captain," Sulu said softly, "and we're not even going to wait to be thrown in."

"No, but the other guys are going to get scratched as badly as we will," Jim said. "Worse, because they don't have *you.*"

Sulu grinned, and indicated a small bright blot on the screen. "Sir, is that the dilithium processing facility?"

"That's it," Jim said. "Some strange motions on some of the asteroids in that area."

"They're probably nudged around a lot by casual propulsion effect from the ships servicing the facility," Sulu said. "You'd be surprised how even just chemical jets can affect these asteroid systems over time. And all kinds of other random perturbations occur in a setup like this. Sometimes the rocks even bang into each other." He looked thoughtfully at the schematic. "Sometimes, you can *make* them bang into each other." He glanced over at Chekov, raising his eyebrows. Chekov's eyes narrowed, and he produced the shadow of a nasty grin.

Jim began slowly to smile. "Mr. Sulu," he said, "maybe you want to talk to some of our—" *Enemies? Allies?* In a situation like this, terminology could too easily slip and cut you . . . now, or retroactively. "—cocombatants out there about what you see as possible options."

Sulu nodded. "Uhura, would you get me Antecenturion Khiy over on *Bloodwing*?"

"Right away."

Shortly thereafter Jim sat in bemusement while Chekov immersed himself in a very comprehensive recalibration and fine-tuning of the controls for the ship's tractor and pressor arrays, and Sulu and Khiy immersed themselves more and more deeply into a discussion about very-large-set-enumeration algorithms and best-guess mass determinators and other flights of what sounded like technological fancy—except that Sulu was plainly in deadly earnest, and so, to judge by his voice, was Khiy. Their voices and Chekov's held something of the barely contained excitement of children who have found a new and interesting way to break things, and have been told by their too-permissive elders to go find out how well it works. Jim got up out of the center seat and glanced at the chrono. It was at least two hours until anything would start to happen, and he was already in that paradoxical state where he wished it would happen now, while also wishing he had at least another day to prepare.

He sighed. "Engineering."

"Scott here."

"How's it going, Scotty?"

"A bit busy now, Captain. I'll get back to you."

Stop jostling his elbow just because you want something to do, Jim thought. "Sorry, Scotty. Out." Then he remembered something else he had been wanting to do. "Sickbay."

"McCoy here."

"Bones, how's your patient doing?"

A long sigh came from the other end. *"Jim, if Gurrhim recovers it's going to be the clearest possible case of 'we treat them, God cures them.' M'Benga is good with Vulcans, and over a good while I've learned a fair amount about the physiology from my experience with Spock—"*

" 'Experiments' might be a more accurate term," said a dry voice from behind Jim.

"I heard that. But Vulcan and Romulan physiologies are not exactly the same anymore, and some few changes have gone down to the cellular level. The time's too short for drift to be involved. I would expect that some of the genetic tinkering that went on in the Ruling Queen's time might be the cause. But the Rihannsu themselves haven't been very forthcoming with medical information in the past, which I suppose I can understand. Anyway, the patient is doing as well as can be expected in a facility that isn't primarily equipped for his species."

"So he'll live."

"Oh, I'd say that seems likely enough—until we get into the next battle, anyway. After that it's up to you."

Jim raised his eyebrows. "I'll do what I can."

"He wants to see you, by the way."

Jim blinked. "He's conscious already? Shouldn't he still be in the Romulan version of a healing trance, or some such?"

"Oh, he went straight into that as soon as we killed the

anesthetic field, and even then the state only lasted him about nine hours. Nearly decked M'Benga, too, when he was waking up. But after that he started having a sequence of micro-trances—not sure whether this is a typical occurrence or something secondary to the severity of his condition when he came in. I need to talk to Ael's surgeon about that. Anyway, when he's been conscious, the Praetor hasn't said much—doesn't surprise me, he probably feels pretty awful—but that request to see you has come up a couple of times, and it's been emphatic."

"Well, if he wakes up again in the next few hours, tell him I'm glad he's still with us, but I'm likely to be busy for a while. After that he and I can have a chat in sickbay, or some other venue. Not, I hope, a hotter one."

"I'll let him know. But there's no rush. I'm not going to take the chance of unduly disturbing his healing cycle. Meanwhile, Jim, we've been getting ready for casualties. When the balloon's about to go up, let me know."

"Will do, Bones. Out." There was one more matter on his mind. "Uhura, what have we heard from Starfleet recently?"

"Nothing's been directed at us, Captain. There's a lot of data traffic passing in Federation space at the moment, though, using the new code."

Jim breathed out. *They're waiting for me to report before sending me any further information,* he thought. *Maybe I should be grateful.* "When you can, see what you can discover about what's going on back in home space. Passive means only."

"Yes, sir."

Jim turned his attention back to the schematic on the screen. Less of it was showing now, as *Enterprise* and *Bloodwing* followed *Sithesh* into the asteroid belt. Jim watched Sulu with some interest; he was both piloting and carrying on his discussion with Khiy, though more sporadically now. "We don't need to itemize them farther out than a hundred thousand kilometers on either side, Khiy. The odds are too low of our being able to do accurate just-in-time predictions of crossthroughs out there, and I bet you they won't bother. The action's going to be closer to the facility—"

"But if we notate a few of the big ones, Hikaru, it'll surely do no harm."

"Oh, why not. Pick your favorites. I've got most of mine in the machine at the moment. We'll sync the databases and start an automated scan—"

"Mr. Sulu," Jim said, "some elucidation would be of assistance to me. As well as reassurance." Some of the rocks they were passing, at nearly half impulse and rather closely, looked very big.

"Yes, Captain. Khiy, finish up at your end, I'll get back to you." Sulu turned as Jim stepped down to look over his shoulder.

Spock straightened up from his scanner. "Mr. Sulu, one caution. The abnormally high dilithium content of these asteroids is likely to make an automated scan give incorrect results for the medium-size bodies' mass-volume ratios. You must correct for this when you process your statistical sample."

"I've got a correction for that in the program already, Mr. Spock. I'm passing it to you now. If you'd evaluate it . . ."

Spock glanced up at the screen over his station, which instantly started to fill with figures.

"Mr. Sulu," Jim said, "I can't avoid the impression that you're counting all the asteroids in this neighborhood."

"Not counting them as such, Captain. We're building a recognition database, tagging the asteroids with nominal IDs, and noting their masses for future reference. If you know an asteroid's mass within a couple of significant figures, you can very quickly calculate what kind of forces would need to be applied to it to make it move. Once Khiy and I get them all tagged, or all the ones in this area, we can get the ship's computer to alert us when an enemy vessel is getting close enough for one of the asteroids to be a threat. Then either *Bloodwing* or *Enterprise* gives the necessary rock a pull with a tractor or a push with a pressor . . ."

Jim grinned. In slower-than-light combat, the lightspeed-or-faster weapons came into their own, as long as you kept away from the higher, near-relativistic impulse speeds. "You're concentrating on the asteroids nearer to the processing facility, I see."

"Yes, sir—a sphere about a hundred thousand kilometers in diameter, including almost the entire breadth of the belt in this area. Any ship outside that diameter isn't going to be a threat to us at subwarp speeds. If they want to engage with us, they've got to drop their speed and come inside the sphere."

" 'Come into my parlor, said the spider to the fly . . .' " Jim said. "Get on with it, Mr. Sulu. In a situation like this, every little bit helps. Are you going to be able to have this ready by the time the 'flies' arrive?"

"We'll do our best, Captain. There are some inconsistencies between the ways *Bloodwing*'s computer handles large amounts of data like this, and the way ours does. We've got to solve them on the fly." And Sulu chuckled. "But give us at least an hour or so before we're ready."

"Very well." Jim turned. "Uhura, I'll be in my quarters for a while if anyone needs me." He headed up toward the lift, hearing behind him the sound of *Enterprise* getting ready to defend herself. Now all he had to do was work out how best to help her do it.

Ael stood behind her command chair and watched as *Bloodwing* and *Enterprise* came in behind *Sithesh* and took up station-keeping positions near the dilithium processing facility. It was a great insectile-looking place, its central core based inside an oblong, hollowed-out asteroid some five kilometers long, with fourteen subsidiary-process struts reaching out above and below the core in a delicate and fragile-looking construction of gantries and spars. The fragility was much on Ael's mind, for this facility was the major economic "engine" of this whole part of space. Other systems in this part of the Empire brought here what little dilithium they managed to mine on their own worlds, glad enough to take home the thirty percent of processed crystal, which was all the Empire allowed them, keeping the rest itself. *That is going to change,* Ael thought, *one way or the other. One might suspect that the economic threat was as much a factor in those nine ships' appearance here now as anything else. Commandeered ships or not, they would have come eventually. I am not the only excuse being invoked here.*

Aidoann stepped down beside Ael and looked out their little viewscreen. "It looks all too breakable," she said. "Nine ships would make short work of it."

"They will not attack it until they think they are in danger of losing it to us," Ael said. "And then, with everything they have. But how much they will have—there is the question." She looked down at Khiy. "How goes it there?"

"We are devising some automated routines, *khre'Riov,*" Khiy said, "while the databases finish building and synchronizing. Sulu and I will be busy with other things all too often, but the systems will be able to suggest useful options to us as we work."

"Good. How long now?"

"Perhaps an hour."

"The fleet will be here that soon," Aidoann said.

Ael glanced over at tr'Hrienteh. "Il'Merrin's buoys have reported now," the Master Surgeon said. "They will be the last warning we get. But they report the fleet on the same course, no change."

"Good. Let *Enterprise* know, and *Sithesh* also, if they have not heard already. And I would welcome a word with tr'Mahan, if he can spare me the time."

"Calling him for you now, *khre'Riov.*"

Ael nodded. "Then you had best get young Kiel up here, tr'Hrienteh; you will be needed in your own infirmary."

"Elements, I hope not," tr'Keirianh said, looking wryly at Ael. "But that's my place indeed."

The screen lit with tr'Mahan's image. How he could sit himself so still in his chair when combat was breathing down his neck, Ael could not tell, unless inexperience simply rendered him immune to the fear. "Courhig," Ael said, "you have the latest tracking information?"

"I do. They will be within local sensor range in about fifteen minutes or so. After that we can perform more exact predictions, and once things start, their cloaks will not much matter. They must uncloak to fire."

"The question now becomes, Courhig, how much you are prepared to reveal to *Enterprise* about how exactly you can predict those positions. Not to mention about how you plan to keep those ships from self-destructing. The captain is no fool, and too much accuracy on your part without proper disclosure will cause him to ask difficult questions. I daresay he's thinking of some already."

"Ael—" Courhig bowed his head in uncertainty. *"You know the question my people are all asking. Can he be trusted?"*

She breathed out. "His ideas of honor," Ael said, "are not constructed like ours. There are so many differences. But for my own part—yes, I trust him. His actions will have to make that plain to you. Then you will have to consider your economic and political needs in light of them. For the moment, though, let us fight our fight. Blood speaks, as we know. Let's see which language his uses today."

Courhig nodded. *"Let us do that. For the moment, though, I prefer you not mention planetary defense as such to him. Nor anything of the remote-operations modules; indeed, we dare not use those today until it's plain no description of their use can make it back to Grand Fleet. One use, Fleet might mistake for some kind of disaster or accident. But they've had some days to think about what might have happened, and if we give them any further hints, they'll find a way to nullify this weapon. As for the rest of it . . ." He sighed. "Nothing more to say but, Elements be with you and yours in what we do today."*

"And with you and all of yours, Courhig."

The screen went black.

Ael turned away from it in some distress, clasping her hands, and looked up to see Aidoann watching her with a very still and controlled look.

"*Khre'Riov,*" she said quietly. "It was not the captain he was inquiring about, was it. Not really."

That thought had been in Ael's mind. *It is me they fear,* she thought, *even while they use me for their purpose. They are afraid of him not only because of what he has always been, but because of what use they feel I am making of him. And they fear me because of what I may become. Perhaps they have wisdom on their side, to fear how sharply the sword may cut. But not during a battle; there is no wisdom in that . . .*

It was bitter to be so distrusted. Yet she had to realize that this was how it would be between her and her own folk from now on, how it would always be, unless she died now.

"Aidoann," Ael said after a moment, "how can I blame him? The future is dark for all of us right now, and he has more to fear than we. Meanwhile, let us wake up the active sensors and see what we see. We have only a very little time left. Khiy?"

"Nearly done, *khre'Riov.*"

"Good." Once again she clenched her hands on the back of the chair she could no longer sit in, and stared at the screen, now once more showing the dilithium processing facility. Kiel came in to relieve tr'Keirianh, who headed off to her surgery. "Kiel," Ael said, "give me all-call now. Battle stations, now, my children. Stand to battle, and the Elements with us!"

The hooting of the sirens drowned out the furious beating of her heart.

"We've got the asteroid database implemented," Sulu said. "Captain, this procedure's going to be on the opportunistic side. If the computer sees a target ship about to get into a situation where we will in turn be in a position to use a rock or two on it, it'll alert us, then there'll be two or three seconds for the hit/no-hit decision before we have to use the tractors or pressors."

"All right, Mr. Sulu," Jim said. "We'll call them as they come up. If I don't specifically countermand you, or you, Mr. Chekov, then go ahead and use your rocks as you see fit. But understand the priorities. I'd love to help tr'Mahan out, but if someone is threatening *Enterprise* and there's a rock handy, or even a phaser beam . . ."

"Yes, Captain," Chekov said, and "Understood," said Sulu.

"There's one other thing," Jim said. "About banging these rocks together, as opposed to simply banging them into enemy ships—what happens when you do that?"

"A lot of heat, maybe some light. Possibly even some transient alpha," Sulu said, "assuming you bang them together hard enough. Naturally plenty of fragmentation, some melting and fusing along the impact sites."

"That I would have expected. But, Mr. Sulu, a whole lot of these rocks have crystalline dilithium in them."

"Hmm," Sulu said.

Spock turned around from his station, looking interested. "In asteroid-sourced dilithium, the common dihedral form predominates by some ninety-eight percent. And under certain conditions of heat and pressure, the dihedral form can become moderately unstable. Normally the rarity of dilithium militates against wasting it on casual experimentation. But with threshold masses, and sufficient density of crystal or crystalline ore—and adding energy-state stimulation with phasers—impacts might result that could at the very least be characterized as . . ." He paused, looking for the right word. ". . . emphatic."

Jim grinned at that. "Mr. Spock, establish the thresholds for Mr. Sulu so that he can pass them to the computer. Emphasis can be a good thing. And I have to confess to a strictly empirical interest in what happens when you knock two such bodies together."

At that both Sulu and Spock gave Jim looks that at the very least were skeptical. "All right," Jim said. "Maybe I really just want to know how far away we should be when it happens."

"Yes, sir," Sulu said, and Spock nodded and turned back to his console.

Uhura looked up suddenly. "*Sithesh* is hailing us, Captain."

"Put tr'Mahan on."

The Artaleirhin commander appeared on a bridge that was now dark as well as cramped, damped down to blue-green crisis lighting. *"Captain, the fleet is on its way in, and will be in-system within thirty minutes. IDs and coordinates are being fed to you now."*

"Thank you," Jim said. "Have you had a chance to speak to *Bloodwing* about what we've been doing out here?"

"Yes, Captain. It is . . . unique."

"Not as unique as you being able to feed us the coordinates of cloaked ships," Jim said, "but we'll discuss that later. Good luck to you, sir, and good hunting."

"The like to you, Captain, and triumph over your enemies." The screen went dark.

Not that it's all that easy anymore to tell just who those are, Jim thought. "Battle stations, red alert!"

The sirens began whooping through the ship.

"Nine ships as promised, Captain," Sulu said as Uhura passed him the information. "Configuration data is embedded. Four heavy cruisers incoming—*Elieth, Moerrdel, Arest,* and *Berouinn*; two so-called 'super-heavies,' *Gauntlet* and *Esemar*; and three corvettes, *Llendan, Chape,* and *Sumpter.* Those last ones are probably more lightly armed, and intended for supply and support work."

"Those'll be the easiest targets," Jim said, sitting down in the center seat again. "For which reason I assume they'll stay farthest out of the way if they can. But one thought. Mr. Spock—" He glanced over at the Vulcan. "—if I remember correctly, 'sumpter' is a word for a mount that's carrying extra cargo."

Spock nodded. "I will be scanning it for the new cloaking device waveform, Captain, as soon as the ships drop conventional cloak and come within range."

"Good. If any of them are carrying another little surprise like the one they pulled out of their hats at 15 Tri, I want to know soonest. Mr. Sulu, off station-keeping now. Manage us a more or less circular course around the station, one eighth impulse. No rush at all."

"One eighth impulse, aye," Sulu said.

"*Sithesh* is signaling the smaller vessels to get ready to move," Uhura said.

Jim hit the intercom. "Sickbay."

"McCoy here."

"I see your balloon, Bones, and it's a big fat one. Hope you've got everything fastened down."

"No fear of that, Jim. You be careful."

"Believe me, it's on my mind." The thought of what kind of weapons a "supercruiser" might be carrying concerned him, but even when outweaponed, *Enterprise* had speed and agility to count on—not to mention her crew, without whom no hardware was more than just a heap of wires and data solids. "Hang on tight, Bones. Out. Engineering!"

"Here, Captain," Scotty said. He sounded as if he wished he were elsewhere.

"Status."

"Ready on impulse, Captain. But we've no warp."

"None at *all*, Scotty?"

"Not if you want to use the warp engines again anytime soon. We're not done with our recalibration. The new crystal has too many irregularities to deal with in such a short time."

"Scotty," Jim said, allowing himself to sound deeply disappointed. It was not entirely an act.

"Captain, don't make me promise you something I cannot deliver!"

"No," Jim said sadly. "I'd never do that. How's impulse?"

"At a hundred and ten percent," Scotty said, sounding only marginally brighter.

"That's where we need it," Jim said. "One last check on weapons systems, Scotty."

"Just finished now, sir. All systems are fully charged and all tubes loaded, ready to go hot."

"Captain," Spock said. "We are getting a tactical-systems feed from *Sithesh*. The incoming ships are going to lower warp speeds, preparatory to dropping out."

"Distance?"

"I am having some slight difficulty converting distances with the desirable precision from the Artaleirhin data feed," Spock said. "Closest estimate would be two point six three light-hours, closing fast."

Jim nodded. Even just a few billion kilometers' worth of warning was of value. "Feed Mr. Sulu the coordinate data. How are they tracking cloaked ships even that precisely at this distance?"

"I would very much like to know," Spock said.

And so would the Federation, Jim thought. But for the time being he put the question of his sealed orders aside. The point now was to both survive to be in a position to use them, and to get *Enterprise* into a position where using them would be easy. "*Bloodwing.*"

There was a pause. Then Ael's voice said, *"Ready, Captain. They are close."*

"We're ready for them. Good luck, Commander."

"And the Elements with you as well—" She broke off. Jim raised his eyebrows. She sounded tenser than usual; revealing in itself, in an officer usually so self-contained and self-assured. Jim sat back and waited the last, hardest few seconds.

"The incoming fleet is beginning to drop out of warp, "Spock said, as calmly as if reporting the weather. "*Gauntlet* and *Esemar* have come out first."

"The heavy guns," Jim said, "ready to break up an ambush. Let's see the tactical, Mr. Spock."

Spock transferred the tactical view to the front viewscreen. Jim saw what he thought he would, the two big ships plunging into the system almost at right angles to the ecliptic, as Courhig had predicted. Already Jim's heart was pounding with the thought that the Romulans had made one of the three great errors of this kind of warfare, that of dividing your forces before you have adequately assessed the danger—though there were some naval tacticians who claimed that any division of a fleet into subsections was already an error, whether the threat had been correctly assessed or not. By that standard, this incoming fleet was already in trouble, though whether they knew it or not was at issue, not to mention how the forces waiting here would exploit the error. If the Grand Fleet ships rejoined to work again as a more closely aligned group, that would be a problem. *But a mistake they made once, they might make again.*

"The Grand Fleet vessels are all now in system," Spock said, as the two tagged shapes of light that represented *Gauntlet* and *Esemar* slowed further, and one after another, the other points of light popped in behind them, in a loose globular formation. "We are being scanned."

"No response," Jim said. "We shouldn't be able to see them; let's let them suppose we can't." He stared hard at the tactical. "Let me know if they make any changes in acceleration or vector suggesting that individual vessels or a sub-group may be about to break away."

"No indications of that as yet, Captain. They are shifting formation somewhat, however. Heading directly for Artaleirh; none appear to be diverting toward us."

"Keep an eye on them, Spock. Especially for any sign that some of them might be about to try to seed that star." It was the smaller vessels in the group that made Jim most suspicious in this regard; the corvettes would almost certainly have more than one function here, since they would be only of secondary use in a fight among starships of any size. *Not that we won't seed that star ourselves if we don't have a choice,* Jim thought, and was once again left very uncomfortable by the concept. How must this moment feel for the people on the planet, knowing that either the enemy or their own side might suddenly make their homeworld uninhabitable?

"We have two of our cruisers out in abeyance at the moment to interfere with them should they start such a run, Captain," tr'Mahan's voice said.

Jim let out a brief breath of relief that he hoped no one heard. *Dammit, we ought to be able to handle it ourselves,* he was thinking. *Damn crystal anyway!* "Good man," he said to tr'Mahan. "We need to stay still for the moment. We'll protect your fallback position here. If they make a move, they're all yours."

"I understand your reasoning, Captain. We are ready now. Here they come."

Jim's hands clenched on the arms of the center seat.

THREE

ON *BLOODWING*, Ael stood behind her command chair, watching what lay there glittering in the dark blue light of the tactical display. Nine ships were arrowing down from the night at Artaleirh, and the thought of what that world might be about to suffer filled her with pain. But if they did not suffer it, much worse pain would yet befall all the people on that world, and many others. *If only this works . . .*

"Course change as they go into lower sublight speeds now," Aidoann said. "All their weapons are going hot, *khre'Riov.* They are initiating big hyperbolic least-expenditure curves, with Artaleirh as their common locus."

They are giving us a chance to regret our intentions, Ael thought. *I hope we can return the favor.* "They plainly think this engagement will be over quickly," she said to Aidoann. "So it may, but not as they intend." Ael glanced down at the seat of her chair, considering that she might prefer to sit this one out. It was likely to get lively. But that would mean moving what lay there now.

I will not. She glanced up at the screen. "Aidoann, hail the flagship. See that they have visual. I do not care if they return it."

Aidoann bent over her console, spoke to it softly. The screen at the front of the bridge remained dark, but the slight hiss of carrier was audible. "*Esemar* is listening, *khre'Riov,*" Aidoann said under her breath.

Ael nodded. "Imperial vessels, stand away from Artaleirh and take yourselves out of the system immediately, on pain of destruction. Your intentions here are known, and will be prevented."

There was a long silence before an answer came back. *"Traitress,"* a voice said, *"you and yours will now pay the price of your perfidy. Speak to the Elements now; you'll have no other chance. Then come out from where you hide and find your death. Else we will take its price from those you have deluded."*

She grinned. "By the Sword and its Element, I tell you I know it will not happen so. Take yourselves away from here and live, or stay, and leave your Houses sonless, motherless, orphaned!"

There was no reply, not that she expected one. "Now," she said softly to Aidoann and Khiy and the others on the bridge, "they must make the first move, and so damn themselves."

"And if their move works, *khre'Riov*?" Aidoann's voice was a little more testy than usual; the tension was working on her as well.

"We will at least send some of them ahead of us to make plain to the Elements the need for proper revenge," Ael said. She watched the curves outlining themselves on tactical: there was no change in them.

"They're going for the planet," Aidoann said.

"We have always thought they would at first," Ael said. "It is a feint. They seek to draw the straw before the *dzeill,* as it were, but that will not help them. For the moment, the *dzeill* lies still."

The curves continued to draw in toward the planet, closer every second. The bridge filled up with the warnings that the Grand Fleet vessels were broadcasting on every available wavelength to the planet below them, blanketing the place. *"This is the Grand Fleet of the Rihannsu Star Empire. All cities and settlements of the Rihannsu Imperial subject world*

Artaleirh are herewith placed under martial law. All manufacturing facilities will henceforth be managed and operated under direct control of Imperial officers. All civil vessels are to ground immediately and prepare to be boarded and either disarmed or inactivated. Gatherings of more than three people in any public place are now forbidden. Hostages . . . reparations . . . a new military government . . ."

The recitation went on and on, a litany of such trammels to liberty as no free culture could possibly bear. Yet the Artaleirhin were expected to bear it. Their lives, which they had been allowed to run in various small ways as long as they fed goods and monies back to the homeworlds and obeyed the whims of their rulers, were now, if not forfeit, to be lived in cages, virtual or real, under the threat of the scourge or the blaster. *"Immediate acceptance of these terms is required. You may choose spokesmen to replace your political leaders, who will give themselves up to the authority of the Fleet to endure the rigors of Imperial justice. Your new spokesmen have one planet's hour to signal acceptance. This is the Grand Fleet of the Rihannsu Star Empire—"*

Ael looked around the bridge at her crew. They were staring at one another, and at the speakers from which the sound came, with expressions of bitter distaste. "This is what we could have become, my children," Ael said, "had we remained too thoughtlessly true to our old loyalty. I will wear the scorn of such as these with pride, as an ornament far surpassing any mere battle honor."

Aidoann looked over at Ael, then, and flipped a switch at her comm console. A voice spoke, a Rihanha's voice, not amplified across multibands like the flat, self-assured voice speaking from the sky, but single, simplex and passionate. *"—needs not one hour for an answer,"* she was saying, *"no, not one breath! This is the Free Rihannsu world of Artaleirh. We are the tool of no empire anymore, and the toy of no Senate. We are our own world under our own sky, and we now*

*take that sky back to ourselves, in arms with those who know
what freedom is worth, and who will help us be slaves no
more. Live or die, we have nothing more to say to you, tools
in the hands of tyrants!"*

The announcement from the Grand Fleet ships persisted
only a few moments longer, then simply broke off, in mid-
playback, as if whoever had been playing the recording
simply could not believe the response. Behind Ael, Aidoann
listened to the silence that followed, and let go a soft hiss of
anguish. *"Khre'Riov,"* she said, "if this doesn't work, all
those cities, all those many people—"

Ael sat silent and watched the curves of the starships'
courses become more acute as they neared the planet.

"Khre'Riov, can we not stop it? Let us stop it!" Aidoann
whispered. "If we move quickly enough, we could seed the
star—or have tr'Mahan give the order."

Ael shook her head. "I will not," she said, her voice terribly steady, far more so than her heart. "You heard Courhig.
You heard our kinswoman down there. The Artaleirhin have
made their preparations. They know how this battle must unfold, for their freedom's sake. Their choice is made. Now we
must honor their intention, or condemn them to the loss of
their own honor, forever."

"But Ael—!"

She would not answer.

On the *Enterprise*'s bridge, the whole bridge crew was
watching the same view in slightly different colors, and a
stillness had settled over them too as they heard what the
translator was making of the Grand Fleet's announcement
to the planet Artaleirh. "Captain," Sulu said, "those orbits
will have the capital ships in disruptor or phaser bombardment range within three minutes."

Sulu was trying to keep his tone of voice neutral, but the
edge showed in it regardless. Jim shook his head, knowing

just how he felt, wishing he could indulge the desire to go and help, but this was one of those moments during which tactics ruled, no matter how it hurt you personally. "I have no interest in going over there, Mr. Sulu," Jim said, doing his best to keep the edge out of his own voice, though he suspected the minutes to follow might give him nightmares for decades. "I'm not going to throw away what advantage we have by allowing them to draw us out. They fight us here, or not at all."

"Yes, Captain," Sulu said, his voice flat this time. Jim had heard that subdued tone from his bridge crew before—the disappointment, the dread. But he was not going to allow that to affect him either.

"Thirty seconds to bombardment range," Chekov said softly.

Jim had used his own phasers on planets' surfaces occasionally. It was very difficult to be delicate about it, and when the ship firing was bent on *not* being delicate, the destruction could be terrible. With time and persistence, even large cities could be rendered not merely uninhabited, but uninhabitable. And then there was the matter of the phasers' effects on the local ecology, on terrain and atmosphere: derangement of the local weather, destruction of water tables and even activation of earthquake faults if any were in the vicinity. But generally the hundreds of thousands of burned and blackened corpses, and the dust of the uncountable vaporized, were no longer in a condition to be able to be concerned about the environmental consequences. The thought left Jim's mouth drier, if possible, than it was already.

The alternative to disruptor or phaser barrage, of course, was no better in that regard—possibly worse. Yet there would be many more survivors of seeding this star than a full-scale planetary bombardment would leave. Jim rubbed his forehead, hit the comm button on his chair. "Scotty."

"*Aye, sir.*"

"If we *had* to break away for the star—"

"*We can't do it, Captain,*" Scotty said. "*Not without warp, and I haven't got that for you. Another two hours. If anyone's going to do it, it's got to be* Bloodwing, *or one of the other lads out there.*"

Jim was watching the little tagged light in the display that was *Bloodwing*. She was not moving in the slightest; she stood to her position. "Uhura," he said, "get me Ael."

Uhura touched her console, nodded at him.

"*I hear you,* Enterprise," Ael said.

"We can't just let them sit there and take what's coming," Jim said.

"*We can and* will," Ael said, "*as they have insisted is their right to do. I like this no better than you do, Captain, but we have had this out with Courhig, and neither he nor those people on Artaleirh will thank us for changing tactics now.*"

Jim sat up and pushed his back against the back of his chair. Finally he nodded. "I just want you to know . . ." he said, and trailed off.

"*I too detest this,*" Ael said, "*should you be in any doubt.*"

Spock was looking down his viewer. "The Imperial vessels are moving into low orbit over the planet. Analysis suggests the initiation of a series of attack runs."

"*I grieve for their folly, Mr. Spock,*" Ael said. "*But for nothing else.*"

Jim sat there, feeling the sweat trickle down his back inside his uniform. *Those people down there have to know what's going to happen now,* he thought. *They're braver than any human population I know would be, under the circumstances.* The problem was that such bravery, in humans, was often closely coupled with fanaticism, and had in the past been associated with many terrible deeds. It was hard, now, to view such stoicism as strictly sane. *But these people aren't human, just humanoid, and it does no one any service to project our ethos onto them.*

Now *Elieth* and *Moerrdel,* two of the cruisers, streaked in past LPO levels, and lower still, deep into the upper levels of the Artaleirhin atmosphere, and began to fire. Jim would have closed his eyes, except that doing so was the coward's part. *The least I can do is watch their sacrifice.*

The first target was a large city down there on the side of the planet most visible to scan, a city by a big bay. Jim looked at it and thought, rather sickened, of how very much it resembled San Francisco. As the disruptors struck down from *Elieth,* he thought, *It's my job to prevent this kind of thing, to protect civilians from being killed in this kind of fight. And I can't do anything.*

A haze of smoky blue fire rose up from where the disruptors were striking. Jim could have wept—

—until he realized that the disruptors were having no effect on what was *underneath* that blue fire. He stared at the screen as the disruptor fire briefly stopped, and the blue glow shrugged itself up and away from the city into a bump, a wobbling half bubble, an immaterial dome.

Jim straightened in the center seat, then looked around at Spock. At his station, Spock was gazing down his scanner intently. "Force field," he said. "Unusual waveform, hexicyclic. Quite robust."

The blue dome covered what had to be hundreds of square miles. A renewed hail of disruptor fire fell upon it from *Elieth,* and then from *Moerrdel* behind it, and a spread of dissociator torpedoes came down as well. Jim found himself holding his breath again, waiting for the blinding light and the kicked-up dust and smoke to disappear.

"The fields are holding," Spock said, still gazing down his viewer. "The Imperial vessels are scanning the planet, probably looking for the power sources of the fields. But I suspect that search will be futile. The power sources are too well shielded—I cannot detect them either."

To Jim's practiced ear, Spock's voice betrayed a hint of what sounded like amusement. The obscuring dust and smoke was already clearing away from the second bombardment, and once again the blue-glowing force fields pushed themselves back up into shape. *Moerrdel* and *Elieth* arced away from the city they had been attacking, heading toward another city in the planet's northern hemisphere, this one sitting on the banks of a great river.

"Keep them in view," Jim said. Sulu nodded, touched his control panel. The tactical view shrank while the scan view pulled back to show the two Imperial ships as they made for the upper atmosphere, tracing great-circle routes toward that second city. It lay near the terminator, drifting into dark. Minute after minute it lay there, with no light about it but the faint hazy greenish glitter of what might have been city streetlights, far below. *Elieth* and *Moerrdel* dove, disruptor fire stitching down through the shadow of oncoming night—

—and the blue domes sprang up, at the last possible moment, almost as if in mockery. All around the cities, smoke and fire leapt up, the local atmosphere going almost opaque with dust. The Imperial vessels swung about, fired again, and again.

Nothing. The dust passed away in a blast of local wind provoked by the sudden heat pumped into the area's air; the fields outside the domes were pitted and crevassed by the disruptor barrage, even molten in places. But the cities stood.

"Most interesting," Spock said, as calmly as if he were passing comment on the progress of some experiment in a test tube. "The hexicyclic wave is a variant on one of several emitted by the device that tr'AAnikh brought us along with the wounded Senator." He straightened. "There is some truly fascinating technology coming out of the Rihannsu colony worlds, Captain."

Kirk filed that statement away for further consideration as he watched the Grand Fleet ships head across the planet again, past the terminator and into Artaleirh's night side, apparently to see if there was some city on that world that they *could* successfully attack. Jim shook his head at such dogged commission of outrage. "Mr. Sulu, keep an eye on them," he said. "I don't think they'll waste much more of their time there. I want to know when they come out of close orbit again. Where are the big ships?"

Sulu increased the size of the tactical display. "*Gauntlet* and *Esemar* have been hanging back, Captain. They were expecting us to come out after them, I'd guess. *Arest* and *Berouinn* have been moving slowly toward the asteroid belt, scanning, but not getting too far from the capital ships."

Jim's smile was bitter. "Wondering what other little surprises we might have in store. Well, they won't hang back for much longer. Uhura, what do their comms sound like—and the comms from the ships attacking the planet?"

She looked over her shoulder and gave Jim an amused look. "Nothing you'd benefit by hearing, Captain," she said, sounding dry. "If my grandmamma was here, she'd be telling me to go find a bar of soap to wash these people's mouths out with."

Jim wondered briefly how long it had been since soap came in bars, and hit the comm button on the arm of his seat. "*Bloodwing!*"

"*We hear,*" Ael's voice said.

"I wish you'd warned me about what was going to happen on the planet, Commander!"

"*The people on Artaleirh were themselves none too sure it was going to happen, Captain,*" Ael said. "*The technology had not yet been quite so vigorously tested. It would not have made any difference to how we had to behave for Grand Fleet's benefit.*"

It would have made some difference to my state of mind,

Jim thought, but wasn't going to say. He was all too aware that, though Ael might trust him, he had another level of trust to achieve with the Romulans in this system and elsewhere, no matter how welcome they said he and his ship were.

"But now the Fleet knows that the planet is of no use as a target," Ael said. *"Now they must engage us. Indeed, they cannot return home* without *having engaged us, at peril of their lives. All we require now is patience, of which we have plenty, and they have little."*

And luck, Jim wanted to say, but once again he restrained himself.

"Captain," Sulu said, "the Grand Fleet ships are rearranging battle order. The two that were attacking the planet have come 'round the far side now."

"Joining up with the supercruisers?" Jim said.

Sulu shook his head. "Coming our way, to feel us out, I'd say. The corvettes are hanging close to the supercruisers. It's another split of forces."

"Thank the Elements!" Ael said from *Bloodwing.* *"Can it be they're not even aware what they're doing?"*

"In normal circumstances, I'd wonder what they're teaching people in the Strat/Tac classes at Grand Fleet," Jim said. "Maybe they're nervous about what happened to the ships they sent in and haven't heard from again. I guess I might be, in their place. But meantime, whichever Element makes people throw away good sense or good battle order when they're angry, let's definitely thank *that* one. Mr. Sulu, this is what you were waiting for."

"Aye, Captain," Sulu said; and in his voice Jim heard something he had heard only very rarely before—an edge of anger, and of relish in the anger, that would have been out of place anywhere but here. Sulu was a kind man, normally, but he had seen things today that, from the sound of it, had at least for the moment wrung some of the kindness out of him. "Khiy?"

"Tr'Mahan signals that the smallships are ready to take the field," Khiy's voice came from *Bloodwing. "Are you?"*

"Going now," Sulu said. "Turn them loose."

In the background, from Uhura's station, Jim could hear a faint chatter of messages, all speaking one or another dialect of Rihannsu—the traffic between the little Artaleirhin ships as they moved into position. "Uhura," he said, "is all that in the clear?"

"Yes, Captain."

"Is that wise?"

She looked over her shoulder and smiled very slightly. "Captain," she said, "have you ever been to Glasgow?"

"Uh, once." It had been one of those long-weekend holidays; Scotty had taken him. To Jim's embarrassment, he could remember very little of the weekend.

"Did you understand the locals?"

"Now that you mention it . . ." That was one of the things Jim *had* been able to remember about the weekend: that Glaswegians, after a few pints, sounded unnervingly like Klingons. He had found it difficult to believe that he and they were all speaking the same language, and their tendency to greet every sentient being in the street with the phrase "Hey, *Jimmy!*" had already given him a crick in the neck by the end of the weekend's first night.

Uhura grinned. "Captain, children at school in the Rihannsu outworlds all learn the 'made speech,' the original recension of Rihannsu, as a *lingua franca,* but their local and planetary dialects vary from it hugely, not just in idiom but in etymology. Not to mention vowel shifts and other complications unique to a constructed language turned out 'into the wild,' where the 'wild' is light-years wide rather than just thousands or tens of thousands of miles. If any of the Grand Fleet people *not* from this system can make out more than one syllable in ten of what these people are saying, you buy me a hat and I'll eat it."

"Let's worry about the hat later," Jim said. "How many of the Grand Fleet personnel *are* likely to be from this system?"

"Captain," Ael said, *"not nearly enough, or we might not now be in this position. The Hearthworlds always have the advantage in placement and promotion in Fleet. To get past the barriers set in their way, commanders must be most extraordinary—and all too many of those are winnowed out early."* Now it was she who sounded bitter. *"No one at command level in these ships comes from Artaleirh. No ships with such command would be sent here in the first place, the suspicion being that they would likely revert to their outworld allegiance."*

Jim found himself suddenly having uncomfortable thoughts about some things Commodore Danilov had said to him about his own relationship with Starfleet—or rather, Fleet's perception of it—and he pushed them aside.

"Captain," Sulu said, *"Elieth* and *Moerrdel* are on approach. High and low."

"Got anything ready for them, Mr. Sulu?"

"Full spread and hot conduits, Captain," Sulu said.

Kirk nodded. "Save the rock-throwing for a little later. No use in showing them the rest of the cards in our hand until later."

"A little slow on the approach," Sulu said. *"Elieth* edging ahead a little. Her scanners are hot. She's looking at the processing facility."

Looking for the same shield waveform as on the planet, Jim thought. "Don't let them pursue that line of inquiry, Mr. Chekov. Fire at will!"

Enterprise's phasers lanced out and splashed against *Elieth's* shields. *Elieth* veered away from both *Enterprise* and the dilithium processing facility, and Chekov sent a couple of photon torpedoes after her for good measure. *"Elieth's* shields down five percent," Spock said, looking down his viewer. "Torpedo hits on her shields. Shield integrity down ten percent. *Moerrdel* is firing—"

Jim gripped the arms of the center seat as *Moerrdel* flashed past, firing en passant. "Our shields down three percent," Spock said. "Reinforcing. The small ships are giving pursuit."

A hail of little vessels, maybe fifty of them in the first wave, burst out from hiding behind various asteroids in the belt and went after both *Elieth* and *Moerrdel,* firing small chemical-explosive missiles and low-level energy weapons after the cruisers. Jim thought it was probably galling for relatively heavily armed ships like the two cruisers to be chased at sublight speeds by little vessels that a cruiser would normally disdain to use even as a gig. *But which of those is carrying, secretly, whatever it was that took down the first flight of Romulan vessels into this system?* Jim thought. *Have to give them a chance to get the job done.*

"*Bloodwing,*" Jim said. "The smaller ships aren't going to do any good until the cruisers' shields degenerate a good deal."

"*I hear you, Captain,*" Ael's voice said. "*Let us deal with it, so long as the supercruisers stay out of it. They may not do so for much longer.*"

"Let's see if we can increase their enthusiasm," Jim said, casting a glance back at Spock and not waiting for a reaction. "*Bloodwing,* we're going to take them for a little ride and soften them up a bit, while letting them think that what we use on them is all we've got."

"*An admirable suggestion, Captain. We will be doing something similar.*"

"Don't get too far out of range of the processing facility, though. I wouldn't like them to strike at it while we're out of range. Mr. Sulu—"

"Captain?"

"The roller-coaster scenario, if you please. I want whoever's directing this engagement to get the idea that even without our aces in the hole, it's going to take a lot more firepower to handle us than they're using at present—and that they're going to have to come in here and do it, not just coast around outside the belt and take potshots at us. Mr. Chekov, gunnery at will."

"Aye, sir," Sulu said.

"Aye, Captain," said Chekov.

Jim settled himself as securely as he could in his seat. It wasn't that he didn't trust the artificial gravity—like any other wise captain, he had ceased to trust it long ago. But his inner ear would occasionally betray him at odd moments when his body insisted it was sitting still, and the viewscreen, on which he was having to concentrate most intensely, insisted that he and others were doing anything but. Every now and then, in such situations, Jim had to remind his stomach just who was running this show, and being well settled in place was always a help.

The view in the main screen lurched and spun to starboard as Sulu's hands began to dance over the helm controls, and he threw *Enterprise* away from the dilithium processing facility and directly toward the nearest large rock. *Elieth* had come about and was firing at them again, but Sulu had already evaded the first spread of phaser bolts and was now in the process of evading the second, lurching from side to side but always heading for the same asteroid, a big one that was rapidly getting too big for Jim's liking in the viewscreen. Sulu hit another control and tactical view came up to overlay the live image, outlining the asteroid, showing the tag number that he and Chekov had assigned it, with wireframe gridwork showing any unusual mass concentrations inside the asteroidal body. There were several, but at the moment this wasn't an issue. Sulu threw *Enterprise* around the ragged curve of the asteroid's limb at an acceleration that was probably nothing her designers had anticipated, to judge by the way the ship's substructure started to groan. *Elieth* came after, still firing, but she came more slowly.

Enterprise dove and twisted away from that asteroid, flashed past a smaller one, and headed for a third, a big, tumbling, potato-shaped chunk of nickel-iron, flickering here and there in Artaleirh's sun with the violet or red-violet of dilithium ore. Over it Sulu sent the ship, and past it and "down," at right angles to the ecliptic and the orbit of the asteroid belt; and *Elieth* came after them, narrowly missing the asteroid as it tumbled.

"They must think we're suicidal," Jim said.

"There's a home-field advantage in every engagement," Sulu said, not looking away from the viewscreen, his hands roving over the helm console like those of a pianist sight-reading a score. "If they'd been here before we were, they could have had it."

He selected another of his tagged asteroids, one shaped like a lumpy letter *L* or *V,* and headed toward it. This asteroid was tumbling far more unpredictably than the last, its wire-frame tactical image showing a number of irregularly distributed concentrations of mass inside it, probably pools of heavy-metal ore or pure lanthanide metals such as were frequently associated with dilithium in the natural state. But the tumble wasn't unpredictable for Sulu: readouts in the tactical display, three sets of swiftly changing six-digit numbers, were showing exactly what the asteroid would be doing by the time Sulu got close to it. *Enterprise* was diving straight at the corner of the *V,* a spot that did not seem from this angle to be moving at all. Behind her, the other side of the split tactical display showed *Elieth* getting closer behind, and closer still, gaining confidence in her pursuit of this foe who would not stand and fight.

Sulu grinned and pounced on the helm console. *Enterprise* shot through the angle of the *V,* then to port and down, groaning in her bones. Behind her, the asteroid skewed in its tumble, and one of the legs of the *V* was abruptly coming straight at *Elieth*. She frantically threw herself sideways, and in so doing came out directly above *Enterprise*'s present position.

Chekov's hands had been hovering over controls on the weapons console. Now it was his turn to pounce. First a full spread of photon torpedoes went out, leaping away from the ship in the tactical view. They struck *Elieth* in the belly, right where the bird-of-prey shadows would have concealed a heart; and as the ship's shields flared with their simultaneous impact, Chekov fired all *Enterprise*'s forward phasers at the spot.

Elieth's shields flared brighter, then flickered in a sickly way. Chekov ceased phaser fire instantly. "Her shields are down," Spock said from his station, straightening up from peering down his viewer.

Enterprise veered away to port and "upward" through the asteroid belt. In her wake came about twenty of the little ships, which began peppering *Elieth*'s nacelles with explosive torpedoes.

"Not a bad start, Mr. Sulu," Kirk said, sitting back in the center seat again. "Let's see what *Bloodwing*'s up to."

Sulu pitched the ship forward a hundred eighty degrees to orient the main sensors back toward the dilithium processing facility. In the distance, past the facility, the tactical display showed the small red light that was *Bloodwing* as she twisted and dove among asteroids there, some thousands of kilometers away.

"Mr. Sulu," Jim said, catching sight of one particularly hair-raising maneuver that *Bloodwing* executed in and out among the bulbous projections of a particularly large asteroid, with *Moerrdel* in pursuit but rapidly dropping behind, "you really have been corrupting Antecenturion Khiy, haven't you?"

"Didn't take much corruption, Captain," Sulu said, rather absently, as he pulled *Enterprise* around the pocked limb of yet another asteroid, one that for just a second, to Jim's eye, had about the same shape as the state of Ohio, and then lost it as they dove past. "He has a natural talent. I just encouraged it. . . ."

"Uhura," Jim said. "Response from the other ships?"

"They're not pleased, Captain," Uhura said, sounding grim. "Engagement command on *Esemar* is ordering *Elieth* to self-destruct. *Elieth* is responding that—" She broke off, listening. "Their comms have gone down, Captain."

"A malfunction secondary to the damage?" Jim said.

Uhura shook her head. "I don't think so, Captain. But there's nothing further from *Elieth*—" She broke off and glanced over at Kirk, one hand to her ear. "*Esemar* has ordered the other ships to go silent, Captain."

"Getting ready to come in and deal with us themselves," Jim said. "Good." *I hope!* He was still uncomfortable about what kind of weapons those supercruisers might have on board. "Mr. Sulu, when the big ships start firing at us, I want to be elsewhere whenever possible. Make them show us what they've got."

"Yes, sir!"

Jim's insides jumped again as Sulu accelerated *Enterprise* to just under half impulse, weaving and darting among the asteroids that lay in their path. He almost wanted to protest. It would be simpler to take *Enterprise* up out of the asteroid belt for a short straight run, but more hazardous. They would be giving up both cover and advantage. *My stomach is just going to have to like it,* Jim thought as Sulu hurled *Enterprise* at another asteroid.

Jim's stomach leapt again. It did *not* like it. "Mr. Sulu, you could miss some of these rocks a little more widely."

"I'd hate anyone watching to get the idea this wasn't easy for us, Captain," Sulu said, sounding cheerful.

Jim sighed. "As you were. Just don't get overexcited and go relativistic on me."

"No need, Captain," Chekov said. "No one in the belt is exceeding one hundredth c."

"Let's keep it that way," Jim said. In particular, phasers and other energy-based weapons behaved very oddly when you got up into near-relativistic accelerations, and he had no desire to be anywhere near such events should they accidentally occur. "*Bloodwing?*"

"*One moment,* Enterprise.*"

They watched her curve and weave among the tumbling asteroids at speeds that would have made Kirk uncomfortable even were Sulu handling them. *Moerrdel* came after *Bloodwing,* as fast as she dared, but not fast enough. *Bloodwing* vanished around the curve of one asteroid, blocked from *Moerrdel*'s sensor view. *Moerrdel* continued along the course that *Bloodwing* had been pursuing, realized her quarry had vanished, but realized it too late, as *Bloodwing* came whipping back around the asteroid to a position directly behind *Moerrdel,* and fired both disruptors and photon torpedoes at *Moerrdel*'s rear shields, point-blank. The shields flared and went down, and as *Bloodwing* arced away, another flotilla of the system's smallships came boiling in from all directions and began to attack *Moerrdel*'s nacelles.

It was impossible, with all the Romulan ships now keeping silent, to tell whether the same loss of communications that had afflicted *Elieth* was now affecting *Moerrdel*. If, as Jim thought, it was a symptom of what had happened to the first vessels into this system the last time Artaleirh was attacked, then the ships were probably in the hands of Ael's allies already. Certainly neither of them had yet self-destructed. "Two down, seven to go," Chekov said.

"Hurray for our side," Jim said, his eye still on the supercruisers, now slowly moving in toward the dilithium processing facility. "*Bloodwing?*"

"My apologies, Captain, we were busy," said Ael.

"So I see. Nice shooting."

"I agree, though Khiy much desires to do something to our enemies besides shoot." Ael's voice was amused.

"Not just yet," Jim said. "Why tip our hand? But he'll have his chance pretty soon, I think. The big ships are moving in."

"As we see. I am uneasy about them, Captain. It's in my mind that they've been better equipped than usual, the better to make an example of us. Especially you."

"We're thinking alike," Jim said, "which on this subject makes me uneasy. Any thoughts on what they might be carrying above and beyond the usual?"

"There have been no great breakthroughs in weapons technology that I have heard of," Ael said, *"at least, not in Grand Fleet. Such things take time to test and install, and by the time that has happened, whatever secrecy might have initially surrounded the project is normally long gone. Though it must be said that I am lacking some of my old sources of intelligence."*

"You couldn't be blamed for that," Jim said.

"For which I thank you. Esemar and Gauntlet are closing, Captain. We must continue this discussion later. But tell me quickly—why would we need not to tilt our hands?"

" 'Tip,' " Jim said. "Uhura is really going to have to do some more work on idiom in the translator. It's a game, Commander. We'll discuss it later."

"May it be so. Here they come."

"Out," Jim said. He glanced at tactical, looked at the three ships closing on *Enterprise.* Two of them were the corvettes *Llendan* and *Chape.* The third . . . "Spock," Jim said, "that big one—"

"It is very overpowered, Captain," Spock said, looking down his viewer again. *"Esemar*'s version of our 'skinfield' and structural integrity field is much enhanced, with shields at initial analysis approaching the power configurations of those on Artaleirh's surface. But the shield implementation is otherwise standard. I see no indication of the waveform we have come to associate with the technology brought us via our 'defectors.' I would judge this to be merely a brute-force variant of earlier weapons technologies."

"Bigger, tougher, but not new," Jim said, watching the slow, steady approach of the big ship. It looked rather like *Bloodwing,* as an expression of the original "bird-of-prey" design, but the primary hull was twice as thick, arguing a much bigger crew complement, or much heavier weaponry.

"I would say so," Spock said. But his own expression, as he looked up from his sensors, suggested to Jim that he was viewing his own assessment with some caution.

Jim felt the same way. He glanced at tactical, saw that *Gauntlet,* unescorted, was presently heading toward *Bloodwing. But it may not* keep *doing that—and I dislike the idea of having two ships like that ganging up on me when I have no warp drive.* "Mr. Sulu," he said, "while I'm unwilling to restrain your display of expertise, maybe this is a time to pretend to be exercising the better part of valor."

" 'Pretend' to exercise it, Captain?" Sulu said, not turning his attention away from the viewscreen.

Jim grimaced at Sulu's amused tone of voice. "God forbid we should ever run away from anything for *real,* Mr. Sulu."

"Aye aye, sir," Sulu said. Jim watched that big ship keep on bearing down on them. *It's as big as* Enterprise, he thought. *A class of Romulan vessel that the Federation knows nothing about. Another reason to make sure we get out of this alive.* "Uhura," he said, "prepare a squirt for Starfleet Command."

"Done already, Captain," she said. She had been watching the screen as carefully as any of them had. "But I don't know if I'm going to be able to get it out. Subspace is full of jamming."

"What's the source?"

"Artaleirh, Captain."

Whatthehell? "Dump it to a microbuoy and prepare to get rid of it that way," Jim said. "Dump my personal logs to it as well, and all Mr. Spock's scans and other pertinent data. We'll need to make sure that the news of what happened here has a chance to get out, even if we don't."

"Handling it, Captain."

"*Esemar*'s weapons are going hot, Captain," Spock said.

"Mr. Sulu," Jim said, "a little more discretion, if you please!"

Sulu whipped the *Enterprise* around the back of a nearby asteroid just as *Esemar* fired her disruptors. The fire blasted the back of the asteroid into magma, tracking toward *Enterprise,* but missing her as she continued around the far side. *Llendan* and *Chape* came streaking around the asteroid to either side, firing as well, but Sulu had already gone diving steeply in z-axis, down through the plane of the asteroid belt. The two corvettes followed, *Esemar* coming after them.

"Disruptors on *Esemar* are running at approximately one hundred seventy-five percent the power of a standard Romulan Grand Fleet cruiser's," Spock said. "Higher even than *Bloodwing*'s, and she has had her gunnery conduits clandestinely augmented."

"And in comparison to our own phaser banks, that would be?"

"About a hundred and forty percent," Spock said. "The comparison, of course, cannot be exact, due to the differences between Federation phaser technology and—"

"I get your drift, Mr. Spock," Jim said. "Mr. Sulu?"

"Running like hell, Captain," Sulu said. And so he was. Jim swallowed as the view on the viewscreen began lurching and swooping in ever more creative and unlikely directions. Jim began to think it was true that some people never really learned to think in three dimensions, and that some people, on the other side of the divide, were born to it. He thanked heaven one more time that Sulu appeared to fall into the second category. Jim's stomach, though, continued to express its own opinions as Sulu found more and more interesting ways to use asteroids for broken-field maneuvers in vacuum. *Esemar* was dropping behind, which would have made Jim happier if its weaponry wasn't so much on his mind, and if the smaller, nimbler corvettes weren't beginning to gain on them.

"Mr. Spock," Jim said. "An analysis of any weak spots in *Esemar*'s shields would be useful at this point."

"Working on that, Captain," Spock said. "Unfortunately the brute-force implementation makes it all too easy to cover such. Elegance of design was not . . ."

He trailed off.

Esemar was firing at them, the initial disruptor bolts splashing off *Enterprise*'s screens without too much effect: but as she got closer, Jim knew this would no longer be the case. "Mr. Spock?"

No answer came back. Spock was peering down his viewer, though hardly lost in thought—Spock was less likely to get lost in his thoughts than anyone Jim knew. "Mr. Sulu," Jim said, "buy us some time, would you?"

"I'll dig down deep, Captain," Sulu said, "but with something like that chasing us, not to mention its two little friends, my budget's limited."

Now we're up against it, Jim thought. But Spock was still gazing down his viewer, one hand working over the controls at his console, and Sulu was hammering away at the helm, corkscrewing among the asteroid field's flotsam and jetsam, while *Esemar* and *Llendan* and *Chape* hunted them behind. Disruptor bolts jolted past them on the viewscreen, Sulu avoiding them by whatever synthesis of skill and instinct. For lack of anything else to do, Jim hit the comms button on the command chair. "Scotty?"

"Aye, Captain?"

"It's heating up out there, Scotty. It'd be nice to have warp capacity sometime soon."

If a voice could break out in a sweat, Scotty's did so. *"Fifteen minutes, Captain."*

"Right," Kirk said, and hit the button again.

Sulu flung *Enterprise* into a ninety-degree angle to the plane of the asteroid belt, and plunged along "upward," into regions where there were fewer asteroids, smaller ones, easier to evade. *Esemar* came along after her, not even bothering to evade the smallest ones anymore, taking them on her shields, pulverizing them in passing.

"Mr. Sulu!"

"Working on it, Captain."

Sulu flung *Enterprise* into what would have been a hairpin turn on Earth, if the hairpin was being bent in three dimensions instead of two. Jim wondered briefly how long it had been since anybody on Earth had used a hairpin, and watched the viewscreen hard, that being the best way to keep his stomach under control. The two smaller ships arced out wide and came along behind *Enterprise* again. *Esemar* matched the turn, much wider, rather slower, and came hard along behind again, blowing the smaller asteroidal chunks and fragments into glowing dust against her screens as she came.

Spock was still gazing down his viewer. "Indeed," he said abruptly.

Sulu grinned. "As Mr. Spock said, the relative rarity of dilithium makes some kinds of testing difficult. Or impossible."

Spock was working at his console again. *Don't jog their elbows,* Jim thought, *let them get on with it.* But it was so hard!

This is what they always said was the hard part of command, Jim thought, holding himself still, though it was torture to stay that way. *The delegation. To command, and sit back, and let those who've been commanded get* on *with it.* He watched as *Esemar* came howling along behind them, firing again now, disruptors splashing against *Enterprise*'s shields, but for how much longer? *But it's rarely been as hard as this to command, and do nothing else.* "Mr. Sulu!"

Sulu was twisting and corkscrewing among the asteroids, bigger ones now, and bigger ones yet. Once again the tactical array was outlining one or another of the asteroids visible on the viewscreen, showing masses, compositions. They were in "friendly" territory again, getting closer to the dilithium processing facility, and *Llendan* and *Chape* were soaring in from port and starboard, hounds in front of the hunter. In the distance, on tactical, *Bloodwing* could be seen executing the same kind of desperate evasive maneuvers in the van of the two other Grand Fleet heavy cruisers. *But how desperate are they?* Jim thought.

"*Bloodwing!*" Sulu said suddenly, as in the now triply split screen view *Esemar* could be seen getting closer and closer behind *Enterprise*, holding its fire as if waiting for one really good shot.

"Enterprise," came the reply, and it was Antecenturion Khiy, not Ael, "*are you seeing the annihilation spectra I am?—4551 angstroms and better.*"

"Confirmed," Spock said. "If rocks are to be thrown, this would be the time to start. But not those originally planned. Vectors will naturally add, and large masses will not propagate the effect correctly, so you are enjoined from using anything bigger than 1.4 to the third kilograms at this point."

"You're a spoilsport, Mr. Spock," Sulu said, but he glanced at Chekov. "Twenty seconds," he said, and threw *Enterprise* into a new set of maneuvers.

The screen subdivided again, bringing up a map of wireframed asteroids no more than a few tens of thousands of miles from the dilithium processing facility. "No chance you could get *Gauntlet* to follow you in there, is there, Khiy?" he said.

Half the asteroids in the display flickered dark, losing their computer overlays. Then another half. Then half those again. "Best solution," Chekov said. "Take it or leave it."

"We can only try," Khiy's voice came from *Bloodwing.*

"Go for it," Sulu said.

Bloodwing came arcing up out of the plane of the asteroid field in a long, lazy curve that displayed her belly to the pursuing *Gauntlet* as if she were a big fat cat with legs splayed, waiting to have her tummy scratched. "Oh, Lord," Jim said, half in terror that an ally should so expose herself; half in admiration, for no attacker worth his, her, or its salt could possibly refrain from such a target, so insolently displayed. *And what is Ael thinking about this?* he wondered. It was an issue better left alone at the moment.

Gauntlet dived after her. "This is even better than the fastball option," Sulu said. "And it leaves us the option for slow-pitch afterward. Got your target, Khiy?"

"Three of them."

"Choose your best one, and let's jump together—so they don't have a chance to warn each other."

"Counting back," said Khiy's voice. On *Enterprise*'s tactical display, one asteroid's wire-frame outline came alive, blazing red—picking it out from all the others but two, which pulsed darker, slower. *Enterprise* raced toward that asteroid, seemingly a small one, only a little bigger than many that *Esemar* had pulverized without noticing.

"Angstroms four five five one point three six two eight nine eight, at this mass," Spock said, glancing at Sulu. "Angle to the shields, along the longitudinal axis, fourteen degrees six minutes for *Esemar.*"

Sulu didn't speak, just nodded. From *Bloodwing,* Khiy said, *"Close approximation for* Gauntlet, *sixteen degrees twelve point one minutes."*

Jim held on hard to the arms of his command seat.

Esemar was swelling in the rear view that Sulu had running on the main screen. She filled nearly all of that view window, and the sweat broke out on the back of Jim's neck. He could just hear disruptor conduits going hot.

In tactical, *Bloodwing* rolled once more, exposing her ventral side, and without warning let off a full spread of photon torpedoes at *Gauntlet* while also reaching out with a tractor beam for another of the wire-framed rocks ahead. Whether anyone on board *Gauntlet* realized what was happening with that tractor, there was no time and no way to tell, for she put on a burst of speed, trying to angle up and away from the torpedo spread, firing as she went—and so went exactly where Khiy had plainly intended her to go. The tractor arced up over *Bloodwing*'s belly, swinging the asteroid up against *Gauntlet*'s shields at that sixteen-degree angle as she passed—

Bloodwing rolled again and threw herself up and to port, firing her phasers at the asteroid as she let it go. Behind her, as the asteroid struck them, *Gauntlet*'s shields flared and failed—and the asteroid, crackling with sudden surface fires and the violet glitter of destabilizing dilithium ore, plunged past where the shields had been and into *Gauntlet* itself, smashing into her starboard nacelle and shearing it away.

Shields down, bleeding silvery air and glowing plasma from the stump of the nacelle, *Gauntlet* plunged through the roil and tatter of dust from the asteroid impact. Out of the darkness, a swarm of the smallships came streaking in to surround her. *Gauntlet* fired at them, but with not much more effect than someone firing at a swarm of bees with a rifle. In the big screen, Jim stared at *Esemar,* still coming fast as *Bloodwing* swung back toward her and *Enterprise.* Without warning, *Chape* broke away, leaving only *Esemar* and *Llendan* in pursuit.

Uh-oh. Quick now, before they can figure it out. "Now, Mr. Sulu!" Jim said.

As *Bloodwing* dove at her, *Enterprise* swung up and to port. *Bloodwing* dove starboard and down. *Esemar,* shooting along behind them, veered ever so slightly toward *Bloodwing,* and began to fire disruptors.

As the green fire lanced out from *Esemar,* Sulu's and Chekov's hands came hammering down on their respective boards simultaneously. *Enterprise*'s tractors flashed out, fastened onto another of the remaining wire-framed asteroids, gripped it and swung it around and back. The ship wallowed a little, decelerating, and her course skewed as the mass she was manipulating turned her briefly into a two-body system. Jim hung on to the arms of his seat, expecting to be thrown out of it at any moment. But *Esemar* had no time to shift her field of fire, which she found suddenly blocked away from *Bloodwing* by the swiftly swelling shape of yet another asteroid, swung at her from the other side. In a flash of empathy, Jim could imagine himself seeing what *Esemar*'s bridge crew now saw on her screens. More green fire, lancing out without effect at that sudden and horrible rock as it got closer and closer, and on her bridge, orders being shouted, but hopelessly, no time to see them enacted, and the desperate thought, *The shields held this long, against rocks nearly that size; maybe—maybe—*

But these were not just any rocks. They caught *Esemar*'s forequarter shields solidly between them, crushing through them, crushing into the hull beneath; the ship's kinetic energy combined with the asteroids' combined velocities, the resultant energy discharging itself disastrously through the ship's structure. And the asteroids kept on going, crashing into each other.

Things blew. Things blew beyond even what one might have expected in an explosion involving a failure of a big ship's matter/antimatter drive. A little sun bloomed where *Esemar* had been, and scarlet-shot, violet-sparked clouds of dust and gas and half-vaporized dilithium ore blew outward from the primary explosion, following the self-annihilating remnants of *Esemar* as it kept plunging along its original trajectory. *Llendan,* still close to *Esemar,* tried to veer off, but not fast enough, not far enough. The outward-boiling explosion caught it, battered it, and as the particulate, ionized dilithium hit its shields, it took them down. The explosion blew through where the screens had been, and shattered *Llendan* like an empty eggshell. Its own warp core failed, exploded, and in its turn, as it plunged past, the remnant ignited two more of the asteroids that Sulu had had wireframe–tagged in his last sample. More of that bright-shot smoke blasted outward.

Emphatic, Jim thought. "Once again your choice of adjective is right on the button, Mr. Spock. Mr. Sulu, my thanks—that was the first thing on my wish list. Engagement command and control is gone."

"They'll have transferred it," Uhura said.

"If they had time, they transferred C&C to *Gauntlet,*" Jim said. "Which is doing nothing."

"Its comms are down too, Captain," Uhura said. "Not silence anymore; carrier is absent."

I don't know what Courhig and his people are doing, but maybe I shouldn't complain, Jim thought. *I'd sooner have Grand Fleet think that we're using some obscure secret weapon on them than have the word get back that all we did was run away and hit their ships with rocks.* "Where are *Arest* and *Berouinn*?" Jim said.

"Heading sunward at warp six," Chekov said. "On an interception course for *Sumpter.*"

FOUR

THE HAIR STOOD UP on the back of Jim's neck. "Uhura, get me *Bloodwing!*"

"Hailing her, Captain. No immediate response. The other ships are maintaining silence."

Jim began to sweat again.

Spock, looking down his scanner, suddenly looked more tense than he had. "Their screens are shifting frequency, Captain."

Tuning! "Engineering!"

"Bloodwing's on, Captain," Uhura said.

"Scotty, one moment. Ael!"

"My apologies for the delay, Captain; we were busy."

Jim had a look at the tactical display that Sulu had just refreshed for him. *Bloodwing* was arcing away from a trace that had been *Chape,* and was now an expanding cloud of air, cooling plasma, and debris. "You hit him with one of Sulu and Khiy's little presents?"

"No, I fear that he dodged the wrong way, and into an asteroid that had nothing more special about it than mass."

"Mass counts for a lot at even a hundredth of *c*."

"So we find. They are regrouping, Captain."

"With intent," Jim said, studying the tactical. "They don't dare come after us: they saw what happened to *Esemar* and *Gauntlet.* They're out for revenge now."

"I see their shields tuning," Ael said. *"Khiy!"*

"Following them, khre'Riov.*"*

"One moment, *Bloodwing.* Scotty!"

Scotty's voice sounded ragged, but relieved. *"Warp now, Captain!"*

Finally! Jim didn't say. "Thank you, Mr. Scott. Sulu, go!"

Sulu went, kicking the ship into warp so suddenly that it almost felt as if someone had hit the ship's screens with a spread of torpedoes. But Jim knew the difference in the feeling, and smiled a slight, grim smile. *"Captain,"* Scotty said from engineering, *"keep her under eight until the crystal settles in!"*

Jim watched the three ships ahead of them hurling themselves at the star, with *Bloodwing* plunging after. "No promises, Mr. Scott," Jim said. "Just deal with it, because we're off to the races. Can we catch them, Mr. Sulu?"

"I'll give it my best shot, Captain."

"That's Mr. Chekov's job," Jim said. "Sulu, do what you have to do. Uhura, that squirt—"

"I'll refresh the buoy's content, Captain."

He nodded. "Mr. Spock?"

"Sumpter, Captain," Spock said, "as we thought. Another set of power readings coming up."

"She's pulling away from the others, Captain," Sulu said, suddenly alarmed. "Warp six. Warp seven."

They're going to seed that star and take their chances on killing a whole planetary population, Jim thought. *If they can destroy us, someone can always come back later and reoccupy the system at their leisure, because they know Ael's here, and they figure killing her will take the wind out of the rebellion's sails. And as for all the people on Artaleirh, that's just tough.*

Indeed, *Arest* and *Berouinn* were approaching Artaleirh now, while *Sumpter* kept on pulling ahead. "Their weapons are going hot again, Captain," Chekov said. "Preparing another barrage."

"But they can't do anything to the cities."

"Approaches suggest they are heading for the polar caps, sir," Chekov said.

Those sons of— Jim swallowed hard. *Insurance. If something goes wrong with the seeding, they'll make the planet uninhabitable another way.* "Bloodwing."

"It is the old aphorism about the lleirh *and the hunters, Captain,"* Ael said. *"Either choice is deadly."*

Arest dove in first, and Jim's hands clenched on the arms of his center seat. "Sulu—" he started to say.

He was completely unprepared for the hot blue beam that came ravening up at *Arest* from the nearest city on the planet's surface. Jim's eyes went wide. *Arest* threw herself to one side, just barely avoiding the blast, and rather than falling into orbit, hurled herself onward and away from the planet in *Sumpter*'s wake. *Berouinn*'s course, too, changed in haste, following *Arest*'s.

"Augmented disruptor-type weapon," Spock said, looking down his scanner, "with that hexicyclic also involved in its generation."

"Ael!" Jim said.

"Captain, I tell you, that came as a surprise to me as well," Ael said, and her surprise did sound genuine. *"Plainly Courhig forgot to tell* me *something."*

The tone of her voice was unusually rueful. *He didn't forget,* Jim thought. *They don't quite trust you, either, do they? Something else you're going to have to deal with in due course.* "He's been a busy man," Jim said, as offhandedly as he could. "Meanwhile we have other problems. Mr. Sulu?"

"Helm's still sluggish to respond, Captain," Sulu said. "I've got warp six, but no better."

It wasn't going to be good enough. "Bloodwing," Jim said, "this one's going to have to be yours."

"Which one?" Ael's voice came back, somewhat desperately, as the three ships suddenly became four.

"There is the new reading we were expecting, Captain," Spock said. "Same velocity and trajectory as *Sumpter* for the moment. Now accelerating away. Warp eight point two— eight point three—"

Arest and *Berouinn* broke to port and starboard, but both of them were still heading generally sunward. *Any one of them could seed the star,* Jim thought, *but that little splinter off* Sumpter, *that's the best candidate for my money.*

Though could it be a decoy?

He threw his doubts aside. "The new reading. We'll take *Arest* for the moment and cover your back—then take *Berouinn* if there's time, after you've handled what just jumped off *Sumpter.* Mr. Sulu?"

"Aye, Captain," Sulu said, and *Enterprise* veered after *Arest,* but still too slowly.

"New reading," Spock said. "Coming uncloaked."

Oh, now *what?* Jim thought, and tried to swallow, but his mouth was just too dry. He watched *Bloodwing* arrowing after the reading that had separated itself from *Sumpter.* She was making a little headway, catching up to it, but too slowly. Artaleirh's star was getting close.

"Free Rihannsu ID," Spock said. "One of their captured ships, a cruiser. Closing on the new reading."

A bloom of fire erupted abruptly in front of them. Chekov said something fierce and satisfied in Russian. Sulu looked up with a feral grin as he threw the ship after *Arest,* which had begun veering toward the sun again. "Oh no you don't," he said.

Chekov fired a spread of photon torpedoes ahead. *Arest* veered again, away from the star, and Sulu followed her, closer now. "Warp seven," he said. "Seven point five."

"Mr. Sulu!"

"It's all right, Mr. Scott," Sulu said to the voice on the comm, almost absently. "We're not redlining. She's settled in now. Seven point nine."

"Enterprise," Courhig's voice said, "*this is* Sithesh." He sounded shaken. "*Tactical detection imaging has been down for some minutes, secondary to jamming artifact, but we've just recovered it, and we have new traces inbound. Six—*"

"Six *what*, Courhig?" Jim said.

"*Indeterminate. The readings could be* K'tinga-*class, but whether Imperial or—*"

In streaks of blue fire fading to red, the uncertainty was resolved. Spock glanced up from his scanner. "Klingon, Captain," he said, and even his controlled tone managed to communicate a sense of alarm. "IDs show six vessels. KL776 *Kartadza,* KL6044 *Tevekh,* KL908 *Melikaphkaz—*"

Six, Jim thought. *Oh my God. And here I was thinking that we'd gotten off lucky this time.* "I don't care who they are, they can't leave the system. *Bloodwing!*"

"*I see them, Captain,*" Ael's voice said. "*System jamming is holding, but we must engage them and not let them leave!*"

Jim shook his head. *Us.* Bloodwing. *Two, maybe three of the Free Rihannsu vessels capable of taking them. Against six of them?* The odds were uncomfortably long. "Sulu!" he said.

"*Arest* is breaking off, Captain," Sulu said. "*Berouinn* is following. Heading out of system fast, along the ecliptic. *Melikaphkaz* is following—"

Enterprise shook violently, and Jim clenched his hands on the arms of the center seat again as the *K'tinga*-class vessel fired at them en passant. "Number three shield down to fifty percent," Spock said. "Other shields are holding. Compensating for three."

The ship shook again, and again. "Mr. Sulu, abandon pursuit of *Arest,* form up on *Bloodwing.*"

In the tactical display, a light winked out. "No point in chasing *Arest* anymore," Sulu said. "*Melikaphkaz* got her. He's pursuing *Berouinn* now." And another light curved in on a last green-colored one in the display: two lights became one. "That was *Sumpter*," Sulu said. "*Tevekh* got her—"

Comms was suddenly full of a clamor of voices from all over the system. *This is a mess,* Jim thought, with entirely unnatural calm, as if watching all this in a classroom. *We need much better C&C for these mixed-force engagements. Must sit down with Uhura and design something a little less jury-rigged for the next one. If there* is *a next one.* "Bloodwing!" Jim said.

"*Truly I dislike having my problems solved for me in such a manner,*" Ael said, sounding, for one of the few times since Jim had met her, distinctly rattled.

Four of the Klingon vessels came arrowing toward Artaleirh. One of them peeled off to the side to make a run at the planet. *Well, they're going to have to take care of themselves. We have other problems.* The other three ships continued past, plainly targeting *Bloodwing* and *Enterprise*. "Wouldn't you say their timing's awfully good?" Jim said. "It's almost as if they expected to find a battle in its late stages."

"*It is a matter of common knowledge that there are Klingon agents in Grand Fleet,*" Ael said, sounding unusually grim. "*We have always killed any we found, but in these latter years, treachery roots too deep to dig it all out. I will take the foremost one.*"

"We'll take the two behind. Sulu, go!"

Sulu didn't even nod, but tactical display and the wild veering of stars in the viewscreen showed *Enterprise* breaking hard to starboard and "under" the approaching vessels as *Bloodwing* broke to port and "over." The Klingon vessels broke right and left to follow them as if it were all a maneuver choreographed well in advance.

"Two to one," Kirk muttered, his smile grim. "Their kind of odds." He watched the twisting, spiraling course that Sulu was tracing down between the two closest Klingon vessels, heading for system nadir and spinning *Enterprise* on her longitudinal axis as she went, firing the phasers from both under and over the primary-hull conduits and spraying phaser fire in a deadly pinwheel at the Klingons, now trying to close from either side. The phaser fire hit their screens without effect. One of the two ships, *Zajikh,* fell slightly behind.

"Sulu!" Kirk said.

Again Sulu didn't respond, but the *Enterprise* came out of the spin and curved up, and up, and back the way she had come in a huge arc that left both *Zajikh* and its brother vessel *Pefak* behind her and briefly going the wrong way. Another half spin and a lurching tightening of that arc, and now *Enterprise* was behind the two Klingon vessels. They started curving up in arcs of their own to get back the advantage.

Sulu grinned and broke hard aport, but let *Zajikh* drift into range in front of him. As he did, Chekov fired everything he had, phasers and photon torpedoes both. *Zajikh*'s shields bloomed with fire on the port side, then flickered in one spot. Once again Chekov hit that spot with phasers.

The beams stabbed through to the port nacelle. *Zajikh* blew. Sulu threw *Enterprise* just enough to one side to miss the worst of the expanding debris cloud, but now *Pefak* was hard on their tail.

Sulu swung back around, threw *Enterprise* into another of those bone-groaning turns, and headed in the nadir direction again—but this time the plane of the asteroid belt was under them. Sulu fled toward it. *Pefak* came after him, fast.

Chekov pounced on his board again; a spread of torpedoes sprayed out of the aft launchers. "We're empty until recharge," he said. "Cycle in five minutes."

Jim shook his head. It wasn't going to be enough. Sulu poured on the speed as *Pefak* took some hits on his forward screens, slowed a little.

Bloodwing came swinging in to plant a spread of her own torpedoes all over the same shields Chekov had just hit.

Those shields flared, went down. *Bloodwing* fired disruptors.

Pefak coasted on by with engines failed, but before she could fire again and finish it, *Bloodwing* had to veer off once more as *Kartadza* came in firing, and pursued her away from the stricken ship. *"Captain,"* Ael said, *"I would say we have a problem here."*

"You would say right," Jim said, not taking his eyes off tactical. "Sulu—"

"Coming about, Captain."

But not for more than a second, as *Kartadza* swung around, abandoning *Bloodwing* and coming after *Enterprise* instead. Once more Sulu headed nadirward, for the belt, but only a few seconds later *Melikaphkaz* was arrowing straight at *Enterprise,* cutting her off. Sulu had to veer away, twisting, to avoid collision, and *Enterprise*'s hull groaned from stem to stern as he did it. As the Klingon fired at them from behind, and the ship shuddered with the impacts, Sulu dove back down again, but once again *Melikaphkaz* got between them and the belt, and once again Sulu had to veer away.

Jim let out a bitter breath. The burning clouds in the asteroid belt and the peculiar spectral readings coming from them had told the Klingons perfectly well what had happened in the belt. They were not going to allow any ship to take refuge there. *They're going to make us fight in the open, cut us to pieces.*

In the tactical display, *Bloodwing* was describing another long arc that would bring her back toward *Enterprise.* She started firing at *Kartadza,* but without effect—the range was too great. Jim watched her come, wondering how much longer they had. *Kartadza* was swelling in the screen's view aft. "Shields," he said to Spock.

"Down to thirty percent, Captain."

Spock did not have to say, *We cannot take any more of this.* Jim heard it quite clearly in his tone, and swallowed.

It only remains to see how many of them we can take with us. "Mr. Sulu," Jim said.

"Enterprise," Courhig's voice came suddenly. "Blood-wing—*we have incoming.*"

More Klingons, Jim thought. *All right, this is it.*

It was always strange, how being about to die made you feel more alive. None of that nonsense about your life passing before your eyes. The last breathing seconds of life *now* were too intense and dear to waste on retrospectives. Jim sat up straight in the center seat, took in what was happening on the tactical display. "Let's sell ourselves dearly, Mr. Sulu," he said. "*Kartadza* first."

Sulu spared him just a glance. "Aye aye, sir," he said, and turned back to his console, then said, suddenly, "Warp ingress, Captain!"

Chekov added, "*Massive* vessel, Captain." He actually sounded a little shaken. "Decelerating hard."

"Onscreen!"

The view changed. Jim looked out into the darkness—and stared.

He had never seen anything quite like it. Big ships, yes, and tremendous habitats and facilities like *Mascrar* and the starbase at Hamal. But this was something else entirely. It was a triple-hulled design, all three of the huge backswept, cylindrical hulls mounted in parallel, at hundred-and-twenty degree angles, in a mighty central framework. Each main hull had to be at least three kilometers long. If *Mascrar* had been a city, this was more like a county, or even a very small country. And a well-armed one, as a swarm of smaller vessels came bursting away from it, bright small sparks shooting toward the ships that had been arcing in toward *Enterprise* and *Bloodwing*—and were now already beginning, entirely understandably, to veer away.

"Uhura, hail that vessel!" Jim said. "Find out what it's called."

"The cavalry?" Sulu said under his breath.

Jim was half inclined to agree. Uhura was speaking softly to her console. "Captain," she said after a moment, "they ID themselves as the Free Rihannsu vessel *Tyrava*."

"Greet them," Jim said, "and tell them we'd be glad to talk to them when things quiet down."

"They acknowledge," Uhura said.

Jim nodded and watched the ship flash past. Away behind them, as Sulu spun *Enterprise* in yaw on her central axis to bring her best weapons to bear, the five Klingon vessels still able to move took one look at *Tyrava*, flipped themselves, and fled.

Not fast enough, though. *Tyrava* fired. Jim's eyes narrowed against the blinding blue burn of phased disruptors at least as violent and powerful as the ones that had arrowed up from Artaleirh, if not more so. The first three of the Klingon ships simply vanished, leaving blooms of plasma where they'd been. *Kartadza*, running fastest, was enough out of range so that those beams didn't simply annihilate it, but left some debris, all molten. *Pefak*, trying to limp away, suffered the same fate seconds later. A fraction of a second later, one last bolt lanced out toward *Melikaphkaz*—but it was gone, gone into warp, escaped.

Jim sagged back in the center seat and stared at the screen, while listening to a sound he hadn't had leisure to notice all this while: his heart pounding. *Where the hell are that thing's nacelles?* Jim thought. *What have these people been doing to warp technology?* His mouth, dry before from nerves, was now getting drier still as he realized this was a matter over which Fleet would have his skin if he didn't get some answers. *And I thought I knew what the sealed orders were about before,* Jim thought. *I didn't know the half of it.*

"Captain," Uhura said. *"Tyrava."*

Jim stood up, holding on to one arm of the center seat for

just a moment to see if his legs were shaking. They were. He braced himself still. "Put them on," he said.

The screen cleared out of tactical to show what Jim assumed was *Tyrava*'s battle bridge, though the space looked to be the size of one of *Enterprise*'s rec rooms. Nearest the pickup stood a small, dark man in a plain, dark gray one-piece uniform much like Courhig's. The man was lean, with black hair, a long, lined, somber face, and eyes in that face that were nearly black. Jim was strangely reminded of Ambassador Sarek, though this man's expression was both far fiercer, and in a strange way, more settled. *"Captain Kirk,"* the man said in a light, soft tenor.

Jim inclined his upper body in a slight bow.

"I am Veilt tr'Tyrava," the man said. *"I am chieftain-designate of Tyrava Ship-Clan, as it has been reconstituted for this new time and circumstance in which we find ourselves. As clan chief, I command this vessel; though in the Starfleet structure you would conceive of me rather as an admiral than a commander."*

"Sir," Jim said, "whatever the details of your rank, let me say that right now, you are most welcome."

Just a slight smile warmed that long face. *"So are you,"* tr'Tyrava said. *"Here begins a new age for us, for good or ill, and your presence has made that beginning possible. May we meet, after you've recovered from the exigencies of battle? We have a great deal to discuss."*

"I agree," Jim said. "It would be my pleasure. Perhaps in a couple of hours?"

"Of course. Bloodwing *will give us the length of the hours you use. We look forward to offering you our hospitality."*

"It will give us great pleasure to accept it," Jim said, and once again bowed just slightly.

The screen went dark, and Jim straightened.

Here begins a new age . . . Jim thought about his sealed

orders again, and put aside for the moment the question of how in the world he was supposed to implement them now.

"Captain," Uhura said, "*Bloodwing* is hailing us."

"Put her on."

Ael was standing there in front of her center seat, over which lay that still, glinting shape.

"Commander," Jim said, "well fought. And thank you for your defense when we needed it."

Her look was wry. "*I had hoped to thank you first, Captain, for whatever I might have done was as nothing to what you did. Your presence in this engagement was instrumental in buying us the time we needed for* Tyrava *to arrive. And had she come only to avenge us, the message that this battle will carry to the Imperium would have been a much different one. We are now much stronger than we were, because of you.*"

"Strength by itself's not going to be enough, Ael," Jim said. "You need leverage, too, to turn strength to appropriate use. *Tyrava* is certainly more than welcome. But tactically speaking we're still far short of what we need to go into Eisn's space and make changes there. When we're over on *Tyrava*, I think we need to sit down with Courhig and whatever other of your confederates are on hand, so I can start choosing among the options now before me."

She nodded. "*I understand you,*" she said. "*I will see you on* Tyrava *in two hours. They will contact you with the appropriate coordinates.*"

"Thank you," Jim said. "*Enterprise* out."

He turned away from the screen and looked over at Spock. Spock had finally straightened up from his viewer and was looking at the image of *Tyrava*, which now filled the main viewscreen.

"Fascinating," Spock said.

"I have this feeling it's going to get a lot more so," Jim said. He sat back down again, as much from sheer weariness

as from any wobble in his legs. Formally, he said, "Lieutenant Commander Sulu, Lieutenant Chekov, you two are up
for commendations for today's work." Then he grinned.
"Don't try to talk me out of it."

"No, sir," they said in near-perfect unison.

"Uhura," Jim said, "get the relief helm and weapons officers up here." Jim jerked a thumb at the turbolift. "And you
two, go take the rest of the day off. You've earned it."

"Thank you, Captain," Chekov said, and "Thank you,
sir!" said Sulu. They both got up and stretched.

The intercom whistled. "That's another thing," Jim said.
"I should get down there and see how Dr. McCoy's patient is
doing."

"He's fine," came the rather irritated voice, *"much to
my surprise, the way you threw us around. At least the
power didn't go out on us, I'll give you that much. Did we
win?"*

"Uh. Bones, if we hadn't, we would now be exploring
some other plane of existence, I guarantee you."

McCoy snorted genially. *"Well, whatever else I can say
about sickbay, it's hardly heaven. Gurrhim woke up for
about ten minutes and gave me rather the opposite about the
noise and vibration you were inflicting on him, then fell
asleep again."*

"Everybody's a critic," Jim said. "I'll apologize to him
later. Kirk out."

He hit the button. The relief helm and weapons officers
came in, and Sulu and Chekov ambled toward the doors, followed by the muted congratulations of most of the bridge
crew. "A regular roller coaster," Chekov said as they went,
sounding completely satisfied. "Invented in Russia, of
course."

Sulu rolled his eyes. Everybody else on the bridge
groaned.

Chekov looked stricken. "No, but really, it was!"

Laughter broke out, and all around the bridge people went back to work. "Truly!" Chekov said. "In 1766—"

"Pavel," Sulu said, getting into the turbolift, "don't push your luck. You did a great job. Let's go get something to eat and congratulate ourselves on a *genuine* Russian accomplishment."

The doors closed on the two of them. Chekov's expression was a little woebegone.

Jim smiled to himself and just sat there in the center seat, listening to the sound of his bridge calming itself down. Once again the unexpected had occurred around him, as he'd seen it happen before. The very nature of space itself had changed, and a volume of empty vacuum had suddenly become a battlefield, and a matter of history. Ten minutes, maybe twelve, was all it had taken to turn the surroundings into the Battle of Artaleirh, something that would be analyzed and pored over in the future by historians, and by other officers who would look over Jim's shoulder with the comfortable augmentation of twenty-twenty hindsight and say, *He made a big mistake there. If only he'd done such and such . . .*

Feeling something, he glanced up. Spock was standing by the center seat, gazing at the viewscreen, and *Tyrava*.

"We got lucky today," Jim said.

"Random elements of chance," Spock said, and raised one eyebrow. "The wise tactician knows they are not to be depended upon."

Jim smiled half a rueful smile. "Well, on the other hand, it's not every day you get to have a fight in an asteroid field full of raw dilithium. *That* at least was interesting."

Spock nodded. "Your adjective, too, is apt, Captain. But the next fight will be of an entirely different order. Grand Fleet sent to Artaleirh what they considered more than ample force, and we demonstrated to them that their reckoning was faulty. Next time they will make no such mistake. The next engagement will feature crushing force, administered not from arrogance, but anger, uncertainty, and fear—a much worse configuration to face."

Jim nodded slowly. "Meanwhile, sufficient to the day are the victories thereof."

Spock's expression was neutral. "I would not quite describe this one as Pyrrhic, yet its consequences are likely to be complex in the extreme. For all of us—but most especially for you."

Jim nodded, and said nothing more.

FIVE

AEL STOOD with her hands on the back of her center seat, staring at the viewscreen, in which the dark of space was completely blocked by *Tyrava*. She was finding it hard to do anything but tremble, and not entirely because of the battle. Out there, hanging huge and dark, a great mailed shadow, her future had come for her. And perhaps, in the shadow's shadow, death . . .

She took a long breath and thrust the feelings of ill-omen away from her, stepping around from behind the seat to step up to the viewscreen. *Nothing ails me but after-battle shakes, and lack of a meal or two,* Ael thought, trying to become annoyed with herself. That was always her way, to cope with a crisis first and react to it later. This battle was like any other, if only a little more complicated.

But the darkness hung there and said to her heart that this battle was different—and the others to follow would be more different still.

She glanced over her shoulder. Her bridge crew were putting themselves to rights without comment. Aidoann had been slammed against a console during the battle, and stood there now with her sleeve up, examining a bruise on her arm that was already coming up most splendidly turquoise-black. Others were dusting themselves off, leaning back in their seats or against their stations; Khiy had his head down on his console. Ael peered at him and heard a slight sound that shocked her. He was snoring. And there behind him, glinting in the normal day-running light, lay the Sword, right where she had left it, across the arms of her command chair, nearly an eternity ago.

Ael could only shake her head. "Aidoann," she said softly.

"Khre'Riov?"

She glanced at Khiy. "Have you seen him do this before?"

Aidoann stepped softly down beside her. Together they stood looking at Khiy: he emitted a snore rather louder than the previous ones, then subsided again. "Never *during* battle," Aidoann said quietly, and smiled.

Ael had to smile as well. "It is reaction, I'd say," Aidoann said. "He did not sleep at all last night, and I think not much the night before. And then to go from such a pitch of action to peace in the space of a few breaths . . ."

"I envy him the ability," Ael said. "Nonetheless, we have business. Get me *Tyrava*; and if Khiy does not wake by the time I'm done and out of here, then find some way to rouse him that will not let him know or suspect what we've seen." Aidoann started to step away, and Ael halted her with a hand on her arm. "And one thing more," she said quietly. "Have Surgeon tr'Hrienteh have a look at him afterward; but not a word as to why. Let it be said that I have asked all crew to be checked after such an encounter. Indeed, that's not a bad idea. Have her see to it."

"Ie, khre'Riov."

Aidoann stepped back to her console. A moment later, the screen flicked into a view of *Tyrava*'s vast battle bridge. Ael had never seen the place before, but had heard tell of it, and now she marveled at a space into which it seemed all of *Bloodwing* could have been fitted. In the background of the view, people moved about their business, dressed in the somber work-clothes of an ostensibly civilian environment. But Ael saw the occasional glance thrown at the screen as the dark shape she had been expecting came walking up to it, and she read those looks to mean that those who gave them were wondering whether they would shortly be in the military—*some* military.

Veilt tr'Tyrava came to a stand before the viewer and looked at her. Ael gave him a second's worth of bow more than was strictly required of her, for he was worth it. Here, embodied in this slight, unassuming shape, was a whole Ship-Clan in a single package: wealth, power, and a very specific turn of mind. Greater names than she had come to this man's door seeking his support, and had gone away with empty hands. Now Ael found her hands full—perhaps too full. She was not easy with the circumstances.

"We are beholden to you, tr'Tyrava," she said, also addressing him more formally than she needed to.

"Yes," he said in that light, casual voice, *"so you are. But let us not start reckonings yet. There are many more screenfuls of figures before us, and the full value of some of them is still to be decided."*

It was one of those cryptic utterances of his that could mean one thing, or a hundred. Ael had gotten used to the sound of them over much time, but was not yet entirely sure that she was capable of winnowing out *everything* behind one. For the moment, though, Veilt smiled that small sword-edge smile of his, as much humor as he normally exhibited to anyone not one of his intimates.

"Yes," Ael said. "Well, you were late, Veilt. We were expecting you rather earlier."

"You are to count yourself lucky we came at all," Veilt said. *"Indeed matters could have gone well otherwise had we not detected, on our way in, the* other *part of the Klingon task force sent to deal with you—but fortunately, they had divided their forces."*

Ael looked at him in shock. "There were more?"

"There were," Veilt said, *"another ten heavy cruisers. I should not have cared to meet that whole task force at*

once—it would have stretched even our resources—but for-
tunately for us, the Elements have been making our enemies
too sure of themselves in these early engagements. They will
not stay so for much longer, however."

Gazing at Veilt, Ael bowed once more—a much deeper bow, much longer than the last one. "I misspoke myself," Ael said. "My apology to you."

"You could not have known," Veilt said. *"No apologies are needed. Yet we must take warning from this, as our ene-mies doubtless will."*

"They'll take more warning away from this than would have pleased me," Ael said. "Woe to that last ship that got away!"

"Oh, I think it may not do us such harm, at least not right away," Veilt said. *"Only consider that ship's position. They emerge from warp and return home in disorder from an en-gagement in which they should have had marked numerical superiority, and in which they should have been, if not easily victorious, at least certainly so. And no other ship comes back to tell any tale. Only they—with an outrageous story of some unidentifiable monster ship that came from nowhere and cut them all to pieces. However true it may be, that's not a story they'll have any joy in telling their superiors."* Veilt raised an ironic eyebrow at Ael. *"Dearly I would love to hear them make that report, and hear what their superiors have to say. That sixteen cruisers were dispatched to deal with* Enter-prise, Bloodwing, *and perhaps five or six light cruisers—as-suming they do indeed have spies in this system, we may safely conjecture that they know that much, and nothing more than a motley flock of little single ships, not fit to clean out their phaser conduits."* Veilt smiled. It was a wintry look. *"And then all of those big ships were destroyed by such a paltry little band? If I were in the Klingon High Command, I would find it hard to believe a word that ship's commander said. Indeed, I'd suspect that they had turned and fled in the*

face of forces not nearly so overwhelming—just because
Enterprise *was there. You know what effect that name has on*
Klingons as well as I. Enterprise *would be assumed to have*
done yet another of its sorcerer's tricks on the task force.
That they would believe. But that last poor ship's command
would be assumed to have run for their lives, and then made
up the rest of the tale about giant ships out of nowhere to jus-
tify their cowardice. Were I the Klingon admirals in their
High Command, I would have that ship's officers all shot."
That smile became more wintry yet.

Ael had to smile herself, a touch ferally, at the truth in
what he said. "Yet no word will come back to the Klingons
from the other fifteen ships," Ael said. "They are going to
have to explain their loss to themselves eventually."

"By the time they find out the truth of what's happened,"
Veilt said, *"we may hope it will be too late for them. They*
will already have committed more forces using tactics now
outdated, and those forces will again be too scattered to deal
with Tyrava *properly. The big engagements to come, in the*
space outside Eisn's heliopause, those give me concern in-
deed; but at those, I think we will have help."

Ael's heart leapt in her side. This was the news she had
not dared ask, for fear it would be bad. *"Divish, then?"*

"Not only Divish, *but* Taseiv *as well. Both ships' comple-*
ments were overwhelmingly in favor." Veilt gave her one of
those obscure looks that had always made Ael so uneasy in
the past. *"It will have had a great deal to do with the com-*
pany you are keeping, and the way he has performed so far.
The news that will come to them from Artaleirh will only so-
lidify their decision."

"Are you going to tell *him* that?" Ael said.

"Should I?" said Veilt.

It was that question of trust again. *Sharpen the knife cau-*
tiously, lest it turn in your hand. So the saying went. *But at*
the same time, Ael thought, *a knife that's not sharp enough*

does no one any good, and can be a danger when you try to cut.

"I think you should, and must," Ael said. "The alternative makes us look like fools, or makes us seem to think him one. Or it gives the impression we fear what Kirk will do if he comes to know himself indispensable to what we do. Like it or not, Veilt, indispensable he has been, and is. Pray the Elements with all your heart that *Enterprise* lasts until we get at least as far as Eisn space, otherwise I much fear all of this, and all of us, will come to nothing at the last."

Veilt was silent for a while. *"He has kept faith,"* he said at last, *"so far."*

"He is no dayside fighter," Ael said, "to slip away when the dark makes it easy. You will see, when you meet him. And then you will ask yourself how you could have thought I would deal with such a one for more than a single engagement."

Veilt held up his hands in a gesture of mock alarm. *"Cousin* thrai," he said, very mild, *"keep your teeth for better use. I am willing to be convinced, if you're right. For the moment, though, I need to make things ready for our guests to come."*

"The doctor," Ael said, with a slight smile, "is fond of ale, and well he's earned it today, it seems. Gurrhim tr'Siedhri lives."

At that, Veilt's half-lidded look went just briefly wide-eyed. *"We had heard he was like to die."*

"So he was," Ael said, "had he been left in *Gorget*'s infirmary. But he was snatched out of it and delivered straight into Kirk's hands, and McCoy did the rest."

Veilt nodded, and the bland look on his face, Ael knew, was suddenly just a mask over calculation, reassessment, some whole new nest of obscurities which, if she were lucky, she would be able to puzzle out eventually. *"He shall have ale enough to swim in, if he wants it,"* Veilt said at last. *"A*

*good turn past believing, he's done us today. This makes
many things much simpler."*

Ael smiled. "So see how saving us has done you good
after all," she said, much more lightly in tone than she might
have. "Veilt, I am all of a muck sweat with fighting, and must
go make myself ready to be in company with beings that
have noses. Your pardon."

"Of course. But Ael—"

She paused.

"Perhaps the apology should have been mine."

"Wait until you meet Kirk," she said, "and then tell me so
again. Out."

"It's a monster," McCoy said.

"It's a monster that saved our lives, Bones," Jim said.

They stood on the bridge, looking at the viewscreen.
Spock was over at his scanner, taking readings; McCoy and
Jim and Scotty all stood gazing at *Tyrava.*

Scotty shook his head. "What have they done with that
thing's nacelles?" he said.

"I was hoping you could give me an answer to that,
Scotty," Kirk said.

Scotty examined the tripartite hull of the ship with a practiced eye. "If you were dead to caution, and had a population
made up of suicidal maniacs, then maybe . . . *maybe* you
could run the warp conduits down the centers of those hulls."
He looked skeptically at *Tyrava.* "But you'd have to be absolutely certain that you had a warp technology that wasn't
going to fail you. And if you *had* something like that . . ." He
shook his head.

"Could 'something like that' be derived from the little device that Arrhae sent over to us from *Gorget*?" Kirk said.

"Captain," Scotty said, "it's too soon to tell. I haven't had
time to find out the half of what that wee thing *does* yet.
There's not just one, but at least three new technologies con-

tained in it. The first one has similarities to the transtator, but entirely differently conceived. The other two—" He shook his head again. "K's't'lk is taking some time off the Sunseed business to look at it now. She may see something she recognizes; the Hamalki have a whole different view of their sciences."

"I've noticed," McCoy said. "Let's just hope that whatever she sees in that little gadget doesn't give her any strange ideas. The last thing we need right now is to wind up in some other reality, getting all transcendent."

"I've already warned her about that," Jim said. "I think we can assume we're safe from that eventuality. But we may have worse ones to deal with." He glanced at the chrono. "Come on, we'd better get over there."

They made their way to the transporter room and climbed up onto the pads. McCoy rolled his eyes expressively at the ceiling as the transporter tech worked the sliders. The world dissolved in dazzle.

When the brief storm of light faded, they found themselves standing in the center of what appeared to be a huge, round, empty space several hundred meters across—a black glass floor, gray walls, and a domed gray ceiling apparently about forty meters up. Jim looked around him with astonishment and appreciation, and a bit of unease at all this empty space inside a vessel. *But is this perhaps the wave of the future?* he thought. *Really big ships? Are starships on the present scale just a temporary aberration? Or, at least, starships the way we have them now.*

His unease, as he stood there looking around him and waiting to see what would happen, wouldn't quite go away. *I wonder,* Jim thought, *if this is the way Ael felt the first time she came aboard* Enterprise. *A little outraged at the sheer size of things, compared to what she was used to.* He gazed up and around again, trying to judge the size of this vessel by using the size of this waste space that seemed to have simply been thrown away. *Yet perhaps . . .* Jim looked around again, looked at the floor. "Spock," he said, gesturing at the floor.

Spock nodded. "Yes, Captain." He had his tricorder out, and was scanning the floor. "All of this," Spock said turning slowly in the circle, "is one large transporter pad."

"With a multiple array underneath?" Kirk said. "Or—"

"No, Captain," Spock said. "This is all a single pad. Extremely flexible, extremely programmable, able to transport one person, or an entire shuttlecraft." He looked around him. "Or something much larger."

"I can believe this ship would have power to burn," Jim said softly. "But *that* much? That they could transport whole vessels, instead of just using normal propulsion?"

"I have no doubt of it, Captain," Spock said. "There are certain economies of scale to be achieved by using such strategies—if one can afford them."

That was the whole point, of course: *if* you could afford them in terms of volume and power. The thought that had first occurred to Jim after seeing *Tyrava*—well, all right, the second one, after the intense relief of seeing it start slicing up the pursuing Klingon vessels as if they were so much baloney—was, *How much did it cost to* build *that thing?* No one went around building generation ships without a massive capital outlay. And this was much more than just a generation ship, a tin can full of people. Here, in front of him, he saw a secret as strange in its own way as the little *Gorget* gadget that Scotty was trying to understand. *Normally,* Jim thought, *we tend to think of the Romulan colony worlds as poor places, struggling for survival. Yet here* this *is. And what are we supposed to make of it? Either these people have access to wealth, or sources of wealth, that we don't know about or understand—*

—or what we're seeing here is the result of every single person on several planets, everyone who can work, privately or publicly donating—how much? He shook his head. *A sig-*

*nificant amount. For the promise, or even the mere chance, of
leaving their homeworld and finding a new one, somewhere
else, very far away—and if not for themselves, then for their
children.*

Off to one side came another sparkle, this time the telltale
golden-red of a Romulan transporter. Ael shimmered into
shape on the shining floor, and as transport completed, she
looked around her with an expression of nearly the same
borderline unease as Jim had felt.

She walked over to them. "I hope you gentlemen have not
been bored."

McCoy raised his eyebrows at her. "Bored? Us?" he said.
"Not a chance. We've just been wandering around, picking
up the vases and looking underneath 'em for the price tags."

Ael smiled at him, though the smile was not entirely without an edge. "How one so occupied with the weighty business of life and death can find time for such drollery," Ael
said to McCoy, "not to mention such acuity in the economic
mode, I hope someday to understand. McCoy, how does
your patient?"

"Better than can be expected," McCoy said. "I detect certain reassuring diagnostic signs in Gurrhim—specifically,
that he's a mean old coot who's too stubborn to die while he
still has things to do."

Ael smiled. "I am none too sure of what a 'coot' is, but
otherwise I think your diagnosis is correct. But he's full of
wiles and guiles, is Farmer Gurri, and has his own acuities.
Beware that, while you are gone, he does not strip sickbay to
the walls and sell the parts off secondhand."

"Farmer Gurri?" Kirk said, bemused.

"I cannot tell you the half of it now, Captain," Ael said,
"but he makes much of what he would call his 'rough country ways.' They are at least partly a disguise. On ch'Havran,
they have a saying that the Siedhrinnsu did not become as
wealthy a clan as they are by giving anything away. With his

own hand, almost, that man built up a moderately well-off set of family businesses into a mighty trading empire—at least, as we reckon such things. Some people will tell you that he owns half of ch'Havran. It would not be too far from the truth. Gurrhim is a force to be reckoned with: not only rich, but honest, and with a strong ethical streak, though sometimes, without warning, those ethics skew in favor of family or business priorities. Beware of getting yourself entangled with him—he will twist you 'round to his ways of thinking before you know what's happened."

"He's not going to be twisting anyone into much of anything for a few days at least," McCoy said. "But he said again that he wants to see you, Jim, and Ael as well, when she has time."

Jim nodded. Ael glanced to one side; he followed her glance, and saw coming toward them, across the broad, shining floor, Veilt tr'Tyrava.

As soon as he was close enough to speak without shouting, he said, "Gentlemen, Ael, I hope I have not kept you waiting long."

"It's a long day's walk to anywhere in here, from the looks of it," Jim said, not bothering to take the slight edge of envy off his tone. "I don't think we mind that it took you a few extra moments to get here."

"Normally, we use transporters," Veilt said. "While I dislike keeping any guest waiting, the master of a ship like this has many responsibilities, which routinely interfere with one another. I pray you hold me excused." He turned. "Ael—"

She bowed to him slightly, her left fist against her heart. "Elder and cousin."

That brought Jim's head around. "If I may ask—you're related?"

Veilt smiled a thin, slight smile. "The Commander General has some Ship-Clan blood, Captain. We are kin from afar. There would be those in Grand Fleet who would explain all her past disaffections in terms of that circumstance—as if being of Ship descent automatically made one a potential traitor. I wonder sometimes if those Hearthworlders ever consider, these days, that without our ancestry, there would have *been* no Hearthworlds. But these days, the division runs deep." He glanced around. "You will hear enough of it in the days to come that there would be no point in keeping you standing here while I educate you. Will you follow me to where we may sit and talk?"

"Gladly."

Within a very short time, Jim realized there was no point in trying to keep track of where they were being led. It was like being in a new city. Ael walked along with him, a little ahead of them, as they made their way down long high-ceilinged corridors and through wide hallways, up lifts, down long escalators through vast public spaces. The place was bigger than Starfleet Command, far bigger than any en-closed space Jim had ever been in. Yet, people went about their business; small children ran and played; and all around them was the quiet, comfortable buzz of people at home in an environment that had been their home for—

"Sir," Jim said, "how long has this ship been inhabited?"

"Its population has been in training for this inhabitation for about three years," Veilt said. "We have enough memo-ries of the last time our people were in generation ships that we have no desire to throw them into such an environment without some practice. Especially since, if things don't go smoothly as we hope, they may be spending a matter of some years in such an environment. Not that we have to spend so long in transit any more, now we have warp drive. But all the same, it can be a long time between worlds, find-ing the one that's right for those who travel with you."

Down a hall ahead of them was a pair of black glass doors. Veilt led them toward those doors, which slid aside as the group approached. Inside was a roomy, handsome, modern conference room with a black glass table in the center, and abstract art hung on the warm, gray walls. "Very humane," McCoy said. "And a lot more cozy."

Veilt smiled. "Like most other people, we desire some intimacy in our personal areas, Doctor. We don't throw away space merely in order to impress. There would be no logic in that." He gestured at the table. "Cousin, gentlemen, please be seated and tell me if there's anything I can get for you to make you comfortable while we talk."

They all sat down. Water in pitchers appeared on the table, along with glasses; and also pitchers of something blue. McCoy smiled.

"On the job, Bones?" Jim said.

"This is strictly social, Jim," McCoy said, reaching for the pitcher and pouring himself out a tot of ale. He lifted the glass to Veilt, and said, *"Ei e'hraaintuh na'hwiufvteh, emeihet'!"* Then he knocked the ale back in a gulp.

Both of Veilt's eyebrows went up. Ael smiled slightly as McCoy pushed the pitcher over to her, glancing at him with humor but apparently declining to take any other notice of the way his eyes were watering. She poured herself a small glass of the cloudy blue stuff and eyed it with appreciation.

Jim gave McCoy a look, then turned to Veilt. "First of all, I want to thank you for a very timely rescue. We are in your debt."

Veilt looked at him speculatively. "Not many commanders I know would be so quick to put themselves under obligation to another. Among our people, it tends to be a sign either of uncertainty or unusual confidence."

"I would hope to avoid either," Jim said. "The situation in which we are soon to find ourselves will not be improved by either state."

"And that situation would be?"

"Well," Jim said, "we *are* in the early stages of a war. While with your help we've just successfully completed its first engagement, successive battles are likely to be less straightforward. Uncertainty can be healthy enough in its place, but too much of it in the days to come is likely to be as dangerous to us as too much confidence." He leaned back in his chair and gave Veilt a look as speculative as the one he had been given. "Not that this ship isn't one to inspire confidence."

Veilt laughed so softly as to hardly make any sound at all. "Believe it or not, there are others that may yet inspire you even more. But more of them shortly. Captain, we were glad to be of help to you, but our major role is not offensive. *Tyrava* is a habitat first and a battle station second. In fact, we always hoped to avoid battle. None of the people you see living here would have chosen the shipboard life had on-planet life not become intolerable for them. This ship holds some three hundred and eighty thousand souls from far-flung colonies of the Empire, planets like Gahvenn and Thalawir. Some of their worlds were sparsely populated, and nearly abandoned by the Empire; some were closer in, but more harshly treated. But in every case, the people who now populate *Tyrava* were willing to take the chance every day of dying, rather than live under the Empire any longer. With such a crew and population, one can do much. Or rather—" Veilt looked amused. "—they can do much with me. Their will with me, often expressed, is to do anything that would make the Empire a place where we could live again. Until recently, 'anything' meant 'anything but war.' But no longer. All over the Empire, the uprisings are beginning. This is the time for which many of us have waited. And this is the gamble on which we must now stake everything we have. If after the conflict to come the Empire still has not fallen, then we must seek our lives elsewhere. But in the meantime—" He looked at Ael. "—we must take our best chance."

Ael bowed her head. "We did well enough here. But we must do better yet. In particular—" She glanced at Jim. "The too-timely arrival of the Klingons suggests that they had spies at Artaleirh—as we long suspected. Desirable as it would have been to keep any Klingon ships from escaping the battle, in terms of intelligence, I think that has become a nonissue. The High Council will hear soon enough what actually transpired in these spaces. We must move forward, and quickly; so we must determine in what directions to move, in what force and strength—and to what purpose."

Jim folded his hands on the table in front of him. "I've been considering some initial planning, if you would be willing to hear it."

"More than willing," Veilt said. "We also need to give some thought to what disinformation we can spread in this system before we move on. As for the rest—" He looked thoughtfully at Jim. "Your skills as a tactician have gained you the esteem and curses of our people often enough before. Few of us will have looked for the chance we see now, where you employ those skills on our behalf."

"Not just yours," Jim said. He glanced up from his hands. "No sane man willingly goes to war. But it seems that once every generation or so comes the war from which it would be cowardice to turn away. At the moment, this looks like that war." Jim sighed. "And there are other issues. The proliferation of the Sunseed technology . . ."

Ael looked over at Veilt, frowning. "They were ready to seed that star. They would willingly have destroyed all life on a Rihanssu Imperial world, and used that fact to put the fear of such destruction on other worlds, where warships can no longer do so."

"Or in cases where the Empire's resources are spread too thinly to allow the dispatch of a task force," Spock said.

Ael nodded. "I fear also that Artaleirh would have been a testbed in other ways. My concern is that they have been attempting to refine the technique to make it more predictable, or more deadly—or both. It is almost horrible to hope that they are blind to the dangers of using such a thing repeatedly. Far worse is the concept that they are *not* blind to them."

Veilt nodded, and looked at Kirk. "Ael has told me that you are attempting to devise some technique that may be used to keep the Sunseed technology from being implemented in a given star system."

"That's right," Jim said, and threw a glance at Ael.

"I'm relieved to hear it," Veilt said. "Even the possibility will give some hope to the many millions who could not make their way onto a ship such as this. In the meantime, such work may prevent the Sunseed technique being used as a weapon of war, as opposed to a mere tool of oppression. If you will share your research with us, we will give you whatever help we can. Meanwhile, we must choose our next destination quickly. Though what has happened here will throw the Klingons briefly into disarray, we cannot count on that state of mind lasting long. They will come after us in fury, and seek to strike where they can do the most harm—not just to us. To you as well."

The hair stood up on the back of Jim's neck. "A two-front war," he said softly.

"It is always a harrowing prospect," Veilt said. "And I must ask—does *your* front have more than one ship in it?"

It was the question for which Jim had been waiting, and the one he could not be sure that he would be answering correctly. "At the moment, no." He paused for a long moment. "Strictly speaking, I shouldn't be here. Strictly speaking, if Starfleet manages to get in touch with me again . . ."

Veilt shot a look at Ael. "I take it that you have been having some persistent communication difficulties."

"Well," Jim said, and smiled just slightly, "there *has* been all this jamming . . ."

Veilt smiled. "I have a feeling it may continue. Meanwhile, let me put to you a question of strategy. We have yet to gather to us all the resources that the Ship-Clans can bring to the conflict to come. Two other ships like *Tyrava* exist, one of which is willing to meet us and lend its assistance to the next major engagement. Now we must decide where that is to be."

He touched the table, and a large holographic map of Romulan space appeared in the air above it, rotating slowly. Jim looked at it.

He stood up. "There," he said, and reached out a hand to point at a spot inside the display.

Veilt looked at him in silence for several long moments, then glanced at Ael as he stood up as well. "Not here," he said, indicating another star, "or here?"

Jim shook his head. "Too far away. Those targets—Lelent, and Biriha, I think?—would be too easy for the Senate to write off while they concentrated on other things. And they're too far away from our final goal. Wasting time attacking them would merely give Grand Fleet more leisure to reinforce the Eisn system, and in strength, after this defeat at Artaleirh. Right now my estimate is that the Senate has their 'force-projecting' assets scattered across half the Empire, trying to put down, or keep down, the rebellions that are starting to spring up all over. Why give them so much time to call the assets back? Let's concentrate their minds by attacking them much closer to home, so that they feel they have to divert most of Grand Fleet *there* to stop us, and ideally to break us. Let's make them draw the line in the sand where *we* want it, not where they choose to." He looked at the little blue-white star. "Augo."

"The system is resource-rich, strategically placed, and a home to several large Grand Fleet refueling and resupply bases," Spock said. "Additionally, it is a system that would need to be secured first by any force intending to make a major incursion into Hearthworld space, both to make Augo's resources available to the invading forces, and to deny them to the defenders."

"You would not merely go straight in to ch'Rihan?" Veilt said.

Jim laughed. "I may be the captain of the *Enterprise,* but even *my* one ship doesn't make a fleet, any more than yours does, sir, with all respect to you and *Tyrava*'s size. What we've got now isn't anything like enough force to take ch'Rihan and ch'Havran, especially with the intelligence I've got at the moment. If I were the admiral in charge of this operation—"

"You are," Ael said.

Jim had to work to keep himself from showing any outward reaction. "—then I would use Augo, once the system was secured, as a staging point for the attack on ch'Rihan and ch'Havran. I would use the system as a place where reinforcements and previously unaligned forces could gather from the colony worlds. I would use its location, the timing of the system's acquisition, and the events themselves as tools to gather the most recent possible intelligence from the Eisn system before I went in. I would use it as a base for initial strikes on the outer planets in the Eisn system, the domed bases, and defensive satellite arrays. And *then* I'd attack the Hearthworlds themselves. Time's on our side at the moment, but not for long. The more we waste, the more Grand Fleet and the present Rihannsu government will benefit."

Veilt nodded. "Captain, you have the true tactician's eye for where to start work. So far, at least, we are in agreement."

"So far, but no further?" Jim said.

"There is the issue of what happens when we *reach* ch'Rihan," Veilt said. "Strategy for that has yet to be devised."

"Sir," Jim said, "we have a saying: it's hard to describe the multiverse while standing on one foot. I've been giving that matter some passing thought. I have more thought to give it yet, since no planet is reduced *merely* from space. At least, no planet that hominids hope later to inhabit. I expect to have a master close-planetary and ground-assault plan ironed out . . . oh, within a few hours?"

Veilt smiled very slowly. "I am reprimanded. A few days, certainly, will do. Even a tenday or so. For one thing, I have as yet given neither you nor the Commander-General any realistic assessment of non-Ship assets that will be available to us. That information would only become concrete when the engagement at Augo is done. And after that, you are quite right, there would be a need to move swiftly."

There was a little silence at the table. "Captain," Veilt said, "there is one thing I must say to you. There will be many of our people who will distrust your motives in assisting us. There will be those who would distrust them no matter how spectacular a victory we might achieve at Augo, indeed, no matter if you offered them ch'Rihan and ch'Havran on a salver. Betrayal will be constantly on such people's minds, and however well-intentioned you prove, they will be looking to see how the Federation might be exploiting you for its own purposes. Your leadership will be constantly scrutinized and second-guessed at every level, examined for ulterior motives. But you're not to feel as if you are being singled out in that regard, for there are Rihannsu who feel passionately about this uprising, this chance for freedom, but still fear and distrust my kinswoman, your colleague." He looked at Ael.

She raised her eyebrows in a weary way. "We will liberate them whether they like it or not," Ael said, her voice edged with humor. "Certainly they will like it better when they become sanguine enough to take part in the endeavor. For the meantime, I will go on as I have begun; I too am conscious of being used to a purpose, in some quarters at least, but I do not intend to let it stop me." The look she gave Veilt was difficult to read.

"Sir," Jim said, "the question does need to be answered. If we attack Augo, and fail—"

"Then *Tyrava* will make her way to other spaces," Veilt said. "This ship was not built and populated with the desperate children of ten worlds to be destroyed in a fruitless conflict. We will try to make the Empire a place where we may remain. We all love our homeworlds; the decision to part from them was not casual. But most of us are past desiring to die for them. We are well armed, yes. The Clans who have near-beggared themselves to secretly build these ships have always understood that we would have to fight our way free of the Empire. But none of us ever planned for sustained campaigns inside Eisn space itself. Our weaponry was designed for flight into other spaces—not for taking on all of Grand Fleet in repeated battles. You have a chance to prove yourself at Augo. After that, if worse comes to worst, we go our own way."

Jim nodded, and stood up. "With that understanding, perhaps I had better get to work. For the moment, I think we'll be remaining where we are for at least a short time." He glanced at Mr. Scott. "Scotty?"

"'Twould be wise," Scotty said. "I'd prefer to stay here a day or so at least, for we've still a lot of replacement components to install as a result of that long run at high warp, before the battle. Our new dilithium crystal looks to be settling in nicely—aye, and this would be a fine place to lay in some spares; I'd guess the mining and processing facility will be glad to accommodate us. But I want to run some more tests on the main crystal to make sure she's bedded in for more high-warp running. I have a feeling we'll be needing it."

He didn't say anything about what Jim felt sure Scotty was thinking—that more time spent in *Tyrava*'s neighborhood would possibly give him a chance to investigate its warp technology more closely.

Veilt, for his own part, rose as well, and merely smiled that slight, somber smile again, nodding. "We too had thought to stay for a short time. Planetside provisioning has been something of a problem for us in recent months; we have had to take unusual care not to be seen by any force, Rihannsu or otherwise. But our secret may safely now be assumed to be out, so we will use our time here to our best advantage. And as you say, extra dilithium is always welcome; and we will be in a position to be of assistance, if only as backup, while the Artaleirhin put their newly captured ships fully into commission, and make contact with other systems that are as active in rebellion."

Everyone got up and headed for the door. "Sir," Jim said, "perhaps we might invite you over to *Enterprise* in the next day or so? Purely socially."

Veilt's smile abruptly lost its somber quality. "I had been hoping you might ask," he said. "Believe me, Captain, while our ship may seem impressive to you, *Enterprise* is impressive to us for entirely different reasons. Big ships are nothing special by themselves. Some vessels act bigger than they are, and produce bigger results."

"I know," Jim said. "The real trouble comes when they're routinely *expected* to."

As they made their way back to the transporter hall, that thought kept coming back to haunt Jim. It could sometimes be useful for your enemies to think that you were more of a danger than was really possible. But when your friends and allies thought so too . . .

Jim began thinking in earnest about Augo.

SIX

IN A TAPESTRY-HUNG ROOM on the Klingon homeworld, a man was swearing.

"Where are my ships?" he said. *"Where are my ships?!"*

Four other Klingons were in the room with K'hemren, the Chancellor's chief counselor. Two of them wore the all-black uniforms of Imperial Intelligence, and stood before him in varying attitudes of disdain or annoyance. Another was a servitor, standing in the rear, awaiting orders. The fourth was on his knees, stripped of his armor, his hands bound behind him. His head was down, and though he was not trembling, it was plain that he shortly expected that head to be severed from his shoulders.

"It is as I told you," he said. His voice had gone dull; he seemed to have passed beyond desperation. "The great ship came—"

"From *where?*" K'hemren roared at him. "You got no weapons or engine telemetry from it, not even a scan of the direction from which it came."

"Lord," said the kneeling man, "it was cloaked. The cloak was of a kind we'd never seen before. It leaked no signal, no waveform whatsoever until the ship was fully revealed. And by the time it was—"

"You would have me believe," said K'hemren, "that they destroyed at least *five* heavy cruisers—the whole rest of your complement! Yet you alone managed to fight your way out of this situation?"

"Sir," the kneeling man said. "It was not fair. It was not *fair!* We had them! And we would have had *Enterprise!*" Some hints of outrage began to illumine the deadness of his voice.

K'hemren merely snorted in disbelief. "Greater men than you have tried that and failed. It stretches my imagination intolerably to believe that boot-stickings like you could ever even approach such a feat." He looked over at the two Imperial Intelligence operatives.

One of them, gazing down at the kneeling man, shrugged. "Local space was full of jamming signals. It was affecting local scan and telemetry unusually badly. Yet something did show through in the initial analysis. However unlikely it seems, his ship got a brief glimpse of something very large—very massive. On the order of two hundred eighty million *tieks.*"

"There are no ships of such a size." K'hemren made a disgusted face and waved the suggestion away. "Though doubtless there are those who would like us to believe there are. This is some kind of propaganda trick, some ploy or illusion, some alteration of the scans so that they seem to reveal the impossible. *Enterprise* has been involved with such trickery before."

K'hemren stared at the man on his knees for a moment longer, then gestured to the servitor, who started silently toward them.

The second Imperial Intelligence officer looked up. "Lord," he said quietly, "*where are the other ten ships?* And where are the other five from this task force?"

"The other ten had orders to run under silence, as you know. As for these five . . ." K'hemren chewed his mustache briefly while looking down at the man who knelt before him;

behind the kneeling man, the servitor drew closer, with something in his hands.

"Suppose there *were* ships of that size?" K'hemren said softly. "It might well suit our enemies to have us disbelieve this report. More: it might well suit them to have us believe that the ship is not a Federation vessel, but Romulan."

"The Romulans could never afford such a thing!" said the second security officer, with a scornful laugh.

"Indeed," said K'hemren, "they might like to have us believe that too. Well, I think we need more data. This undertaking has already become more complex than I would like. For the sake of the attack on the Federation that we're contemplating, we can well afford to throw away a few more ships to discover the truth of this 'great ship'—who it belongs to, what weaponry it might have. Whether indeed it's reality, or just some propaganda ploy."

The servitor now stood directly behind the man who knelt. He lifted one hand, raised his eyes to those of the Chancellor's counselor. "Truth we must have, and that quickly. No," K'hemren said to the servitor. "Not right now. You!"

The man who knelt realized that he was being addressed, and looked up for the first time since the start of their meeting, though not with any expression of hope. "Take yourself out of my sight," said K'hemren. "And stay in whatever wretched bolthole constitutes your quarters here until you're sent for. I may, if you're lucky, send you to your death in some more honorable fashion than the skulking, whining exit you made from your most recent battle."

The kneeling man scrambled to his feet, bowed deeply but hastily, and left with the servitor close behind him. When the chamber door boomed to again, K'hemren looked at the two Intelligence officers. He leaned back a little, stretching his arms along the arms of the chair. "The coward," one of the two Intelligence men said.

"Even a coward may tell the truth," said K'hemren. "I give you leave to access all archived sensor data from our fleets for the last half year. Examine all downloaded scan data for any traces or signs of massive vessels such as our frightened friend claims to have seen. Correlate the data, and have it on my desk by tomorrow morning. In particular, look for sudden emergences of signal or losses of signal such as we have heard described. In this case, things not seen, or half seen, may prove as revealing as things seen clearly—assuming that our poor friend here did not lie."

"And if he did not?" the second Intelligence officer said.

"Then we have a problem," said K'hemren. "But not so severe a problem as one we did not know about until it was too late."

"Should this encounter have been genuine, do you anticipate that it will affect the second front of the battle?" said the first Intelligence man.

The man in the seat breathed out. "Oh, most likely not. My first guess would be that the poor cowards got a glimpse of some ship of the Lalairu, or one of the other ragtag traveling species, while they passed through the Artaleirh system. They are no threat if they're left alone; they do not seek out wars or enter alliances. However, if the vessel as described and armed does indeed exist, and is a Federation one, it might to some extent change the thinking of the High Council. Certainly it would change the Chancellor's."

The two Intel officers frowned, looking scandalized. But K'hemren only laughed at them. "Death in glorious battle is one thing," he said. "But death that throws ships away thoughtlessly, decreasing our ability to project power, that's another. There are those who say that the Chancellor is the highest expression of the Klingon ethos. But in my experience, he values his power, and the power of the Defense Force, too highly to throw them away for merely ethical considerations." K'hemren's smile was supremely ironic. "Now go—correlate that data. I expect to hear from you first thing tomorrow morning."

In an office in Paris, another man, too, sat in a chair, looking out the window at his view of the Eiffel Tower.

It was night, and the top of the hour. The Tower was ablaze with a storm of glittering white lights—the old illuminations that had been put up late in the twentieth century for the Tower's hundredth birthday, and had become so popular with Parisians that they refused to allow them to be taken down at the end of the centennial year. The old electrics had been replaced with pulsestrobes long ago, but the effect was much the same, and now that same white light raced down the tower like liquid lightning, outlining the graceful curves of the structure, dying away again. The lights in the room were dimmed, as usual, so that the man who watched could better enjoy the effect. But the dimness inside, and the brilliance outside, did nothing to help the President lose any sense of the anger of the man who stood behind him, waiting to regain his attention.

"He's done exactly what some of us thought he might," said Fleet Admiral Mehkan, the Starfleet Chief of Staff. "He's gone native."

"You have no proof of that," the President said.

"We don't need proof at this point," said Mehkan. "He hasn't been heard from for two days. That whole part of space is full of jamming. Romulan SIGINT and Klingon SIGINT are both up ninety percent. The war is about to break out in earnest. And *Enterprise* is still on the wrong side of the Zone. You heard Danilov's last conversation with him! You heard what happened."

"I heard what *seemed* to have happened," the President said. "As did you. That Danilov got no reply doesn't necessarily mean that *Enterprise* has gone over to the other side."

"Sir, with all due respect, you always knew this was going

to happen," said the Fleet Admiral. "Up to a point, that served our purpose. And now the war between the Klingons and the Romulans is breaking out, as we had hoped, while the Romulans themselves are in the throes of a revolution even as they declare war on us."

"Dai, you can leave me out of the 'we' regarding that particular hope," the President said. "And I'm not yet certain that hostilities have broken out in exactly the manner that Starfleet, or the Strat-Tac department, would have planned." He looked at Fleet Admiral Mehkan rather acerbically. "If it had, they would've completely annihilated one another by now, and Kirk would have been home. But as I told you, it was never going to be that simple, and as you say, Kirk's not back. And it would seem that neither of the two other combatant sides is entirely as eager for war as you would've credited. As I read it, the Klingons and the Romulans are both still jockeying for position, trying to avoid fighting with each other, while the Romulans hope to be allowed to concentrate on us, and the Klingons are looking to see which way it will best benefit them to strike. Though, as far as I can tell from the intelligence I see, the Klingons are suddenly having some second thoughts not only about us, but about the Romulans."

Mehkan was silent for a moment. *He's wondering,* the President thought, *for the hundredth time: Do I have access to intel that doesn't come from Fleet?* But the President of the Federation stood there looking innocuous, and after a few moments the Fleet Admiral turned away, frowning. The President held his face quite still and said nothing further for some moments. A gift for looking innocuous had gotten him elected in the first place; since then it had turned out to be more useful than he could possibly have believed.

"I'm still afraid we're going to have to hunt him down and bring him home," Mehkan said at last.

"Regrettable," the President said. What he was regretting

most emphatically was the image of *Enterprise* being re-solved to her component atoms, which was—he firmly believed—what the Chiefs of Staff had in mind rather than a court-martial. "Shot while trying to escape," was one of the things the intervention in question had often been called, once upon a time, whether escape had actually been involved or not.

"I need your sanction," Fleet Admiral Mehkan said.

The President gave the Tower a glance, and then faced the Starfleet Chief of Staff full on. "You do *not*," he said. "Under the uniform code, you already have the sanction you need for what you contemplate. I can quote you chapter and verse, if I must. What you *want* is the tacit approval of the office of the Commander in Chief."

Mehkan watched him. The President absorbed his gaze stolidly, not changing expression, not moving a muscle. Finally, the Chief of Staff looked away again.

"In a perfect world . . ." the President said then, turning to look back at the Tower. "But never mind. The world's not perfect, is it? What we seek, theoretically, is that there should be peace. And what we get, usually, is war. Isn't that strange? Sometimes I think that maybe we're just a little too willing to let our old natures assert themselves over the new one we're trying to build. That man out there—he said, once, 'We're not going to fight today.' And he was right, to the annoyance of a lot of people in Starfleet. Now he thinks he *has* to fight, and goes about doing it the best way he can—and you're *still* annoyed at him." The President shook his head.

"Oh, he's a thoughtful man in his way," said Mehkan, "and one who doesn't obey orders blindly. Once or twice this has served our purpose, I'll admit that. But when forces on this scale are involved, the lack of discipline ceases to be an advantage. If one portion of a team doesn't interact pre-dictably with the others, doesn't react as it should in a crisis, it endangers the others as well."

Not that I can tell you what orders besides yours he is obeying, the President thought. *Or how much trouble it's going to make for you when he really gets going.*

The dim lighting in the room let the President see, reflected darkly in his window, the face of the Chief of Staff behind him—the man's already dour Centauri expression now impassive under the shadow of a distasteful task he now felt he had to do, one for which he now realized he was to be given no backing. "You know my preferences," the President said. "And you know the realities of this situation. Come war or come peace, any scenario that ends in the destruction of the *Enterprise,* any scenario whatever, will cause this administration in particular and the Federation in general a great deal of trouble. That ship has become a symbol for something very basic, something at the root of what we do, which is why, I would guess, some people in Fleet are so uncomfortable with it, and its command." He allowed himself one small smile. "It's always troublesome to try to deal with archetype when it rears its head in the middle of what passes for reality. But if we deal with it in the wrong way, the results echo for years. Be very careful what you do. And under all circumstances, break your backs to bring her back safely, because if she doesn't come back safely, you're the ones who're going to have to answer for it first. And not to me. To *them.*"

He looked out into the night. A last splash and spatter of light ran up the Eiffel Tower and seemed to leap into the sky along with the pure white laser that burst up and out of the Tower's peak to mark the end of the evening's last display. That line of fire burned upward, like an upheld lance, and then slowly faded. By the time it was dark, and the Tower with it, the President glanced up to see that Mehkan was gone.

He let out a long breath and sat down at his desk, leaning back in the chair. He squirmed a little in the chair, but the chair was not comfortable. This was no surprise: long ago, he had insisted on it.

The President put his hand down on the surface of the sapphire-glass desk, gazed down into it. The desk read his handprint, and the red line of the laser flickered up into his eye, making him blink as it read his retina. It always made him blink. *I can never believe the damn thing isn't going to make me blind eventually,* he thought.

The surface of the desk went bright, then, with windowed readouts and piled-up "documents." He searched in vain for one that he had been waiting for, one which should have been blinking for his attention.

Come on, he thought. *Show me a sign. I can't save you now if you don't help me do it.*

But the message he looked for wasn't there, and was most unlikely to appear while he sat there waiting for it. Finally the President of the Federation got up and stretched, shut the desk computer down, and left his office. The office lights dimmed themselves down to darkness as he left; and behind him, through the window, the City of Light's illumination burned steady, starlike, unmoved by the deepening night.

SEVEN

THE DREAM was a strange one. There was a great deal of noise in it, a commotion of people running in all directions, alarms, the sound of disruptor fire. Through it all, Arrhae walked with unnatural calm, gazing around her bemused as the lights flickered and the ship's engines roared. Crewmen with guns ran past her; she brushed by them as if they hardly mattered. Screams came from ahead and behind. Arrhae floated straight on through it, making her way toward the place where they would finally have some answers for her.

She stopped at a closed door and lifted her hand to the door signal. She pressed it, though she couldn't hear whether it was working; the noise of gunfire down the hall was too loud. She waited while more people ran past her.

The door slid open. And there was Gurrhim, standing there and looking at her with a kindly expression. Unfortunately, there was a great hole in his chest where his heart should have been. He bled green, not in great gouts, but in a slow, sad seepage that ran down the front of his tunic.

Arrhae was briefly shocked, but then she realized that, bar the blood, there was nothing really that terrible about the way Gurrhim looked; and more, he was waiting for her to speak, a courtesy that a Praetor hardly had to extend to so junior a Senator as she. Finally, all Arrhae could find to say was, "I don't have it. I gave it away. Please forgive me!"

Then she clapped both hands over her mouth as she realized, in absolute terror, that she had spoken in English.

Gurrhim merely smiled. "Nothing is revealed. Nothing I didn't know. I will keep your secret as you have kept mine."

For some reason, Arrhae found herself completely relieved by that, utterly reassured. She nodded, and gave Gurrhim a little bow. Then she turned and walked away again through the corridors full of shouting people, singing softly to herself in relief as she went. "Take me out to the ball game," she sang, "take me out to the crowd; buy me some peanuts and Cracker Jack; I don't care if I ever get back . . ."

In the fabric of the ship around her, she heard the groaning begin. *We're going very fast,* she thought. *We'll be going into warp soon.* The low, insistent shout of the battle-stations' alert, a dismal basso hoot, was throbbing right through everything now. And without warning, the corridor before her was empty. She turned to look behind, but no one was there either, and Gurrhim had closed his door. Only Arrhae remained, and at last she turned again and headed down toward her quarters. "And it's root, root, root for the home team," she sang softly, "if they don't win it's a shame, 'cause it's one, two, three strikes you're out at the ol—"

Bang! went something in the room, and Arrhae's eyes flew open. She sat up on her couch, her sleeping silks sliding off her in all directions. The source of the bang, she now saw, was merely old Mahan, the door-opener of House Khellian, who had dropped the empty handbasin that he had apparently tiptoed into her room to fetch.

"*Hru'hfe,*" he said, "I'm so sorry. Did I wake you?"

Arrhae sat there among the silks, rubbing her eyes for a moment, and then looked around her. Visible through her bedroom window was a gray, early morning; mist lay over the gardens to the side of the house. "Mahan," she said after a moment, as she woke up enough to realize what was going on, "that's no work for you! Go get one of the house servants to do that."

"I don't care to have them in here when you're sleeping, *hru'hfe*," Mahan said, picking up the dropped basin. "Sometimes—" He turned the basin over in his hands, looking at it thoughtfully. "Sometimes," Mahan said, more softly, "you say things in your sleep. Gibberish, mostly, but—"

Arrhae went cold. "Mahan," she said, grasping after the fading tatters of her dream, "was I singing?"

"Might have been," Mahan said. *"Hru'hfe,* I need to go fill this." And off he went.

Arrhae i-Khellian sat there for a while in distress, being careful not to show it. *Since when do I talk in my sleep?* she thought. *Much less sing.*

She let out a long breath, getting a last fading glimpse of the dream—the people running around, the noise. And poor Gurrhim. *Since* Gorget . . . , she thought.

Arrhae reached to the footstool beside her bed for an over-robe. Hastily she shrugged into it, got up, and stepped over to the window. It was hard to believe that the mad events in which the conference had ended had occurred only three days ago. *Gorget* had fled home to ch'Rihan at speed, as if a whole battle fleet were behind her. No one truly feared that; though everyone knew that the Federation would now declare itself at war with the Empire, no one thought they would begin the war's first battle right at the moment. With the negotiations for which *Gorget* had left ch'Rihan now collapsed in complete disorder, and indeed any real need for them submerged in the realities of imminent hostilities, the higher-level military and diplomatic staff on board had ceased to have any need to speak to the lesser personnel such as Arrhae and the other observers aboard *Gorget* with them. All such folk had been left strictly to themselves for the few days it took to get home to the Hearthworlds while (Arrhae supposed) the military staff busied themselves with what preparations they could make for war at such a distance from ch'Rihan.

Arrhae had been left with plenty of time to catch up on her reading, if indeed she'd had the composure to do any such thing. For the first day or two, she had found it difficult to do anything but sit in the chair by the door of her suite on *Gorget,* waiting for someone to knock—that someone expected to be the horrible Intelligence officer t'Radaik, or someone sent by her. Every one of those nights, Arrhae had awakened sweating and trembling, remembering the sudden improvisation in which she had put Gurrhim's tiny personal cloaking device into the hands of those who would use it to free him from *Gorget*'s infirmary and flee with him to the *Enterprise.* At any moment, Arrhae had expected the security people to come back and start asking her the questions that she had been dreading. But no one came near her at all. She had sat in her quarters all that while quite unmolested, with nothing to fear but her suite-steward Ffairrl, who at that point seemed to feel he had license to feed her until she was three times the size she'd been when she first boarded *Gorget.*

Arrhae gained a pound or two, but nothing else happened at all. *Gorget* finally set down at the great military landing field outside Ra'tleihfi, and from every direction a flock of little flitters came to settle around her and take away the delegates to the negotiations. Arrhae had stepped out to find a flitter waiting for her as well, and within a matter of minutes she and her luggage were in it, and on their way home. Perhaps ten minutes after that, Mahan had opened the door of House Khellian to her, and shut it behind her again when the flitter crew had brought in her bags and once more departed. There Arrhae had stood with her back to the massive door, looking around her small Great Hall. It was all over; it might all have been a dream. She was still a Senator; she was still alive; and she had come away from the middle of an armed engagement at RV Trianguli, physically not a whit the worse for wear.

Her nerves, though—those were in tatters, and even then, barely over her own threshold, she had thought they'd remain so for some time. *And now this,* she thought, *talking in my sleep. I was more right than I knew.* Arrhae shook her head. She would have been glad enough to seek professional help, but there was no one on the planet to whom she could safely go. The one professional who might possibly have done her any good was back there at RV Trianguli.

Or probably not, Arrhae thought. Enterprise *would hardly have lingered there, not with a battle breaking out all around her, and more fighting yet to come. But still, oh, Dr. McCoy, could I ever use you now!*

Arrhae leaned on her forearms on the wide windowsill and looked out at the gardens, breathing deeply and trying to maintain her composure. The gardens weren't big—any more than most things about House Khellian were—but they were beautiful this time of year, especially now that the long, drooping crimson branches of the *sserayl* trees around the walls had come into leaf, so that they looked like long tongues of flame where they swept the short, trim turquoise lawn. And the turf—it was not grass, but something more like creeping chamomile—was just beginning to come into bloom. Like chamomile, *wevet* turf had a strong aroma, and in the morning mist the spicy scent of it was quite pronounced. Arrhae breathed it deep, several times, and waited for her old steadiness of mind to settle in again.

Slowly it started to reassert itself. The memory of the last week's unsettling events, of the security people searching her room, of t'Radaik trying to trick her into saying something self-incriminating, of tr'AAnikh's hands on her as he kissed her violently, of the last chilly session between Federation and Rihannsu personnel before all Areinnye broke loose—all these did not fade, but they started to assume more proper proportions in her mind.

One image, though, still took the forefront. *Tr'AAnikh.* Arrhae put her head down on her forearms, gazing out into the garden, but mostly seeing his confused face as he came to Arrhae's quarters and received from her something that would have been her death had she been found with it, and for all she knew had been his.

The thought of the kind of death he would eventually have been dealt had tr'AAnikh been found with Gurrhim's toy made Arrhae's flesh creep. *Yet there was no news aboard ship of any such thing happening,* she thought. *Gurrhim's escape, yes, but nothing more. Of course I was not going to ask anyone directly. But Ffairrl was forthcoming enough about the gossip he got from the other nobles' servants—the flight home from that part of space, the rumors and news of the war to come. Try as the Intelligence people might to keep things hushed up, intraship gossip still often defeated them.* So there was a chance, at least, that tr'AAnikh had gotten away with his life. Arrhae suspected that more definite news would likely be a long time coming, so for now, all she could do was put the matter out of her mind.

There are more important things to think about. It would most likely be today that her political patron, Praetor tr'Anierh, would send for her. The only message Arrhae had had from him since her homecoming was that he wished her to prepare a report for him; he would analyze it and send for her to answer any questions when his schedule permitted.

Arrhae had spent the previous afternoon and evening on this piece of work as a way of settling herself back into the house and starting to regain her calm; she had finished it and transmitted it last night just before taking to her couch. The report began as a fairly dry recitation of events, followed by a more detailed and perhaps juicier discussion of personalities, conflicts among members of various parties, factions, and Intelligence services who had gathered around the negotiating table. Arrhae might not have access to supersecret bugging devices, or be a touch telepathic, but she had eyes, and a good ear for nuance in what might otherwise seem casual conversation. It was—she smiled to herself—part of a good *hru'hfe*'s art to be able to intuit a master's or guest's wants or feelings without a word spoken, sometimes before they knew what they wanted themselves. It was an art she had brought with some skill to the negotiating table, and as far as she could tell none of those on whom she'd practiced it were much the wiser. Most of the upper-echelon people had hardly noticed her anyway—a Senator almost entirely by courtesy rather than by birth, and as far as the talks themselves went, merely an observer with no power of her own.

They would all, of course, have known whom I was going to be reporting to. At least they would have if they were wise. But beyond that, all they saw when they looked at me was a tool.

She smiled at that. Such perceptions could do nothing but protect her. If she—

She heard the low gong of the door signal go off, and immediately Arrhae woke up completely. "At such an hour!" she muttered. "Don't praetors sleep? And I am nowhere near ready."

Arrhae hurried over to the chest in which her better clothes lay. Some of them had been cleaned and pressed by the house staff since she came home. The rest were of fabrics too fine or too ornate to be handled at home, and had to go to town to be groomed by a professional cleaning firm. *And naturally those are the ones I want today! Ah well. The dark silks, then. They can pass for formal daywear, if a little on the somber side.*

She snatched the silks up out of the chest and was halfway to the 'fresher when the knock came at her door.

Damn! "Mahan," Arrhae said, sounding crosser than she meant to, "tell the pilot he must wait for me ten minutes, and that's all there is to it. I am not a—"

The door opened just enough for Mahan to put his head in. *"Hru'hfe,* what pilot? That was just a delivery car, bringing a package. It looks like a welcome-gift."

"Oh!" Arrhae laughed then, and draped her clothes over the top of her sleeping silks for the moment. "Well, I wonder who would send me such a thing?"

"Doubtless there'll be a chip in it to say. I will put it on the hall table for you, *hru'hfe.*"

"Thank you, Mahan. And would you get me some draft?"

"Of course, *hru'hfe.*"

He went off to get it, and Arrhae padded out to the hall. On the side table, where the commset and a scribing pad and various other business supplies were kept, there now sat a square package perhaps a cubit on a side, done up in a golden wrapping all spattered with ornamental sparks of brighter and darker gold. She went over to it, picked it up to test the weight: somewhat heavy. Arrhae shook the box, then smiled at herself. Nothing rattled.

She wandered back into her chamber with it, pushed her clothes aside, and sat down on the couch. Carefully Arrhae unwrapped the paper without tearing it—the old habit of a household manager, not to waste anything that might be useful later—and set it aside, revealing a plain golden paperboard box inside. A seal held the closing-flap down. She slit the seal with one thumbnail, opened the box, and found inside it some white tissue spangled with more golden spots, all wrapped around something roughly spherical.

Arrhae pushed the padding-tissue aside to reveal a smooth clear substance, a glassy dome. Reaching into the box, she brought out what revealed itself as a dish garden of clear glass: the bottom of it full of stripes of colored sand, and rooted in the sand, various small dry-climate plants, spiny or thick-leaved, one or two of them producing tiny, delicate, golden flowers. Attached to the upper dome, instead of a chip or tag, was a small, white, gold-edged printed card that said, FROM AN ADMIRER — WELCOME HOME.

Arrhae laughed softly to herself, got up, and went back into the Great Hall, holding the old-fashioned card in her hand. *It's not as if he can fool me,* she thought. This present bore the hallmark of her former master, the Old Lord of House Khellian. Hdaen tr'Khellian was up in the little patch of land that still belonged to House Khellian, a "shieling," or remote summer pasture for the house's herdbeasts, amusing himself with the renovation of the old shieling-house there, and also cleverly avoiding the oppressive summer heat down in the city. Previously he would have been unreachable up there, but when Arrhae's assignment to the negotiation team aboard *Gorget* had come through, she had prevailed upon him, for the sake of the household staff, to keep a mobile commlink with him. He had muttered and sworn about it, but finally he'd given in. And now Arrhae had to smile at the thought that he was doing what he'd sworn he wouldn't do: use it on his own initiative. *How like him to think of me,* Arrhae thought, and touched the control that would connect her to the old man's private commset.

"What?" was the first thing that cranky voice said.

She laughed. "Hdaen, do you always answer the link that way?"

"Mostly I don't answer it at all," he growled. But the gruffness was feigned; Arrhae knew the tone. "So you're home at last, are you?"

"I am indeed. Are you well?"

"Better and better, now that I won't have to answer this thing anymore when it rings. It screeches just like the one in the front hall, but louder, since the staff insist that I keep it in my pouch all day. You've got to crack your whip over that lot, girl. They don't know what to do when you're gone. Every little decision that's to be made, they call me. At least I can have some peace now you're home!"

"I should think so," Arrhae said. "How is work coming on the house?"

"The workmen try to overcharge us every day," Hdaen said. "The world is full of cheats and chancers, young Senator. You should go get some laws passed to make them behave."

"The first chance I get," Arrhae said. "But that wasn't why I called. I wanted to thank you for the present."

"Present? I didn't send you anything, silly girl. It must be from one of the ten thousand suitors angling after the most eligible woman in the Tricameron."

Arrhae laughed—and in the middle of the laugh, it came to her in a rush of terrible realization exactly what this was all about. She suddenly saw that the last thing she could do now would be to agree, on a line that was almost certainly monitored, that she had received a mysterious package from she knew not where. Nor could she give him a chance to say anything further about how this *hadn't* come from him. "You are such a tease," Arrhae said, chuckling, "that I don't know how I put up with you. And—oh, now, here comes another car, doubtless with more of the same. You are a scandal, noble sir! I'm sorry to have disturbed you. I'll speak to you shortly." And she cut off the communication without letting Hdaen say another word.

Arrhae stood there by the commset for a few moments, thinking in the empty quiet of the hall. That package, whatever else it might be, would not be merely a present. *It's more trouble*, Arrhae thought. *Why must all this be happening to* me? *And why now? Can't I have a moment's peace?* But this was why she had been emplaced here, all that while ago. So what if no one could have predicted the position she now occupied? She was in it, and peace was for other people. It was *her* job to cope, now, come what may.

Arrhae let out one last long breath, then went back into her sleeping room. There she stopped in the doorway, hearing a sound. For a moment Arrhae couldn't think what it was.

Peep.

A tiny sound like an insect, or a bird. Arrhae stood there—
Peep.

Against the far wall stood her second travel case, the one that the household staff hadn't unpacked, and which contained her "business" tools: her chipreader, her notepad.

Did I leave the chipreader on all this time? Arrhae thought with annoyance. *No, of course I didn't. I remember turning it off.*

And inside the case, the chipreader said *Peep.*

She swallowed, then, as the sound gave independent confirmation of what she had been thinking about while on the commlink. Arrhae's chipreader was not quite the standard model. Under some very specific circumstances, it could activate itself.

Arrhae closed the door behind her, shot the bolt, and then went over to the case. She opened it and took the chipreader out. It appeared to be off, but in her hands it said *Peep* again. Slowly she nodded, and "woke it up" fully with the single extra keypress that let the reader know its clandestine features were authorized.

The little screen lit. Arrhae let the reader draw itself an image of her room, and then superimpose on that image a diagram showing where any as yet unfiled data might be located. Instantly the diagram showed her the location that matched where the neatly folded wrapping paper lay on the bed. Arrhae went over to the bed and looked closely at the paper, smoothing it out until she found the place where the microdot lay, in a folded-under spot where the bright and dark gold sparkles buried in the paper made it seem like just one more dark one.

She got up and went into the 'fresher for a pair of tweezers, came back, sat down by the paper, and carefully pulled the dot off. With care Arrhae dropped it on the chipreader's scan pad. The screen filled with words. Arrhae started to read—

—and what she read made the blood thump in her veins. She could feel herself going pale, almost faint.

No, she thought. *No!*

Arrhae sat there frozen on the bed for long moments, then slowly turned to look out the bedroom window, where Eisn's light was beginning to break through the mist. *How one takes that light for granted,* she thought. *Here, or in any other star system, whoever looks at it and ever seriously thinks of losing it, someday? Oh, tens of millions of years from now, yes, when civilization's gone and the world's a dry scorched skeleton, all the life long gone from it. But not now. Not in months, or weeks.*

Or *days!*

She had been able only to send home the most general warning, last time. But there was nothing general about *this.* Here were times, dates, courses, frequencies, intents—the kind of detail that would make the difference between billions of lives saved, or the same billions lost.

The sudden knock on the door brought her bolt upright, and the sweat burst out all over Arrhae a second later.

"Hru'hfe?" Mahan said.

She breathed out, then put the chipreader aside, with its screen blanked, and got up to unlock the door. "I beg your pardon," she said to Mahan, taking the beaker of herbdraft from him. "I was in the 'fresher."

Mahan nodded and closed the door again.

Arrhae took a big drink of the draft and held still, forcing herself into quietness, forcing herself to think. *Do normal things when you've had a shock,* one of her crisis counselors had told her long ago, when she was first training for this job.

Let reflex do its job until you recover a little. Then don't linger over your choice of intervention. Often the first thing you decide to do will be the right one. Trust your own judgment, once it's been proven trustworthy.

So Arrhae drank her draft, and then started to do normal things. She went into the 'fresher and washed, at the usual speed. She saw to her teeth and her hair, and her basic skin care. She got dressed, and did a couple of more things with the chipreader in private. Finally she opened her chamber door again and strolled out into the Great Hall. Mahan was there, gazing out the door into the summer morning.

"The paperwork," she said wearily to Mahan as, hearing her, he came into the Hall again. "It never seems to be done. Here's a message I forgot to send yesterday." She dropped it on the hall table—a plain little roll of paperboard with her reply to the received message inside, and the anonymous preprinted Imperial franking seal for that weight of container capping one end. "It's for a city address."

"Shall I call a courier, *hru'hfe?*"

"Elements, no, the day-post is more than sufficient. Just dump it in the post-tube down in the market when you go to do the morning errands. You *are* marketing this morning?"

"Third-day is the best day for vegetables," Mahan said, in a tone of slight reproach, as if Arrhae had no business forgetting such things just because she wasn't acting as household manager anymore.

"Of course it is. I didn't know if you were going yourself, though, or sending someone."

"I'm going, *hru'hfe.* Teivet can't tell if a fruit's ripe or sour, no matter how she squeezes."

Arrhae smiled slightly and went back to her room, ostensibly to relax. But there would be no relaxation for her until Mahan came back from market and reported that message sent. So she waited, and an hour passed, and two. Again and again Arrhae resisted the urge to reread the horrible message she had passed on to the contact given her, in a time that now seemed a lifetime ago, as a use-once-and-never-again option. She went about the house, greeting the staff, checking on how things had been going during her absence, keeping herself by force from reacting to the terrible thing she had learned. It was hard.

Mahan came back from his marketing, but it would be a while yet before Arrhae could relax. Morning had shaded into noon before, without warning, the commlink in the Great Hall shrieked.

It shrieked just once. Mahan was starting toward it to answer it, but when it didn't ring again, he turned away muttering. Arrhae, at the door of her chamber, turned away and let out the breath she felt as if she had been holding all morning. The city's tube-post was quick; the ancient pneumatic system had been augmented with local transporter service so that even out-of-the-way branch offices received many deliveries a day. Someone had stopped in to one of those branch offices and collected her message—and the commlink's single shriek, followed by the breaking of the connection initiated at some public link terminal, was Arrhae's confirmation that the message had been received and read, and would be passed to where it would do the most good.

But quickly, Arrhae thought. *Quickly!*

Then she sighed, for there simply was nothing more she could do. Earth's safety was out of her hands now, had passed to others. *And if I'm eventually to be of use for anything further, I should get something to eat.* Arrhae headed for the kitchen.

The door signal sounded again. Mahan opened the door, and there outside it, on the near flat, stood what Arrhae had been expecting earlier: the dark flitter with the arms of the Praetorate on its side. Earlier it would have been an innocent thing. But in the past few hours, everything had changed. Now the sight of it terrified her.

Standing outside the open door in the hot brilliance of midday, the pilot saw Arrhae and bowed to her; Arrhae much hoped that, through the cool dimness of the Great Hall, he couldn't see how pale she was. "Noble *deihu,* if you will accompany me."

Recent habit rose up and overcame fear for the moment. "I am not quite ready," Arrhae said. "Ten minutes, if you please."

The pilot bowed again. Arrhae let Mahan close the door on him; then he turned to her and gave her an approving and complicit look. "Do him no harm to prop up the wall for a little while," Mahan said, "whether he needs to or not."

"You're quite right," Arrhae said, and went back to her room. Into the 'fresher she went, and shut the door, and sat there on the convenience for some moments, with her eyes closed, just breathing. *Betrayal,* her fears shouted at her, *despair, death! The timing's too coincidental! What if they've already caught your one-time contact? What if—*

Arrhae breathed, and breathed, and breathed once more until the terror faded, though it did not pass.

If I am going to die today, Arrhae thought, *I will do it with my composure about me.* And there were other things about her as well that would be useful at the last need. Starfleet had not left her without last defenses, though it seemed like years since she'd even thought about the issue.

Arrhae thought about it now, as she got up to see to her cosmetics and scent before going out to get into the dark craft that would take her into the jaws of the Praetorate.

EIGHT

AT A GREAT DISTANCE from ch'Rihan, aboard *Enterprise,* James Kirk sat alone in the officers' mess. In front of him sat the empty plate that had contained his third chicken sandwich. The first two had vanished as quickly as if tribbles had been at them; but the third one had taken a little longer, and the edge was off his hunger now. *There's nothing like being shot at,* he thought, *to sharpen your appetite. At least, after the shooting stops.*

He got up and got himself a second cup of coffee, and put much more milk and sugar in it than usual, and sat down, stirring it.

Admiral, he thought.

It was a word he had used with varying degrees of respect, or disrespect, over his career, when thinking or speaking of other people. Some admirals were very good. Some of them were, frankly, inept. Too often the admiralty was something into which ineffective captains were kicked so that they could do less harm. And even the best admirals didn't usually command a ship proper; normally they "rode" ships that carried them around while they directed what was going on outside them. It was a curious kind of command, in which one's "flag" or personal influence counted for more than the ship in which it rode. For a man as used to a very personal relationship with his vessel as Jim was, the whole concept seemed peculiarly abstract and thin-blooded, and not particularly desirable.

Yet when that dubious honor had finally descended on Jim, he had accepted it—and the acceptance had been founded in a straightforward awareness that to refuse such an increase in rating could constitute career suicide, even for such a relatively successful commander as he. Jim had of course taken the exams associated with the change in status—one did not ascend into the ranks of the admiralty without proving a grasp of the theoretical aspects of the job as well as a talent in the field that suggested the potential for it. And as he'd expected, at the exam level he'd done quite well.

But then Jim had fallen foul of that least predictable of factors: current events. *Or more precisely, a lack of them,* he thought. He had come to understand why the favorite toast of sailors in wet-navy times had been to "a sudden plague or a bloody war," since both were seen as the surest route to promotion via the death of your immediate superiors. *Real* admirals, in Jim's opinion—and just about everybody else's, he suspected, though at Starfleet no one said so out loud—commanded fleets. But there were only so many fleets to go around, especially in times of relative peace. And as luck or the lack of it would have it, Jim's promotion coincided with one of those somewhat quiet times when the usual old troubles are simmering away, but not actually breaking into a boil. With conflict at something of a minimum, there was what—from any other angle—would have been considered a blessed lack of attrition among Starfleet ships and crews. At the same time, none of the older admirals showed any signs of retiring, and no younger ones, newly come into fleet assignments, got any sudden urge for planetside duty. As a result, the command of which James T. Kirk took charge on the day he put on his admiral's insignia was a large and shiny new desk.

And there he stayed for entirely too long, in his own opinion—until V'Ger came along and changed everything—at a time when he should have been out in the galaxy doing his first real admiralty work.

But now, Jim thought, *that gets to change. The situation doesn't* look *anything like I ever thought it would, but that's beside the point.*

For Artaleirh, there had been no time to devise anything but very general plans that would suit the available personalities and materiel. But for Augo, something far more complex was going to be necessary, or Ael and her people would be courting disaster. Now Jim would get to act a wartime Fleet Admiral's part, designing and directing the progress of a significant part of a campaign. *Just in an entirely different Fleet than the one that commissioned me,* he thought, and smiled a smile that was fairly grim. *Even if we win, I'll be lucky if I don't get keelhauled. Or the yardarm.*

But that was a problem for the future. At the moment, a great deal rested on his seeing further than most, so Jim was going to have to find the tallest giants he could, and climb on their shoulders in a hurry. He would have to sit down over the next couple of days and whip his initial thoughts on the upcoming campaign into some kind of order, some shape that would stand being closely examined and picked at, not just passed as an exam essay, with a commendation on the clarity of his writing style. And even then, even assuming Jim could design something that would work, the enactment of the plan would be no classroom exercise, nothing that could be played out in the simulator, to victory or destruction, and then walked away from afterward. Real blood, red and green, would be shed, and Jim would need to consider every drop as precious as his own; for the game wasn't just to win, but to do it with the least possible mortality and destruction. *This isn't just some "give 'em hell" proposition. You're fighting* alongside *the antagonist side. This is more like breaking an occupation than anything else.*

He had a long drink of the coffee, and put it down again, making a face: too much sugar. The door slid open, and Spock, McCoy, and Ael came in together.

"Thought we'd find you here," McCoy said. He looked at Jim's empty plate as he went to the food processor hatch. "Second one? Third?"

"Third," Jim said.

"Stop there," McCoy said. "Commander? What's your pleasure?"

Ael threw a glance at Spock. "I suspect you have plomeek soup, or an analogue?"

"We do," McCoy said. "Large or small?"

"Large, if you would."

"It is underspiced," Spock said. "However, I will have one as well, Doctor."

"Two it is," McCoy said. "But, Spock, you've never mentioned anything about the seasoning before."

"I would not have considered adjustments to the cuisine to be part of your job description, Doctor," Spock said. "I have occasionally attempted to discuss the matter with Mr. Scott, but the discussion inevitably degenerates into something to do with haggis."

Jim grinned. "That happens entirely too often whether you're discussing food or not," he said, as they all sat down and McCoy brought the dishes over from the hatch. "Probably it's wisest not to provoke the response on purpose." He sipped at his coffee again, threw an amused look at Ael; seeing her had reminded him of something Uhura reported having heard on the local planetary comms networks. "So, Commander," he said, "how does it feel to be the Savior of Artaleirh?"

"Please, do not," Ael said softly, spooning up some soup. She tasted it, and made an approving face. "In your world as in mine, salvation often has unsavory aftereffects on the one seen to have done the saving, for only the powerless need to be saved, and routinely they hate to be reminded of it."

Jim smiled, though only a little; she had a point.

"And being too successful is likely to produce trouble as well," McCoy said. "I doubt the Praetorate is best pleased with you at the moment."

Ael had a little more soup, then nodded. "Both they and Grand Fleet will be in turmoil. Recriminations will be flying, for under no circumstances would they ever have expected our cause to come so far, with such success. The next blow they deal us will be intended to be infallibly mortal, for we've done far worse than merely inflict a defeat upon the government and the Fleet. We have made them look ineffective, perhaps even foolish, and there could be no deadlier affront to their egos, or threat to their power."

Jim nodded. "That's what I've been thinking too. We might have been the hammer this time out, but next time we'd better be ready to be the anvil."

There was quiet for a time as everyone ate. Jim sat back, drinking his coffee, and gazing out into space. The ship was presently orbiting Artaleirh, and through it, the few cities on the nightside could be seen rotating lazily away toward the planet's limb—demure little spatters of light, with no sign about them of the sudden blue glow that had saved them from destruction.

"Jim," said McCoy, as he finished the small Caesar salad he'd chosen for himself, "you already look like you've lost a credit and found a cent. You should try to let your successes stay with you a little longer before you declare them worthless and chuck them out."

Ael looked up at that, glancing over at Jim to see how he would take this. Jim could only shake his head. "Bones, this was just one victory, and in the scope of the campaign to come, a relatively minor one. While we've done well to reduce the Empire's available forces by as much as we have, they won't make any of these mistakes again. The next engagement will be massive, involving an investment of really serious force—tens or even hundreds of vessels. To counter that, we're going to need more than a scattering of cruisers, a Really Big Ship, and a swarm of little ones. We need a conventional fleet—"

"Well, didn't Veilt say that they were going to send in another really big ship like *Tyrava?* That would have to make a difference. That thing went through those cruisers' screens like a hot knife."

"It did, Doctor," Spock said, "but bear in mind the other purpose of such vessels. They must be preserved to take their people away to new worlds, if the body governing the old worlds cannot be liberalized or overturned. The Free Rihannsu have done much to reveal the presence of even one of these ships to the Imperium. They will not readily reveal the existence of too many more of them. They have been built at too high a cost, and the hopes of whole peoples ride on them. Unless all other hopes vanish, and there is no choice, risking the great ships would be folly."

Ael nodded.

"But even *Tyrava* and its companion ship," Jim said, "can make one big difference, without firing a shot. They can deliver ground forces."

McCoy looked at him with a slightly perplexed expression. "Just use them as troop carriers, you mean? I don't get it. If our side has a bunch of ships armed and defended like *Tyrava,* then once the Eisn system's safe for them, why not just put them all in orbit around ch'Rihan and blow up everything on the planet that doesn't surrender?"

Jim shook his head and had to smile gently.

"Leaving aside the tremendous undesirability of war itself," Spock said, "barrage from space except in the 'surgical' sense is an error of scale—a massive waste of energy.

Whatever we have seen on the small scale in the past, attempts to permanently reduce or subdue a planetary population by attacks from space are inevitably doomed to failure."

That made McCoy sit back in his chair.

"Bones," Jim said, "when you've got a patient with a viral infection, do you flood his whole system with an antiseptic?"

McCoy gave him a look that was both bemused and barbed. "Hardly. Besides making the client sicker than he was, it wouldn't do a thing to viral entities hiding inside cells. The preferred tactic these days is to teach the patient's own immune system to get smarter about destroying the infection. Tailor the phagocytes' antigenic response to the bug in question, equip them with tailored RNA-cutting seek-and-destroy modules, autoclone an 'exploded population' of them, and then turn 'em loose to attack the viruses *in situ*."

"Exactly," Jim said. "You've just described the only effective kind of planetary invasion. It has to be appropriate to the medium in which or over which it's conducted. We can improve space-based technology until all the galaxy's cows come home, but when all the ruckus in the sky dies down, the surface of a planet can *still* only be taken, held, and secured by ground troops. Naturally you do need to achieve local-space and atmospheric superiority first. But after that, everything comes down to people holding small arms—or not-so-small arms—as the situation requires." Jim shook his head, smiling rather grimly. "Believe me, there've been a lot of attempts to get around this problem over the last few centuries. Mostly they've resulted in the participants having to have a war two or three times instead of once. Leaving aside the question of our limited resources and relatively constricted timeframe, if we have to have a war, I'd rather have it just once and get it over with."

He stretched, leaned back in his chair. "But Spock's point,

as usual, is the most important one. The whole idea of this attack is not to destroy the infrastructure of ch'Rihan and
ch'Havran, but to destroy the power of the present government to rule."

He looked over at Ael, who was still working on her soup.
Despite her present position of potential power, she continued to look uncomfortable when he discussed this very basic
goal, which somehow, for the moment at least, made Jim
more comfortable, rather than less. People who wanted too
much to be running things were all too often, in Jim's opinion, the wrong people for the job. The reluctant ones could
often surpass everyone's wildest hopes.

"Anyway," Jim said, "we now have at least a partial answer to the troop-movement problem, in *Tyrava*."

"Yes," Ael said. She finished her soup, placed the spoon
alongside the bowl on its tray, and pushed the tray away,
leaning back in her chair and gazing out into the night.

"Correct me if I'm wrong," Jim said, "but all the data I've
been able to find in the Starfleet general-intelligence databases suggests that the Imperium has very few vessels
specifically constructed for troop transport."

"Not few," Ael said. "None."

Jim's eyes widened slightly. Spock, finishing his soup,
looked up with sudden interest.

"Over the last few decades," Ael said, "what vessels
might have been used for such purposes have not been replaced as their 'useful lives' came to an end. There have been
any number of reasons for this: budgetary cutbacks, the desire to invest the funds in other infrastructure projects more
useful to the Hearthworlds, various political moves by certain parties in Tricameron and Praetorate to keep money in
their own hands and out of others'. And there will always
have been a significant number of both military and political
analysts to advise the Praetorate and Grand Fleet that, with
the danger of Klingon incursion into our spaces always pre-

sent, what was needed was not large-scale ground-force support, but strike-force support—more and bigger ships, better armed, to interdict any possible incursion before it could get a foothold at the bottom of any world's atmosphere. At any rate, for at least the last decade, the Imperium has relied almost entirely on small- or medium-scale fleet actions to keep the outer systems in line. And for the most part these have been sufficient to the purpose."

" 'For the most part'?" McCoy said.

"Oh, there have been occasional rebellions among the most distant outworlds," Ael said, "but one might say that those happened too soon. Some of their causes were similar to the causes being cited now by the worlds that are in uprising, but support from others could not then be counted on, and the Imperium suppressed those earlier rebellions brutally."

"Surprising that *this* rebellion's doing so well, then," McCoy said.

Ael raised her eyebrows. "I think it is at least partly because the last couple of decades have seemed so quiet on the 'home front,' and the governments of the period simply did not believe that any new rebellion would take root for the foreseeable future, or perhaps ever. As a result, they have been slow to act. Additionally, I believe the Praetorate erroneously assumed that the outworld colonies' fear of invasion and subjection by the Klingons would always invariably outmatch any possible anger over the stringency of the Empire's rule. Their own arrogance may now prove to be the present Praetorate's downfall, for as you say, Captain, the Empire has deprived itself of the ability to actually handle any such problem where it must be handled: on the ground."

Jim nodded. "It's a weakness we're going to exploit as quickly as possible. Also, as regards the Klingons, *Tyrava* will have upset them a great deal also. They plainly expected to find a system half-subdued by the Imperium, ready to fall into their hands as soon as they got rid of the Grand Fleet cruisers. Instead . . ." He brooded for a moment. "I wish we'd been able to keep that last ship from getting away."

"You are thinking," Ael said, "that a mission from which no ship returns, and no news, is far better than a disastrous one from which news returns of an enemy far stronger than had hitherto been thought."

"Yes. Fear of the unknown is a whole lot more useful for our purposes." Jim let out a breath. "Well, nothing we can do about it now. The Klingons know about *Tyrava,* and when they hit us next, it'll be with absolutely everything they've got. They're in the same position as the Praetorate and the Grand Fleet. They have not only a defeat to avenge, but an embarrassment."

Ael nodded. "At least, I doubt they intend to put troops into the Eisn system. I think their intention, should they come so far, would be wholesale destruction—to try to cut off the old enemy's head, with the certainty that the body would fail soon after. We must be aware of them, and seek whatever intelligence we can quickly find to determine their objectives. Meanwhile, we must both unseat the government and still leave ch'Rihan and ch'Havran sufficiently capable of defending themselves that the Klingons, evaluating the situation, will decide that the space around Eisn is still too much trouble for them. The outworlds may yet fall under attack, but that will be a separate problem. Right now what is right before us—Augo first, and then Eisn—will be challenge enough."

The door opened. Scotty came in, surveyed the group at the table. "May I join you?"

"Of course, Scotty," Jim said. "We were just talking about you."

"We were just talking about *haggis,*" McCoy said, making a most expressive face.

Scotty gave him an amused look as he went to the food

dispenser. "Burns Night's not for months, Doctor. No need to break out the antacid just yet."

McCoy smiled a sardonic smile as Scotty sat down with a large ham sandwich.

"And meantime," Jim said, "we have one more problem to consider . . . and it's potentially a worse one than anything that's been happening here, or is about to happen in Eisn's space." He glanced over at Ael. "Commander, you won't have had time to hear about this, but the information came to us from a ch'Rihan-based source that we both know."

Ael looked up at that. "You mean our young Senator? So *Gorget* got back safely home out of that stour."

"We don't know that," Jim said, "though I hope it did. Terise sent us this information before *Gorget* departed. We were warned by her of 'an imminent, clandestine attack of a major and devastating nature on Federation space.' "

Ael nodded slowly. "That is something I was half expecting," she said. "The Empire's uncertainties about this upcoming war are great; they are none too sure, I would guess, of their ability to manage two fronts at once. But the technology . . . Is it something to do with Sunseed, perhaps?"

"We have only guesswork at the moment," Spock said, and the flat sound of his voice left no doubt as to how little he disliked guesswork. "But one piece of data has commanded my attention since we parted company with the rest of the Federation task force at RV Trianguli." He folded his hands, with the fingers steepled, and looked past them. "You will recall my scans of the vessel *Pillion,* eventually revealing the second cloaked vessel 'riding' on the first."

"Yes," Jim said.

"Then you will possibly recall that there were two such vessels in that engagement that displayed doubled readings. *Hheirant* was the other."

"*Hheirant* was destroyed!" Scotty said.

"Yes, Mr. Scott. But I have no evidence that the source of

the secondary reading she was carrying was destroyed as well. In fact, I have circumstantial evidence, though no better, to suggest that it was *not*. I have carefully reviewed my scan records. My last successful scan for the 'new' cloaking waveform, just after the battle began, shows the secondary scan still present, but somewhat dislocated from *Hheirant* herself."

"Jettisoned," Jim said.

"Possibly," said Spock. "The data is difficult to read. As you know, the energy discharges of a battle situation can adversely affect scan, and local space was full of phaser discharge and stripped-ion artifact at that point. In any event, the object, let us say vessel, producing that waveform cannot be accounted for as destroyed in the engagement. I would estimate fairly high odds that it escaped under cloak. I would also speculate that that is exactly what it was intended to do."

"They were holding those vessels in reserve right under our noses," Scotty said. "One to use to attack *Bloodwing*. The other—"

"It is impossible to say exactly what its purpose is," said Spock. "But I am nearly certain that it left that area under cloak, having been missed in the confusion."

"Probably exactly as someone intended," Jim said. He sat there, brooding darkly for a few moments. "Let's assume it was carrying some new kind of weapon. But God only knows *what* kind. They got it as close as they could to Federation space, under cover, and then . . . Would that vessel be manned, do you think, Spock?"

Spock frowned. "Logic would seem to suggest so. Indeed, if that vessel carries the prototype of a new weapon sufficiently powerful to endanger Earth despite all the planet's mobile and static defenses, I cannot believe the Romulans would be so reckless as to send it off into enemy space on a critical mission without either escort or supervision, especially if the technology is new."

Jim sighed. "Well, as we've agreed, this is information we must get back to Starfleet. But if you're right, and even the new codes have already been compromised . . ."

Then Jim paused. Codes or no codes, someone inside Starfleet Command had purposely sent Ael to a place where she would be ambushed. Someone inside Starfleet Command, too, had sent them out these new communications ciphers. Once again the hair stood up on the back of Jim's neck at the thought that, somewhere, very high up in the command structure to which he was subject, and unsuspected, treason was quietly festering.

"We have to find some other way to get this news home," Jim said. "And there's no time to waste with message buoys this time. The message has to move at least as fast as subspace radio. But it has to be something that can't be read by anyone else but Starfleet." *Though how do we make sure that information won't be somehow denatured when it gets there? Made safe, or unavailable, by the same person or persons who's been secretly working against us.*

Scotty looked uncomfortable. "You're not asking much."

"Miracles, as usual, Scotty. Nothing more."

Scotty sighed. "I'd go out for a quiet stroll on the lake to think, but there's none handy. Still, I'll do what I can. I'll have a chat with K's't'lk as well; she may be able to suggest something novel."

" 'May' be able to?" McCoy muttered, and shook his head.

Jim nodded. "Good enough." He turned back to his first officer. "Spock, was there anything else in Lieutenant Haleakala-LoBrutto's data that might give you even a *guess* as to what the nature of this weapon might be?"

"There was only the suggestion that it would be able to devastate Earth's whole solar system if it reached its target," Spock said. "I can think of various ways to produce such a result, given near-infinite power. But as for imagining a device so capable, which can also be attached to a ship like *Hheirant,* and successfully cloaked . . ." He shook his head. "At best, all we can be sure of is that even at high warp, Sol's system is distant enough from RV Trianguli that it would take a vessel at least ten days to reach it. But if we are to warn Starfleet to any effect, much less to be able to suggest a defense against whatever this weapon may be, we need much more data."

They all sat quiet for a few moments. "Well," Jim said at last, "we have at least a couple of 'halcyon days' to sit quiet here and rummage around in our hats for some rabbits. Let's make the best of them. Scotty, how are your repairs coming along?"

"At good speed, Captain. We've got another eighteen hours or so of spares replacements and recalibrations to do, then we're fit to run at full speed again."

"Good. Spock?"

"Gentlemen—"

They all looked over at Ael.

"The soup was excellent," she said, "and so is your company, but the last forty hours have been unusually wearing, and I have briefings aplenty waiting me aboard *Bloodwing.* I should get back there and take them, before I do you all the discourtesy of dozing off at table. May we meet tomorrow?"

They rose as she did. "Whenever you like, Commander," Jim said. "Call when you're ready."

She bowed to them all, with a weary flash of smile for Jim, and left. McCoy looked after her. As the door closed, and they sat down again, he said to Jim, "That's an admission you wouldn't usually have heard from her."

"What? That she's tired?" Jim said. "Why wouldn't she be? Adrenaline can only take you so far. It's within the few hours after you finish an engagement that the reaction sets in really hard. I'm tired too. And we're all going to feel more or less that way before we're done. *You* can't be any better.

How many hours did you and M'Benga spend in surgery?"

"Believe it or not, barely one and a half," McCoy said. "But it does feel like months, afterward." He stretched, rubbed the back of his neck. "There are a few steps I can take for all of us: help manage the lactose buildup in the muscles, some other things. Myself, I favor meditation. But the best treatment for the fatigue is to see that it was all for some good purpose. That man down there is alive, when he wasn't meant to be."

"That's another thing. When can I see him?"

"I'd let him alone for a while more, Jim. Though when he's thinking about the subject—Gurrhim's urgent enough about wanting to see you—his strength's not up to long conversations right now. He tends to drop off in midsentence. While he's still that tired, I prefer to let him keep on sleeping and healing, and not provide him with stimuli that're likely to impair his ability to rest."

"No problem. It can wait a little while more."

"There were other matters I wished to discuss with you, Captain," Spock said, "but I was not entirely willing to do so with the Commander here. To begin with, we will shortly be hearing from Starfleet, and I suspect the communications will be rather . . ." He trailed off.

"Tense?" McCoy said. "Why in the world would *that* be?"

"Bones," Jim said. "A little too much irony in your diet lately? Spock, the issue's been on my mind. I have a few messages I need to get off before we leave this area of space where communication has been so, shall we say, difficult. After that we will run 'silent' until we reach Augo. And after that . . ."

"They can court-martial us *in absentia,*" Scotty said, and his tone of voice was almost cheerful.

"I'd like to prevent that if I could, Mr. Scott," Jim said, "but it's nice to see you taking it so well."

"You are expecting," Spock said, "that matters at Augo will so transpire as to leave Starfleet willing to—"

"Keep on giving us rope," McCoy said.

"Our legal status is complex," Jim said. *And that's putting it mildly!* He regretted once more not having had some time to sit down with Sam Cogley, while they were all at RV Trianguli, for the purpose of discussing with him some completely hypothetical situations that were becoming less hypothetical by the moment. *Well, it'll have to wait.*

"I'm going to speak to the crew tomorrow evening," Jim said. "Apparently there's already some kind of gathering planned down in recreation; I'll call them together at the end of it. We're rapidly getting into a situation their service oaths don't cover, and this short time we're spending near Artaleirh is the best time to deal with the problem."

The others around the table nodded.

And there Jim had to stop for the moment, for he was left staring at the question of how much to say, to whom, and when. *Because* your *service oaths are as much at issue.* He got up and went over to the hatch for another cup of coffee.

Sealed orders, he thought, *are always a poisoned chalice.* If they hadn't been sealed in the first place, you would at least have witnesses to the fact that you had been instructed to try to pull off something nearly impossible. But when no one had seen the orders but yourself and the President of the United Federation of Planets, it left you in a nasty spot. Yes, he was your Commander in Chief, but the heads of the Services still didn't care to have him going over their heads, even in the most unusual circumstances. And if they put enough pressure on the President, and he bowed to it, then suddenly you could find yourself with a "plausible deniability" problem, and a President who "did not remember" giving you these orders, and could make a case that they were forgeries. Regrettable, of course, but what technology could devise, other technology could subvert. *And then you find yourself staring down the big end of that court-martial Dan mentioned.*

Jim let out a breath as his coffee arrived. Now he was going to have to act without any further sense of the reaction of upper-ups in Starfleet, but would still have to take those reactions into account, no matter what he did. And judging what they would be, without data, would be difficult. Even without data, though, Jim was increasingly certain that either the Federation or Starfleet—possibly both—were ambivalent about Ael, and the Romulans backing her, actually winning this war. Her certainty, her skill, and perhaps worst of all, her growing popularity, would be difficult for them to manage. *It would be less problematic for her to go down trying very hard,* said a more cynical part of his mind, *leaving a power vacuum that they could manipulate.* And bearing in mind that someone in Starfleet, or someone with access to their messaging, had purposely sent *Bloodwing* into harm's way once already, it would be foolish to assume that they wouldn't do so again if they could.

He picked up the coffee and carried it back to the table, sat down. *Still, any kind of war, no matter who wins, is going to mightily destabilize the Romulan Star Empire right now.* Even if the powers at the top of it were merely shaken rather than toppled, Jim thought the Federation ought to see that as a good thing—either the harbinger of change to come in the near future, or eventually. *And you'd think it would be that much for the better if the present regime fell completely out of power, and Ael became part of the new order.* Then there would be someone high up in Romulan politics who would owe the Federation a tremendous favor . . . and (as the Federation and the Fleet knew very well) someone who would actually pay off on such favors and neither ignore them, nor stab the Federation in the back afterward.

Yet would they see it that way? *And what about me?*

Jim thought. *They ought to know I will do what duty requires of me.*

But they're balancing off the question of my loyalties, and from Danilov's not-very-veiled warning to me, they're worried about what I'll do. There are probably some people up in Fleet who are quite happy for me to help Ael to succeed, but are also looking at whatever I do to supply them with an excuse to court-martial me . . .

"Captain—"

He looked up. The others were watching him.

"The commodore's orders to you were quite explicit," Spock said.

Jim was silent for a long moment, and then made up his mind. "They were," he said. "Unfortunately . . ."

McCoy got up, went over to the mess door, and locked it.

Jim's eyebrows went up.

"You're going to tell us that you're running under covert orders again," McCoy said, sitting down. "To which the only possible answer is, so what?"

"Aye," Scotty said.

Jim looked over at Spock. Spock raised one eyebrow. "The doctor's methods of deduction often defy any logical analysis," he said, "but they do occasionally work."

" 'Occasionally'? Why, you—"

"Bones," Jim said, rather sadly, "does it show that much?"

"To the crew at large? I doubt it. But this is part of my job. And those two—" He looked at Spock and Scotty. "—they just know you. You should lay off so much caffeine, by the way."

Jim could do nothing but laugh helplessly. "Well, I suppose this little chat is a good thing, because it saves you having to relieve me of command because you think I've gone nuts."

"I still may do that," McCoy said, "if the need arises. But it won't have anything to do with your sealed orders."

Jim sighed. "I guess I should be grateful. Bones, though a ship's commander may be exempt from Starfleet's wrath when the details come out, the crew may still possibly, and rightly, become insubordinate at some of the things I may order them to do. That's where the legal implications get sticky. Theoretically, if we all come out of this with our skins intact, Fleet will forgive all. But if they decide not to, if someone in a high place has a lapse of memory, it could get very bad for the crew. Those of them, that is, who aren't already dead of some other trouble we're about to get into. Augo, or later."

"And so you've paused as long as you could over the choice you now have to make," McCoy said, "but now you can't pause any longer."

Spock looked from McCoy to Jim. "And we are, I surmise, about to ignore your orders from the commodore, and to go on to assist in the overthrow of, if not the whole Rihannsu government, at least the main personalities presently determining its policy."

Jim looked from Spock to McCoy. "Yes," he said. "I feel that that's the best way to fulfill both the letter and the intent of the sealed orders. While I can't say much—"

"I don't think you need to," McCoy said. "Sunseed and the forced-telepathy project were an indicator of some pretty advanced science being done in Romulan space these days. What we've just seen at Artaleirh is more of the same, though the source may be slightly different. Don't think I haven't heard you babbling about *Tyrava* and its wonderful new warp technology," he said, glancing at Scotty. "Taking everything together, I strongly suspect that the whole purpose of this exercise—besides the liberalization of the Romulan regime, which of course would be seen as 'nice'—" McCoy snorted. "—is another smash-and-grab raid of the kind we're all too familiar with, the kind that got us tangled up with Ael's niece in the first place. Find new technology, bring it home. So that even if the present rebellion is quashed, and Ael fails, and even if—worst case—the Federation is forced into a premature peace after this war stalemates, we'll still have enough technological 'booty' at the end of the day to make it all worthwhile. And to see to it that some kind of technological parity is maintained between our two forces, so that the Romulans won't be tempted to push into the tactical vacuum that would accompany a ceasefire without attestable victory for one side or the other." He leaned back, stretched a little. "And if the Klingons catch a little punishment during the proceedings, well, so much the better. In any case, the technological advantages to be obtained from our little *razzia* will work just as well against them. We get a maximum result with minimum logistical outlay."

Spock blinked. "Doctor, you have been reading the classical strategists."

McCoy shook his head. "No, just the *Analects*. It's all in K'un-fu-tse."

"I would have thought it was Sun Tzu," Jim said.

McCoy shook his head. "Overrated. Man only had one book in him. In the course of which he repeats himself about fifty times. Jim, we're going Viking, in a very selective way, and we can't tell anybody. Not even Ael. Isn't that so?"

That was one aspect of all this which had been rubbing part of Jim's conscience raw. "That's most of it."

"It would be safe, I believe, to conjecture that there are aspects of your orders that you are not permitted to divulge even to us," Spock said.

Jim said nothing, just looked at him.

McCoy folded his arms. "Jim, we've all been in some pretty awful crunches between duty and necessity, over time, but by and large we've managed all right so far. Obviously the mission, and the ship, and the people who make both mission and ship work, come first for all of us. That helps.

But in case you were worrying, I think we can count on you not to take us anywhere we won't be able to support you in going, knowing what we know. And I think you can count on us not to let you down when it gets tight, though we may have to give you a hard time occasionally, if only to keep up appearances."

"For once, unusual as it may seem," Spock said, "the doctor speaks for me." The two of them exchanged a glance that was quite devoid of the usual edge.

Jim breathed out. "Gentlemen, that is all I could possibly ask. And when we finally get out of this mess . . ."

"I am going to prescribe us all a rest. I know this little place on Vesta," McCoy said, "where the girls . . . well, *theoretically* they're girls . . . well, all right, if you take into consideration a little monkeying around with the thirteenth chromosomal pair, they're probably more like—"

Spock was gazing at the ceiling as if profoundly interested by it. "Doctor," he said, turning his attention to McCoy again, "what recreation would you recommend for someone less enthusiastic about indulging in relationships with the genetically enhanced?"

McCoy gave him a look. "Chess."

Jim chuckled and got up. "I need to get busy. Bones, when I'm finished with this next piece of work, I'll come down and see Gurrhim."

"I told you, there's no rush. Right now I prefer to let him sleep—which is, incidentally, a condition I recommend to *you*. Otherwise I'll come and administer you some sleep whether you like it or not."

"Noted and logged, Bones."

Jim went out.

NINE

THE FLITTER brought Arrhae to tr'Anierh's great house as it had before, but this time she had no appetite for the food and drink laid out in the little cupboard in the passenger section. Her stomach was tying itself into knots, and even though she kept telling herself it was ridiculous to feel so, that there was no way she could have been betrayed so quickly, she couldn't believe it.

She sat there with her hands folded in her lap for those fifteen minutes, every one of which seemed to crawl over Arrhae's skin with excruciating slowness while she excoriated herself for being so foolish as to have used the public posts to send her message. *Well, what else could I have done?* she thought. *Any other kind of transmission would have been immediately traceable to me.* But at the same time Arrhae knew quite well that, in troubled times, the Intel people sampled the posts randomly, looking for just the kind of message she had sent: something without a return address on it, something that tried to pass itself as a message of no importance, trying to lose itself in the mass of normal postings. Now Arrhae saw what she'd done as utter folly. And she had done evil as well in asking poor Mahan to post the message for her. Now *he* would share whatever punishment came down on her. The whole household would. All the servants, and even her old master, would be hauled in and questioned, possibly tortured, for evidence that they had been complicit in her crimes. . . .

The flitter grounded. Arrhae swallowed, trying to get some control over herself. *It's ridiculous,* she thought then, trying to steady herself. *If your contacts, whoever they are, had been caught already, do you think it's to the Praetor's house they'd have brought you?* For the door had opened, and there was the walk up to the broad porticoed frontage, just as before, and no unusual guard-presence to be seen— not even the honor guard that had greeted her the last time. *That could be a bad sign too,* she thought, as the pilot handed her down. Yet at the same time, conditions might have changed. Possibly this visit was meant to be less public, less noticed, than the last one.   ...+. .

She walked up the paved path behind the pilot with her head up, greeted the door-opener of tr'Anierh's house with a small polite nod, and followed him as he led her once more across the huge Great Hall to the side room where tr'Anierh's office was. The door-opener touched a control, so that the office door swung open for Arrhae. He bowed her in.

Arrhae crossed the threshold, smiling, ready to greet tr'Anierh—and then froze. He sat behind his desk, and was rising to meet her. But two other chairs were set on either side of his side of the desk; and in them sat Urellh tr'Maehllie and Ahrm'n tr'Kiell, the other Two of the Three.

Arrhae couldn't help but swallow once in sudden dread. Thinking that tr'Anierh was kindly disposed to her merely because he had treated her kindly was a great danger, and the sudden presence of these others reminded her of that all over again. And now here she was alone and defenseless in a room with the three most powerful men in the Empire. Fleets moved at a whisper from them; an annoyed look from one of these men had caused people to vanish without a trace and never be seen again. Any one of them by him-self could potentially be deadly if you spoke the wrong word, and even under normal circumstances, it would take all your concentration to make sure that you did not. To be caught in the midst of all three of them at once would be like being trapped in a quaking bog. Too many directions in which you could misstep and be lost, too many things that one of them might take well, but one or both the others might take ill.

"Don't freeze there like a bird under a *thrai*'s eye, young Senator," said tr'Kiell. "Sit down. We have some questions for you."

Arrhae made her way to the one empty chair that stood facing the other three, and sat down. Her mind was shouting with alarm at the way things looked, more like a setup for an interrogation than anything else.

Of course that's what it is, you nitwit, said some chilly, matter-of-fact voice at the back of her mind. *These men haven't sent for you to have noonday herbdraft and wafers with them! Now* concentrate, *because you could possibly do more good during this meeting than those who sent you here ever dreamed possible!*

She made herself as comfortable as she could, and tried to get the measure of the other two men without seeming to stare at them. Tr'Kiell probably looked the least threatening of the three—short, round, with bushy eyebrows and a broad face; but that look would be as much a weapon in his hand as anything he might pull out of a holster. Tr'Maehllie looked so like a nonentity that the effect had to be purposeful. Neither too tall or too short, too dark or too fair, with nondescript dark hair and eyes whose color was almost too neutral to make out, his features regular and unremarkable, it was easy to more or less discard him after you had summed him up. But by all accounts, this man was the most dangerous of them all, though tr'Anierh might look taller, more striking, more impressive in his broad-shouldered blondness. All three of them had their subtleties, and their dangers, or they would not be where they were now.

"*Deihu,*" tr'Anierh said, "be comfortable. There's nothing

to fear. But you do look unwell. Were you ill on the trip? Do
you have trouble with space travel?"

She looked at him in surprise, almost with gratitude; he'd
offered her as good an excuse as any. And suddenly Arrhae
saw what to do, all laid out clearly before her. *They're treat-
ing me the way they would if I were truly a* hru'hfe, *just some
charlady that they'd sent off to space—a creature essentially
out of her depth. Whatever I may have feared, they have no
idea I might be anything more than I seem. Play into it!*
"*Fvillha,* it seems I do," Arrhae said. "And the last few days
of the trip were . . . unusual. Perhaps more exciting than I
had expected."

"Yes," said tr'Kiell. "Well, put that out of your mind, as
we have other things to discuss."

"We have all read your report," tr'Anierh said, "and my
colleagues have questions about some of the details."

"The tone," said tr'Maehllie, "was unduly gossipy."

Arrhae suspected that she was supposed to be scared by
this reprimand. She let her reply sound subdued, but not
cowed. "*Fvillha,* so was the tone of those whose conversations I reported. At first I didn't know how to take it; we tend
to think of the great ones, our political masters, as being
above such. I thought at first that I ought to improve the delegates' tone in the report, so as not to seem disrespectful. But
then that seemed a disservice to my patron," she nodded, not
too deferentially she hoped, at tr'Anierh, "who looked to me
straightforwardly for news of what I saw, not my own gloss
on it. If those on the mission with me seemed to be acting
badly, that was the honorable Praetor's judgment to make,
not mine."

Arrhae watched them. She saw tr'Anierh glance at his
colleagues, especially number two, with just the slightest expression of a man not only satisfied with an answer, but more
satisfied because it had proved him right about something.

"Let the tone pass for the moment, then," said tr'Maehllie.

"There are some details that seem to have been skirted in your discussion of the negotiation sessions."

"Sir," Arrhae said, "whatever you desire to know, I'm at your disposal."

There followed a difficult half hour or so during which Arrhae was grilled over the general attitudes and specific responses of nearly every delegate who had been involved in the sessions Arrhae had attended. *This was all in the report,* she thought quite early on. *They're just judging my off-the-cuff responses, trying to see whether what I wrote was composed, figured out after the fact, or genuine observation. And probably they're also interested in how my impressions compare to reports from the other spies they had there.* Though the other Two of the Three were at great pains to seem in control of the questioning, the thought kept occurring to Arrhae that they were uneasy, uncertain about something. *Uncertain, perhaps, about their own spies?* she thought. *Amusing. Uncertain even about the people they had spying on me? Entirely possible. And now I wonder, did they indeed have someone else spying on me besides tr'Radaik? Ffairrl the steward would have been a perfect candidate. Or that poor little chambermaid I saw about twice.*

She put the thought aside and concentrated on answering these men's questions. Tr'Anierh did not say much, except to occasionally ask Arrhae to expand on an answer or two already given. Mostly he seemed to be watching his companions. *And they, for their part, seem mostly to be watching each other. I may be a pawn in this game to some extent, but I have leisure to see here something that perhaps only few Rihannha ever perceive: how little these three trust one another, and how divided they are.* That insight turned Arrhae's thoughts in another direction entirely. *Is it possible that either tr'Kiell or tr'Maehllie is interested in seeing whether I would be worth subverting to his own uses, as a weapon against tr'Anierh?* The idea produced an obscure annoyance in her, but this too she put aside for later examination. Answer their questions for the moment. *There'll be time to analyze this later.*

There came a brief lull after that first half hour or so. "There were some events that were rather scantily covered in your report," said tr'Kiell after some moments' thought. "I speak particularly of the gathering before the first negotiating session—"

"There were quite a few people there, *Fvillha*," Arrhae said, "and it was difficult to watch them all at once, especially without being seen to do so."

Tr'Kiell looked amused. "So tell us about that. Who was uncomfortable at that gathering? Who stood in corners speaking furtively?"

"Mostly the Intelligence operatives," Arrhae said, "because how else would they be seen to be doing their jobs?"

Even tr'Maehllie's chilly look broke a little at that, and he produced a small smile, though an edged one. "I would be as interested to see who did not look uncomfortable," he said. "Especially among the Federation people."

Arrhae spoke briefly of Kirk and McCoy, and was not surprised to see how interested they all were in Kirk, but the more she spoke, the more she got a feeling that there was something more they were waiting to hear about him— ideally, something bad. "He did have perhaps more ale than was good for him," she said, sheerly to see how they would react. "The Praetor Gurrhim tr'Siedhri inveigled him into it."

Tr'Kiell snorted. Tr'Maehllie looked grim. Tr'Anierh had no reaction at all, merely watched the others.

On a sudden urge, Arrhae said, "Sirs, if I may ask: what became of the Praetor?"

"You may not," said tr'Maehllie, brusque.

"Oh come, Urellh," tr'Anierh said. "The bruit of it was all over *Gorget,* you know that." He looked back to Arrhae.

"Dead. He was in no condition to have survived being moved so much as a cubit, and the kidnappers haled him off a support-bed and through disruptor fire, and then who knows where else aboard that ship, before they all vanished at last. It was unfortunate. He will be a loss to the Senate."

A lie, Arrhae was suddenly certain, *on top of a lie, with yet another lie beneath.* Yet at the same time she got a sense that tr'Anierh knew perfectly well that *she* knew this was a lie. *This could become dangerous,* she thought. Did the others know he was lying? If they did . . .

She put the complications away for later pondering. If she had trouble sleeping that night, the puzzle would at least be entertaining. The Three looked at one another. "Well," tr'Anierh said, standing up, "we have at least one meeting to attend within the hour, so I think we must end now, unless the two of you have questions still unanswered."

The other two rose. Arrhae rose with them, bowed a little. "Senator," Urellh said, "our thanks for your time. Your service to the Empire is appreciated."

"That the *Fvillhaih* asks it, honors me," Arrhae said, as tr'Anierh came out from behind his desk. She bowed again, turned; he saw her to the door.

"Arrhae," he said very quietly, when they were at the threshold.

"Fvillha?"

"You did well. A bad business, being caught amid the three of us."

She was tempted to agree with him to his face, but restrained herself. "If I gave satisfaction," Arrhae said with one more slight bow, "I am content."

"You did. One word before you go, however. The news today may have some unusual items in it. If you wish to be of use to me, I will be needing your reaction to that news, and the reactions of others in the Senate over the next few days. Obviously you will keep this business between us."

"Fvillha," she said, very softly, "you may rely on my discretion."

"I know that. I thank you. You will hear from me shortly. There is one more piece of work I would like to entrust to you."

He turned away from her, back to the room, and the door shut behind him. Arrhae made her way out into the building's Great Hall, nodded a courteous good-bye to the door-opener, and made her way out to where the flitter waited for her. Arrhae climbed into it and rode home, too preoccupied even to look out a window at the view.

The household was quiet. It was time for daymeal, and most of the staff would be down in their own quarters. Only old Mahan was still at his post, and as she came in he locked the door and looked at Arrhae closely. "A long day," he said.

Arrhae felt as if she had had about three long days at once. Her body ached with her earlier terror and its abrupt relief, and her brain was buzzing with unanswered questions. She could not get rid of the feeling that something had been going on in that room that was more than a mere elucidation of her report. Once again tr'Anierh had been at the heart of it, and Arrhae was at a loss to know what it had been about. "Mahan," she said, heading for her sleeping chamber, "maybe you would leave me some ale and a little bowl of stew in the retiring room? Or something cold from the larder. I have to catch up with the news."

"There's some stew of fresh *theirnh* and skyroot from the market today, *hru'hfe.* And last week's ale is just ready. I'll put a tray on the sideboard for you presently."

Arrhae went into her sleeping chamber, changed into a long comfortable tunic and trews and some soft slippers, then went out and made her way down the corridor that led from the Great Hall toward the back of the house. Here was the retiring room, a comfortable place that housed the library and mediascreens, with windows that opened onto the peace of the back garden. To Arrhae's surprise, Mahan had been in and out already; ale in a goblet, and the stew, steaming gently and sending a most appetizing scent of goldspice and *desiv* into the air, sat on a tray beside the hardwood panel behind which the viewer was hidden.

Arrhae touched the control that would pull up the concealing panel, and the screen came on and showed Arrhae the menu of available entertainments for that afternoon and evening. *Where has the day gone?* she thought, looking out over the lawn at the lengthening shadows of the trees. She picked up the bowl of stew, tapped the screen several times to scroll out the menu of news channels, selected the most sober of the lot, and went to sit down in the comfortable chair facing the screen.

She put up her feet on the nearby hassock and had the first few bites of stew. The crunch of the vegetables, the savory gravy, and the relief of being alive and well to eat them, were too wonderful for the first few seconds for Arrhae to pay any attention to what was happening on the screen. The sound of shouting, though, made her glance up.

She found herself looking at an urban landscape, parkland surrounded with tall structures. Smoke hazed the view of what was happening; flames licked out of buildings' windows, vehicles plunged through the chaos and out of view again. People were fleeing in all directions, shouting, screaming. *Where is that? Has there been some kind of disaster?*

"—*has occurred in a number of cities on ch'Havran,*" the announcer was saying. "*Security forces were obliged to move in to pacify the areas where the disorder broke out. A number of arrests were made of ringleaders of the gangs that declared themselves responsible for the disruptions. Other citizens are assisting the authorities with their inquiries.*"

Arrhae watched as helmed and armed men and women,

dark-clad in the subdued uniforms of the security forces, dragged away Rihannsu who struggled and cried out. Some of these were being beaten by the security people pulling them along. One man dashed in front of the pickup of the crew recording the incident and cried, *"The Empire's making slaves of us all! Rise up now, take back our sun, take back your freedom and your* mnhei'sahe! *The Sword is coming, follow her, follow—"*

A truncheon descended. The man who had been shouting in front of the recorder fell abruptly out of view. The recorder was jostled, went sideways, went dark. The next shot showed the same streets quiet, empty of everything but some litter scattered about; but smoke still hung in the air, like the echoes of the cries that had been silenced. *"Local authorities say that the disruptions were short-lived, and were the actions of a minority of malcontents and seditionists in the Havrannssu population."*

Without looking away from the viewer, Arrhae put the bowl down on the little table by her chair, staring at the images in near disbelief. She couldn't remember ever having seen anything like this on the news services. But there had been rumors in the Senate of late, whispered even in the hearing of relative newcomers like Arrhae, of places where there had been demonstrations, even riots, against some of the government's more repressive actions. The increase in surveillance, the new war tax—there had even been demonstrations in favor of a certain person—but no one would say the name out loud. It had, after all, been thrice written and burned. The rumors said *those* demonstrations had been put down most brutally of all.

But what Senators whispered one tenday, people in the street would be whispering the next. Soon enough they wouldn't be whispering. *And now,* Arrhae thought, *possibly because there'll soon be no way to cover it up anymore, I'd guess the news nets have been told that they may show these "disruptions." Or* ordered *to show them, and how they're handled. The population's meant to take warning from what they see.*

Arrhae then thought of what tr'Anierh had said to her, and shivered a little. *He has found me satisfactory as a spy, able to operate without causing suspicion in a small group, and so now he extends my role a little further, to a larger group. The Senate. I am meant to see what they think of this, and to betray those who aren't in favor of it.*

"Loyal Rihannha are urged to notify the government of such treasonous actions, which only give comfort to our enemies in this time of war. The following commlink addresses can be used to contact local authorities to notify them of suspicious activities."

Arrhae could not get out of her mind the images of burning buildings, the police craft and military police flitters firing disruptors at fleeing figures on the ground, the shouting, running people, fists shaken at the sky. She could feel outrage building in her, the reaction of other Rihannsu who would see this. *How could* all *those people be spies and traitors?* they would be thinking. *Something's gone wrong here, something's the matter with the government.*

Arrhae shook her head. She knew well enough from her own studies that the best time for external forces to become involved in a revolution was when a government was already having internal problems. *People in the Fleet will be seeing at least some of these images of civil unrest,* Arrhae thought. *Censorship in the military services is often more relaxed than it is for the general public, if only because the military have access to more ways to break it if they start to become interested in doing so. And gossip travels fast. One reason the noble Praetor dislikes it so.*

The newsreader had gone on to some less loaded topic, something about preparations for the departure of the in-system portion of Grand Fleet for the Outmarches, the

Neutral Zone, in preparation for hostilities. *So now it begins,* Arrhae thought. *And as for spying on my fellow Senators— well, it seems I must do it, for the time being, to maintain my position with tr'Anierh.* But she would also be keeping her eyes open for anything that would make a difference to those who had originally sent her here. How she would get *that* news out, if she found any, she had no idea. Her one-shot contact was gone forever. *No matter. If I must, I will improvise something. In the meantime . . .*

She sat and tried to shake the images of the smoke rising up, while also thinking of one much worse: night falling over a planet far away, a night that, unless a miracle happened, would be followed by no morning.

Light-years away, in his quarters, late in his local night, James Kirk sat gazing at a blank spot on the wall with his feet up on his desk, invoking the Gods of War.

They had names like Clausewitz and Imessa and Xenophon and Kalav and Churchill and Kościuszko and Patton, and they were all full of good advice. But his problem was figuring out which parts of their advice to take. They often contradicted one another on details, due to their coming from separate time periods and in some cases separate planets. The padd in front of him was covered with notes about some of the things they agreed on, but there were too few of these for the peace of mind of a man who found himself doing his "admiral's work" under such peculiar circumstances.

After all, an admiral normally had a fleet he could depend on—*well, theoretically, anyway,* Jim thought—commanded by beings with whom he had previously served. But this campaign wasn't going to be anywhere near that simple. Jim was presently devising a battle plan that was going to be executed by people he'd fought against in the past (and often beaten, which didn't strike him as a recipe for incipient cooperation), people who didn't trust him, people who, even under the best circumstances, were going to want to get rid of him just as soon as possible. Some of those people might even like to see parts of his planning fail, regardless of whether they themselves took some damage from the failure. One of the War Gods had said that no battle plan, however well-laid, survives contact with the enemy. *In this case, though,* Jim thought, *I'm going to be lucky if it survives contact with my own side.* So his goal was to construct a plan that could not be damaged even by his cocombatants' direct hostility, let alone the always unavoidable potential for sudden idiocy in a crisis.

Jim sat and looked at his padd. There, in neat order, were what he considered the Top Four Helpful Hints of the War Gods—at least, in the present circumstances—what Jim judged the most basic tactical necessities.

First, and most important: destroy the enemy's ability to attack.

Second, as a way to bring the first goal about, destroy the enemy's command and control structures to whatever extent possible.

Third, put the enemy into "shock." Shock produces or facilitates unconsidered or uncoordinated actions on the enemy's part. Such actions are usually to your advantage and almost always to the enemy's detriment.

Fourth, destroy the enemy's communications, his ability to predict what's going to happen, his ability to see.

That implied four (a): *destroy whatever he has by way of an early warning system.*

Considering that particular principle of war, Jim frowned at the blank spot on the wall, turning over possibilities in his mind. The pathway of the Free Rihannsu fleet in toward Augo was not as problematic as its later course toward ch'Rihan and ch'Havran would be. Subspace jamming, and physical interdiction of the space between Artaleirh and

Augo, would do the job well enough for the first leg. The process, according to Veilt tr'Tyrava, had already begun, with the dispatch of some of the ships captured by the Artaleirhin to patrol and secure the invading fleet's projected course.

But Jim had other concerns. He had been thinking hard about the Romulan monitoring satellites on their side of the Neutral Zone, which lay not too far from the course that would lead from Augo to Eisn. He was also thinking about the Federation monitoring satellites, on the other side of the Zone but not so far away, which would be under threat as soon as war broke out.

Assuming that they haven't already been compromised. There was a thought that had been troubling Jim for some time. Those satellites were a long way from Earth, and the Romulans were very technologically creative. Jim suspected that it was at least a fifty-fifty chance that they had been tapped, and that everything they saw was possibly already being piped straight through to Grand Fleet and the Romulan High Command. But there was no way to destroy *that* early warning system.

Or is there?

The wall suddenly seemed less blank than it had, as Jim's line of reasoning made a big jump into laterality. He could suddenly start to see a way to go, mapping itself out step by step and branch by branch, a growing tree of potential decisions. But that first branch was a doozy.

The Zone monitoring satellites, on both *sides, have to be destroyed.*

The unmanned ones, anyway. But those were by far the most numerous. There were thirty of them between the Federation and the Empire, scattered in a best-solution configuration over a geodesic "surface" spanning some fifteen light-years. It wouldn't be necessary to destroy them all, just the ones that would be closest to the areas through which the

Free Rihannsu fleet would be moving. And if possible it should look coincidental. It would even be useful—and Jim grinned rather ferally—if it looked like Grand Fleet itself had done it.

Certainly the Romulans would think of the loss of the satellites, in general, as a good thing. They'd gone out of their way to demand their removal, during the talks. An accident? Or a strategy? Hard to tell. But when the Romulans would hear about the destruction of Federation satellites, the last thing that would occur to them was that the Federation was behind it. The concept would be just too outrageous, as they considered the Federation to be impossibly conservative and afraid to do anything risky. *They might, of course, think the Klingons did it.* That'd *give them something to chew on too.* The implications needed more thorough consideration: but making the fog of war a little denser, in this situation, might be smart.

And of course Starfleet would go pale at the very thought of us destroying our own satellites, even if it does *serve their best interests.* Jim folded his arms and considered the logistics of destroying, say, ten or fifteen monitoring satellites. *Without going near them, since we're going to be busy elsewhere. And we somehow need to make sure that the Federation has adequate feed of tactical and strategic data from inside Romulan space when Starfleet is ready to move.*

He'd talk to Mr. Scott about it. One more impossible thing to do before breakfast was the kind of thing that Scotty thrived on. Jim turned back to the general principles, once more considering that blank wall. *Deny the enemy's supply of attacking forces from outside the Hearthworlds.* That would be the next big problem to handle, and *Enterprise* and the ships traveling with her would be in no position to do anything about it, nor indeed would it be an appropriate tasking for them. Smaller and more lightly armed vessels could do the interdiction. The Romulans would quickly run low on vessels to spare for convoying. Very soon after the beginning of any civil hostilities, they would be forced to expose their supply and troop movements, and Ael had told him what he really wanted to know, that big troop movements were going to be a problem for them. That would make it much easier for little rebel vessels to harry the ships that would be moving people and supplies. *With almost all the participants carrying cloaking devices of one kind or another,* he thought, *this turns into real twentieth-century stuff, "submarine" warfare—surface, fire, vanish again.*

He considered whether there might be some paradigms from that earlier time that would do the attackers good. *Something to consult with Spock about,* he thought, *and Sulu.*

Jim sighed. That would start getting into the shallower waters of attack design, detail that could be added after he sat down with Ael and Veilt on *Tyrava,* and with the other Free Rihannsu commanders now gathering in the system, Courhig and his ilk. But now Jim thought he saw the way to present them with a strategy that would reflect both what they thought was most likely to happen next, and what was most likely to go wrong.

Now all he had to do was keep his self-confidence in place. Desperately important as this work was, Jim thought he could do that. After all, how many other admirals' campaigns had he taken apart, first at the Academy and then later, for his own pleasure—and time and time again said, softly, or sometimes loudly, "I could do better than that!" Well, now was his chance to prove it. And how far wrong could you go when you had Sun Tzu and Clausewitz and Linebarger and Damins and hr'Teeilih behind you, all concurring on the most important things?

Pursue one great decisive aim with force and determination.

And don't be distracted.

Jim nodded to the War Gods, pulled the padd over, and got to work.

When he next glanced at the chrono, it was hours and hours later, but strangely, he felt less tired than he had when he'd started. The bare screen of the padd was now showing the "topmost" of a series of pages—mostly text, but with many diagrams of the Augo and Eisn star systems as well as some others. Now embedded in the text were numerous images and maps of ch'Rihan and ch'Havran, large-scale and small-scale, all heavily annotated with "warfighter choreography" symbols indicating the mooted positioning of all forces from brigade level up, with first-draft conditional movement parameters all laid in.

Jim sighed and got up, as he had been doing at frequent intervals, to stretch and have some water. He looked down at the padd. *This is all I can do for the moment,* he thought. *Spock needs to look at this, and then we'll meet with the Free Rihannsu side for input and feedback in the next day or so. The delay's useful; if I've forgotten something important, it'll give me time to realize what it is, assuming Spock hasn't already caught it.*

He sighed. Though the plan for dealing with the battle itself was making more sense, the business of *Enterprise* actually being at Augo was the sorest point for Jim at the moment. That was the point at which it would become plain that he was flouting Commodore Danilov's orders, and he would be in no position to reveal why. *The only question remaining,* Jim thought, *is this: when we finally make contact with Federation forces, after Augo, will they attempt to destroy* Enterprise *on sight, assuming that I've turned?*

And what will the crew think?

Strangely, that mattered more, and Jim had kept coming back to it as he worked. It wasn't as if he didn't value Danilov's good opinion. But he was not responsible for

Danilov. He *was* responsible for his crew. *Tomorrow night,* Jim thought, *we'll find out. And after that, however many of them are left following me, we'll get out there and start doing business. The President's business.*

Jim bent over and touched his toes once or twice to stretch his back, and then did a couple of squats and stretches. *The man is taking the long view of the Federation's relationship with the Romulans,* he thought, *that Fleet, for whatever reasons, is not. After all this is over, even if we win, I have a feeling the Federation and Starfleet are going to find themselves in the middle of a constitutional crisis concerning the President's powers as C-in-C. After that, things may change; sealed-order missions like this may become illegal. But right now the chain-of-command issue is clear enough to me.*

And he truly felt that the President had the right of it on this issue. The Romulan Star Empire could not be allowed to collapse as a result of the civil war to come. The balance of power between the Klingons and the Federation would be too seriously deranged, and all hell would break loose. *So,* Jim thought. *"Into the valley of death," but for a good cause.*

Jim wandered back over to the padd, touched its controls, and scrolled through the pages again. It all looked so neat and tidy here. Little bright lines and symbols, arrows and boxes, and all the pages of description. These ten thousand people here, those five thousand there . . . *It's all just fiction now,* he thought. *Bloodless and neat. But it won't stay that way. It'll start becoming real very soon now. Too soon.*

He paused at that one page in the middle. *Except for this,* he thought. *Everything turns on this, and no matter what the Rihannsu say, it's got to happen. Better do now what I've been putting off. It won't wait any longer.*

Jim sat down again, made sure the document was properly archived, and cleared the padd, then brought up the private commlink address he had been told to use only once. At first he was about to send the message by voice, but then he reached for a stylus and wrote:

You said I had one favor coming. I'm calling it in.
Here is what I need . . .

TEN

LATE THE NEXT MORNING, after sending his message and getting some sleep (though probably not nearly as much as McCoy would have wanted him to), Jim went down to the mess again, found it empty this time, and had some breakfast, then headed up to the bridge.

Spock was in the center seat, looking with a speculative expression at a front-screen view of *Tyrava*. As Jim came in, he rose and handed him a padd. "Captain, the post-battle assessments are in from all departments now. We sustained very minimal structural damage; repairs are already being made. Mr. Scott tells me that ETA for the completion of repairs is about six hours from now."

"Very good, Mr. Spock," Jim said, looking down the list on the padd and handing it back to him. "Anything else that needs my attention?"

"Nothing here, Captain. Though I believe that Mr. Scott wishes to see you as well, to discuss something he and K's't'lk have been working on."

"Fine," Jim said. "I'll go down there after I hit sickbay and find out if McCoy will let me see his star patient. He's being as protective of the Praetor as a hen with one chick." He looked out at *Tyrava* and shook his head. "I really should see if I can wangle Scotty an invitation over there, though. Any thoughts on the warp technology as yet?"

"Some conjectures," Spock said, "based on some early

remote readings. But my preference is for firsthand observations, as you know, and Mr. Scott's is probably for blueprints, or the original engineering drawings. I fear right now we have time to procure neither, even if the commanders of *Tyrava* would let us have them."

"Yes," Jim said. "Even after Artaleirh, it's going to take them a little while to trust us. But they'd better hurry up. If they're still not sure of us by the time we get to ch'Rihan . . ."

Spock nodded. "There is always that possibility. And if other aspects of our mission are to be successful as well, that would seem to be a necessity."

"Yes," Jim said.

He headed for the turbolift, glancing over at the comms station, where Uhura was running a diagnostic. "Commander Uhura," he said, "have we heard anything from *Bloodwing* this morning?"

"Not as yet, Captain," Uhura said. "I'll hail them if you like."

"No need," Jim said. "They're probably just as busy with after-battle cleanup as we've been. If they haven't checked in by a few hours from now, call them and ask Ael if she has time to meet me before the crew get-together tonight."

"Yes, sir."

Jim nodded and got into the lift. "Sickbay," he said, and it whooshed off. Now that he had his suggestions for the battle of Augo down in "hard" form, all the other concerns of the last couple of days had come pressing in on him—especially Arrhae's warning about whatever was closing in on the solar system to threaten the Earth. *I'd give a lot for more data,* Jim thought. *But I have a feeling that Scotty's and Spock's conjectures are on the money. The Romulans have Sunseed, they know it works, they know that under certain circumstances it can be made deadly at a planetary level. I could spend hours trying to figure out what else they might have up their sleeves, but why bother? If I were them, I'd use what I had.*

Unless of course they expect us to think that way.

Jim sighed. There was no point in trying so hard to antic-ipate your enemy's complex and twisty strategies that you tied your own brain into knots and distracted yourself from the obvious, leaving your enemy with leisure to come up be-hind you and do something straightforward like bash you over the head with a club.

The lift stopped, and Jim got out and went down the cor-ridor to sickbay. As its doors opened he was greeted by the sound of someone laughing and then suddenly stopping with a kind of wheeze of pain, and then laughing and stopping again. "You should cut that out, Praetor," he heard McCoy saying, though there was something strange about his voice. Then Jim realized that he was hearing the doctor through his implanted universal translator chip, and that McCoy was speaking Rihannsu. "The sutures are robust, but you'll pop them if you keep it up."

"If you will tell me such jokes, in such an accent," came the reply, "the fault is yours, not mine!"

"Now what's wrong with my accent?" McCoy said, as Jim came into the diagnostic bay. The doctor was looking up at the readouts, and on a mobile bed below them lay Gurrhim tr'Siedhri, propped up about halfway and clutch-ing his abdomen. For a man who had so nearly expired only the day before, he looked in surprisingly good shape. He was still rather pale for a Romulan who had been more on the swarthy side normally, but his eye was bright as he saw Jim come in, and if Gurrhim wasn't moving easily, he was at least moving.

"Praetor," Jim said. "How are you feeling today?"

Gurrhim gave him a wry look. "I am Praetor of nowhere and nothing now, Captain, so you had best omit the title. But otherwise, I feel far better than I did when they shot me. I may now say that being shot is greatly overrated, and an experience I could safely have forgone." He shifted a little on the bed, and winced. "But then, for the moment, so was death, for which I owe the doctor here a debt."

Jim leaned on the bed opposite and looked up at the readings. He was no expert, but they looked fairly steady. "All part of our basic service package," McCoy was saying idly, as he studied the readings himself. "But you won't be needing my attentions for that much longer, Gurrhim. I want to patch in a second layer of autoplast venal grafts tomorrow, but I can do that while you're conscious, and you can watch and critique my style."

Gurrhim shook his head in wry wonder. "You do a thing as routine with which our people seem to have great difficulty. I wish we could establish some kind of medical exchange program."

"I wouldn't mind that at all," McCoy said, "assuming our respective governments can get the details sorted out. But that's what this is all about, isn't it?"

"You may be right," Gurrhim said, looking over at Kirk. "Captain, I must thank you first for giving me refuge. You would not have been blamed to have refused delivery on so abruptly delivered a package."

"Well," Jim said, "that kind of behavior wouldn't normally be our way. And anyway, the package came with unusual, shall we say, wrappings."

Gurrhim got a sly look. "That surprises me most, that the little trinket I gave to another has now come into your hands. You will keep it safe, I hope."

"My chief engineer has it now," Jim said, "and from what he's said to me about it so far, I think it couldn't be in better hands. When everything calms down again, we'll return it to you. I take it that the doctor has filled you in on the circumstances under which you arrived."

"I am glad he did," Gurrhim said, "for I remember little of it. One moment I was reading in my quarters. After that—"

He raised his hands to shrug, and then winced again. "—very little."

"Standard partial global amnesia," McCoy said. "Disruptor shock has a hydrostatic-shock element as well. The abrupt increase in intracranial pressure alone knocks most people out as soon as the beam-field hits. And you can't remember after the fact what you weren't conscious enough to have a memory of in the first place. I'd say it's a recollection you wouldn't much miss."

"There are flickers of other memory, just disjointed scenes, from later on," Gurrhim said. "I hurt most abominably. I fear I used bad language, and that to the young men who saved me."

"One of them, by Rihannsu reckoning, is now where he understands what you were going through even better than you do," McCoy said, "and the other's long since forgiven you." He looked over at Jim. "Young tr'AAnikh's asleep now. He was worrying himself into a decline, so I took it on myself to slip him a mickey."

Gurrhim tilted his head to one side as if listening to something. "You gave him a rodent?"

Jim smiled.

"I stuck an intradermal translator in the Praetor this morning," McCoy said. "Sorry, Gurrhim, I just can't stop calling you that. But, Jim, we've got to get the translator system's damn idiom-handler looked at again. Every time we think we have it pretty much running right, something new pops up."

"I'll speak to Uhura," Jim said. "She mentioned it to me herself, but she's got a lot to do right now. Gurrhim, you're our guest for the time being, and until our situation clarifies itself after our next stop—"

"Augo?" Gurrhim said.

Jim stared at him.

"It would seem the logical next step," Gurrhim said,

"judging only by what the doctor has told me, that we are at Artaleirh, where we have won a battle with a small but significant segment of Grand Fleet. But even after Augo, Captain, my personal resources are limited enough by circumstance that it would not benefit me to try to go home. Not just yet."

"They'd just try to kill you again," McCoy said, "and this time, they'd probably manage it."

"Even if 'they' did not desire to simply kill me," Gurrhim said, "whoever 'they' were—I would guess that one or more of the Three are somewhere behind the attempt—then there would also be the possibility of being arrested and tried for treason."

"Which treason in particular?" Jim said.

"Well, escaping from my assassination," Gurrhim said, and smiled slightly. "To a Federation vessel, yet. And by now 'they' would have had time to assemble plenty of evidence of whatever treachery it was that impelled them to try to assassinate me. Probably I will already have been arraigned for such in my absence on ch'Rihan. The end of such a proceeding would be for the government to seize my assets and properties on ch'Havran and elsewhere, and take control of my various corporations. But then, on the other hand, if the government assumed that I was dead . . ." He trailed off, thinking, and a dry, amused look started to spread across his face.

"Is this preferable?" Jim said.

Gurrhim shook his head. "Well, were I alive and attainted a traitor, and my name written and burned, then the government would simply seize all my properties and funds. I estimate that such an outcome would harm the revolution that is to come, which I know in advance my family will support. We have spoken of it often enough in private. But if I am dead, then control of my chattels passes to my children. And my son and daughters, while naturally having to seem to acquiesce with the Imperium's demands as to what needed to be done with them afterward, would have their own opinions about how to handle such demands. We feel strongly about our holdings; they were hard-won, in the face of much interference from that same government. In particular, even if the Empire might eventually become frustrated with my children's noncooperation and seize one or another industry from us, they would hardly know how to *run* it right off, and during that transitional time, many things might go missing, or otherwise astray." He raised his eyebrows, an innocent look. "Funds. Physical plant."

"Might be smarter, then," McCoy said, "if you stayed dead, for a while, for tax purposes."

Gurrhim stared at McCoy, then guffawed, and then stopped and groaned and clutched at his gut. McCoy raised his eyebrows, reached behind him, and handed Gurrhim a pillow. Wincing, Gurrhim hugged it to his abdomen, and then, properly splinted, began to laugh again, more circumspectly. "True it is," he said, gasping slightly, "that medicine is the cruelest art. But you cut to the heart of the matter, Doctor, as might be expected." Now it was McCoy's turn to groan. "Let me, then, remain dead, by all means. For the time being, at least."

"Your family . . ." Jim said.

Gurrhim's face went grim. "I dislike bringing such suffering on them," he said. "But I must balance that against what joy they will feel, once all this is over, to find that I live after all. And if accident so falls out that, after Augo or whatever follows it, I die at last, well, then no more harm is done. They are most unlikely to learn that I died twice."

Jim thought about it for a moment, glanced at McCoy. McCoy nodded. "All right," Jim said.

He went over to McCoy's desk and hit the comms button on his desk monitor. "Bridge. Commander Uhura."

She looked at him from the screen. *"Uhura here."*

"Commander," Jim said, "send a message in the clear to *Bloodwing,* to Ael's attention. Regret to inform you, and so on and so forth, that the Praetor Gurrhim tr'Siedhri has unfortunately died of his injuries."

"He has?" But then, as she studied Jim's expression, a very small smile appeared on Uhura's face. *"I mean, of course he has, Captain."* And the smile vanished again. *"Such a shame."*

"No incoming communications from *any* source are to be directed to the Praetor without clearing them through me first," Jim said. "Nor is he at any time to be referred to as if he's still breathing. Meanwhile, pass this to security and flag it for Mr. Spock's attention: sickbay is to be off limits to all *Bloodwing* personnel but Ael until further notice."

"Yes, Captain," Uhura said, though looking somewhat bemused. She made a note on her padd. *"Shall I have guards posted?"*

Jim threw a glance at McCoy. McCoy shrugged. "I was going to move him out of the IC area this afternoon anyway, and into one of the private rooms. But then again, we're having a gathering tonight, aren't we?"

Jim nodded. "Hold off on the guards until guests start boarding the ship this evening," he said to Uhura. "Then post them only inside sickbay. And they're not to be obviously identifiable as security." He glanced at McCoy again.

McCoy raised his eyebrows. "I can always use some 'extra staff' to haul things around. We can put them in medical uniforms for the time being."

Jim glanced at Uhura. *"I'll take care of it, Captain,"* she said, turning to her station to begin instructing the computer accordingly. The screen went blank.

Jim nodded and turned away. Ael's comment, some time back, about being none too certain about all of her crew— not even now—was on his mind. *Though I wonder exactly where her suspicions lie.*

"You'll want to leak some 'evidence' to support the claim," McCoy said thoughtfully. "I can do you some images of what Gurrhim looked like when he came in, and process them a little, but not so most people would notice." He grinned. "We can even do his autopsy."

"I will be glad to help you," Gurrhim said.

"You will *not*," McCoy said. "You may have a rubber brain inside a cast-iron skull, Praetor, but even your people aren't immune to psychological damage from this kind of image. You just lie there and I'll find you some other kind of entertainment. Something to read, perhaps."

"I cannot think when I would have last had time to simply enjoy some reading," Gurrhim said, his face suddenly acquiring a nearly angelic look of delight that sorted oddly with the lines of calculation and deviousness in that face. "Perhaps there is something to be said for being shot after all."

"Praetor," Jim said. "Yes, I know, don't say it, I don't care. I have a feeling that if things go well, you'll be entitled to the title once again someday. I just want to ask you one thing before I go, though I do want to talk to you more about this some other time, when you're feeling better. Right now I have little other opinion to go on. Ael's I've heard plenty of. I've heard some of Veilt's, and I hope to hear some more. But your opinion would interest me. Not as a Senator or Praetor, but as a Rihannsu citizen. When this revolution starts, are people going to support it?"

The blissful look faded somewhat. "Captain," Gurrhim said, "were I so talented a prophet as you seem to think me, I would be many times richer than I am, by mere gambling, rather than having had to work so hard for so long. This matter is complex. Our people are oppressed, overtaxed, overgoverned by a structure that once was far looser and more forgiving, but has been tightening on them little by little, like a noose. That fact, hardly any of them would deny. But the oppression has been *our* oppression, if you follow me. It is native. Some there are who will see your involvement and instantly assume that what seems a revolution from within is actually being controlled from without, by our old enemies. Or those whom we have been taught are our enemies—for it's been a century and more since the Empire and the Federation have been involved in anything more but the merest border skirmishes—an old war gone cold, but 'warmed up' at intervals when the government needs it for something, such as tightening that noose a little further."

Gurrhim frowned. "The Klingons are another story. We have warred with them more or less constantly over the last three decades, and many people see the Empire as it's presently constituted as being the only realistic defense against being overrun by the larger Empire next door. If the government was wise, it would invoke that fear as a reason against the revolution to come. But is it wise enough to do that? There lies a danger for you, if it does. And there is always an additional unpredictable factor in such a situation: the Fleet. Finally, the armed forces are the ones who will decide what happens to any revolution. The government itself has no guns; it depends on Grand Fleet and the ground security forces to do its bidding. Once upon a time it held them bound to it by *mnhei'sahe,* the desire to keep the given word to something that was worth serving. Now those bonds are weaker, or are constructed of money or power or fear, rather than virtue. Will they hold under stress?" Gurrhim started to "shrug" with his hands again, then thought better of it and dropped them.

"So," Jim said, "you genuinely don't know."

"I think perception will matter a great deal," Gurrhim said. "I think the actual conduct of the war will matter a great deal. It must do no more harm to Rihannsu people and Rihannsu property than it absolutely must. It must leave Rihannsu sovereignty intact. And it must not take too long, lest

it start to recall memories of all those years of border skirmishes, and become a 'normal thing.' If that happens, we are
all doomed: the Rihannsu and the Federation together, and
maybe even the Klingons."

Jim nodded slowly.

"But beyond that," Gurrhim said, "there is a chance. If
you take the opportunities offered you, and if your ally with
the Sword does not back away."

That remark surprised Jim. "The favorite Rihannsu tactic," Gurrhim said, "is to hit and run. But comes a time when
you cannot run, when you must stand. The Commander-
General has had little practice at that. To do her justice, because of what the Fleet did to her, on the orders of their
political masters, she has had little opportunity. Now, though,
she must exercise that virtue. I hope she has it to use."

Kirk nodded again. "Jim," McCoy said, glancing up at the
vital signs monitors, "you go on now. I want this man to get
some rest."

"Right," Jim said. "Gurrhim—thank you."

The Praetor nodded and put his head wearily back down
on the pillow.

Jim left sickbay and headed for engineering, deep in
thought. When he arrived the place was in its usual state of
seeming busy even though nothing in particular was going
on, with crew hastening in all directions. Scotty liked to see
his people on the hop, and Jim knew that the engineers hu-
mored him in this regard. They also seemed to get a lot of
work done in this mode, so everybody was happy.

He paused just inside the doors to look around, and
caught the sound he had been listening for: the Scots burr
mingled with a sound like a sporadically shaken wind chime.
Jim followed the sounds into the center of engineering,
where, over by one of the larger control panels, a design
table had been set up. There the chief engineer and what ap-

peared to be a giant twelve-legged glass spider were examining the holographic projection, rotating gently in the air, of a star's limb and corona, with a superimposed spectrogram—a long rainbow band with dark lines through it here and there.

"It's a bonny setup," Scotty was saying to K's't'lk. "Just look at those iron lines. You could use them for crowbars."

Jim raised his eyebrows as he came up behind the two of them, looking up at the spectrogram. "I take it this is a good thing?"

"Oh, good morning, Captain," Scotty said. "Aye, it is."

"What are we looking at?"

"This is 553 Trianguli," K's't'lk said. "It's a star we'll be passing on our way to Augo. Well, not precisely passing, but we'd like to make a stop there."

"What for?"

"Remember the little problem you tossed me last night?" Scotty said.

"Oh, Scotty!" Jim said. "You've found a lake to walk on *already?*"

Scott's smile had that slightly self-satisfied tinge that had often made Jim feel happier than any number of citations from technical journals.

"In a manner of speaking," Scotty said. He stood back from the holographic representation of the star's corona and shifted to another display, a long strip of spectrum interrupted by thin lines all down its length, and most markedly by two of them, like railroad tracks, right in its middle. "There are the Fe IX lines, Captain. You need strong ones if you're thinking of seeding a star. Robust lines mean the coronal plasma's of the right minimum density, which in turn is a diagnostic that tells you the star's core is stable."

"After 15 Trianguli," Jim said, "the star's stability would definitely be on my mind." He gave K's't'lk an amused look; she jangled gently, embarrassed.

"Well, we did the best we could with what we had," Scotty said. "And that on short notice. But the situation's much more clear-cut here. And we've time to prepare."

"I'm glad to hear it, Mr. Scott," Jim said, "but why exactly do we need to seed 553 Trianguli?"

"So that we can experiment with how to stop the process at a distance," K's't'lk said.

Jim blinked. "You really have a method that doesn't involve another ship running into a star's corona and destroying the one that's doing the seeding?"

"Yes," K's't'lk said.

Jim sat down. "I take it this isn't something that you two did since yesterday."

"Captain," Scotty said, "we're engineers, not miracle workers."

Jim was tempted to laugh at them, and restrained himself. "Go on, tell me what we're going to have to do."

Scotty actually shrugged. "We're going to have to build some field generators. They're going to be heavy on exotic parts, and labor-intensive as the dickens. But beyond that, all you need is enough power to produce the field effect. We can use the warp engines to kick-start it. After that the generators will take care of business."

"And you have to know which star your opponent is trying to seed," K's't'lk said. "Once you know that, you go to the nearest star of roughly equivalent stellar type, within a class on either side. Then you power up the field generators and 'unseed' the target star."

Jim stared at her.

"You go to the nearest star *of roughly equivalent type?*" he said.

"I know," K's't'lk said, sounding rather embarrassed. "It's so clumsy. If we had more time, we would be able to work out how to do it with *any* handy star. But since we're in something of a rush—"

Jim leaned over and looked the Hamalki in the eyes, or as many of the twelve as he could manage at once. "T'l," he said, "that was *not* intended as a criticism!" He looked up at the chief engineer. "Scotty, are you sure this is kosher?"

"Aye, well," Scotty said, and it was his turn to sound embarrassed now, "I'm still looking closely at the math myself, for it's more at Mr. Spock's and K's't'lk's level than mine. As for the parts of it I do ken, it'll take a wee while before we have all the uncertainties shaken out of the equations, and as usual, the test will tell us better than anything else where we've gone wrong. Or right. Mr. Spock's double-checking the parameters right now. Once he signs off on the equations, I can pull together a design team and we can build the hardware."

"Do we have everything you need?" Kirk said.

"What we don't have, we can fabricate," K's't'lk said.

"And you really think you can have this ready by the time we leave in a couple of days?" Jim said. "Just so you know—I don't contemplate taking long in transit to Augo. Just long enough to meet at one outworld rendezvous point to pick up the other small outworld fleets that'll be going in with us and *Tyrava*."

"We'd thought as much," Scotty said.

"No, we'll be ready, Captain," K's't'lk said. "It was the instrumentality that had us stymied, but we've got that worked out now. At least the theory's as sound as theories usually get before anyone tests them to success and makes further theorizing a pastime rather than a necessity."

Jim shook his head. "I can see you two are going to be making the technical journals again."

"Well, we might get an article out of it," K's't'lk said, "but not for coming up with anything new. This physics is a few hundred years old, on your world, and about six hundred years ago on mine."

"We use one aspect of it on the ship already," Scotty said,

"to manage the inertial damping fields that keep the *Enterprise* from turning into a lump o' twisty girders at warp speed."

"And keep us from turning into so much pulp inside her," Jim said. "That far I follow you. Are you using the technology to play with the star's gravity somehow?"

"Well," Scotty said, "it's not quite as simple as that . . ."

He caught his captain's warning look, and trailed off. K's't'lk, though, just laughed. "It's not that bad, Captain. The inertial damping fields are just an outgrowth of the warp-field equations. They pull limited amounts of directed 'virtual mass' out of the quantum vacuum, the electromagnetic zero-point field that fills the universe—what they used to call the plenum. The star-unseeding protocol just takes the same principle a little further, exploiting the 'heresy' that grew out of Einstein's original principle of equivalence."

"I remember you mentioning that a while back," Jim said. "It sounded like a strange term for a physicist to be using."

This time Scotty laughed. "It gets stranger. Einstein thought gravitation and electromagnetism were connected somehow, and finally gave up on the idea because he couldn't get the math to support it. But then some later theorists thought that maybe the electromagnetic zero-point field was what gravitation was *really* connected to."

"And this was heretical?" Jim said.

"If you were a physicist on Earth at that point, yes," K's't'lk said. "But later practical work bore the 'heresy' out. Our own version of it goes a step further yet. It states that the so-called 'quantum leap,' in which you do something *here* and something similar happens *there* without any direct spatial connection between the events, can be caused by mediating the events inside the zero-point field. So we pick a star, denominate a target star, then do something to *this* star, and something happens to that one over *there*."

The possibilities began spelling themselves out in Jim's

mind. "If you were right about this," he said, "you wouldn't have to build field generators in every solar system to protect that system's own star from being seeded. You could build just nine or ten of them, each near a candidate star that would represent one of the main stellar classes, and then wait for news that someone was trying to seed a given star. Set your 'good' star to target the one being seeded—"

"And stop the process," K's't'lk said. "You also need to be close enough to a given star system, in terms of subspace radio communications, that a call for help will arrive quickly enough for the 'unseeding station' to *do* something in a timely manner. But any one set of stations could protect stars for some hundreds of light-years around. And the whole system, once in place, will prevent the 'seedstorm' effect which so concerned Mr. Spock."

Scotty reached down to the design table and touched a control, shifting the image of the spectrogram to an image of the star itself, all blue, with prominences standing out in blue-white and white. "You get a reading of the star's general coronal state from the Fe IX lines. Those lines give you warning of any sudden fluctuation of the star's gross energy state—you match those with other diagnostics from mass gravimetry. Then you turn the field loose, using some of the star's own energy to power the outreach stage of the 'sync' between the control star and the target. The zero-point field propagates the progressive resonance between the two stars until the target's fully affected. Then the two stars go into sync. And the gross energy state of the control star then overrides the gross state of the target star, killing the seeding effect."

"Side effects?" Jim said.

"We won't know until we try," K's't'lk said. "That's what we need 553 Tri for. It's barren of worlds."

"What star do you have in mind for the target?"

"Well, 658 Tri has no planets either, and is only eight

light-years further on," K's't'lk said. "It's just on the Federation side of the Neutral Zone. We can observe it directly."

"All right," Jim said. "Now here comes the big question. Could this technique *itself* be used to seed a star?"

Scotty and K's't'lk looked at each other. "I'd have to think so," Scotty said. "But it doesn't matter if you can also use it to *stop* the seeding as soon as its starts. With the dissemination of stations of this kind, and information on how to build them, the technique ceases to be strategically useful—which is what you asked us for."

Jim nodded. "If it works. We'll give it a shot. Meanwhile, there's something else I need to talk to you about, something we might need to do."

Scotty and K's't'lk both looked at him attentively. "What did you have in mind?" Scotty said.

Jim took a long breath. "I think we need to destroy the unmanned monitoring satellites in the Neutral Zone." As Scotty opened his mouth, Jim said, "On both sides."

Scotty closed his mouth again. After a second, he said, "Captain, I hate to blow up technology that someone might need again later. And that's something else I've been needing to discuss with you. It can wait a moment, though. How would it be if the satellites just stopped working?"

Jim's eyebrows went way up. "No data in or out, to either side?"

"Until you give the word."

Jim thought about that. *It would really be preferable,* he thought. "But no—there would be a certain psychological effect to be achieved by actually *destroying* the satellites."

"Captain," K's't'lk said, "without asking you for more detail, think about this. Those satellites are all a long way from anywhere, and both sides, we must assume, are shortly going to be very, very busy fighting each other. What if only *one* satellite was actually destroyed—say one on each side—but all the others just stopped working at the same time? The obvious assumption for all concerned would be that they were *all* destroyed, and two parties at war are hardly going to waste valuable time sending starships to see if all the rest of the satellites had really been blown up."

"Hmm," Jim said. "All right, supposing you can deliver, on both counts. Just how are you planning to produce this wonder?"

"Ah," Scotty said.

He went over to a console and keyed in a sequence on a touchpad on the top, then turned back to Kirk with something in his hand. It was the gadget that tr'AAnikh had brought back from *Gorget* with him.

"I promised the Praetor that we'd give that back to him," Jim said.

Scotty looked at the little green metal sphere and sighed. "Captain, this wee bobble is potentially worth more than this whole ship and everything in it. Or more accurately, perhaps not the creature as a whole, but *this*."

He took the little sphere in both hands and twisted it slightly. It popped open and laid itself out in his hands in two hinged halves. The inside glittered with jewel-like data solids and dazzlingly machined metal, producing an effect like a giant Swiss watch of the old type with "intensive complications." One or two of the solids burned inside with power, the light of them burning bright, fading, burning bright again, as if with a pulse.

Bu Scotty's attention wasn't on them. Set slightly off center in the device was what looked like a shiny, blunt push button sticking up from the core. With great delicacy Scotty pulled it out of the body of the sphere and held it up, glinting in the lights of engineering. It looked like a mere cylinder of charcoal-colored metal, just a few centimeters long.

"This wee beastie," Scotty said, turning it from side to side, "may be as important to us in the future as the transtator was to us in the past, and the transistor a long time before that—and fire, first of all. If you scan this in any normal way, it presents itself as an inert body, just a gadolinium casting. Scan it more aggressively, and you get a sense that it could have data encoded in it at the crystal-lattice level, though you cannot read it. You have to look at it much more deeply to discover that the encoding is happening at the atomic and subatomic levels, in the very shells of the atoms, and inside them—using the Heisenberg 'space' and all its associated uncertainties as if they were as reliably programmable as the on/off, one/zero states of a quartz atom when it vibrates. But it seems to implement quantum mechanics in ways that I cannot understand without far better tools for analysis than we're carrying aboard *Enterprise* at the moment, so it's best not to meddle too far." He looked at the little thing with admiration.

"Captain," K's't'lk said, "it's this gadget that started us thinking about the zero-point field as a solution to the Sunseed problem, for this construct—it's an insult to call it a machine—accesses the quantum vacuum for its own power. There are endless implementations possible for this technology."

"We've seen a couple," Scotty said. "One would be the force-domes that were protecting the cities on Artaleirh. Another is a way to cancel out local transmissions of any kind of messaging, in realspace or subspace. Not jamming—*cancellation,* as if the transmissions'd never gone out at all, until you tell the effect to stop. I won't trouble you with the details, but that implementation's what the two young lads used to get Gurrhim off *Gorget.* That much of this creature's operation I can duplicate, so that we can do what you're asking as regards the monitoring satellites. But this prototype is too precious to spend on such; it contains implementations of the basic technology that'll take a whole team of physicists and engineers to understand. This technology could change our whole civilization, given time."

This, Jim thought, *is what we were sent to find and bring home. And the presence of this here implies so much more.* "I think you may be suggesting," Jim said softly, "that if our destruction or capture seem imminent, this should be sent off on its own, with the intent to get it back to Starfleet at all costs."

"Aye," Scotty said. The look he was giving the little sphere was one Jim had occasionally caught him wearing in less fraught circumstances: that of a man privileged to examine the engineering version of the pearl of great price, ready to do anything to see that it is passed around as widely as possible to do the most possible good. "Now if this had been stolen technology . . ." He made a face. "Well, we've been down that road before. I've aye disliked taking another person's work without seeing they're credited with it and paid for it. And duty's forced us into that path once or twice. Well enough. But this came to us, as it were, as a gift, and it wants using. Many a world that's barren now could become livable with the technology underlying this to help dome its cities and protect its ships, and eventually to make terraforming far easier than it is now. Maybe there wouldn't be such a scramble for planets that are naturally livable. Maybe there wouldn't be a need to fight so many wars."

Jim's expression went just slightly wry. "Our people will probably keep doing that for a while yet, but if this thing will make that big a difference . . ."

"It could, if we can get it home and study it. But it's not secure here, Captain. If we're lost—"

"Work out something, Scotty," Jim said. "We've replaced all those signaling buoys we used heading in to Levaeri V, so you might want to prepare a couple as decoys as well."

"I had thought of that, Captain," Scotty said. "But two problems with that. One—what if this bauble's lost in the sending? And two—you've promised to give it back to the Praetor. I don't like to break a promise."

"Neither would I," Jim said. "Well, I'll leave the problem with you for the moment. Meanwhile, good work, you two. Get started on the monitoring satellite problem. And I'll schedule a stop at 553 Trianguli."

"Aye, sir. Thank you."

Jim headed back to the bridge.

In a retiring-room deep inside the ancient House-home of House tr'Maehllie, in what were now the suburbs of Ra'tleihfi on ch'Rihan, an argument was in progress. It was an outgrowth of the argument that had begun, in much quieter mode, almost as soon as the young Senator i-Khellian had left tr'Anierh's study and the door had shut behind her. But nothing had been settled there, and now, more than a day later, the argument had gained speed and urgency.

"I *told* you the Intel people were becoming more useless by the day," Urellh was growling. "What was it about? *What was that message about?*"

The retiring-room was nothing like as well furnished as tr'Anierh's study, where he now very much wished himself to be. It was bare, lean, as devoid of ornament as the mind of the man who lived in it. But there was no avoiding passing on this news, and no avoiding suffering tr'Maehllie's reaction to it in a space so acoustically bright that tr'Anierh was already on the edge of a headache. He shook his head. "We will never know now," he said, "since as you say, the Intelligence people seem to have allowed the poor fool to help them a little *too* enthusiastically with their inquiries."

"By my name, they'll go the same way he did," Urellh said, glaring out the window. "But much more slowly. In the meantime, I'll assign a new team and find out every last moment of the wretched spy's last few days. Where he went, who he saw and spoke to—"

"Urellh," tr'Anierh said, "possibly we have other concerns right now. I have some strange reports from the Fleet of late. Ships delayed in reporting back, or in making scheduled planetfalls in the Outworlds."

"Indeed, and there's another issue," Urellh said under his breath. "The ships that went out to Artaleirh: *Where are they?*"

"The Klingons destroyed them," tr'Anierh said.

Urellh's head snapped around. "What?"

"So they say; I have copied you a transcript of the message. Another department of Intel entirely from the one that has been so cheerfully killing off our potential informants has today received a message through one of their go-between agents on the Imperial homeworld. The Klingons say they destroyed the task-force fleet at Artaleirh, as well as 'other alien vessels present at the engagement,' whoever *that* may mean; we can only hope they meant *Bloodwing*. It would be too much to hope for to assume they also meant *Enterprise,* assuming she was still in pursuit. The Klingons have had no better luck with Kirk than we have, and if they'd truly destroyed that damned ship, they would have shouted the brag to everyone who'd listen. At any rate, the Klingons also say they have annexed the Artaleirh system." Tr'Anierh couldn't keep his face from twisting as if he had a mouthful of something bitter. "The message claims that the Klingons have offered to give us a discount on dilithium processing if we acknowledge the 'changeover.' "

A brief and complete silence ensued. Then tr'Anierh spent the next few minutes thinking, rather clinically, that no one would be surprised if his fellow Praetor suddenly fell over one day, seeing that he kept on indulging himself in rages of this kind. It was some little while before tr'Maehllie was fit for anything but kicking the furniture and smashing up various inconsequentia of his daily life, and tr'Anierh thought, *It would not take much. His blood pressure is probably already too high. If it should be chemically assisted in*

being raised somewhat, and then someone should spring a
piece of news of this kind on him . . .

He sighed as tr'Maehllie flung himself into the only other
chair in the room and started to calm himself. "They can't
have done it," he said under his breath, glaring at the floor.

"They could have," said tr'Anierh. "And we cannot now
spare the resources to send another task force to drive them
out of that space, even if they are still only there in whatever
force they used to take it. The situation is worsening on the
other client worlds, and there are persistent rumors out of
Augo that something is about to happen there."

"The Klingons wouldn't dare come so close!" tr'Maehllie
said, almost in a hiss, and tr'Anierh knew he was meant to
take it for another rage starting, but he knew by the sound
that tr'Maehllie's reaction wasn't anger. It was fear.

Tr'Anierh knew that fear too, but was not going to waste
time railing against circumstance. "This is what we have always hoped would never happen. Civil unrest at home while
we start to prosecute a war."

"War I don't mind!" Urellh shouted. "Elements only
know we've been waiting for a chance to deal with the Federation once and for all, and it's almost upon us—a matter of
days only—but why does this have to happen *now?* We cannot handle both them and the Klingons at the same time!"

Perhaps this is something you should have considered
earlier, tr'Anierh thought, and did not say. *You were always*
so sure that they were not capable of moving quickly, but
that's not what the monitoring satellites tell us. "It's a pity
that we cannot get the Klingons to attack the Federation instead of us," tr'Anierh said. "A shame that our diplomatic
contacts have always been so ineffective and short lived."

"*Au,* they despise us," tr'Maehllie said. "Possibly even
more than we despise them. They would do nothing that
would help us, no matter how much it benefited them." He
got up and started pacing again. "And for once the *vhai'd*

Federation is not moving with its accustomed sloth. No, ships are coming into the near-border starbases from all over. They are going to enter our space in strength, in a matter of days, and overrun all the near side of the Outmarches! All those planets will be lost at least for supply purposes, the only other reliable supply for dilithium except Artaleirh—"

"That is not what the cipher traffic indicates," tr'Anierh said. "The latest dispatches suggest that they will come through the Outmarches, yes, but then hold on the near side and try another diplomatic initiative to keep the war from going any further."

"That's the old cipher," Urellh said, annoyed. "They know we've broken it; we're being fed disinformation."

"No," tr'Anierh said. "This is the new one. It was more susceptible to breakage than they believed. Someone got lazy, or hurried, about the code, and reused elements of the last one, so we have an advantage they were not suspecting."

"Well, wonderful," Urellh said. "But this is no better. 'Diplomatic initiative!' Do they truly think we'd ever agree to such a thing while they were inside our own space? I'll tell you what it is, tr'Anierh. They're going to block our escape on that side, and then sit there and wait for the damned Klingons to come down on us and do their work for them! And when that's done, and the Klingon fleets are well reduced by the exercise of destroying *us*, then the Federation will come down on the Klingons in their turn and finish *them!* Nothing will be left for thousands of parsecs around but space that the Federation owns—and all our worlds in ashes, to be terraformed by them and their culture planted on top of ours, as one plants the alefruit tree where the volcano's been!"

Urellh lurched up out of his chair, and tr'Anierh saw that he was about to start breaking things again. "There's time still to avoid that eventuality," tr'Anierh said, "and that's done by ending the civil unrest, and stopping the fight that's about to happen at Augo. There we will meet them, and there we will destroy them, and the Klingons will think again about meddling with us—*if* we can but hold our nerve. Both Empire and Federation look for us to panic, now, and I for one do not intend to give either of them the satisfaction. Time enough for that when we actually see the Klingons in our own space, rather than just hearing them boasting about it at a distance. If they did destroy *Bloodwing,* fine; they've saved us a job. We can broadcast the news that the woman's been reduced to plasma, and the Sword with her. Cut off the head and the body may stagger about for a little while, but it'll fall down at last; the rebellions will disintegrate, and whatever anger remains for the theft of the Sword can very profitably be laid at the Klingons' door. Then we deal with the Klingons if they do indeed make any incursions into our space."

"I should prefer better Intelligence of *Bloodwing*'s destruction," tr'Maehllie said.

"So would I, but we have no leisure to send a forensics team out there right now," tr'Anierh said. "Let us wait and see what we hear over the Federation's monitoring satellites. That particular keyhole is proving very profitable to listen at, and whatever else we might say about them, the Federation's intelligence network is nearly as well developed as ours. If the Klingons did indeed destroy our ships at Artaleirh, and *Bloodwing* with them, then I'd wager we will soon hear confirmation about that from the Federation side. I'd think they'd be relieved, for the damned woman has been as much an annoyance to them as to us, almost. With her dead, they might even be willing to look aside from the loss of life at RV Trianguli, once we'd driven the Klingons away, and they saw which way the wind was blowing. Meanwhile, we have the Senate to manage, defenses to man, work enough to keep us busy until matters clarify themselves. Grand Fleet in particular is growing restive with the recent losses; they're preparing battle plans for Augo already. We'll need to spend this afternoon doing our own research on the system, so they don't think we're going to simply take their word for everything; that's no way to run a military."

Urellh sat still for a moment. Then he looked up at tr'Anierh. "For all your annoying ways," Urellh said, "you are a steady head when there's trouble. This will not be forgotten."

"That's as may be," said tr'Anierh. "But whatever happens, we have no time to tear at each other's throats right now—there will be teeth enough at them shortly. We will be wanted in the city shortly; come ride with me."

"Let me take a moment to change," Urellh said.

He went out of the retiring room. *That I much doubt you'll do,* tr'Anierh thought. *But let's see if you manage at least to contain yourself over the days to come, so that it doesn't become necessary to raise your blood pressure one last time.*

ELEVEN

THE GATHERING in main recreation was scheduled to start, as usual, around the time alpha shift came off duty. Only a little after that, Jim slipped in. It was an early arrival for him; he'd had a long day, what with getting caught up on paperwork that had been allowed to slip since the unfolding of events at RV Trianguli and Artaleirh. Now he wanted a while to unwind, and also to watch the crew come in. But at least forty people were there before him, starting the business of denuding the buffet tables and gossiping at maximum speed. Jim knew what they were gossiping about.

There's a leak somewhere in the command crew, was always his first thought, but the truth was simply that the *Enterprise*'s crew were intelligent people, who could read the gestalt and feel of their vessel nearly as well as Jim could. They knew something was up. *Even just looking at it from the strictly logical point of view,* Jim thought as he paused by one of the tables to get himself some iced tea, *everyone understands what we've just been through. These people know their history and their politics. You don't get assigned to a starship by isolating yourself from the doings of the planetbound. It is, after all, the planetbound who determine, at a remove, what we do.*

He stood there watching as more people came in, heading straight for the food and drink, laughing, hailing friends from other departments. From behind Jim a voice said,

"Smart move to get here early. You'd think nobody ever fed these people."

Jim turned to see Harb Tanzer, the head of recreation, watching the increasing numbers at the tables. "I thought you said you usually kept some of the best dishes for later in the evening."

"It's becoming a challenge," Tanzer said, and nodded at a small group of crewmen gathered down at the end of one of the tables. "Scotty's bad kids down there keep sneaking in and reprogramming the food delivery systems when they think I'm not looking."

His smile was just a little more somber than usual. "How have they been?" Jim said.

Tanzer shook his head. "I doubt you really need to ask me. You can feel the air."

"A little tense."

"A little tense," Harb said. "But let's give it a while and see how things go. Look, there come the first instruments."

Jim glanced off to one side and saw that Lieutenant Penney from data analysis had come in with a guitar over his shoulder, closely followed by an ensign Jim didn't immediately recognize, carrying an electronic violin. "Always a good sign," Harb said.

"Mostly of off-key singing." Jim smiled a little.

"If I ever heard any of that in here, I wouldn't admit it," Harb said. "Is the Romulan contingent coming in this evening?"

"Ael will be here," Jim said, "and some of her people, but probably not for a while yet. There's still a lot of tidying up going on over on *Bloodwing,* I understand."

"Fine," Harb said. "We still have a separate processor set up for them. I'll see that they know where it is. Forgive me, Captain, I haven't got all the conversation pits set up yet."

"Go on," Jim said, and Tanzer headed off across the room. Jim got himself that iced tea, settled into an unoccupied conversation pit over at the edge of things, underneath the huge windows that looked aft of *Enterprise* into space, and did his best to relax.

It took some doing, for both the threat to Earth and the upcoming battle at Augo kept coming into his mind, and Jim kept finding himself trying to think of measures he ought to be taking, things he had missed. He had to keep pushing those thoughts out of his mind again. *This is recreation,* Jim thought. *This is where you're supposed to let that go, if only for a little while. So recreate yourself!*

He leaned over the media table that sat in the middle of the pit and tapped at it to see what Harb had loaded into the master rec computer at the moment. There were all the usual games—endless card games, including the rather bizarre "four-and-a-half-handed" module of Fizzbin that Chekov had been building for some months now; every kind of board game, including a huge volume of "fairy chess" variants, in two, three, and four dimensions; and games of every other kind, including roleplay, historical, strategic, geometric, spatial manipulation, and thousands of others, imported from no telling how many other planets.

"Looking for something in particular, Captain?" said a voice seemingly out of the air. It was Moira, the personality that Harb had had added to the rec computer the last time *Enterprise* was in for a major refit.

"Peace in our time?" Jim said under his breath.

"You might as well ask for the Holy Grail while you're at it," Moira said.

Jim laughed under his breath. The "For Argument's Sake" personality module was an out-of-the-box augmentation that could be applied to most stand-alone computer systems with enough memory. But Moira's sense of humor, and "her" tone of voice, always made Jim think of McCoy—and since recreation was a department of medicine, reporting directly to the ship's surgeon, Jim wasn't particularly surprised by this. "If you *did* have it stashed around here somewhere," Jim said, "I'd be nervous about keeping it on board right now."

"If I understand the stories correctly, if it was here, it could probably take care of itself. Is there anything else I can get for you, Captain? There are some new things added to inventory over the last couple of weeks. Something in a poker simulation, perhaps?"

"Why bother *simulating* poker?" Jim said.

"It's an interactive tutorial. Some of the Romulans were inquiring about it."

"Aha," Jim said. He looked across the room and saw Spock approaching, with his Vulcan harp under his arm. "It can wait for the moment, Moira. You might want to bring up a chessboard, though."

"How many dimensions, Captain?"

"Three," he said. "Bring up the last game that Mr. Spock and I didn't finish."

"A week and a half ago," Moira said, *"before we arrived at RV Trianguli."*

Jim shook his head in mild astonishment. That seemed about a year ago, but then life had been seeming to pass at a rather accelerated rate lately.

Spock, about to step down into the pit, paused. "Captain, if you are otherwise occupied—"

"Not at all. Please sit down, Mr. Spock. Why the *ryill?* Are you playing tonight?"

"I think not," Spock said, "but Mr. Scott and K's't'lk are deep in discussion of some rather abstruse physics, and I think Commander Uhura may want to continue following the Hamalki version of the discussion in the musical mode." Spock put the harp down a few feet away on the cushions of the pit and examined the 3D chessboard that Moira had used the media table's transporter to materialize. "You are sure you wish to resume this game, Captain?" Spock said, giving

him one of those looks through which the amusement was
absolutely not supposed to show, yet did. "I predict mate in
twelve."

"Ah, but *whose?*" Jim said.

Spock raised an eyebrow and said nothing.

"Go on, Mr. Spock," Jim said. "White to play."

They played, not hurrying. The room kept on filling up.
Within fifteen or twenty minutes, there were maybe eighty or
ninety people in there, a significant proportion of alpha shift,
and the noise level was approaching what it ought to have
been at one of these functions. *See,* Jim thought, *they're re-
laxing. You should too.*

"Check, Captain."

Jim looked down at the board with annoyance. "Sorry,
Mr. Spock."

Spock briefly glanced up at the room. "Doubtless the
noise level is making it difficult for you to concentrate."

"Spock," Jim said wryly, "I don't think that's the problem,
but thank you. It's actually mate in six, isn't it?"

"After that last move," Spock said, "yes."

Jim turned his attention back to the board. After what
seemed like only a few moments, an amused voice said from
behind him, "I have studied his games as carefully, but it
does me little good. *Your* tactics, at least, I can understand."

Jim looked up, surprised. Ael was leaning on the back of
the conversation-pit sofa, looking down ruefully at the board,
while Uhura leaned over the other side of the pit to pick up
Spock's *ryill.*

"I thought I would have spotted you coming in," Jim said.
"My apologies."

"Captain, none are needed," Ael said. "How you could
have spotted anyone through this crowd, *that* would have
been the mystery." She looked over toward the buffet tables,
where new food was constantly materializing, and vanishing
nearly as quickly. "And more are coming, I see."

Jim glanced at Spock. "Maybe we should resume this later?"

Spock nodded; Jim reached down to touch the table, and the board and pieces were transported away. Ael slipped into the pit to sit a little apart from Jim. "I received a copy of the proposal you sent to Veilt tr'Tyrava," she said.

Jim nodded. "And?"

The look Ael gave him was quite matter-of-fact, so much so that Jim wondered if she were trying to get a rise out of him. "Well," she said with a very slight smile, "we already have evidence of what you are worth as a tactician in the small scale. But now I see you have increased the aunt significantly."

" 'Upped the ante,' " Jim said. "Commander, have you been taking language lessons from K's't'lk?"

"No," Ael said, and laughed. "But there have been some poker lessons. After Mr. Scott discussed the game with my master engineer earlier, he and his crew became enthusiastic, so Mr. Scott was kind enough to send tr'Keirianh some tutorials. They took my fancy as well when he showed them to me. The game is complex and interesting, and from my crew's point of view, any new way to redistribute their personal wealth is always welcome. But the idiom—I was sure I had it right. Or is the translator failing again?"

"It's the homonyms," Uhura said, glancing up. She had been checking the harp's stringing; now she touched its "on" control to give the old-fashioned solid-state electronics time to warm up. "They're always a weak point in the present implementation of the translator. They keep promising they'll fix it in the next version." She glanced over at Ael. "I'll have a word with it, Commander—patch you in a module of games terminology to suit those tutorials, and a translation of *Hoyle* as well, if I can find one I can adapt quickly."

"Thank you, Commander. I take that very kindly."

Uhura wandered off into the crowd. Spock glanced at

Jim, asking without words whether he should leave. "No, stick around, Spock," Jim said.

Ael gave him another look. "I thought our language was rich in peculiar idiom, but yours is far more so. I would not have thought of Mr. Spock as particularly adhesive."

Spock bowed his head to her slightly. "That reassures me, Commander."

"English is like that, I'm afraid," Jim said, "It doesn't so much *borrow* words and idioms from other languages and cultures as chase them down dark alleys, bludgeon them into submission, and go through their pockets."

Ael raised her eyebrows at that. "Well, Captain, one bit of business before we abandon it for the evening. I heard from Veilt earlier. He continues to analyze your proposal along with Courhig and some other members of his own crew. Doubtless he will have some suggestions, and I will have some for you as well. We must meet tomorrow to discuss them. But this I can say . . ."

She paused. Jim looked at her, then realized she was indeed hesitating for the sake of his reaction. "If I'd made *you* wait that long before we fired at those torpedoes running up your rear at RV Trianguli," he said, "we wouldn't be having this conversation right now."

Ael laughed. "Captain, you're right. You deserve better of me. Your plan excels. Of course there are always things that can go wrong, but we cannot be sure what those will be until we reach Augo. I gather from your initial scheduling that you expect that to happen the day after tomorrow, by *Enterprise*'s time."

"No later," Jim said. "Every second we spend here is a second that someone on ch'Rihan may be spending getting ready to meet us there, and I grudge them every second of that time."

"Still," Ael said, "even if the strategists at Grand Fleet had read your whole plan while we were reading it, it would still take them a matter of some days to gather the materiel to handle us at the kind of odds they prefer. I have high hopes for this engagement—to a point."

Spock gave her a thoughtful look. "But no great pleasure."

"No," Ael said, "I am well past that point, Mr. Spock, if ever I was there for long. War is a means to an end. The possibility of a good end to it—that thought sustains me. But the means itself . . ." She shook her head.

They looked out into the room again. "Captain," Spock said, "I see Mr. Scott over there, and I believe he is looking for me."

"Go on, Mr. Spock." As Spock got up, Jim said, "By the way, I just had a thought about that mate in six."

"Only one, Captain?" Spock said. He nodded to the commander, and moved away through the crowd.

"And what was the thought?" Ael said.

"That I ought to resign while the resigning was good," Kirk said. "But now he'll spend all night running the scenario in his head and wondering whether he missed something."

"Mr. Spock? All night? Hardly," Ael said. "Getting him to do that for an hour would be an accomplishment, I would think."

"You're probably right," Jim said. "But with Mr. Spock, you take your advantages where you can. Come on, Commander, we're taking up space for ten. Let's go up to the gallery level. Would you like an ale to take with you?"

"I would like that very much."

Jim spoke to the menu on the media table, and a few moments later it produced a tall cold glass of blue for Ael and a shorter glass of whiskey for Jim. He handed Ael her glass. She looked at it in some bemusement. "Is this a message?" she said.

Jim pulled the bamboo-and-paper cocktail umbrella out

of the glass, looking at the Chinese characters on it and then folding it up and leaving it on the table. "Only that Scotty's kids need watching," he said. "Come on."

Together they made their way out of the pit and toward the stairs that led up to the gallery, which stretched straight across the middle of the huge glasteel windows that looked aft. As they went, Jim paused and looked down into the crowd, which now contained at least a hundred fifty of the crew. From the midst of it came some sounds that suggested it was not physics being discussed in the musical mode, at least not yet. Someone was playing an electronic keyboard, and a male voice rose above the hubbub, singing:

"*—drunken spaceman,*
What do you do with a drunken spaceman,
Ear-ly in the stardate?
Beam him down into liquid methane,
Beam him down into—"

The singer was interrupted by cries of "Naaah!" "Oh, please!" "*That* old thing again?" "What else have you got?"

Various people began shouting suggestions, some more helpful than others. Jim raised his eyebrows and continued up the stairs. Chairs were scattered here and there up on the gallery; he led the way over to one pair, down at the far end, where they could overlook the refreshment tables and the pits at the center of the main recreation floor. For a few moments they just sat quietly, and Jim lost himself briefly in the stir and noise from below.

"Now that we are in private . . ." Ael said. "Captain, I heard about Gurrhim." She paused, looking down at the crowd, and very softly said, "It is not true, is it?"

"No."

She nodded, satisfied; but the look in her eyes was strange.

"How did you know it wasn't?" Jim said, suddenly suspicious.

Ael looked at him without that odd expression changing much. "Because Dr. McCoy was involved."

Jim nodded. "You'll forgive me for not telling Bones about that, because he'd become insufferable for days. But I see your point."

"Others who have less confidence in McCoy's skill," Ael said, "or know less of his stubbornness, will find it easy enough to believe. Otherwise, they will find it equally easy to believe that Gurrhim left *Gorget*'s infirmary with such injuries as were not *meant* to allow him to survive long." She leaned back, stretched a little. "But now perhaps you will tell me why you so suddenly chose this action. It does not sound like something you contemplated for long."

"Ael," Jim said, "you told us yourself, not so long ago, that you weren't entirely sure there wasn't someone else in your crew who—" Thinking of Ael's son Tafv, and a memory that must still be bitter to her, Jim swiftly discarded the phrase "was a potential traitor." "—whose loyalties might waver under stress."

"Or who had been planted there by Grand Fleet a long time ago," Ael said. She sighed. "Mine would not be the only ship with such. Once they were out in the open, actually called 'political officers' or 'loyalty officers.' Did you know that? But then Fleet stopped that practice, for the accident rate among such officers became unaccountably high, and personnel would seek transfer or demotion rather than hold such posts." Ael smiled gently.

"I believe you," Jim said. "Anyway, I'm curious to see whether this particular piece of misinformation spreads. No harm in it, anyway, since I think I'd rather have Gurrhim out of the public eye. Leaving aside the completely crass and self-serving idea that he might be extremely useful to you later on, there's no telling whether someone might not pop up and try to kill him again, and I wouldn't care for that."

"Nor I," Ael said. "He is a good old man, of a type we have too few of anymore in our world."

"Old?" Jim said. "Well, maybe as you reckon these things. But he doesn't come across that way."

"No," Ael said. "Which makes him all the more valuable."

"Anyway, Dr. McCoy asked me to reassure you about the Praetor's status. He says Gurrhim is doing remarkably well for someone who has suffered the equivalent of having his heart, as McCoy put it, 'pulled out of him and stamped on.' "

"It is a great heart, that," Ael said. "I am glad he survived."

"That's more or less what McCoy said, on both counts," Jim said. "And I agree with him. Meanwhile, he has elected to stay 'dead' for the time being, which means he will remain our guest. Which leads me to my next question: What to do with young tr'AAnikh?"

"Well," Ael said, "does he know that Gurrhim is alive? If so, then to keep the secret, he cannot come back to *Bloodwing*. When the secret is secret no longer, then we will be glad to bring him wherever he wishes to go. And the same for Gurrhim, as well. But I would lay a small wager that where he would want to go, is where we *are* going."

Jim nodded. "I'd put my money right down by yours. Meanwhile, let's put the issue on the back burner. In two weeks, who knows, we might not need to worry about it. By then we might be the conquerors of ch'Rihan and ch'Havran."

"Or plasma," Ael said.

"Optimist," Jim said.

They sat and watched the crewpeople below them. In the middle of the group that had been doing most of the singing, a guitar started to strum hard, a series of swinging chords, and another joined it, and voices went up together in song. Jim smiled a little and reached for his whiskey, while Ael gazed down at the crowd gathering around the central conversation pit. The raised voices got considerably louder with the end of the first verse, and a fit of melodious yodeling broke out after the chorus. Jim looked over at Ael's expression with some amusement.

"How can they do this?" she said softly. "Seeing what they have just endured, and what lies before them."

"It's how they cope," Jim said. "And how they remind themselves who they are." He leaned back against the cushions and stretched a little. "Ael, do me a favor."

"If it's in my power."

"Tell me what's on your mind *without* stopping to think about the tactics of revelation."

She had to smile at that, though the smile was sad. "I think that perhaps some of these people will not do this again," she said, so softly it could hardly be heard. "That for some of them, this is their last time to sing together."

"You think they don't know that?" Jim said.

Ael shook her head. "No. But the fact is no less bitter in my heart for all their recognition of it."

He watched her watching them. *The prospect of their danger hurts her as much as that of her own people,* Jim thought. *Possibly even more. Interesting. And something about her that Starfleet would never believe.*

"Third verse!"

"There *is* no third verse."

"That's not what I heard—"

More shouting of suggestions followed. Jim let out a long breath and said, "That's not all that's on your mind, though."

She glanced at him. "How can you tell?"

"Because it's not all that's on mine, and we are too damn much alike, some ways."

Ael was quiet for several breaths. Then she said, "I have been having second thoughts about your presence here."

"A little late for that," Jim said.

"Yes, so Aidoann tells me," Ael said wearily, "and tr'Keirianh as well. But I have these thoughts nonetheless. I would ask you not to needlessly endanger *Enterprise* on behalf of my cause."

"I would never needlessly endanger her for *any* cause," Jim said, "so you can put your mind to rest on that count. But as for the rest of it—there comes a time when you have to make a stand."

He waited.

"Yes," Ael said after a long while. "That is what I have been thinking about. There has been so much running, in the last few years."

Jim kept quiet.

"I am afraid," Ael said finally. "Afraid of it all having been for nothing, if I die. Or, even worse, afraid of being turned from my path afterward, if we succeed. If the old government of the Empire does indeed fall, if it is replaced by a Senate and Praetorate committed to the kind of changes I have been dreaming of, then I fear to be paid off, given a medal for my great contributions to my people's culture, and sent away for a 'well-deserved rest.' Or perhaps not *that,* so much, as being too tired to come back from the rest afterward. Finding myself saying, 'Not today. I have no stomach for the fight today. Tomorrow.'"

"And tomorrow never comes," Jim said.

"True. And then, slowly, everything goes back to the way it was, after the fervor dies down," Ael said. "And it all turns out to have been for nothing. The last stands and the first ones, the betrayals and the heroism, the great battles and the small. Despite them, everything ebbs back to what it was before. Oh, a few things are improved, some of the tyranny scraped away—but elsewhere it accretes again, and everything is as it was before. *That* is what I fear."

"The inertia of history," Jim said.

She glanced at him. "Is that what your people call it?"

"I don't know," Jim said. "But I know what you mean. The fear of not mattering, of having made no difference."

"Yes."

They sat quietly for a while longer. When Jim looked at her again, Ael's expression was rather drawn. The admission had cost her something.

"What does one do at such times?" Ael said.

Jim shook his head. "Stick it out, and see what happens."

Ael laughed. "Yet more adhesives."

"Maybe. Sometimes they're all that makes the difference." Jim looked down into the crowd. "Hear that?"

Ael listened. "Hear what?"

"The change in the noise level."

She shrugged. "That happens once every forty *t'stai* or so in any gathering, my people say."

Jim nodded. "It's something cyclic. Practically everything in human life—excuse me, hominid life—has some kind of cycle attached to it. So why is *this* one surprising you? You carry the banner up high for hours at a time, then after a while you have to let it fall, but not forever. You push and fight and make your way forward in a battle, and then sometimes you have to fall back a little, until the moment comes to start pushing forward again. The uncertainty, the difficulty—you've been there before, in battle. So have I. The cycle's just a little longer than usual this time. But it's still a cycle. Ride it out."

Below them, the sound started to come up again. Ael had a long sip of her drink, and then turned slightly to look over her shoulders at the stars, and at the air-blued curve of Artaleirh sliding by under them as *Enterprise* made her way toward the terminator, and night.

"That cycle is longest, though," she said. "Worlds around their stars, stars in the long flow through the galaxy's arms, as all the little spirals fly apart. And then perhaps back together again." She looked over at Jim with just a little humor showing in her eyes again. "Or have they changed the theory again, this year? Sometimes the scientists say the universe is 'open,' and the cycle can never repeat, then two or three years later they reverse themselves."

"We could ask K's't'lk," Jim said. "But if you ask me, I think we should just stick it out, and see what happens."

Ael looked at him for a moment, and then raised her glass to him. Jim clinked his against it; they drank.

They sat there for a great while longer, talking about all manner of things, while underneath them sunset and dawn and sunset passed over Artaleirh at the usual accelerated rate. Every now and then they got a glimpse of *Tyrava,* like a shadow in deeper night, pacing them above and behind, glinting now and again in planetlight, or the light of Artaleirh's star slipping up through the atmosphere in yet another dawn. Below the gallery, the singing and the laughter went on, coming to crescendo and fading, and always coming up again in another wave of sound. Jim was not aware of actually counting the cycles, but he knew that at a certain point he would have to stop merely being aware of them. One of those silences would be meant for him, and the crew was waiting.

"I cannot think how they all fit in here," Ael said. "And who is running the ship?"

"It takes fewer people to run *Enterprise* than most people would think," Jim said. "But you know that. I would rather the news didn't get around too much, though."

He stood up and leaned on the gallery railing. There had to be at least three hundred and eighty of the four hundred and thirty down there; people of many species, eating and drinking and talking like there was no tomorrow. *And maybe there's not,* Jim thought. There was no point in putting it off any longer.

"If you prefer," Ael said, "perhaps I should go back to *Bloodwing* now."

"Why bother?" Jim said. "About a third of your people are down there already. What happens here, you have a right to hear."

She bowed her head to him, then, and lifted her empty glass, but said nothing more.

Jim went over to the stairs and started to make his way down. As he went, he noticed how quickly the room was starting to go quiet. *Not just twenty after the hour,* he thought. *Not this time.*

He made his way over to the side of the room where there was a one-step dais used for informal theatricals, dancing, or the occasional performances of the *Enterprise*'s jazz band. As he stepped up onto it, the quiet settled down hard over the room, and held.

"Thank you," he said, and then had to stop for a moment, because his throat suddenly dried up on him.

Jim swallowed. "Some of you will in recent days have been discussing among yourselves the correctness, in view of our oaths to Starfleet and the Federation, of the actions I've taken, and which I am about to take."

There was no sound, no rustling. His people were still, watching him.

"I am convinced that the course we are about to pursue is in the best interests of the Federation. I am willing to face a court-martial, if necessary, at the end of all this, to justify my actions. And I'm almost certain, even at this point, that I'm going to have to. I stand on the brink of a series of actions that at the very least will make me extremely uncomfortable about the future, but which I believe my oaths demand of me."

More silence. He took a long breath and went on. "I am aware that some of you are going to find my actions questionable. I am therefore taking this opportunity to offer you a choice to act on your own consciences. If at this point any of you feel that what has been happening, or is likely to happen, will conflict with your oaths, I want you to disembark and be returned to Federation space." He looked around at all the terribly immobile faces. "The Artaleirhin have undertaken to send a ship back to RV Trianguli. There they will transfer anyone who wants to return either to *Mascrar*, which is still there, or to one of the Starfleet vessels shortly scheduled to be coming into that neighborhood in the pursuit of the war."

Silence. They looked at him.

"Captain—"

Sulu.

Of all the voices he would not have expected to hear raised, *that* voice spoke up now, and the sound of it bit him deep. Jim looked over at his helmsman, wondering what to say *now*, wondering how *Enterprise* would possibly cope without him. And if Sulu, veteran of so many difficult and dangerous situations aboard *Enterprise* until now, felt this way, how many others would feel the same?

"Captain," Sulu said. "We *have* been talking, some of us." The voice sounded a little shamefaced. "We thought—"

Here it comes.

"—that we should give you something, just so that you understood our feelings."

Sulu turned to Chekov, standing in the crowd behind him, and then the pair of them stepped out of the crowd, holding something dark in their arms.

They unfolded it, shook it out. Black, with a flash of white in it, settling as Sulu and Chekov grabbed the upper corners and held the silken shimmer of the thing up to show it.

Black silk. A skull, white. Crossed white bones underneath it.

Jim, very slowly, began to smile.

"Mr. Sulu—" he said.

"We're not leaving, Captain," Sulu said. "We've stuck

with you for a long time now, when things looked bad, or strange. You've never given us reason to regret that. We're not about to change the pattern now."

Jim looked up. "Is this unanimous?"

The response deafened him. Not that he cared. He was blinking hard. *My eyes don't work at the moment. Why should my ears?*

He swallowed once more, then assumed the sternest expression he could muster under the circumstances and said, "Mr. Sulu, Mr. Chekov, put that away. For now," he added, unable to restrain a flash of a crooked smile. "Meanwhile, ladies and gentlemen . . ." Thanks was almost demeaning in a situation like this: more, it could be taken as a suggestion that he had believed things might go otherwise. Finally Jim simply looked over the crowd and said, "Let's bring the evening to a close in a while. Don't rush, but we have a busy day tomorrow."

There was a murmur of agreement. He would have said "Dismissed," but it seemed unnecessary. People nodded to him and then began saying their good nights (or good mornings) and filtering out as if they'd been planning this all evening.

Jim stood there and watched them go. There was no movement behind him, but as the last of the crew left the room, he turned and saw Spock and McCoy standing there, shoulder to shoulder.

McCoy looked at Jim. "Yo ho ho," he said.

"Declined," Jim said, "with thanks. Come on, Bones, let's go get some rest. We have to be up early in the morning. Haven't you heard there's a war on?"

Then he went straight out, trying not to look as if he were hurrying. But behind him he could feel Spock and McCoy looking at each other, and McCoy was grinning. Near the doors, he paused just briefly to look at the woman up in the gallery, who stood there, leaning on the railing, silhouetted

by starlight, watching him go. At this distance, in the subdued evening light of main recreation, Jim couldn't make out
her expression, but he thought he didn't need to. She was
standing straighter than she had all day, and though her face
was shadowed, he could feel the edge of her smile.

Jim headed for his quarters.

TWELVE

A DAY AND A HALF LATER, *Bloodwing* and *Enterprise* set out together for Augo. They did not go alone.

With them went the nine Grand Fleet vessels that the Free Rihannsu had captured so far. They might have been hastily crewed and short on supplies, but their weapons were in order. All had been newly equipped with the same quantum-vacuum shielding that had protected Artaleirh's cities and armed the planet against its enemies. As important as the weapons, or more so in the eyes of the ships' Rihannsu crews, every ship had ceremonially had its old name stripped from it—respectfully, for the ships had done nothing to disgrace themselves. The old names' charactery had been scoured from the hulls and chiseled or burned off their inner keels, and every one had been renamed by her crew—all the Elements' names and natures being invoked in the appropriate manner, and plasma borrowed from Artaleirh's corona to hold the space in their drives for what would later be used when they were recommissioned into a fleet based out of Eisn or, if necessary, some other star.

It was that image, more terrible than almost any other, that kept recurring in Ael's mind as they made their way out of the Artaleirh system and into the longest night. Rihannha had a great love of place. Years in time and light-years in distance removed from her long-lost home, Ael still had to do no more than close her eyes to see the way the light fell over the hillsides and fields of her family's old farmstead, the hole in the outbarn wall where the *sivit* wandered in and out between grazing times, the overgrown orchard with the fifth tree in the third row from the house fallen down, but blooming stubbornly every year nonetheless. The houseless, wandering life that had been forced on Ael by her personal rebellion against the will of the Praetorate was hard enough for her to bear. But she suffered it far worse in the persons of her crew, who could have cast her off for homes of their own at any time since the attack on Levaeri VII, and still could have as recently as RV Trianguli. For *mnhei'sahe*'s sake they stayed by her, and so her own *mnhei'sahe* required her to do the same by them. Nonetheless, it was hard.

"Aidoann," she said, standing behind her center seat and leaning on the back of it, "where will you go?"

Aidoann looked up, bemused. "When, *khre'Riov?*"

"When ch'Rihan and ch'Havran are liberated, and I am a Praetor."

Aidoann gave Ael a glance half humorous and half annoyed. "I would have thought you intended to find a cave in the mountains above the Firefalls and go into retirement there, *khre'Riov.* 'No more cities for me, no more shipboard life, I'm going to go up the mountain and be a hermit,' that's what you've always said. Have you made a change in career plans and not told us?"

"Oh, of course," Ael said. "Indeed, why stop at Praetor—why not make myself Ruling Queen?" Then Ael wrinkled her nose in disgust; even as a joke there was nothing particularly funny about it. "You must forgive me," she said to Aidoann, "but you tempted me to it. I was serious, though. If there were nothing to stop us—where would you go?"

Aidoann looked a little unfocused all of a sudden. "Masariv again, I suppose, assuming that the Empire hasn't moved all the people off it and scorched its earth. My folk were never terribly cooperative colonists, and we see from the bulletins that much worse has been done to places that hewed far closer to their loyalties than we Marasivsu did." She looked thoughtful. "My House—how many of them are left now, I wonder? We were never a big family, and even so the House-home was small for us. There was always talk about 'fusing' with some other House; but while she lived my mother would never hear of it. And where my father and brothers might be now—"

Aidoann broke off suddenly, before the wistful look became too sorrowful. "But, Ael, my shame to complain. It was far harder for you; you are all your own House now. I feel selfish, saying anything."

Ael shook her head. "Now then, cousin," she said, and for the first time wished the term spoke to a genuine family relationship rather than just one of close companionship. "Don't feel that you've troubled me. I was more curious about where I should look for you when all this is over and we're all rich and free to go where we please."

Aidoann smiled, a wry look. "From your mouth to the Elements' ears, *khre'Riov,* assuming that They have ears. Meanwhile you haven't much farther to look for me than my quarters. Will you be all right alone here for a while? It's coming to my rest time, and Himif should be up here to handle comms, this shift, but I told him not to rush. He was helping the master engineer with something."

"Certainly, go on with you," Ael said. "I won't get lost."

Aidoann grinned at that. It was about as easy to be lost in *Bloodwing*'s bridge as it was to be lost in one of her heads, the main difference being that the heads were far more peaceful. Aidoann lifted a hand to Ael and went out; the lift door shut behind her.

Ael sat down in Aidoann's seat at the comms post, stretching her legs out in the quiet, and looked across her dark, cramped little bridge, watching the stars flow by on the viewscreen. Their reflections glinted in brief flickers on the end of the blade of the Sword, which stuck out far enough from the arms of her center seat for her to see it from there. Ael twitched a little in the hard seat, thinking about how long it had been since she'd sat in her own chair while in command. *What a fool I was to put that there,* she thought—and then laughed softly at herself. Not that she was *not* a fool, but the comms seat was just as hard-cushioned as her own.

The Firefalls . . . Ael thought. Well, it was part of her family's land, though ages and ages ago. Even were she a Praetor, she would have trouble moving in up there now. The Falls were a Rihannsu world cultural site—a rocky place, and a barren one because of the fire, but also a famous and terrible one, because the Firefall cliffs and their valley were the only place on ch'Rihan where the rarest and most dangerous Element occurred naturally and continually. The top of the cliffs was the exit site for a huge upwelling of natural gases and liquid hydrocarbons under pressure; they poured out and down over the stones in an intermingled, toxic solution that constantly shifted states between gas and liquid, and all of which burned. Probably it was a mercy that they did so, otherwise the uncombusted fumes would have made the whole area fatal to any oxygen-breathing life that ventured there. As it was, between the fire and the smoke, no one in their right mind would really want to live there. Ael tended to use the idea of retreating to the Falls as a metaphor for how very much she simply wanted to get away, when everything was over, and be completely alone for a while.

But how likely is that to actually happen? she thought. *Say worst case happens, and you fall in battle. Likely enough, in space, or on the ground; maybe even at those Falls themselves.* For the Firefalls were a strategic landmark as well as a cultural one. The valley of the Fires was the only practical way for a ground force to pass the mountain wall rising to the south of the plain where Ra'tleihfi stood on its broad river. In these days of transporter access and troop transport by air or space, this was less of a problem, but the area was nonetheless one of importance as a matter of perception, land that had been fought over in ch'Rihan's past, and doubtless would be again. *No matter. If you fall, then no quiet time for you first—though whether you'll care, being in the Elements' care at that point, it's hard to say.*

And if she lived? *As a captive, perhaps? You will have little time to rest then.* Anyone who would bother to make Ael prisoner would be best served by seeing her quickly dead. *And otherwise, if you live, and your cause triumphs? Then there will be no rest for you either, for having dragged your people through war and out the other side—or having, in your turn, been dragged so by them—they will condemn you to go on as you have begun. They will lock you in an office in the Senate, or some obscure reconstruction authority, and it will be years before matters are well enough settled again that you might be let out.*

You are *a fool.*

Yet there was no arguing that Ael had felt she had no choice but to do what she was now doing. Kirk had the right of it there. *The trouble is, I did not think things through. I saw an image of my world, free, of the Sword replaced on its proper place under the Dome, and the evil Senators and Praetors cast out, and good ones put in their place. I was willing enough to use myself as a tool to that end, to let myself be used as such a tool by others. And then, I thought, I would slip away.*

Whatever made me think I would be allowed to?

She laughed again, and the comms board chirped as she did, recalling her to the moment. Ael swung around in the seat and touched the control that brought the capsule of the message up on the screen for the comms officer to examine and decide how to handle.

Ael frowned at the screen as only a few lines of code displayed themselves there. The message was addressed to her, but the capsule was not labeled as to origin or time. The structure of it was Rihannsu, but the routing was peculiar; it had apparently come via raw subspace transmission, rather than through one of the much faster transfer satellites. *Of course, if it is something sensitive—but then, at the moment, what is* not *sensitive?*

She told the console to copy the message to her encrypted storage, and then instructed the comms system to break the capsule for her. The screen filled about halfway with green text.

Ael read the message, and within only a couple of sentences found her heart starting to pound in her side. So shocked was she by what she read that she couldn't continue to sit, but rose in alarm and read the rest of the message standing, leaning over the screen, simply unable to believe it.

This is not for me. This is for Kirk—but does he know? He must not. If he did, how could he possibly *have been so calm last night?*

But whether he had known this menace was coming or not, he did not have *this* much information about it; the message itself made that plain. *I must get this new data to him immediately!*

But she could not. While possible, transport between their ships while they were in warp and running would raise too many questions. It would have to wait for a little while. And there was not much time—

Ael looked again at the coordinates, with the sweat breaking out on her, and did math in her head. *Six days,* Ael thought. *Six standard days—*

She straightened and stood there with her hands clenched together, the message a mere blur in front of her now. The back of Ael's neck prickled with reaction: horror, terror, rage. *Suppose it was Eisn,* she thought. *Dear Elements, only suppose! How can anyone actually* order *such a thing? Their hatred of humans, or else their mere callousness, is unbelievable. Or their fear.*

It was more likely to be fear that was at fault, for aliens had been the great terror of the Rihannsu since before they left their ancient homeworld and went out into the night. *And shortly that fear will become worse yet, in some quarters at least,* she thought. *For into the battle for the Homeworlds, the aliens will once again intrude. One alien in particular.* Not so much those who rode inside one specific starship, perhaps, but the ship herself, seen as almost a live thing by those who hated and feared her. And curious it was that the captain saw her so as well, and treated her so. *But then perhaps that is why she responds so well to his command. And why she has kept him and his crew alive all this while. It's as the old saying goes: Better treat matter as soul than soul as matter. That way at least no one is offended at a crucial moment.*

The lift door hissed open, and tr'Keirianh came in. Ael glanced over at him as he made his way toward his engineering station. He met Ael's eyes, and she saw something odd about the look on Giellun's face—perhaps a reaction to Ael's own look of distress and disgust. "Ael," tr'Keirianh said, "what's the matter?"

She opened her mouth to tell her friend, then stopped herself. *Not even to him,* she thought. *This information is too sensitive. Should he chance to let it drop—* Yet the shame took her by the throat almost immediately. *We have been at each other's side in a hundred battles, he has saved my life and all the crew's, he has—*

Ael shook her head, clearing the screen as she turned back to it, and erasing what she had just read from the bridge computers' buffers, leaving only the encrypted version of the message in the private storage in her quarters. "My fears beset me," she said, "and they shame me, Giellun."

"You are too hard on yourself," tr'Keirianh said, "and you do not confide enough in those of us who are here to help you." He said it lightly enough, and he had said it a hundred times before. But suddenly today it sounded different.

Ael shook her head. "I must go over to *Enterprise* as soon as we reach the rendezvous point."

"I will have the transporter ready for you," said Giellun, and Ael went out, feeling the strangeness of his look on her back.

I have been wounded, and I have lost husband and son, she thought, *and I have come close enough to death in my time. But this hurts worse than any of those. Au, to lose the very trust that life depends upon, all that was left when everything else has failed . . .*

It is gone. No matter how alone I have been, no matter how alone I would be if I ever did move into that cave up by the Falls, it does not matter. I was never really alone before. Not until now.

They came to the rendezvous point some five hours later, and though she dared not show anything else she was feeling at the moment, Ael was at least able to rejoice at what they found waiting for them in that empty space. There were no less than eighteen vessels of various sizes there, corvettes or bigger. Some of them, as at Artaleirh, had been purloined from the Empire after they had attempted punitive missions in other systems. But there were several of them that, to Ael's way of thinking, were worth much more. Those were the ships whose crews had independently turned against the Empire and had sought out the colonies in rebellion, looking to find ways to be of help.

She could not trust them either, right now, and they would look suspiciously enough at her, those ships' captains who would meet her on *Tyrava* with various people from *Enterprise* and from the Artaleirh system. But that could all keep for the moment.

Ael came up from her quarters with nothing in her

pocket but a data solid with that message's contents on it. "Would you call *Enterprise* for me?" she said to the comms officer.

"Right away, *khre'Riov*—"

Ael turned to the screen and saw Lieutenant Commander Uhura's face. *"Good afternoon, Commander,"* she said. *"How can I help you?"*

"I need to talk to the captain about a matter concerning our approach to Augo," Ael said. "It is rather urgent, and I would like to get the matter handled before we meet with the commanders of the new ships."

Uhura glanced to one side. *"He's free at the moment, Commander; he's down in sickbay. Come on over and I'll let him know you're on the way."*

"Thank you, Commander," Ael said. As the screen flicked to darkness and then back to the images of the eighteen ships hanging in the starlight, Ael made her way to the lift.

"How long will you be gone, *khre'Riov?*" said the comms officer.

"No more than an hour, I'd think," Ael said. "Tr'Keirianh wanted me to come down to the engine room before the captains' meeting this afternoon. Tell him I'll see him there as soon as I return."

"Ie, khre'Riov."

Ael made her way down to her own transporter room and beamed over to the *Enterprise*. The transport technician there nodded to her as she materialized. "Commander, can I help you get anywhere?"

"I am meeting the captain in sickbay," Ael said.

"Do you need escort, ma'am?"

"I think not; I know the way."

The transport tech nodded at her, and Ael headed out into the corridor, heading for the lift. She remembered how huge and overblown this ship had seemed to her once. Now, though, *Enterprise* seemed the right size for the people in it;

it was *Bloodwing* that seemed pitifully cramped. *I have spent too long with these people, they would tell me in Fleet. Yet what is wrong with having enough room for the crew not to have to live in one another's laps?* How wonderful it would be to have an empire rich enough to build ships like this, where *all* the people who served in them had enough room, not just the privileged few who commanded.

She walked into sickbay and paused just inside the door, looking around. There was no one in sight except, against the rear door, a gentleman in medical uniform who did not look particularly medical. Ael thought she detected a bulge under his uniform tunic that the tunic was not modified to handle; and he was looking at her with some interest, though he didn't move. As she was about to speak to him, the door to McCoy's office opened, and McCoy came out. "Commander," he said. "I was wondering when you might turn up. It's all right, Geoff, she's with me."

"I was looking for the captain," Ael said, following McCoy into his office.

"I know," McCoy said. "Uhura just spoke to me. You both just missed him, though. Scotty needed him for something down in engineering. He'll be back here shortly—Uhura will let him know you're here. Come on in."

The office door closed behind him, and Ael found herself looking at a desk that reminded her too much of her own master surgeon's. The desk was all scattered with papers and printouts and printed images and data solids and cassettes and books and bindings and the Elements only knew what else. "Sorry about this," McCoy said, picking up an armful of the stuff and depositing it carefully into a large box near the desk. "Every now and then my drawers get too full, and I have to call someone from clerical to come down and help me get it sorted out." He sat down and sighed. "I'm a doctor, dammit, not a file clerk."

Ael sat down by the desk and smiled, for she had heard

something similar from tr'Hrienteh on occasion. "How is Gurrhim doing?"

"He's asleep right now. He's still running on the time they were using on *Gorget;* he probably won't be awake until late this afternoon." McCoy picked up another pile of papers and data solids and other such objects. One object in particular started slipping off the pile as McCoy moved it, and he stopped it from doing so and put it back down on the desk. Ael eyed it as he bent down to put the papers on top of the others in the box.

It was a small rectangular packet, about a finger long and a thumb thick, with colored images on the outside—some kind of pattern. "Doctor," Ael said, "you too play this 'poker' game?"

"What?" He looked at the packet, then sidewise at Ael, and laughed. "Uh, those aren't the cards for playing poker with."

"Another game, then?" She shook her head. "Your people have more ways to play."

"Oh, I bet you have as many ways as we do," McCoy said. "You just think of them differently. These, though—" He sat down again, looking amused. "They're not usually for gaming, no."

McCoy opened the flap at the end of the packet and tipped out the deck of cards, then handed them to Ael. She took the deck from him, turned it over, and saw, not the stylized number-and-symbol imagery that had appeared on the obverses of the cards tr'Keirianh had shown her, but instead, varying images of hominids, some very strangely dressed, or holding curious objects.

"These are derived from distant ancestors of the cards we use for poker," McCoy said. "Once upon a time, they were used as a means to foretell the future. I would say the results were normally equivocal, which is why these days they're usually only used rec:eationally."

"But not by you," Ael said. "Everything is a diagnostic for you. Like the chess cubic."

The look he gave her was amused, but dry. "I find the archetypes useful," McCoy said, as Ael began to riffle through the cards, looking at the pictures.

"But these are human archetypes," Ael said.

"Some," McCoy said. "Not all. Among hominid species, there are a surprising number of similarities in the oldest myths—the things that get down into the bottoms of our psychologies and lie there in the dark, waiting to surprise us." He held out a hand. She passed the deck back to him; McCoy started to shuffle it. "Life and death," he said, "creation and destruction . . . we do a lot of the same things, though the impulses leading to the actions obviously change from species to species. The cards reflect general trends, but not motives. You supply those."

He put the deck down on the desk and reached out to cut it, but she stopped him. "For amusement's sake," she said, and picked up the deck.

"It's never *just* for amusement, with you," McCoy said, "is it? But that's just as well. Go ahead."

Ael shuffled as she had seen McCoy do, taking no more than a few moments to get the hang of it. "Definitely," McCoy said, "they're going to want to get you around the poker table eventually. We can always use another dealer."

"More of that another time, perhaps." She put the deck down on the desk between them. "And now?"

"Cut it twice, to one side or the other." He mimed what he wanted her to do.

Ael cut the deck twice, with the cards facedown, as McCoy indicated. Then she paused. "And now?" she said. "Do I turn one up?"

"As many as you like."

"Three, then. A beginning, a middle, an end."

"That's one of the ways it's done," McCoy said.

Ael turned over the top three cards of the left-hand deck, from right to left.

In the first card a man stood at the top of a tower, looking out over mountains and sea, into a clear sunset sky with stars showing in it, and a waning moon riding high. He was leaning on a tall staff; beside him, from another staff like the first, a banner hung limp. In his free hand, unregarded, he held a small crystalline globe that seemed, in the moonlight, to have the shapes of continents graven on it, but the globe was delicate, almost invisible in the uncertain light, like a bubble.

In the second, a young man in short trousers and a brief tuniclike garment, with a light pack slung over his back, walked toward the edge of a cliff. A small four-legged animal was bouncing along beside him, but the young man didn't seem to notice either beast or cliff. His gaze was directed upward into the mountain air, and the sun burning down on the mist of the mountains all around him whited out anything else that might have been seen.

In the third, a man sat on a low chair in front of a vista of storm clouds, from which a veil of rain trailed over another landscape mostly obscured by mist. He was dressed in some kind of plain uniform, dark-colored, and in one hand, resting on his knee, he held a sharp straight sword upright. His expression was dark and grave, not revealing much.

McCoy sucked in his breath as he took in the cards at a glance. Ael looked at him, and said, "I have heard that sound before, from my master engineer, when he tells me that we must have spares that we cannot afford or make repairs for which we have no time. So the news is somehow bad, but not mortally so." She peered down at the third card. "This worthy—who may he be?"

McCoy grinned briefly, though the expression was sardonic. "The original reference says, 'A doctor, lawyer, or senator.'"

"Indeed." She put up an eyebrow. "Well, there are enough

of the last of those wandering about the landscape back home on ch'Rihan, and most of them wish me ill. Doctors we have in plenty; and legists as well, though in wartime sometimes they are quieter than normal. But there is little here to tell me which one of these is meant, and which will do me harm—if this card is meant as a harbinger of the future."

"No. That's the third one. This one would be the present. As for this . . ." He nodded at the first card. "Been musing on the nature of empire, have we, Commander?"

The look she gave him back was as sardonic as his own. "It would hardly take a diagnostic modality to tell you that. Though it is interesting that such a symbol comes up." She sat back, folded her arms. "Doubts and fears enough, I have had. And much time for reflection in these months during which *Bloodwing* and I have lived the silent life. Much time to revolve in my mind, again and again, what might be done next and what is being done at home. But comes a time when such reflection must stop."

"That's why this card is where it is," McCoy said, "in the past. If you believe in this kind of thing, anyhow."

That left the third card, which he appeared rather unwilling to deal with. "And this fearless youth," Ael said. "But perhaps it is something other than fearlessness. He walks toward the cliff and looks neither left nor right, nor even where his feet are treading."

"The Fool," McCoy said. "Folly, in the classic sense of the word. Choices badly made. Error, confusion, even madness."

She leaned forward to look at it, shook her head. "I would not be sure how to read that."

"Neither would I," McCoy said. "Probably nothing to it, Ael, as I told you."

"But this seems more than just a fool," Ael said. "See, this card is different from the other two. 'Rods,' 'swords.' I would guess these cards are each part of a class within the larger deck. But this young man is of another class."

"A bigger set of symbols," McCoy said, "yes. The beginning of that other class, in fact. He could mean the beginning of a journey—but one into danger. The disorganized, the unknown."

"Every day is unknown until it is over," Ael said. "And sometimes even then. If this means our present is filled with uncertainty, then this too is something we needed no cards to tell us. And the uncertainty will get worse. If the warning is against letting its increase unseat our reason, then I take it as good sense."

The office door opened. Kirk was standing there. "Ael," he said. "I'm sorry. Uhura told me you arrived just after I left. I'm not interrupting anything, am I?"

"Not at all. The doctor was showing me another of his diagnostic tools." Ael got up. "And I thank you for showing them to me. I take it you do not do so often."

"No," McCoy said, "because people might get the wrong ideas. Spock thinks I'm a witch doctor half the time as it is."

Ael blinked. "A doctor surely, but what might a witch be? I have seen none on the ship."

McCoy laughed and got up too. "Probably simpler if you don't."

"Was there something in particular you needed to discuss?" Kirk said to Ael. "I wasn't expecting you until later in the day."

She reached into her pocket and brought out that single small data solid. "There is something here you must see most urgently."

Kirk took it from her and glanced around. "Bones?"

"The reader on the desk is live, now I've got all that stuff off it."

"Perhaps you would rather wait—" Ael said. Then she stopped, embarrassed by her own paranoia.

Both Kirk and McCoy looked at her rather sharply. But Kirk only said, "No, it's all right, Commander." He dropped the data solid onto the reader embedded in the surface of McCoy's desk, and glanced down at the screen.

Then he took in a breath very sharply. "My God."

McCoy looked past him at the screen. "Good Lord, *this* is what Arrhae was trying to tell us about."

"Let's see now," Kirk said under his breath. "They would have launched this, from RV Tri, it's . . ." He paused. "Six days." Kirk reached out to the comms control under the screen. "Bridge, Mr. Spock."

"Spock here, Captain."

"Take a look at what's on the data reader in McCoy's office," Kirk said.

There was a long pause. *"Captain,"* Spock said. *"This confirms all our conjectures. Not only did a cloaked probe leave Hheirant, but information about its course and speed are here. The probe described in this message will reach Earth's solar system four days earlier than I predicted."* His voice was unusually flat, the sound of a Vulcan exerting even more control than usual. *"And it is not as involved an implementation of Sunseed as we thought. It is much simpler, and much deadlier. On arriving in the vicinity of the sun it will transport itself into the sun's core and derange the star's carbon-carbon cycle."*

"A nova bomb," McCoy whispered.

"Nothing so powerful, Doctor," Spock said. *"But to the inhabitants of Earth after such a device was triggered, there would be little difference between Sol going nova and the effect that will be produced. The simulations Mr. Scott produced for us of an enhanced Sunseed effect will be as nothing to it. The resultant hyperflare will blow between a third and a half of the sun's mass into space. Earth's atmosphere will be stripped away within seconds of the main flare-wavefront hitting the planet. The dayside will be reduced to magma in seconds, and crustal heat convection will destroy everything on the far side in massive earthquakes*

*leading to mantle rupture. All life on Earth will be extinct
within hours of the device being triggered."*

The silence that followed was terrible. "I take it that this
news was not accompanied by any message such as 'Call
off your war or else,' " McCoy said to Ael after a few moments.

"No, Doctor. No ultimata have been delivered."

"And I don't think any will be," Kirk said. "I think this is
intended as a 'final solution.' "

Hearing their voices, Ael began to tremble again. *And I
thought I was over that.* "Gentlemen," she said, "I had
thought my people were lost to shame before, but now I
begin to be ashamed to be Rihannsu at all." She looked up at
Kirk. "But you astound me, Captain. I could by no means be
so calm in the face of such news."

"I knew something about it already," Kirk said, his voice
tight and fierce. "This just confirms the details. We're already working on the problem."

"But how? What can you possibly do from here? You
must inform Starfleet at once!"

"I can't, at least not by the normal channels," Kirk said.
"Right now, those channels can't be trusted. There are elements at Fleet that are likely to distrust *anything* I say now,
on the assumption that I've been suborned or turned. And besides that, there are people at Starfleet who've sent you into
ambush once, maybe twice. I'm not sure who those people
are working for. If I simply send this information off to Fleet
in the normal way, I have no guarantee that the same people
who set you up aren't in a position to either discredit or lose
this piece of information. And for the sake of the home of
humanity, that's not a chance I can take."

"I understand you," Ael said. "But what are your other options, besides sending the data home to Starfleet? If you do
not trust them, who else *can* you trust?"

"Present company aside," Jim said.

Ael laughed at him. "Captain—Jim. You flatter me, and I would go if I could. But under no circumstances can I be spared from our present business. Were I and *Bloodwing* to suddenly go missing from either Augo, or our next engagement—the one on which everything rides—then Senate and Praetorate and all our enemies in the Empire would instantly rise up and cry, 'Did we not tell you that the traitress was just a front for the Federation?' The revolution, such as it is, would implode right then. You will have to look elsewhere for your courier."

"You're right," Kirk said. "And there's still the problem of sheer speed. You couldn't get into Federation space before the device would. The message indicates that the thing's got a tailored warp drive that lets it make better speed than a normal ship could; it's almost halfway to Sol already. No, we have other options open to us, back doors we can use. Both in terms of getting the news back home by more devious means, and doing something direct about the problem. Mr. Scott's pursuing that avenue of investigation, to good effect. So right now everything that can be done is being done, besides getting on with our work here. You're going to be at the meeting on *Tyrava* this evening? I've done all I can here as regards my initial take on strategy and tactics for Eisn space. Once you and Veilt and I are in agreement, we should get started for Augo."

"That will happen, I think, within minutes of our meeting's end. For now, I should get back to *Bloodwing*: I would not want anyone to think I had come here about anything serious."

"All right. Meanwhile, obviously we won't be mentioning this to anyone else." He nodded at McCoy's screen. "But one last thing. Who *sent* you this?"

"I do not know," Ael said. "I would much fear, however, that whoever they were, they are dead now. Surveillance on messaging out of ch'Rihan is always tight. In wartime, it will become unbelievably so, and no unauthorized person who has been in contact with this particular piece of news will be spared." She shook her head. "Elements with them, whoever they are, for nothing less will keep them alive." She got up and looked at Kirk. "Now I must go back and try to act as if everything is well. Or as well as it can be, less than a day before battle."

"You'll be fine," McCoy said. "I wouldn't have known that there was anything in particular going on with you when you first came in."

Ael looked at him, wondering whether to believe him. "I hope you are right," was all she could find to say, at last. She nodded to him, to the captain, and went out.

McCoy watched her go, and as the door closed behind her, looked over at Jim. "And as for you," he said. "How are you holding up?"

"Well enough," Jim said. "I'm a little more nervous than I was at Artaleirh, I'll admit that much. We don't have the guaranteed early warning of what's waiting for us that we did before. But we've got a good force assembled for an intermediate engagement like this. Even if they threw all of Grand Fleet at us."

"Perish the thought," McCoy said, in genuine horror.

"Bones, they don't dare," Jim said. "There are still the Klingons to think about. If the Romulans pull everything out of the colony spaces, that whole side of the Star Empire will be hip-deep in Klingons in just a few days. To this extent, but no further, a de facto two front war is a good thing." He rubbed his face.

"You getting enough sleep?" McCoy said.

"I'll sleep in October," Jim said.

"Don't get cute with your old family doctor," McCoy said. "You need your edge more than usual, right now. I'll medicate you if I have to."

"All right, all right." Jim stretched, straightened himself. "Anything else I need to know about?"

"Just Gurrhim's condition. Improving."

"Good. Will he be all right during the battle?"

"You handle it like the last one," McCoy said, "and don't get us blown up, and he'll be just fine."

Jim grinned, nodded, and was gone.

With a sigh McCoy turned back to his desk and looked down at the New Waite deck again, reaching out to put it away. Then he paused. On an impulse, he made a bet with himself, then turned over the top card of the third "cut" deck.

The card showed a robed woman seated on a throne, in profile, very erect and still, and crowned. In one hand, point up, she held a sword. Behind her, in a windy sky, storm clouds blew, tattering past. At her feet sat a small black cat with a thoughtful look in its eyes; not in profile, but looking out of the card at the one who read.

Uh-oh, McCoy thought, and looked at the Queen of Swords for a moment, as thoughtful as the cat. The card was replete with meaning, as all the cards were, from the superficial to the profound. Sorrow, mourning, separation, long absence, those were the general indications. But McCoy was tempted for the moment, however unusual it might be, to take the card literally at face value. The heart of the problem of the moment was a woman with a sword. The card's usual meaning, when read in the personal mode, indicated a woman in a position of power—though not a position that would let her use it. More generally, it suggested that trouble was coming, and a very bad time.

Didn't need a piece of plastic to tell me that, he thought, picking up the card along with the rest of them. He tapped them together, gave them one last quick shuffle, slipped them back into their packet and tossed them into a desk drawer, then went off to check on Gurrhim.

THIRTEEN

IN HOUSE KHELLIAN on ch'Rihan, Arrhae was sitting in her dayroom and sipping a cup of hot herbdraft, trying to get some command of her nerves. It seemed that any chance noise or sudden occurrence could make her start. She lived in fear of the commlink going off again.

There was a scratch at the dayroom door. She jumped where she sat, and then cursed most fiercely at herself.

After a moment the door opened. "Mistress," Mahan said, putting his head in the door, "my pardon."

She found a slight small smile for him. "It wasn't you I was cursing, Mahan."

"I'm glad of that," he said, and managed to sound slightly disapproving of her language. "But, mistress, there's a person here at the door." Mahan looked briefly confused. "He says he desires to speak with the noble *deihu*—and there's something odd about him."

Arrhae looked at him, her heart already starting to beat fast and hard enough to leave her certain it could be heard from right over there. "Odd in what way?"

"Mistress, it's hard to say," Mahan said. "He seems nothing much like the military or government people we've seen in and out, these latest days."

"Perhaps that's a relief," Arrhae said. *Not military.* While she was relieved, there were still too many things that could mean. *Intelligence?* "Of what kind is he?"

"He is a dark-visaged man, and bears himself quietly," Mahan said. "In fact, I may have misspoken myself. He is not in uniform, but he has something of the look of a man who might have been in service once himself."

She shook her head. "Mahan, I will go to the door with you. Perhaps with a precaution or so."

He nodded. Together they made their way through the front hall, and to the door, and there Mahan paused for a moment. He glanced at Arrhae, and then at the little cupboard inset behind the hinge side of the door. She understood the look quite well. In there, finger-locked to her and Mahan and a few other trusted household staff, were several small but highly effective hand weapons. Mahan quietly turned to the little cupboard and put his thumb to the lock. The door popped open.

Arrhae glanced at the cupboard. "If it is an Intelligence operative, and he really wanted me, none of this would stop him. Nevertheless, open the door, Mahan. Let's see this strange caller."

Mahan touched the door open, stepping into place behind it, as was proper when he was opening it in the presence of the mistress of the house. The dark-clothed shape standing on the doorstep now turned as the door opened, looking into Arrhae's face.

For a moment or so, Arrhae's mind went quite blank with confusion. She fumbled for recognition as one will sometimes do on seeing a person from a shop or stall out on the street and out of their normal place. For that frozen moment, as she and the man looked at each other, Arrhae felt disoriented. But a second later, memory locked into place, and she realized whom she was looking at. The only reason she hadn't instantly recognized him was that he hadn't been trying to feed her something. Standing there on her doorstep was Ffairrl.

He gave her a bow of considerable respect, seconds

longer than she was used to, even from a servant. "Gracious and noble *deihu*," he said, as he straightened, "I am sorry to trouble you here on the threshold of your very house."

"You do not trouble me at all, Ffairrl!" Arrhae said. "Please favor me by crossing my threshold. Mahan, this good gentleman cared for me while I was on *Gorget*. He was steward of my apartments, and kept me out of all manner of trouble. Mostly by feeding me until I could barely move."

Mahan smiled, gave Ffairrl a bow of moderate respect, and closed the door behind him as he entered. Arrhae noticed that somehow or other, Mahan had also managed to quietly shut and hide the weapons locker without anyone noticing. "Anyone who has cared for the lady of House Khellian," Mahan said, "is very welcome here." He turned to Arrhae. "Noble mistress—"

What do you want me to do next? he was asking, without saying as much. "Mahan," Arrhae said, "be so good as to lay out a pitcher of ale for us, and some wafers, in the retiring-room." She gestured into the hall. "Ffairrl, please come into the room and sit down for a bit. Eat and drink and tell me how things have been for you."

Privately, she was already beginning to suspect what might have brought Ffairrl here. He had been released from his duties aboard *Gorget*, and was looking for work. She had never been entirely certain of what his formal status aboard ship was, as there had been too many other things occurring on *Gorget* that had been occupying her attention. Certainly, Fleet had many civilian or semicivilian employees, doing jobs on which Fleet did not care to waste its own personnel. *Yet also,* Arrhae thought, *there could well have been many on the vessel who seemed to be such personnel, but were not.*

She wondered if in Ffairrl's case she wasn't being a bit paranoid. It was so hard sometimes to successfully walk the line between paranoia and foolishness. Yet for a long time now, Arrhae had been happy to stay on the paranoid side of the line; it had kept her alive this long. True, sometimes the attitude started to seem foolish. *Possibly,* she thought, *a good sign for my sanity. But also possibly not so good for my survival.*

She walked Ffairrl calmly enough through the Great Hall, bringing him back to the media room where she had previously sat and watched those unsettling crowd scenes unfold. *Terrible,* she thought, *how events can change one. Two nights ago, I thought those were the most frightening things I had seen or heard. Now, though, after the news . . .*

She touched open the door of the media room and waved Ffairrl toward one of the comfortable chairs there.

They talked pleasant nothings about the weather for some moments, until Mahan came in with a tray of ale and wafers and a bowl of soft *khefai* on the side. Arrhae nodded approval at him, and said, "I think we will need no other care than those for some while, Mahan. If the commlink goes, let me know if it's something urgent. Otherwise, let us be awhile. I will call you if you're needed."

Mahan bowed and took himself away, but not without something of a warning glance at Arrhae. She smiled a little as he went out. "You see," she said, "I am well cared for here on my own ground. And I have not forgotten how well you cared for me at so troublesome a time." Then she wondered if she had just said, a little too baldly, *See, I do not need any additional household help right now.*

"I am glad to see you well served," Ffairrl said. "And it doesn't surprise me that perhaps you think that prospective employment is the errand on which I've come. Indeed," and his eyes suddenly acquired a shadowy chill that Arrhae had never seen in them before, "I much hope that others may think as much, for I am sure that I was seen coming here."

Arrhae sipped her ale, and tried to maintain in her face a composure that was definitely not present in her heart or her mind. "Ffairrl, I would not have you in trouble with some

other employer—past or future. If such is the case, tell me
how I can help you."

"Lady," Ffairrl said, "the trouble is not mine, but yours."
He glanced around him. "This room—do you feel secure
here?"

She knew what the question meant well enough. "Ffairrl,
if I may speak to you familiarly—you're not in my service
anymore, if you ever were—yes, we have had some workmen in recently, but they installed nothing but the commlink,
and that only in the front hall. They went nowhere else. We
watched that with some care."

Ffairrl let out a breath. "It will have to do." He looked at
her, and she saw, behind his look, far more than his old concern that she'd grown so used to—the mere matter of when
she'd last eaten or drunk.

There was too much at stake for Arrhae to lose her composure now. "Ffairrl," she said, "bearing in mind the position
to which I've been elevated, it's only to be expected that I'm
being watched. So far, only the certainty that I am a very
minor player in the game going on around us has kept me
from becoming much more unsettled than circumstances already seem to require. I was glad enough to come out of the
madness that beset *Gorget* when its mission came undone. I
was relieved indeed to come back to my own home and shut
the door on all of that. But now I think you may be trying to
tell me that it's not as shut as I thought it was."

He bowed to her a little where he sat. "Noble *deihu,* your
caution is commendable, as it always was. But I think now
you must not pretend to peer at the world's dangers through
your fingers, like a child looking at some harmless game.
The moment requires a different response, so I will be blunt,
to save time." He looked at her earnestly. "I think that perhaps the commlink that you watched installed with such care
rang once yesterday."

Arrhae put down her cup of ale on the tray at her elbow,

folded her hands in her lap, and looked at him with her best expression of mild interest.

"And?"

"They know," he said.

She sat quietly and thought about that.

"Two words," she said, "so brief. But how many folk in this world might panic on hearing them? Just think of the trouble you could cause by sending, to everyone on this planet, a post-scroll or wire-scroll that said, 'All is revealed: flee while you can!' " She smiled at him. "All one would have to do then is sit back and amuse oneself watching all those who have something to hide, running about and revealing the fact. For myself, I prefer to sit still and watch matters unfold."

"Lady Arrhae," Ffairrl said, "that is exactly what I fear you do not have the leisure to do."

"You fear?" Arrhae said. "Or you know?"

It was Ffairrl who was studying her now—an uncomfortably assessing look. She had never seen anything of the kind from him while they were on *Gorget*. He had often seemed embarrassed enough to meet her eyes at all. Yet the look of the moment was frank and thoughtful. "It is always very hard to tell with you," Ffairrl said, "when you are being bold on purpose, when you are bluffing, and when you are simply using your questioner's own thoughts against him. It is a considerable skill, this gift you have for misdirection. It has taken you into interesting places of late. But even the company you have been keeping may not be sufficient to save you from some of the *other* company your company keeps."

He too took a drink of his ale, and put the cup down again. "The man who made that commlink call to you yesterday is dead. He died a silent death, a matter of great annoyance to those who sent him to it. Only the fact that this man had no connection to any Intelligence service anywhere, and no connection to any politician or anyone else of any possible interest—only this has so far kept the Intelligence services from your doorstep. They fear to offend your employer, and they fear that the link might genuinely have been nothing more than a circuit error—in which case they would pay dearly for your assassination. But they are seeking cause against you even as we speak."

"My employer," Arrhae said, and smiled gently. "Well. You are, I think, now to tell me that their fear of my employer grows less, or that the protection he is able to offer me grows less, or both together."

"That is exactly what I would tell you," Ffairrl said.

"It falls to me, then, to ask you how do you come by such information?" Arrhae looked at Ffairrl, trying not to have the look be friendly rather than intimidating.

Ffairrl merely looked at her.

"You're thinking," Arrhae said, "that I would be far simpler than you initially thought had I not long since suspected that you were an agent planted on me by one or another of the Intelligence communities working in *Gorget*. Well, I had that thought, and put it by; for good or ill, I never had any proof. What possible good would denouncing you have done? Besides, who knows if the next spy along would have made herbdraft as well as you do? And that soup you used to make in the evenings!"

For just a moment that shadow on Ffairrl's face vanished, and his eyes crinkled with amusement. "Most would expect you to have had that suspicion, lady, but none expected you to react as you did, as if all your life you were used to being spied on, and took it as blithely as if it were just a fact of life like sun or rain. It was taken in some quarters as evidence of wiliness beyond belief, and in others as evidence of incredible stupidity."

Arrhae had to smile at that. "That you are here suggests some other opinion. I suppose I should be glad."

"Lady," Ffairrl said, "I come to tell you this: you must take measures to protect yourself."

"And what would those be?" She got up and went over to the window, looking out at the trees and the velvety lawn. "Life is sweet to me, Ffairrl; I have no desire to leave it. So I take your warning kindly." She turned, and let him, just for a moment, see the look on her face that told him she really meant what she said. "But what would you have me do? If I do indeed flee, that would be proof that I had cause to. The pursuit would shortly be after me, and I have nowhere to run from them, nowhere to hide. Yet if I sit still, you seem to be saying, they will come for me regardless. Against this, I must balance the fact that my 'employer' yet has use for me; and I like to think, for my own part, that I have some useful part to play in the world as it stands. So I think I must stay here, and work in the spot where the Elements have put me. For this little while, my protection must be that, should I suddenly go missing, the noble Praetor would take notice." She looked at Ffairrl. "Nonetheless, I thank you for your warning. And now, what I must ask you is, how shall we cover your presence here? Should I, perhaps, hire you into the household? Or would that cause as many questions, in its own way, as your appearance on my doorstep in the first place?"

Ffairrl chuckled. "Lady, it was always a pleasure serving you, and it would be a pleasure now. But I think I've today done you as much service as I can. Though I will have been watched, I am not under suspicion—not yet. Those who watch, know no more about me but that I served aboard *Gorget* as a steward. My history—or at least that part of it to which they have access—" He smiled gently. "—will suggest nothing more. But should you hire me, that would be found unusual. Those who watch know your personal finances, and that House Khellian is not overly wealthy. When you turn me from your door, that will be no less than they expect."

He stood up. Arrhae rose as well. But she offered him her hand, and surprised, Ffairrl took it and held it in the manner of one who had been intimate with its holder in ways superior to the merely physical. "I know that you've risked much to do this," she said. "You've done me a great courtesy. And I thank you for the warning; at least now I have some data to back up the paranoia that's been my bedfellow, these last nights."

Ffairrl bowed at the compliment, then straightened. "I'm glad to serve you in that much, at least. I should go. With the noble *deihu*'s permission." He turned toward the door.

"Ffairrl," she said.

He paused, looked over his shoulder.

"Why?" Arrhae said.

He looked at her. "Because you did not treat me like a servant. Because you treated me with the kind of courtesy one reserves for one's equals." He paused. "And because you gave me recipes."

Her eyes widened. "I gave you—"

"You have forgotten the recipe for the mulled ale with *elstekt*," he said. "Or the 'burnt bread.' There were several others. You passed them from your little reader to the desktop machine for me. They were very good recipes; I will not soon forget them. Or the context in which they were offered."

She glanced down and found herself blushing.

"And also," Ffairrl said, "because you sing in your sleep."

Arrhae held very, very still.

"It is a sign of an unusually open heart, I find," Ffairrl said. "Of a soul sunk deep in its own certainties, and its own kind of peace, though the circumstances through which that soul moves may be difficult in the extreme. Such people are too few in the world. It would sort ill with any man's *mnhei'sahe* to allow such a person to be extinguished by the political imperatives of the moment. You do, indeed, have work to do where you are."

He bowed again, and straightened. "I wish that you may

do it well. No, do not; I saw the way out. I bid you farewell, noble *deihu*."

He opened the door and was gone.

Arrhae stood there, and now her hands twisted together in the way that they would have liked to do while he was still there.

And now what? she thought. *Only a few possibilities. Do as I have done; stay as I have stayed.*

Or act as if the letter I was describing has dropped on my own front doormat. 'Flee! All is revealed!' But what would happen is exactly as I described it to him. It would neither help my situation, nor leave me free to continue doing the work I need to be doing.

She let out a long breath.

Or . . .

Arrhae sat down again in that comfortable chair. *It is perhaps time,* she thought, *to start acting like a senator. If I have one of the great Three as my patron, then perhaps it is time to start being a little proactive. He has reposed great trust in me. Now it will be seen if the same can be done with him. If not . . .*

Arrhae began to consider the finer details of the visit she was about to make.

The space around 553 Tri was an undistinguished place. The little yellow sun itself had nothing of any interest around it, just an asteroid belt in the system's far outer reaches that was too sparse to be of any concern. But there was another band of bright bodies closer in, catching the star's golden light and glittering it back at any newcomer. The local space was full of ships.

Ael looked out on the vista her viewscreen showed her with considerable trepidation. *So many.* Then she was tempted to laugh at herself. *I would have been as upset had there been too few. Why am I complaining?*

She turned to Hvaid. "How many now?"

"There are at least a hundred, *khre'Riov*," she said. "The massed armament is impressive. And already we will have exceeded the abilities of the command-and-control structures that Uhura and Sulu and Khiy have been designing."

Ael sighed, leaning on the back of her command chair. "It seems ungrateful of me to look at all this and feel that things are going too well. I am sure that such an appraisal would be erroneous. I feel some stroke hanging in the air over us, something that we will not expect."

"But if you expect it, *khre'Riov*," Hvaid said, "then surely it is no threat."

Ael leaned lower over the back of the chair, looking at the reflection of ships and stars in the blade of the Sword. Then she laughed and pushed herself away from the chair, straightening. "Would it were so simple," she said. "But the question is *where* to expect it." She stood up straight, and stretched, and rubbed her eyes. "Which brings us to the matter at hand. When will they be expecting *me?*"

"Quite shortly, *khre'Riov*. They are gathering now."

"Well," Ael said, "best I should get going, then. Do you run another set of diagnostics on the C&C protocols while I am gone. I am not yet comfortable with how they interweave with our systems. I much fear that in the middle of a battle, we are likely to have the systems crash."

Hvaid opened her eyes wide. "*Khre'Riov*, Khiy would never permit anything so commonplace. For our systems to fail, it would be for some much far more exotic reason."

Ael laughed. "You're right, of course. Mind the bridge for me. I will be back within the hour."

She stepped into the lift, and as the doors closed on her, she thought, *Therein, of course, lies the constant danger. Expect the exotic steadfastly, and without doubt it is the commonplace that will be the end of you.* She rubbed her eyes, and sagged against the wall of the lift. It was something she dared not do anywhere her crew could see her. *Would that there were someone to be strong for me,* she thought, *someone I could collapse on. But I seem to have cast myself in too harsh a role for that.*

The lift doors opened. Ael came out on the level where the ship's transporters lay, and as she walked down that narrow little corridor, her friend tr'Hrienteh came out of the transporter room's door, turned toward her, and seemed a little surprised to see her. "Did you need me for anything, *khre'Riov?* I am just now going back to the sickbay."

"No, cousin," Ael said. "All is well enough with me. What brings you down here?"

"Technician Gioufv's head aches him," tr'Hrienteh said. "I brought him a pain-relief gel."

Ael smiled a little wanly, and massaged her own brow. "I'd wager there's no one aboard who either has not had one of those in very recent time, or shortly will have one."

Tr'Hrienteh looked at Ael sympathetically. "It has been hard for you, *khre'Riov.* Harder, I think, than anyone aboard knows."

"But it would not be their job to know," Ael said. "If they did, I would not be doing my job well as their commander. My work is to bear the burden, and not burden them with it." She looked narrowly at tr'Hrienteh, seeing the circles under her eyes. "But how does it go with you, cousin? You, too, have felt the burden of late—"

"No worse than with many others," the surgeon said. "But for you, *khre'Riov,* I do have some concerns. I have some new stress-relief and biorhythm managers down in my offices. They are adaptations of some equipment McCoy has given us, which I have altered to suit our physiology. Come down, if you have time, and try one of them out. It may give you some relief."

"Had I a moment now," Ael said, "I would do that. But they are expecting me over on *Tyrava.* Remind me of that again in a day or two; I will certainly come." She smiled, and rubbed her head again. "Any relief would be welcome, especially now, when I can take it without feeling too guilty. Closer to the battle—" She shook her head. "—I would be too concerned that I might somehow impair my function."

"As you say, *khre'Riov*," tr'Hrienteh said. She patted Ael on the shoulder and headed for the lift.

Ael made her way into the transporter chamber. There one of her antecenturions was standing, and to her shock she actually had to feel about in her mind for his name, though tr'Hrienteh had said it to her only a moment ago. *Indeed,* she thought, *the stress is becoming a problem. I think as soon as I have time, I must take tr'Hrienteh's advice.* "So," she said, "they require my company on *Tyrava,* Gioufv. Would you do the honors?"

"At once, *khre'Riov*," the antecenturion said.

Ael stepped up onto the pad, and turned. "And are you feeling better now?"

"Much better, *khre'Riov*," he said, and smiled back at her. "The surgeon's remedies are sometimes rather a shock to the system, but they do the job."

Ael nodded. "I agree. Meanwhile, I should go. I will call you shortly for pickup from *Tyrava*'s pad; just scan for my presence there in a while."

The antecenturion nodded. "Ready, *khre'Riov?*"

She nodded, composing herself for the transport.

When *Tyrava* shimmered into view around her, she looked out from its huge receiving pad and then had to exert great control to keep from standing there openmouthed in astonishment. A hundred ships' captains, give or take a few— that she had expected. A hundred ships' crews—that took Ael by surprise. But it occurred to her, then, that they were coming as much to prove to themselves that it was actually *she* who was leading them as for any other reason. *Perhaps the caution is wise.* The Empire had often enough used ruses and hoaxes to trick disaffected individuals into places or situations where they could be easily trapped or taken.

Ael walked off the pad toward where they all stood. There to one side, Veilt tr'Tyrava stood, watching her calm, watching the reactions of those who saw her approach. The look on his face was unusual. He was reacting to his guests' expressions, of course. Many of them looked like people who had not truly believed in the prospect of the fight before them until they saw the slight little woman with the braided dark hair coming toward them. Others looked almost belligerent, though toward whom was difficult to tell at this remove. Others looked astounded, as if they had believed this was going to be a trick all along, and were now put out of composure by her presence.

"So, my associates," she said. The word was one of the more neutral ones in Rihannsu. *Ally* required a commitment she thought was about to be made, but had not been quite yet. "I must apologize for not being here with you sooner. I dislike making people wait for me. And some few—" She glanced around at them. "—would, I guess, have been waiting a long while."

A rustle went through the men and women standing there in their many uniforms—mercantile, private, some of them even old Grand Fleet uniforms—as they waited to hear what Ael had to say. She met the eyes of all the closest, one after another. "But I, too, have been waiting for you," she said. "For a long while now, events have waited upon the people who would finally rise up to take back their Empire. And in that endeavor, I am glad—to lead you perhaps would be the wrong phrase. To be in this battle with you; to be at the forefront of it, yes. But many of you will be there too. To lend, perhaps, a sense of direction. We are all going the same way, led by *mnhei'sahe*." She glanced around them, saw the effect of the word, was heartened. "Too long that word has been absent from the lips of those who govern us, and from their

hearts, and from their actions. Time to bring it back into government and rule again, and into the ken of those who guard
our world, and deal on our behalf with other. If you have
come here on that journey, right gladly I will travel with
you."

Another transporter hum came from the pad behind her.
Ael looked over her shoulder, and saw Kirk appear there, and
the little rustling among the ships' captains and crews before
her now died away to complete stillness. Ael smiled very
slightly to herself. Here, too, was one the assembled group
had not quite believed in, one who might have been a hoax.
Even the sight of his ship, hanging there off 553 Trianguli,
apparently had not entirely convinced some of them. "And
this man," Ael said, as Kirk walked over to her, "has come
much farther than I on this particular journey, and has proven
himself more completely than you can know. To my satisfaction, certainly." She glanced over at Veilt. "And to that of
Tyrava's command."

Kirk came up to stand beside her, and looked out over the
group waiting there. "Anything in particular I need to say
here?" he said under his breath.

Ael raised an eyebrow. "Only what you would normally
say to perhaps a thousand people who were trained not to
trust you, and now find they must."

Kirk nodded fractionally. "Oh," he said softly. "Just like
Starfleet Command. No problem."

He looked around at the crowd. "Ladies and gentlemen,"
he said, "commanders and antecenturions and civilian commanders of all ranks and styles." He looked thoughtful for a
moment. "I'm here to fight alongside you. I'm here to help
you take back your worlds."

"And what then?" someone said, from the center of the
group. The person was safely hidden away among all numbers. There was no telling who had spoken.

Kirk glanced that way. "Then, I expect to go home and

find the best possible legal representation for my court-martial." He smiled, an edged smile with no more curve than Ael's, but considerably sharper. "I have something of a name among my own people for stretching my orders to just the point before they'll snap. I think I may have exceeded my reputation this time, even among my own." He looked rueful. "But for the time being—let's just say that there are some fights that must be fought, at the risk of refusing them and letting the world change much for the worse. This is one of those fights. And if I have a reputation in this part of the universe at all, I hope it's for not leaving a fight until it's finished."

They all stood there quietly for a few moments, digesting that. Then Ael said, "What more needs saying, friends? Events are moving, and so must we. We cannot linger here long."

Slowly a group of about fifty moved forward. The young man at the head of them said, "We need only to swear you our fealty." And he broke off.

Kirk looked briefly confused; but Ael understood the confusion. Even among these people, rebels already in the grain, it came hard to speak the name of someone whose name had been written and burned. Ael looked at Kirk, and her smile grew an edge to match his. "Call me what you will," she said. "I imagine there must be a calling-name for me among the volunteer fleets."

Many of those gathered there looked at one another with slight discomfort, almost nervousness. "They call you," said the commander nearest her, "the Sword."

"The winged one," said another. "The wind," a third said. "The wind that blows, and makes things new."

Ael flicked a glance at Jim. He caught her discomfort, perhaps. "I seem to remember," he said under his breath again, "you telling me something about having to be careful how you choose your names . . ."

She nodded. "And at times like this, more so than usual."
Ael raised her head, looking at the gathered fleet-folk. "At
the moment, there is one Sword on my ship that takes
precedence over any other. From such a naming, I would refrain. The winged one, though," she said, "*Hlalhif:* so let me
be called, for this time. Come and tell me your ships'
names, and your own." Then Ael laughed, and it was her
turn to sound rueful. "There are so many of you, it will go
hard with me to remember you all, at least on sight. I pray
you, be patient with me until I learn all names as well as
they deserve."

Slowly they began to come up to her then, group by
group: large groups, small ones, sometimes little gaggles of
only three or five people, several times just one person by
himself, all sworn to her service. There were no other words
to say on such an occasion; the name was all. Giving it gave
your business, your intention, to a certain extent your life,
into the other's hand. If Ael was a weapon in some other
force's hand, that she had learned to bear; but to have such a
burden of weaponry, a veritable armory of souls, thrust upon
her like this—it was hard. Their lives or deaths, their fates,
were all on her head, now.

Next to her, Kirk stood straight, listening, his eyes
dwelling on all the faces; but he said nothing. Perhaps he was
able to tell from the hushed atmosphere that had fallen
around them that this was not his place to speak. *But it is his
place to be. I am glad that he's here.*

The recounting of names took a long time. Finally it was
over; finally Ael had spoken to them all, giving them in exchange for their own names her new gift-name, in lieu of the
three she could not give and the one she would not. There
was nothing more to do, now, except to go into battle. "The
officers on *Bloodwing* and *Enterprise*," Ael said, "will be in
touch with all your communications and weapons officers
concerning command and control for this upcoming mission.

I beg you, pay the most heed to them, and carefully check the communications and coordination protocols that will be laid into your computers. In a situation like this, our coordination will prove a greater weapon than any phaser or disruptor. If we all do what we are all meant to do, victory will be ours, for our enemy counts on us being a crowd of ragged individualists who cannot set aside our personal visions long enough to cooperate. If we slip—" And then Ael shook her head. "But we will not slip. The weapon is no less sound for being untried. We will shortly teach the Empire that its head is not safe on its shoulders. If we are fortunate, if we teach it well enough, then perhaps our worlds may be spared much grief. Let us fight in that hope, and the commitment to carry on even if hope fails."

A cheer went up from them, muted, but enthusiastic in the only kind of way that mattered. These people were determined. Ael looked at Jim, and turned away.

Standing behind the two of them, however, was Veilt. "There is one word yet to say," he said. "My Ship-Clan is with you; I am with you. But one more thing I can say to you that will make you, and all the others, most sure." He bent over toward Ael, and whispered a word in her ear.

Ael's eyes went wide. Veilt looked out over the assembly. "She has my fourth name," he said. "Should I fall, she is Clan-Chief and Clan-Captain of *Tyrava*. Her word in such case will weigh as heavily in the balance with the other Clan-Chiefs of the Ship-Clans as mine would have were I still breathing. All of you here, know this word, and know that I have given it to her. If I fall, follow her as you would follow me." And as casually as that, he turned and walked off out of the great assembly hall into some other part of *Tyrava*. Ael and Kirk watched him go.

Slowly, the two of them went on to the pad. "Always full of surprises, that one," Kirk said.

"You have no idea," Ael said. If she had thought herself

burdened before, it was nothing to what lay on her shoulders now. "I must talk to you later, if you have time."

"No problem," he said. "Call me just before we leave. We have to do our test on the star."

Ael nodded. "Later, then." She stepped up onto the pad, moved to a decent distance from him, and a few moments later, vanished.

Hours later, *Enterprise* hung there in the darkness, two hundred million miles out from 553 Trianguli, waiting.

Jim, sitting in the center seat, drummed his fingers on its arm and eyed the star. It was big enough to be safely out of the dwarf category, which would have made it a little too closely a twin of Sol. But the sun was much on his mind at the moment, along with other things.

He had come away from his later chat with Ael feeling all too sobered by the newest Intelligence passed to them from *Tyrava*. It suggested that truly massive force was being marshaled against them at Augo, and Jim was already having to think of different ways to handle the increased injection of materiel, ships, and manpower. *If we ever had any kind of advantage of surprise,* he thought, *it's gone now. Whether we have leaks or not in our own ranks—and it's pretty likely, since there are thousands of people on our side whose allegiances and private alliances I know nothing about—somebody at Grand Fleet has got the message: better have a big engagement at Augo than any closer to home.*

Dammit. They were doing such a good job at being stupid until now.

Jim sighed and focused on the task at hand. "Scotty?"

Mr. Scott was leaning over his station, making some final adjustments, straightening up again to look at the screens showing the data input and output from the field-generator probe they were getting ready to drop. "We're all sorted out," he said. The look on his face, though, suggested that his inner calm didn't even slightly match the calm he was enforcing on his voice. "Just waiting for the probe to finish its diagnostics, then we can let her fly."

The turbolift door opened. McCoy came wandering in, looking like a man who was glad to have escaped from sickbay for a while. "Doctor," Jim said. "Got everything strapped down tight in sickbay?"

McCoy's eyes flickered just enough to let Jim know that he wasn't talking about the laboratory glassware. "All's secure." He ambled over to Scotty's station, peering over his shoulder at the status screen above the console. McCoy raised his eyebrows. "Looks like a whole lot of power there, Mr. Scott."

"Aye, Doctor," Scotty said, sounding tense, and not taking his eyes off the display. "Close on a yottawatt."

"A yotta *what?*"

"Watt."

"No, I mean, a yotta *what?*"

"That's what I said."

McCoy said nothing for a moment, but his face suggested that he was counting something inside his head. Scotty looked over his shoulder and saw the doctor's perplexed look. "A great number of watts," Scotty said, with somewhat exaggerated patience.

"Oh," McCoy said. "How many zeroes?"

"Twenty-four."

McCoy made a disgusted face and turned away. "Every time I think I know all the prefixes, they invent another one. It's some kind of plot."

"Bones," Jim said quietly, for he could see that Scotty was practically trembling with the attempt not to hear anything McCoy was saying right now, "let it be."

"*Bloodwing*'s hailing us, Captain," Uhura said from behind them.

"Put her on," Jim said.

"Captain," Ael's voice said. *"Tyrava signals that they are ready to move. The new convoy signals ready as well."*

"That's fine," Jim said. "We'll be ready to leave here in—" He glanced at Scotty.

"Two minutes to launch," Scotty said. "Four minutes until the generator kicks in, and another half a minute for the effect to propagate."

"At this *distance?"* Ael said. *"Mr. Scott, have you managed somehow to repeal the speed of light? Tr'Keirianh will be so disappointed that you did not consult with him first."*

Scotty straightened up again, but this time he was smiling slightly. "It's not a light-speed matter, Commander," he said. "When the effect propagates, it drills down through several layers of subspace; that's why it's going to be able to do the job we want done in the first place."

The turbolift doors slid open again, and this time K's't'lk came chiming in. The chiming was all in the major, a cheerful sound. "I finished its preflights, Sc'tty," she said. "The probe's ready to go."

"Aye," Scotty said, sounding more than slightly reluctant. The tone, however, didn't bother Jim. It was one he'd heard from Scotty many, many times, usually when something was about to work quite well—though that was never anything Scotty liked to admit to himself before the fact.

Scotty looked over at the captain. "We're ready to launch, Ael," Jim said. "Make sure that *Tyrava* and the others are at the proscribed safe distances."

"They are all standing away from the star at a minimum of two hundred million kilometers," Ael said.

It was about fifty million kilometers more than Scotty had said was strictly necessary. Jim smiled, only a little grimly. "The better part of valor," he said.

"'Twill only mean they don't get as good a view," Scotty said. "The star's optimal for our purposes." He touched a last few controls on his console, looked down at K's't'lk. She reared up on her front four legs, looked over the console with the forward rosette of eyes, and made a soft chiming sound of acquiescence.

"Ready, Captain," Scotty said.

"Do it, Mr. Scott," Jim said.

Scotty nodded over at Chekov. Chekov hit a control on his board, and Jim could feel the ship under him make that tiny, barely perceptible sound that said the inertial dampers were compensating for a torpedo launch.

On the screen they could see the sensor-augmented trace of the probe-torpedo as it streaked away from the *Enterprise.* Jim watched its course arcing gradually around toward 553 Trianguli. "Trajectory's fine," Scotty said quietly. "Setting up for hyperbolic orbit."

The screen showed the projected hyperbola. It would be a tight, fast curve around the star, a worst-case orbit. If the probe could do its job under such circumstances, its successors would do quite well when there was enough leisure to put them in more open, more stable orbits around other stars.

"The generators are on line," K's't'lk said. "Solving for the close-in data now." This, as Jim understood it, was the diciest part of the operation. To "unseed" a star correctly, the probe had to set up and then solve a number of extremely complex equations describing the behavior of the star's upper atmosphere, then tailor the field it would generate around the star to suit those equations—and keep changing the field every hundredth of a second or so to keep pace with the changes that had so far been made to the star.

Scotty and K's't'lk were both staring unblinkingly at the console above Scotty's station as the bar graphs and sines there flickered and danced. "There's your baseline, Sc'tty," K's't'lk said, sounding pleased. "Second-order solutions coming now."

Jim glanced back at the main viewscreen. "Push us in a little on that, would you, Mr. Sulu?" he said.

"Augmenting, Captain," said Sulu. The view of the star, filtered to a nonblinding sphere, swelled to fill the screen. It was a fairly quiet star at the moment, only a couple of sunspots flecking it here and there.

"Second-order data's done," Scotty said. "Now the fun begins. Probe's on auto now."

The bar graphs on the display above Scotty's station began to jump around most energetically. Jim looked at this with some slight concern, as was usual when he didn't have a clue how Scotty had the readouts calibrated, or what the calibrations meant.

He looked over at Spock. The science officer had been watching the readouts as intensely as Jim had. Now he put up one eyebrow. "Mr. Scott," he said, and looked away toward the viewscreen.

"Aye, I see it," Scotty said. "It's expected—just a herald effect."

The sunspots seemed to start bobbing up out of the star's photosphere like little black bubbles. And, like bubbles, they started to join up with one another, absorbing each other into larger and larger dark areas. Jim started to get a little unsettled as he watched this happening. There wasn't a one of those spots that wasn't the size of the Earth, and the joined-up ones were a whole lot bigger. "Scotty, is this supposed to—"

"Aye, Captain," Scotty said. "Some amount of this effect is unavoidable, while the star's finding its new equilibrium level and 'syncing up' with the other star. The probe has to readjust . . ."

And Scotty trailed off, watching the screen. Spock, at his station, had been peering down his viewer. He now stood up in what even for him looked like alarm. "Mr. Scott—"

On the screen, the star was going dark. The sunspot-blotches covering it spread, between one breath and the next, to cover maybe fifty percent of the star's surface. By the next breath, they had covered it all. The star had gone from something quite normal-looking to a strange smothered-looking body of an ashy darkness, all threaded with fading, twisting lines of fire.

A flash of furiously actinic light seared the whole bridge like a massive strobe, and whited out the screen. It took the screen some moments to adjust itself back down to normal levels again. When it did, Jim and the bridge crew found themselves looking at a star that was surrounded by a rapidly expanding shell of glowing hot plasma. At the shell's core was a roiling little red body that was rapidly collapsing.

Jim stared at the screen for a moment, then hit the comms button on the center seat's arm. *"Tyrava, Bloodwing."*

"Here," said Veilt, and *"Captain,"* said Ael.

"I think we need to back away from the star a little farther," Jim said. "We'll need to stay in the system for half an hour or so to get some more readings and find out what happened. Then it's time to move out for Augo."

"Agreed," said Veilt. *"Signal us when you are ready for departure."*

"Out," Jim said, and hit the comms button again. He spared one more glance for the rapidly collapsing red dwarf that had been 553 Trianguli, and then turned around to look at Scotty and K's't'lk.

They were both staring at the collapsing readings on Scotty's screen. Finally they both turned to look at Jim.

"It wasn't supposed to do *that*," K's't'lk said, in considerable shock.

"I would suggest," Jim said, "that if this is supposed to be deployed around any stars with inhabited planets, it had better *not* do that."

He stopped himself then, because it did no good to rub Scotty's nose in this kind of thing. The failure itself would drive him far harder than any amount of comment from his commanding officer. *And it's miraculous that he's come this far, even just at the theoretical end of things, under such circumstances.*

The problem is that we're going to need a lot more than theory. We need a version of this thing that works. He looked over at Spock. "Mr. Spock," he said, "can you shed any light on this?"

"We will need to get as many readings as possible in the next half hour, Captain," Spock said. "After that we will be in a better position to hypothesize. However, we have one more piece of data to add to the equation. I now have readings via the Neutral Zone satellites from 658 Tri, across the Zone, which was in sympathy with this star. It too has collapsed."

The silence on the bridge was deafening. Scotty hid his eyes with one hand.

"Very well," Jim said, and got up from the center seat. "Coordinate with Mr. Scott." He went over to the engineering station to glance at the readouts, then at Scotty. "Well, Scotty," he said, "if at first you don't succeed—"

"Aye, Captain," Scotty said, "but between getting to Augo, and dealing with what we find there, and then heading on to the Romulan Homeworlds afterward, we'll not have much opportunity to try, try again except in the computer. And the computer said that *this* should have worked."

Jim clapped Scotty on one shoulder and headed for the turbolift. "You're always telling me that the impossible takes a little longer," he said. "We'll be fine as long as it's *just* a little longer, Mr. Scott. See to it."

The lift doors closed on him.

FOURTEEN

ARRHAE STOOD in the front hall of House Khellian—just stood there silently, for many moments. She was staring across the hall at the commlink.

Behind her, she heard Mahan pass through the hall, and then stop abruptly, looking at her. There must have been something about her stance that kept him from speaking. *He sees the tension,* she thought; *others must not. Nor hear it in my voice.*

She reached out to touch the control pad of the commlink console. "Open channel," she said to the link.

"Open," it said in that unctuously courteous voice it had.

"Praetor tr'Anierh," she said.

"Public listing?" said the link.

"The office listing," Arrhae said. "It is flagged."

Behind her, it was very quiet. Mahan was still standing there and watching her, listening to her. Arrhae acted as if he hadn't noticed. *"Connecting,"* said the commlink. *"Please wait."*

Arrhae did. Behind her, she could just feel Mahan trying to decide whether to leave quietly before she officially took notice of him, or to stand there and discover what she was up to. More specifically, what trouble or danger she was *about* to be up to. Again, she paid him no mind.

"Connecting now," said the link. A second later, a masculine-like voice said, *"Praetor tr'Anierh's office."*

"This is Senator Arrhae i-Khellian," she said. "I wish you a good morning. Perhaps you can be kind enough to tell me when today the Praetor can clear some time from his schedule. He has asked me for a consultation, and I'm ready with the material he asked for."

The voice at the other end sounded a little dubious. *"He did not mention any such consultation to me, noble deihu."*

"I suspect there are many things that the noble Praetor does not mention to you," Arrhae said, and laughed, making sure that the laugh was kind, and meant to be understood as such. She had no intention of alienating tr'Anierh's subordinates, as she knew from her own work as *hru'hfe*, that was always a recipe for trouble. "I suspect it may have slipped his mind; he has been quite busy of late. If you would look into this for me, I would much appreciate it."

She listened carefully for the tone of the response, and was relieved when the young man who spoke sounded not all offended. *"Noble deihu,"* he said, *"if you could come about sixth hour, that would be well. The Praetor has but little spare time today. However, that is normally an optional leisure hour for him. I'm sure he will not mind releasing it to you if you have information he has requested, and if the session will be brief."*

"There is no problem with that," Arrhae said. "Brief it will be. I thank you for your assistance, sir—forgive me, I did not catch your name?"

"Alal tr'Fvennih," the Praetor's assistant said. *"It's my pleasure to be of service to the noble deihu."*

"And mine to speak to you, tr'Fvennih." Arrhae let the smile show in her voice. "I will see you, then, perhaps, a little after the noon meal. A fair morning to you."

"And to you, noble deihu."

Arrhae let her hand drop to the console and touch the link off. There she stood, for a moment or so more, mastering her breathing. At last she turned, and saw Mahan still standing there. Curiosity had overcome caution in him—a tendency of which she had long been aware. "Lay out a suit of midday darks for me, if you would, Mahan. I have a call to pay."

He looked at her with more than just a little concern. "Mistress, where are you going?"

He was rattled. It was unusual for him to ask so bold or bald a question, one so nonnuanced. "To the Praetor's," Arrhae said. "Come, Mahan, he won't eat me."

"Others might." Mahan came slowly over to her, his eyes suddenly full of the shadows of fear. "Mistress—what do you intend?"

"Nothing untoward," Arrhae said. "The Praetor has asked me to look out for some information. And I am about to give him some. Nothing new there."

But Mahan was not fooled. *Silly of me to think that he could be,* Arrhae thought. *We have been together too long, this old wise creature and I.*

She went the rest of the way over to him, and put a careful hand on his shoulder. It was as much intended to be a steadying gesture as one of a restrained intimacy. "Mahan, I have been in far worse danger than this before. I was in far worse danger on *Gorget.* There simply comes a time when one must not wait for the danger to come to one, like a *shauv* sitting in its hole. No point in waiting and watching while the winged shadows cross overhead again and again. Soon enough, one of them will drop from the sky. If possible, the goal of the game is not to be there when it does so. And to have that come about, sometimes one must move first."

She glanced around her. For all she knew, this might be the last time she ever saw the front hall of House Khellian, as either *hru'hfe* or senator, or as anything else that lived and breathed. But she could not spend time thinking about that now; any farewells she made from this point on were going to have to be brief. "Now, old friend, you have other business. You need to lay out that suit for me, and also to act as if nothing unusual is happening. Truly, nothing is. At least, not in the greater scheme of things. I have some other business to attend to right now. See to it that the clothes are ready for me in an hour."

And Arrhae turned and walked briskly away from him, trying with every fiber of her to communicate the message that, while things were going ill, they were not going *that* ill.

She heard no movement from behind her for some time. Finally, as she turned the corner of the corridor leading from the Great Hall to her office, she heard Mahan turn toward her own quarters. She regretted lying to him, but she refused to cause him more pain than was absolutely necessary. *The next day is likely to be difficult enough for all of us.*

And so it was that she came to stand on the doorstep of the Praetor's house. The staff had courteously enough sent a car for her. *See now,* she thought, *what good comes of a moment's kindness.* Had she had to take private transport herself, all kinds of attention would have been paid to her arrival, much sooner than she would have cared to have it happen. Now, though, because she had been courteous to tr'Anierh's assistant, the others who were doubtless watching her moves and his would see this as only another fairly routine meeting, one that had happened a few times before. And who knew? There might even be those who would think that this was the beginning of a relationship less than political, less than platonic. Arrhae smiled slightly as she stood there on the doorstep. Such misapprehensions were always useful as cover. They had been so for her before; they might yet again.

If I live out the week.

The door swung open for her. "Noble *deihu,*" said the young man who opened the door to her, "you are very welcome."

She recognized the voice. "I thank you for your welcome,

tr'Fvennih," she said. "I hope I have not too much troubled you or your noble employer today. But with events moving so quickly . . ." She shrugged. "He will not long have time for such lesser matters, I fear. Best to handle them now, before things become too . . . broken loose." She raised her eyebrows at tr'Fvennih in a resigned way as they walked across the Great Hall of tr'Anierh's residence.

The young man looked at her in a way that suggested he agreed, though it was not his position to be saying so. He opened the door to tr'Anierh's study; she stepped inside. "If you'll wait here for a few moments, noble *deihu*," he said, "the Praetor will be with you shortly. He is finishing his noon meal, and I dislike interrupting him. He has little enough leisure in these days as it is." He gestured over to a pair of easy chairs on the side of the room; a tray and jug and a pair of cups, and several small plates of dainties, sat on a table between them. "If you'll make yourself comfortable there and await the Praetor, he'll be with you shortly."

Arrhae smiled and bowed to him, just a shade more deeply than she needed to. Tr'Fvennih smiled back at her, and closed the door.

She went to sit down in one of those chairs, taking the one nearer the window; she very much wanted to see the light on tr'Anierh's face as she said what she had come to say. Arrhae reached out for the jug, poured herself a very small tot of ale, and tossed it directly off. She was not above using its paired stimulant and depressant qualities to her own advantage at the moment. Then she waited.

While in the midst of pouring a little more into the glass, the door opened again, and tr'Anierh came in. Arrhae made as if to rise and bow; he held a hand to stop her.

She smiled at him and went on pouring, this time pouring into his cup as well. Tr'Anierh settled himself in the chair opposite her, and once again empty pleasantries about the weather were spoken. But after a few moments, tr'Anierh reached out to that cup of ale and said, "Noble *deihu,* while I recall asking you for information, I did not think it would be ready for my attention so soon. Of your courtesy, tell me what you have for me. The rest of the day is going to be fairly busy, and I have not too much time to spare right now."

Arrhae bowed her head to him a little. "Noble patron, I have a small item of news. My sorrow is that I did not come to you with it more quickly. I was unsure how to couch it." She shook her head. "But the brunt of it is: you're betrayed. Those with most to gain by it have spoken a word in the ears of those in whose minds that word will eventually be the most damaging—and so I came to warn you, and to see how I might help you in this."

Tr'Anierh's eyes widened a little. He raised his eyebrows, and at her earnest look, just shook his head a little and slightly smiled. "Arrhae, I grant you have been through much in recent days. But for you, this turn of phrase seems somewhat . . . theatrical?" He said it kindly enough.

"So it might," Arrhae said. "As you say, your day is busy. I will be brief. Indeed, for those who are doubtless watching, brevity is probably best. It will suggest that nothing in particular has gone wrong." She looked up at him from under her brows. "Yesterday, the commlink rang in my house."

Tr'Anierh held quite still.

"The one who rang it," Arrhae said, "is now dead. And those who caused his death are pleased that it should be so. As it happens, his death has not served their purpose. The word that was meant to come to me has done so regardless. And now I bring it to you. If I do so somewhat hastily, it is because I am not sure how much longer they will feel they can afford to leave me alive."

Tr'Anierh still had not moved, not a millimeter more than he needed to breathe. "The import of that call," Arrhae said, "was that information has been planted in the most damaging possible place concerning you and your connection to a great blow that is about to be struck against our enemies." Arrhae got up, casually enough, and went over to that beautiful table—the one that had the long, long stanza of the "Song of the Sun" inlaid with platinum wire just under its glossy top. Idly she ran her hand along one side of the table, along the first verse of the stanza; then she glanced up, expecting him to take the meaning of the glance. "Agents on the far side of the Outmarches have been primed with 'proof' of your instigation of the dispatch of the 'package' that has been quietly making its way into Federation space. When it does its intended job," and she smiled slightly and kept on walking around the table, trailing her hand along the long, silvery verse, "they intend for those long planted in Starfleet Command's extrasolar branches and in the higher structures of the older planetary governments to bring *your* name forward as the one to blame. You are the one at whose doorstep this 'great crime' will be laid. We—" Her eyes flicked toward the chair in which another Praetor had recently sat. "—will be seen to be merely innocent pawns of your plan—victims, as uninvolved as anyone on the Earth was."

Arrhae looked up at tr'Anierh from the far end of the table, its shining expanse stretching between them. In the light from the window, his face looked suddenly rather pale. "The rest of the Federation," Arrhae said, "will come for you, and for the Hearthworlds. They will come to take such a vengeance on these two planets as no one can imagine. The Empire will be shattered, reduced to nothing. Eventually, of course, it will be rehabilitated. And in this your allies, or should I say your opponents, intend to climb up to their new places on *your* scourged back. They have their own plans— of a reconstituted Empire, one more amenable to their bidding—an aggregate of the most cooperative surviving colony worlds. They have been manipulating the intelligence that reaches you to make it seem a certainty that the Federation would come undone with Earth gone and Earth's humanity destroyed." Arrhae shook her head. "But the more accurate intelligence has been kept from you, to serve their purpose. And when the infuriated allies of our destroyed enemy arrive, it is you who, in the sudden capitulation following a few brief battles, will be handed over to them to stand trial for the ultimate 'crime against humanity'—the extinguishing of the Homeworld of a whole species. Those opponents of yours will take up their positions as inheritors of the new Empire, which will rise from the ashes of the old. And you—" Arrhae came around to the bottom of the table again. "Of you, alive in some prison for your life's length, or executed for your crimes, the new masters of a new Empire will count themselves well rid."

Arrhae stood by the end of the table and held quite still, watching the Praetor.

"Why, Arrhae," he said at last, "your imagination does you credit." But he could not quite hide a tremor in his voice.

"Would that it were only so fertile as you think it," Arrhae said. "I would have been better able to conceive of a way out of the situation in which you and I find ourselves today. You, noble patron, have been kind to me. I felt it only right to warn you. Soon, now, those others who until now have commanded your trust will begin coming to you with all manner of tales about how my commlink rang, about what that call really meant. They count on it being as it has so often been among our people before: the best way to discredit the message is to discredit the messenger. The Intelligence people—" She looked at him narrowly. "They do not love you, noble patron. Far less do they love me. To them, I'm a jumped-up housekeeper." And then she smiled. "But how does the saying go? 'It's a poor *hru'hfe* who doesn't know what's in the cupboards.' "

She came away from the table, and sat down once again in the easy chair, on the edge of it, her hands folded in her lap. She leaned toward tr'Anierh, intense. "It will be easy,

noble patron, for them to cast me to you as a traitor. I swear
to you, I am none such. If they are allowed, those others will
see to it, shortly, that I am dead—as dead as that poor man
who rang one ring on my commlink, trying to save your life,
and mine, and the lives of many hundreds of thousands of
people in this world who do not deserve to have the Empire
pulled down around their ears for the sake of someone else's
ambition. Yet this will happen . . . unless you stop them."

"It is all very well—" tr'Anierh began, and then stopped
himself. He raised his eyes to Arrhae. "How do you come by
this data, noble *deihu?*"

She raised her eyebrows. "You put me in the way of it
yourself, noble patron. You sent me to *Gorget,* and to
Mascrar, where many voices spoke, sometimes not being as
careful as they might have about who heard them. Especially
when they thought that the one who heard them was more interested in polishing the furniture." She gave him a wicked
look, finally letting a little amusement show through. "As a
result, I was able to make connections of which they knew
nothing. Many others there, as you intended, undervalued
me, the Intelligence operatives perhaps most of all. That, too,
was as you desired it, was it not? That I should be seen to be
like the bright little insect that sits on the warm wall, fanning
its wings in the sunshine, without enough brain in its head to
carry a thought in. People were to see me as a gesture of your
goodwill, a political gesture perhaps, something guaranteed
to win you support among the common throng of people on
ch'Rihan. And so it has, indeed. But, as you also intended,
your action has provided you with information you would
not otherwise have had. Such as this."

Arrhae held her peace and watched him. Tr'Anierh's eyes
were fixed on something she could not see. Then, finally, he
looked up at her again. "You're right," he said. "I have chosen a sharper weapon than I knew."

"I hope that may be so," Arrhae said. "But now they de-

sire to turn that weapon in your hand. Oh, doubtless that is
the choice I shall be offered, at least, if they're merciful. To
turn traitor, join myself to their cause as the price of my life.
If they are not merciful," she shook her head, "I will be dead
within a week. But at least I have satisfied *mnhei'sahe* by
bringing you the information you need to save yourself from
their plans. Possibly, even to save many more of us. What
happens now, depends on you."

He was looking at the table now. "If all this is true—"

"You will have little time to find proof," Arrhae said.
"Even to do so will start turning your tiles up on the table,
when you least need them seen. But this I would say: now,
noble sir, we must stand together. There is no other hope for
us. If they split us apart one from the other, we're both done.
Together . . . together we stand some chance. And you," Arrhae said, leaning ever so slightly closer to him, "you have a
better chance than they think to turn their plans tails-up in
the air."

He looked at her. *Now,* Arrhae thought, *everything, everything rides on this. This one last throw.* "There is another
stroke coming, as you know. Not that great one, but the im-
pending action that is meant to stave off the threat from the
colonies and the one who is bringing the Federation against
you. The others have tried to keep you from taking any active
part in what's about to happen there."

Tr'Anierh sat there quietly for just a moment more.
"Augo." His face changed.

"Now there lies an opening before you," Arrhae said. "A
way both to put aside the stroke they're aiming at you, and to
take matters—perhaps unexpectedly—into your own hands.
By this action, and the document trail you may now begin to
preserve—though carefully, away from all prying eyes who
might see it too soon—you will be able to prove that you
were the one who saw the wave of the future rising, and prepared for it. You saw the threat coming from the Federation,

and counseled restraint, a careful and conservative response. Negotiation, compromise. But others would not listen; others acted to destroy their enemies utterly. And when you discovered what terrible thing those others were doing in your name, you moved to stop it." She gave him a sly look. "In the most straightforward way, since many of the agents intended to carry word of your 'guilt' to the Federation are part of the complement that is being sent to Augo. It is, after all, on their way."

Tr'Anierh sat still and quiet for a while more. Arrhae could practically hear plot jostling against plot in his mind, chance against chance, gamble against gamble. *But from here on in,* she thought, *it's all gambling anyway. Anyone who thinks otherwise is a fool. Too many forces are moving, in too many directions, for chance not to take its part. The least I can do is help it along.*

For a long time, tr'Anierh sat there, doing the mathematics of paranoia and political calculation in his head. He was astute in that art. Arrhae did not expect him to take long about it. And when at last he looked up at her, his mind was made up, though very few other people could have seen it.

"It has been good having this chat with you, noble *deihu*," he said. "Getting a fresh perspective on old problems. In days to come, we'll meet again. We'll speak more of this in good time, insofar as it's safe to speak of it at all." He leaned back in the chair, turning around and around the cup of ale she had poured for him, and of which he had drunk very little. He glanced up at her again. "You will know—of *course* you will know—how close you have been to death, these last few minutes."

"Noble patron," Arrhae said, rising and gracefully bowing to him, "that old companion rides with us everywhere we go, closer than the vein in the neck or the heart in the side—so the poet says. The whole point of this exercise is, for a short time at least, to draw a little further away from it, for both ourselves and our people. Meanwhile, I hope I have the noble Praetor's leave to depart. His day is almost certainly going to be busier than mine."

Tr'Anierh rose, and then bowed to Arrhae. It was a gesture that both shocked her and heartened her; it was one she had never hoped to see. "I would say that would be true," he said. "If either of us survive the night, I will see you perhaps tomorrow."

He opened the study door for her. Arrhae went out, moving easily, taking the greatest care to keep any of the thoughts in her mind from showing in her body. But there were no guns waiting for her in the hallway, no armed security staff waiting on the doorstep. Only the air car in which she had come sat quietly off to one side, its pilot leaning against it in the sunshine, trying to soak up some of the good weather through his uniform.

Arrhae walked up to the car, unable quite to get rid of the feeling of how lightly she was walking on the earth. She had more or less said good-bye to it when she arrived only—she glanced at her chrono. *Only half an hour ago!* So much could happen in a short time, when the stars were in the right configurations, and one's mind was focused.

Now all that remained was to see whether she had correctly focused tr'Anierh's mind in the direction she desired. But as the pilot handed her up into the car, Arrhae smiled, remembering something her mother had told her so many years ago. *A lie gets stronger the more truth you mix with it.* She had told a lot of truth today, but in such a way as to bounce back ruinously on those whom she was sure were already taking aim at her. Now they would have not one target, but two, and the rebound from the second might be fatal for her enemies, and might buy the friends far out in the interstellar night some time to save their world, and hers.

There was nothing to do now but wait, and think what to do next.

Arrhae leaned back against the cushions of the car as it lifted off, closed her eyes, and began.

Aboard the *Enterprise,* now under way with the Free Rihannsu fleet and making for Augo, Jim sat in the center seat and looked thoughtfully at the strange arrangement that was being erected between the viewscreen and the helm console. Right now there was a framework of light there, just green grid lines in the air, filling the whole space from floor to ceiling, and off to one side of it Sulu was standing and looking at it in a speculative way.

"Two-D isn't going to be enough, sir," Sulu had said to him. "Eventually they're going to have to design better displays for us. There's simply no way any engagement commander should seriously be expected to manage an extensive 3-D encounter in two dimensions. It makes no more sense than if the Academy tried to teach you fleet maneuver tactics by drawing them for you on a chalkboard, or pieces of paper." Sulu shook his head at the idea. "But I don't see why we should be crippled by waiting for what they see fit to install. This rig should help you see what's going on around us a lot more clearly."

"Don't think I'm fooled, Mr. Sulu," Jim said. "This is all just part of your secret master plot to turn my bridge into a tank game."

Sulu smiled a very secretive smile, verging on the archetypically inscrutable. "Those tank games have been played out up here often enough, Captain, and as a result, we're still breathing."

Jim gestured helplessly, shaking his head, and got up out of the center seat, walking around the helm console. Several people from engineering were busily installing 3-D and holographic image implementers in or on all those consoles nearest to the main viewscreen. "Are you sure we're going to have enough room for this to do me any good?" Kirk said.

"It looks like a tight fit for what we're going to have to be able to see."

Sulu nodded. "It's fully and automatically scalable, a lot more so than the viewscreen ever was. Believe me, Captain, you're going to find this an incredible improvement. Mr. Chekov and Khiy and I learned a whole lot from Artaleirh. We were working in 2-D there, and still managed to pull it off. This, though, is going to work a whole lot better."

Jim glanced up at the engineering staffers, who were climbing down from the stepladders or levitating pads they were using. "Looks like we're ready," Sulu said. "Okay, Ali, give it the goose."

Into the green-gridded space between the helm console and the front viewer, the schematic of the Augo system suddenly sprang into being in three dimensions. Jim walked about halfway into it. Immediately, he could see the disposition of the various worlds—the two innermost planets with the Grand Fleet refueling bases on them, the one supply base farther out in the system, and the planets' small orbital defense networks. He could also see, rather annoyingly, a cluster of lights in coded colors, representing about thirty Rihannsu capital ships posted to the area. "The display's showing the most recent data from *Tyrava*," Sulu said. "What you see there will update in real time when we're in the system. Right now we're only getting half-hourly squirts with the ship-disposition details." He stood there, favoring the display with a rather jaundiced look as he walked around it.

Jim was doing the same, for entirely different reasons. "It's a beautiful piece of work, Mr. Sulu. There's only one problem with it."

"What would that be, Captain?" Mr. Sulu said.

"That its very presence here implies that I'm not going to be allowed into the fight," Jim said.

"Ah, well, sir," Sulu said, smiling slightly, "that's the price of admiralty, no matter what the poem says. Not blood; safety."

"Relative safety," Jim said. "Don't remind me." He frowned as Sulu reached over to the helm console, touched a control, and the display rotated. "I enjoy a good session of battle strategy as well as the next man, but having to sit in the background and watch other people enact it? That's another story."

"Don't think we have much choice, in this case," Sulu said. "We're the flag carrier. It'd be pretty careless in terms of the whole engagement for us to allow them to shoot us up. Ael would be annoyed."

Jim raised his eyebrows. "*She'd* be annoyed!" he said. "Oh, well, we can't have *that*."

Sulu chuckled, making his way back around to his proper side of the console to sit down and make a few more adjustments to its controls. Jim came to look over his shoulder. Sulu worked for a moment more, then looked up. "But that's the whole point, isn't it?" Sulu said. "It's not just us we have to keep intact. It's her."

"Particularly her," he said. "Whether Starfleet likes it or not, she's become invaluable to the future stability of the Empire." *And also because,* he thought, *despite the wonderfulness of the little widget that tr'AAnikh brought us, it's not going to be anything like enough to satisfy the parameters in my sealed orders. I'm going to need a whole lot more technology than that. And she's going to be the only one who can give it to me.*

"What's our ETA to Augo now, Mr. Sulu?"

"Twenty hours, Captain."

"Of which I'm going to have to spend about ten getting used to this," Jim said.

"Oh, not more than five," Sulu said. "You wouldn't want to miss the poker game."

Jim put his eyebrows up. "Mr. Sulu—"

"You'd better be there, Captain," Sulu said. "Mr. Tanzer will inform on you to Dr. McCoy if you don't."

Jim sighed. "You people are all plotting against me. I'm beginning to understand how Ael feels."

Now it was Sulu's turn to put up the eyebrows. "Could be dangerous. I mean, in terms of long-term strategic goals."

There was something slightly peculiar about the way Sulu said that. Maybe the strange way it struck Jim showed in his face, for Sulu quickly turned and started being abnormally busy with his console. *Could it be,* Jim thought, *could there be the* slightest *possibility that my crew have seriously started to think that Ael—that the commander and I are an item?*

He blinked. And then he turned away and grinned a rather sour grin to himself. *Well, why shouldn't they? Starfleet certainly does.*

The idiots.

The only thing that bothered Jim was that his crew, as he well knew, were not idiots.

He turned back to look at the nascent tank display. "When will that be ready, Mr. Sulu?"

"About an hour, Captain," Sulu said, not looking up.

"Very well. I'm going down to the mess for some lunch. Give me a call when it's ready." He headed for the lift. "And Mr. Sulu—what time is that poker game?"

"Twenty hundred, Captain."

The lift doors closed.

Twenty hundred came with surprising speed. Jim walked into recreation to find it fairly quiet. There were some people involved with a tank game off to one side—Jim glanced at it in passing and noted a large Klingon war fleet being more or less cut to pieces by some people from biochemistry—and some others having a small impromptu smorgasbord. His attention, though, was focused on a large round baize-covered table over near the main windows, where cards were being dealt. Scotty was there, and K's't'lk; Uhura was there, and Sulu, and Spock, and McCoy; and Ael and her chief engineer, tr'Keirianh. There was an empty chair with its back to the windows. Jim wandered around and took it. "What's the game?" he said.

"Seven-card stud," Sulu said, "jacks are wild."

Everyone was drinking Romulan ale. Jim looked at the jug on the nearby service table, thought of what was going to start happening in fifteen hours, and hesitated.

"Oh, come on, Jim," McCoy said, "you know I can detox you in twenty minutes. Don't be such a stick."

Jim sighed. A moment later a glass was in front of him with three fingers of ale in it. Sulu started to deal.

"Now let me see if I have this correct," Ael said. "Each player receives two cards facedown and one card faceup. Initial bet is twice the aunt—"

"Ante," Uhura said. "Commander, I'm sorry, the homonym routine is still giving me grief."

"Play goes clockwise from the opener," Ael said. "One invokes 'call' or 'raise' if—"

"It's easier to just play," Sulu said. "Come on, Scotty, you open and show her how it's done."

They played. Chips were pushed into the center of the table, and the ebb and flow of the game began. Jim was watching Ael's play with some interest, as was McCoy on the other side of her. She seemed to be doing fairly well. Then suddenly she lost almost all her pot. This happened again about twenty minutes later, and Jim, watching, at that point noticed something strange: Ael was squinting at her cards, not just when she got new ones, but all the time. He leaned toward her.

"Too much ale, Commander?" he said, only slightly teasing. "Need a detox? I'm sure McCoy can tailor something for you."

"No, that is not the problem," Ael said, sounding a little puzzled. "However, I cannot seem to do much with these cards. The symbols really are too much alike for me." She looked over at McCoy. "Perhaps we could use those you showed me earlier?"

Jim was bemused by the faintly shocked look McCoy suddenly acquired. "Uh, I don't know."

Harb Tanzer, passing by, looked down at McCoy. "Problem?"

"Harb," McCoy said, "do you have a spare New Waite deck around here? One that isn't used routinely for more serious purposes."

"I have a few in their original wraps," Harb said. "Half a moment."

Shortly he was back, and not long after that Jim found himself involved in one of the most peculiar poker games he had ever experienced. A full house acquired all kinds of additional nuances when it actually involved pictures of what appeared to be relatives of the crowned heads of Europe, some of them holding extremely sharp objects and looking prepared to use them. The other players seemed more amused than annoyed by the change, and once the extra cards in the deck had values attributed to them, the game proceeded without too many more hitches—except as regarded Jim's hands, which seemed uniformly poor for the better part of the first hour.

"Hit me," Scotty said.

Ael threw him a most peculiar look. "With what?"

"It's just an expression," K's't'lk said. She was studying her own cards with some bemusement. "Do three cups beat two pages?"

"Only in three-trump stud," McCoy said.

Ael's expression got more confused all through this. As the game went forward, Jim saw that she was regarding the cards in her hand with not much more comprehension than she had shown with the standard Rider deck. "I am not entirely sure what to do here," she said at last.

Such an admission was unusual from Ael, and provoked various kinds of advice. "Get a sandwich," Sulu said. "Have some more ale," Scotty said, and reached behind him for the jug.

McCoy put his hand down, got up from his chair, and went around behind Ael to look at her hand. She glanced up at him. He raised his eyebrows.

"Okay," he said, "I see the problem. Let's try something else." He glanced around the table.

"Three-trump stud?" Sulu said.

McCoy shook his head. "Tournament Fizzbin."

Jim opened his eyes at that. *"Tournament* Fizzbin?"

"Dealer invents a new version," McCoy said, and went around the table, starting to collect everybody's cards. "Come on, Scotty, hand 'em over; that hand wasn't so great. Sulu . . . Good. All right. Come on, Ael. You get to invent a version of Fizzbin."

"I do not know the original," she said, looking completely at a loss. "It was not in *Hoyle.*"

"No indeed," McCoy said. "Jim, would you elucidate?"

Jim grinned rather helplessly and took the deck. "All right. So each player gets six cards, except the one on the player's right, who gets seven." He started dealing. "The second card is turned up, except on Tuesdays."

"Is today Tuesday?" Sulu said, suddenly suspicious.

"It's got to be Tuesday *somewhere,* Mr. Sulu," Scotty said.

Spock raised both eyebrows at this, but said nothing. "Stipulated," Jim said. "Now, two jacks is a half-fizzbin, but you don't want three. Three is a shralk. You get those, you get disqualified."

"You do?" Ael said, beginning to smile slightly.

"Absolutely. Now look there: Sulu's got two jacks. That's good. Now he wants a king and a deuce."

"Except at night," McCoy said, looking over at Ael's cards. "In which case he wants a queen and an ace."

"How is 'night' determined?" tr'Keirianh said. "If playing aboard ship, does ship's time prevail? Or is it always considered to be night in space?"

"Yes, and if members of more than one ship's complement are involved," Ael said, "must a consensus of the players be obtained?"

"Only in leap year," Jim said.

"When the moon is full," said Sulu, straight-faced.

"Now wait a minute," K's't'lk said. "*Whose* moon?"

"And why should a year leap?" Ael said.

It went on in that vein for some time, and more ale was ingested to assist the philosophical and scientific arguments that ensued. Eventually a game started, and Jim was none too sure of who started it, but the structure of its rules became unnervingly fluid, even by the somewhat freewheeling standards of the man who'd invented Fizzbin.

Play went forward. It wasn't just a game, but play in the older sense of the word. Jim got a clear sense that none of the people around the table felt like being too rigorous about rules on the night before a day that was principally going to be full of the rules of engagement. *The only thing we haven't done yet is fifty-two pickup,* Jim thought, leaning back in his chair, as the laughter got more sheerly goofy. *Except with this deck I don't think it's fifty-two. Fifty-six? Seventy?*

He shrugged and got on with it. Another round began—Ael started it, this time—and before long the table was foundering in an uproar of laughter, with whole piles of chips changing hands from second to second. Only Spock held aloof from the laughter, but Jim wasn't concerned. He had long learned to pick up on the amusement carefully concealed behind his first officer's eyes. When the deck came around to him, Jim found himself forced to surpass his wildest output of that strange time on Sigma Iotia II.

Much more madness ensued. And it must have been at least two hours later when Jim noticed that Scotty was leaning back in his chair, rubbing his eyes, and tr'Keirianh, to his immense embarrassment, could not quite stifle a yawn.

Jim stood up, stretching. "It's time. Gentlemen, ladies, thanks for your company. I have an early morning, and so do all of you. We'd better go get some rest."

The players rose and started to say their good nights, heading for the doors. Ael paused by Jim and gave him a weary smile. "Not a night I will soon forget," she said, "assuming the Elements spare me for long memory." She glanced over at McCoy. "But a word with you first, McCoy. For you, everything is a diagnostic."

McCoy raised his eyebrows. "Nothing could have been further from my mind."

She cuffed his shoulder in an amiable way. "You are incorrigible," Ael said.

"And you are a talented observer," McCoy said. "Message? If there was one, it would have been just this: in some situations, the only sane thing to do is change the rules. Just make sure you change them *your* way."

She gave him a look. Then, in company with tr'Keirianh, Ael went off to the transporters, and to *Bloodwing,* with an unusual expression on her face. McCoy and Jim stood together and watched them go. The door to the rec room slid shut behind them.

"What was that about?" Jim said.

"Tension relief," McCoy said. "I'd say it worked. And for your part, I think you enjoyed being reminded of a time when the situation was no worse than having a couple of guys pointing machine guns at you."

"Oh, come on, Bones, it was worse than that. The Iotians—"

McCoy shook his head. "Never mind that. What time will

things start getting crazy in the morning? Just so I know when to start securing the various valuables."

"Beginning of alpha shift," Jim said. "We'll be dropping out of warp and going on red alert about an hour after that."

McCoy clasped Jim's shoulder, then headed out. "Call me if you need anything."

Jim nodded and turned to stand for a few moments regarding the stars streaming past the big glasteel windows.

He stood there in the quiet for a while. *"Something, Captain?"* said the voice of Moira, the rec computer.

"No," Jim said. "But thanks."

He went to bed.

FIFTEEN

SIX HOURS LATER, just before the end of gamma shift, Jim was sitting in the center seat, looking into his new tank. *Sulu was right,* he thought. *You could really get used to this. The question is, am I used enough to it now?*

The bridge crew had been coming in early as well. Spock had been there before him, and as Jim had come in, had simply handed him a padd full of status reports. "*Enterprise* is ready," he said, and went quietly back to his station, plainly not wanting to disturb his captain's train of thought.

Jim had gone through the reports and confirmed that they said, in rather more words and detail, simply what Spock had said. In particular, the ships of the joint fleet had checked and double-checked their connections to *Enterprise*'s, *Bloodwing*'s, and *Tyrava*'s joint command-and-control system, and everything was operational. Every ship's movements would be repeated into the holographic tank at the front of the bridge, where Jim would very shortly start his admiralty-level work.

Now he sat in the center seat, watching all his people doing their job in their normal calm, and started to endure the worst part of such an engagement: the waiting.

"Enterprise."

"*Tyrava?*" Jim said, relieved.

"*Warp egress in three minutes, Captain,*" Veilt said. "*We

will be at optimum pre-battle envisioning position, 'above' the system."

"Thank you, sir," Jim said, and went to sit in the center seat again. "Do you have more recent disposition data for me?"

"Coming over now."

The display in the tank changed. Jim walked over, peered down into it, counted the little sparks of light that he saw there. "Veilt," he said, "I'd really like to know where those other thirty ships are."

"Forty," Veilt said.

Jim passed a hand over his eyes. "Another ten?" he said. "When did we hear about these?"

"Within the last hour," Veilt said. *"Captain, I would suggest that the 'fog of war' has begun to descend in earnest. Our earlier discussions suggested that there is no way Grand Fleet has this much materiel available. However, we cannot be certain, as they have not taken us into their confidence."*

"Noted," Jim said. He put out a hand, and without a word Spock stepped up beside him and put a padd into it, with the battle plan already brought up to the correct page. He pulled the stylus off the padd and started making notes. "I'm sending you some emendations to part three that take the new numbers into account."

"We have four versions of part three already, Captain."

"You're about to have six. Do you want to disseminate it, or shall I ask *Bloodwing* to handle that?"

"We will handle it gladly, Captain. We have many more personnel available to double-check the translation."

God knows how many of whom aren't really on our side, Jim thought. But this was no time for paranoia. "Thank you, Veilt. And sir—if by chance we have no other time for this before things get busy—the Elements' own luck to you."

There was the briefest pause. *"Captain, the same to you, and I think the saying is, 'and many more.' "*

Jim smiled. "Out. Uhura, *Bloodwing?*"

"Bloodwing," said Aidoann's voice. *"My apologies, Captain. I am not used to these automatic connections either, but the* khre'Riov *says that they will save us much time."*

"Is the commander there yet?"

"On her way now."

"Egress in two minutes," Sulu said.

"Right," Kirk said. He hit the button on the center seat that gave him all-call; that at least still worked in the normal way. "All hands," he said as calmly as he could, "battle stations, battle stations. This is no drill."

The sirens started to whoop. Jim had to smile at himself at that point. Habit could make you say funny things, especially when this was a scheduled maneuver, and every soul inside this vessel knew perfectly well that this was no drill.

After a couple of moments the whooping stopped. "Ready to drop out, Captain," Sulu said.

"On the mark, Mr. Sulu."

The warp engines died back to a whisper, and instantly the ships and other bodies displayed in the tank snapped into new positions. Jim could see the whole system laid out before him in three dimensions . . . and once again he was pleased at how, for once, random effects had worked in their favor. The two planets around which the Grand Fleet facilities orbited, or on which they were sited, were nearly in opposition to one another—one of them at aphelion, and one of them at perihelion in an orbit that was very skewed from the system ecliptic. "I make that about four hundred million kilometers apart," Kirk said, looking over his shoulder at Spock.

"Affirmative," Spock said, "within twenty-three million, six hundred eighty thousand, five hundred twenty-three point six six kilometers or so."

" 'Or . . . so,' " Jim said.

Spock did not rise to the bait. "Once again, Captain, the ships in-system have divided their forces."

Jim shook his head grimly. "They're slow learners, Mr. Spock. I think we may have to speed up their learning curve a little bit. *Tyrava?*"

"Captain," Veilt said. *"We seem to find them very poorly disposed."*

"You've got that in one," Kirk said. "I'd still like to know where those other forty ships are."

"You would not be alone," Veilt said. *"Nonetheless, we cannot wait to see if they arrive."*

"Agreed," Kirk said. "This disposition closely matches—" He glanced off to one side at the screen. "—variation two-c of our joint plan."

"It does," Veilt said.

"Let's implement, then. And for everything's sake, *Tyrava,* watch out for any sign of the hexicyclic wave we saw on Artaleirh."

"Agreed," Veilt said. *"Out."*

They swept in toward the closer of the two planets, tagged as Thanith, the one around which orbited the smaller of the two Grand Fleet supply facilities. From it, a little swarm of ships fled outward to meet them; the larger capital ships hung back. "They know what's coming," Kirk said, settling back into the center seat. "Fleet A, this is Kirk." He glanced at Uhura to make sure the message was going out. She nodded. "Engage to plan. Go, go, go!"

In the tank, he could see many of the smaller ships, led and protected by two of the captured Romulan vessels, arcing outward in a great formation like an opening flower. It could have been mistaken for a standard englobement, but it was no such thing. Under cover of the Free Rihannsu capital ships, the smaller vessels were arcing around behind the investing capital ships, making their way to where they could start the routines that had subordinated and rendered helpless the present Free Rihannsu vessels. The investing ships might not have been clear about what exactly the smaller ships intended to do; but they fired at them regardless.

This did them little good. As Kirk had anticipated, the sheer numbers and the nimbleness of the smaller ships, especially in intersystem combat like this, made them difficult for the big ships to handle. He also knew that a significant proportion of them, perhaps seven to ten percent of them, would be lost in the attack. But he knew, and Veilt had agreed, that in a situation like this, there were definitely acceptable levels of loss. The small ships would buy time and create a distraction for the still smaller, more stealthy ones that would be fastening themselves to the big capital ships, suborning their systems, and taking them offline. If they could be reduced without being destroyed, that would be useful, but right now the large-scale situation of destroying them, and denying them to Grand Fleet, had become as valuable a goal as keeping them. Either way, the main priority was to render them useless for command-and-control.

Most important of all, now, was to take out the biggest of the supercapital vessels, the ones that were acting as C&C for the capital ships. Rigorous and rigid as Rihannsu command structure could be, Jim knew that the planetside C&C facilities would not easily share power with the capital ships suddenly wished on them by Grand Fleet from afar. Neither would the Grand Fleet facilities take kindly to planetside commands telling them what to do with their ships. Jim had been counting on this split; Ael had let him know about the depth of it. The two rival groups would not easily pick up one another's function, no matter what they'd been threatened with. *Pick off all of one side's C&C, therefore, and both sides get easier to handle.*

Jim watched the biggest capital ships plunge away from the smallships attacking them, like infuriated cattle fleeing a swarm of stinging flies. They were trying to break away from the little ships and come to grips with the larger vessels they saw hanging tantalizingly just out of range. "*Tyrava*," Jim said, "now."

"*As in the choreography, Captain,*" *Tyrava*'s comms officer replied.

Jim smiled, hearing the sound of Veilt reminding him, at one remove, that he understood the battle plan perfectly well. "Thank you," Jim said, allowing the amusement to show in his voice just a little. He gazed into the tank, watching *Tyrava* come coasting in toward the farther planet, a not insignificant bulk even at this distance and scale. *Tyrava* had been well out into the system; now she had swung in fast from the outer portion of the system, as initially agreed. The enemy capital ships, some ten of them, gave up chasing the small ships and turned to engage.

It was a mistake, as Jim had intended it to be. Those capital ships that lost their attention on what the small ships were doing swiftly became vulnerable to them, while *Tyrava,* in a leisurely manner, began carving up the first couple of the capital ships. This, as usual, was the point in whatever engagement he was studying that would normally make Jim nervous: the point where everything seemed to be going according to plan. The dictates of the War Gods were very much on his mind, especially Churchill's old warning that no battle plan survives contact with the enemy.

He cast a quick glance over at the other Grand Fleet facility. Its own ships were holding close, not moving out; they were waiting to see what happened. "All right," Jim said. "Time, I think, to stir things up a little on the other side."

"*We would appear to have things well in hand over here,*" Veilt said, "*at least for the moment.*"

"Understood," Kirk said. "*Bloodwing?*"

"*Here, Captain,*" Ael said. "*We have been monitoring. Beginning sequence two-c.* "

"Go," Kirk said. "And watch out for them."

"We will do that," Ael said.

The secondary task force led by *Bloodwing* and the two other Free Rihannsu capital ships flashed toward the second Grand Fleet facility. Its ships immediately leapt out of orbit and toward the attackers, flinging themselves wide in an attempt to keep the same maneuver that had been used on the first facility from being used on them.

It was all that Jim could've hoped for. The other Free Rihannsu capital ships, finding their enemies so obligingly scattered, were able to take them one-on-one. With their augmented weaponry, the battle began quickly to turn in their favor—though, again, they were being careful to disable, not to destroy. *The question is, of course, how quickly we're going to be able to put those ships back into operation,* Jim thought, watching it all unfold in the tank. *If this fight is conclusive enough, it might actually significantly shorten the final conflict at ch'Rihan. Then again, of course, if it's not, there's always the possibility it will provoke an intermediary engagement somewhere between here and there.* It was a prospect that had been haunting Jim's nightmares for some time. *Yes,* Jim thought, *the choreography is going very nicely.*

That was when he saw a cluster of new sparks of light suddenly pop out at the edges of the tank display—far enough out that it resized itself automatically. Jim tried to count them, and realized he couldn't.

"Incoming," Spock said. "Approximately sixty capital ships of various sizes, including many of the new supercapitals."

Jim swallowed. *Sixty! We are in deep, deep trouble.* "Remind me," he said conversationally to Spock, "not to make the mistake of thinking that anything about this is going to go well."

"I will make a note to do so, Captain," Spock said.

"No warp signatures on those?"

Spock was looking down his viewer. "There were no signatures, as they were not in warp."

Jim felt a chill. "Cloaked?"

"The probability is high," Spock said. "There is nowhere here they could have been hiding, Captain, and no way to approach so quickly on impulse without being detected. I would suggest this is a new cloaking technology that we are seeing for the first time."

Jim swallowed again. "At least they still have to decloak to shoot. See if this cloak has some new signature, or whether it's a variant of the hexicyclic technology. How many supercapitals, Mr. Spock?"

"Fifteen."

Jim sucked in a breath. *Very, very bad. "Tyrava!"*

"Listening, Captain. We see them."

"I may have to retask you."

"But, Captain," Veilt said, *"I thought you told us most strenuously that retasking so suddenly would break your plan."* He managed to sound slightly amused, even under these increasingly grim circumstances.

"A broken plan can be fixed," Kirk said. "A broken fleet is harder. And if you have any other thoughts . . ."

"Three-a, Captain."

Jim weighed the pros and cons of that. It was not an option he relished. He had been saving it for later in the engagement—*much* later. "I'll consider that," he said. "Five minutes. Meanwhile, go!"

"Going," Veilt said.

The huge ship turned with surprising lightness and speed and made straight for the biggest of the newly appeared capital ships. "All vessels," Jim said, "engage at will as per protocol two-f."

A wave of acknowledgments came in as large and small Free Rihannsu ships flung themselves at the capital ships nearest, with special emphasis on the C&C vessels. "Some success with that strategy already, Captain," Spock said. "Two C&Cs have gone down, and five capitals. Two have self-destructed."

"We need more," Jim said softly. "Keep a count for me. Update once per minute for the next four."

He sat there in the center seat and his hands itched. He wanted to be hammering on his comms button to tell Scotty to give him more speed, dammit, more power to the phasers! But this time it was his part to sit, and watch, and wait, while others bore the brunt. *This is hard. Hard. I hate this.*

Tyrava went coasting in among the scattering Rihannsu capital ships, her phasers and disruptors lancing out in all directions. Shields went up, but they were no use against that hyperpowered weaponry. The attacking vessels' shields overloaded and went down, and the phased disruptors reduced them to slag or plasma within seconds. Jim sat there watching it happen, counting ships in his head. The problem was that more kept popping out of cloak at the edges of the display, and diving in toward the fray. "Spock," he said.

"Captain," Spock said, "this is a phased assault. They are uncloaking in waves. It is impossible to tell how many of them might be out there."

"Not many more, I hope," Jim said, very softly. Even with *Tyrava*, there was only so much the present force could do.

"Now ten capitals taken by our side," Spock said. "Two destroyed by their own vessels. Either Grand Fleet has worked out what was happening at Artaleirh, or they are simply suspicious after so many of their own ships went missing."

Jim bit a knuckle and waited, watching *Tyrava*'s rampage. Anything she turned her weapons on was destroyed, but when thirty or so capital ships of all sizes turned and started attacking her in unison, the outcome began to be of concern. *"Tyrava?"*

"Captain," Veilt said, sounding a little strained, *"it may be time for three-a."*

"Spock!"

"Fourteen capitals down now and being suborned," Spock said. "Ten more destroyed by *Tyrava.* Make that eleven. Thirty-four now attacking her."

"Implement one-d," Kirk said. Immediately all the small-ships began attacking the ships that were attacking *Tyrava,* and that whole part of space started turning into a bright inferno of phasers and disruptors and torpedoes. But *Tyrava's* screens were beginning to radiate in the visible spectrum, never a good sign.

Jim made up his mind. "Three-a."

"Implementing," Veilt said. *"Four minutes."*

But one minute went by, and two, and the fire on *Tyrava* increased. Jim began to think, *Oh, no, I've left it too late. No. Please, no.* But the War Gods, if they were listening, gave no sign. *Tyrava's* screens flared brighter, and Jim said, "Mr. Sulu, we can't just sit here."

"Captain," Spock said.

Jim swallowed, and sat still. *Tyrava* began evasive maneuvers. Some of the capital ships attacking her went after her, but some of them now turned toward *Enterprise.* "Mr. Sulu," Jim said, "best evasive."

"Aye, aye," Sulu said.

The warp engines came to life, and *Enterprise* peeled away from the conflict, heading up and out of the system, though everything in Jim rebelled to see her do it. *This is not the better part of valor,* he thought. *I don't care what anybody says.*

"Some pursuit," Spock said, looking down his viewer. "More attention on *Bloodwing,* however."

"Ael," Jim said, "get out of there!"

"I have no leisure for that at the moment!" Ael said. *"We need these capital ships; they will be vital, and the small-ships need cover."*

One minute to three-a, Jim thought. "Lure them up this way, Ael. Let us give you a hand!"

"I do not think that is going to work, Captain," Ael said. *"We can get some cover from* Tyrava. *Veilt is closer."*

There was no arguing with her; she was right. *Enterprise* kept her distance, and Jim sat there in increasing fury and frustration. All he could do was watch the patterns shift as four or five of the capital ships broke away from pursuit of *Enterprise* and turned back toward *Tyrava.*

And suddenly space sunside went dark below *Enterprise* as another huge shape dropped out of warp hardly a thousand kilometers away and dived downward into the plane of the system. "ID coming through," Spock said, as the vessels lit up in the tank. *"Kaveth* Ship-Clan is in the system."

Jim let out a long breath as he watched them come. Veilt had told him that *Kaveth* was even larger than *Tyrava.* He had found it hard to believe until now. He almost dared to smile: the odds were getting evener. "Hail them and feed them the battle log."

Uhura listened for a moment. "They have it, Captain, via *Tyrava.*" Then her eyes widened. "They say we have more incoming."

Jim lost the smile. "Another thirty vessels are uncloaking, Captain," Spock said. "Rihannsu."

Jim went pale. "How many more of those things do they *have* out there?"

"Unknown. The new cloak seems to have no signature."

That's something Starfleet would really want, Jim thought, *assuming that any of us survive to tell them about it.*

Kaveth was down in the heart of the battle, now, chopping up every Grand Fleet vessel within range. Not many stayed there. Some fled instantly into warp and were gone, making Jim curse under his breath. *They've seen what they came to see,* he thought. *Possibly there was no other reason for them to be here at all. They won't be absolutely sure we don't have more of the Clan ships, but they'll have a baseline on what we do have, and what their armament's like.* As he watched, the thirty new ships started an englobement of *Tyrava*. Some of them began to fire, and the beams that lanced out were hexicyclics. *Tyrava*'s screens went white hot in places, just keeping the beams out. She turned and twisted away out of engagement, and a few of the new ships pursued her.

"We have to go in," Jim said.

"Captain!" Spock said.

"*Tyrava!*"

"*We are boosting shields,*" Veilt said. "*Sensors show that not all the new incoming have these weapons. But we cannot defend against these and deal with all the capital ships as well.*"

"How can they have all these, Veilt?" Jim said. "Didn't we adjust for bad data?"

"*And for outright sabotage,*" Veilt said, "*and disinformation, yes. But there is no way they should have such numbers. They must have killed half the labor on the few shipbuilding worlds to produce this kind of result.*"

Jim took a long, deep breath, counting ships. The balance was now almost sixty–forty in the Romulans' favor. They were engagement-cutoff odds. *No, no, this is all wrong, it's not supposed to go like this!* "All right," he said. "Four-a." It was the worst-case scenario: extract forces and run like hell.

"Incoming," Spock said.

Jim wanted to cover his eyes: but he stared into the tank, watching them come.

These lights were not green, however. They were white. His heart simply stopped.

"Starfleet IDs," Spock said. "*Ortisei, Speedwell, Hemalat,*

Lake Pontchartrain, Lake Onondaga, Kilimanjaro, San Diego, Dauntless, al-Burak, Marathon—"

"Hail *Ortisei*," Jim said. He hadn't dared to hope this would happen, having heard nothing for so long.

His screen lit up. There was Commodore Danilov, leaning forward and examining his own tactical display. He looked into the screen, and frowned at Jim.

"Commodore—"

"Don't have time to yell at you right now, Captain," Danilov said, sounding furious. *"It'll have to wait. Hold the flag, and shoot me your log."*

Jim gestured at Uhura. *"Out,"* Danilov said, and the screen went dark.

The wrong end of a court-martial, Jim thought, and shivered. Then he put the thought aside as the Starfleet vessels dived into the fray.

The confusion became complete as *Kaveth* started piling into the capital ships and the Starfleet vessels began weaving and diving through the fight, ganging up on Romulan vessels in the confusion. Jim watched it all with ever-increasing frustration, even as it became plain that the arrival of the Federation vessels had turned the tide. Some of the first Romulan vessels to enter the engagement were now breaking off and running for it; some of the Federation ships pursued them into warp. Other Romulan vessels elected to fight. Mostly they found themselves facing into *Kaveth*'s gunnery. This was always a mistake. The ships with the new hexicyclic gunnery did better, but there seemed to be a problem with their shields. Several of them were destroyed one after another by *Ortisei* and *San Diego*. Together the two ships went after one last hexicyclic-gunned Romulan vessel that was fleeing past the second, smaller of the two Grand Fleet installations.

Another hexicyclic beam lanced up from the installation and caught *Ortisei* on her undershields. She twisted away, glowing—

—and blew.

The breath went out of Jim as if he'd been punched. *Kaveth* swept over, hovered over that installation, and brought every beam to bear on it at once. It slagged down.

Just a moment too late, Jim thought.

More of the Romulan vessels fled, and were pursued at high warp by some of the Starfleet ships and the remaining Free Rihannsu vessels. Most of those who fled never made it out of the system. *San Diego* circled back to join the other Starfleet vessels in the mopping up. In a matter of five or ten minutes, it was all over: the firing finished, the smaller ships gathering together about the larger ones.

Jim sat there in his center seat and looked out at the darkness, feeling both relieved and sick at heart. "Report," he said.

"Forty-eight Rihannsu vessels destroyed," Spock said, "certainly a significant portion of Grand Fleet. Eighteen capital ships co-opted by the Free Rihannsu. Fourteen Free Rihannsu smallships destroyed, the capital ships *Lallasthe* and *Nesev* destroyed, *Sallai* and *Dushill* disabled. A decisive engagement." But his voice, as he said it, was flat even for a Vulcan.

"Decisive, yes," Jim said. He stood up. "Elapsed time?"

"Nineteen minutes, Captain."

Jim just stood there, looking out into the dark.

"My compliments to the ships' captains who've just joined us," he said, "and I'd be pleased to see them at their earliest convenience aboard *Enterprise*. We have some catching up to do."

It did not happen for nearly two hours, while damage control assessments were run and communications were established and other housekeeping secondary to a major engagement was completed. And when they all finally met in *Enterprise*'s biggest briefing room, Jim found it hard to look at the captains gathered there, although he knew almost all of them and was friendly with some. There was one empty chair down at the end of the briefing-room table, to which all their eyes kept being drawn. Jim kept telling himself that it was just a coincidence, that the room just happened to be set up that way . . .

"Afterburner" Gutierrez was there, and Helga Birgisdottir, whom Jim had not seen since *Mascrar.* The other captains, human and nonhuman, deferred to Birgisdottir, as she was the most senior in rank and history. She sat now with her hands folded on the table in front of her, looking haunted; she and the others had just finished reviewing *Enterprise*'s logs with Jim.

"Yet another plan that did not survive contact with the enemy," she said.

Jim nodded. "Our best estimates of the enemy's strength were badly skewed, for one of two reasons. Either we were purposely fed disinformation, or this—which should have been an 'assessment' engagement to see who we were and whether we could fight—had its priorities changed."

Helga looked up at Jim. "You're suggesting that this was not a feint, but a 'last throw' meant to stop us here?"

"A go-for-broke engagement," Jim said, "meant to conceal the fact that there are not enough ships in the Hearth-world system to hold it successfully against us. If I'm reading this correctly, then the war could be almost over, if we can tough it out."

They looked at him with still, grim faces. "We have sustained serious enough casualties, believe me," Jim said. "I would never have called for this kind of assistance if I'd thought that anything like *this* would have happened. Yet now it has, and it remains to me to decide what to do next. So now I have to ask all of you what *you're* going to do."

The expressions they all turned on Jim were uneasy. Afterburner looked up at Jim. "Several of us were given a message by Commodore Danilov to pass on to you after the engagement should the worse come to the worst. Which it has. The message is, 'That's your favor. You're on your own now.' "

Jim sat there and for some moments could think of nothing whatever to say. But finally he shook his head and broke out of the pain that had descended over his thoughts since the end of the battle. There was no time to indulge it now.

"So as for us toughing it out," said Helga quietly, "I'm afraid you are going to have to redefine 'we.' "

He swallowed. There it was. "In other words, Fleet has given you no authorization to proceed beyond this engagement."

"We are to 'report the results,' " Afterburner said, " 'and return to the other side of the Neutral Zone with all possible dispatch.' "

"And what does it say about *Enterprise?*" Jim said.

There was something of a pause. "Nothing," Captain Birgisdottir said.

Jim pulled in a long, long breath and let it out again. He could feel himself being given just one more length of rope, and wondered if he were going to be able to escape the tightening of the noose when he came to the end of it. In particular, he felt sure that his being thrown the rope at all was entirely contingent on the results of this particular battle. If Augo had not gone well, doubtless the orders would have had a lot more to say about *Enterprise,* and Jim, than "nothing."

"I understand you," he said.

"What will you do?" Afterburner said.

"Go straight through," Jim said. "This is an advantage that must be immediately followed up, before the Romulans have a chance to react. If we hit them immediately, our odds of success increase exponentially." He let out a breath. "Meanwhile, I'll be sending a copy of our logs and tactical assessments home with you, and certain other small packages. Regarding the packages—you've got to believe me when I tell you that they are individually more important than all your ships and crews put together. They have *got* to get back to Starfleet. There is also other news in a sealed packet that I would ask you to pass on to your immediate superiors when you get back. I cannot stress enough its urgency."

They nodded, but Jim somehow wasn't sure they were at all convinced, and suddenly he felt deadly tired.

He stood up. "I want to thank you all. You absolutely made the difference in this engagement. A very few more ships on the other side would have tipped it over the other way. We were extremely lucky, and you were the luck."

Some of the captains nodded to Jim, acknowledging the thanks. But the rest sat very still and made no sign.

Just like Starfleet Command, he'd said to Ael yesterday. *No problem.*

The captains stood and filed out. Only Gutierrez and Birgisdottir shook Jim's hand. "Good luck," Afterburner said, but not another word. They went out, and like all the other captains, headed for the transporter room, and their ships.

Jim stood there in the empty conference room for a long while, and learned what "the loneliness of command" felt like at an entirely new level.

SIXTEEN

ON CH'RIHAN, in their shielded room, the Three were meeting.

"How dare you use your personal power to undermine a Fleet action! How *dare* you!"

Urellh was working up to another of his rages. Tr'Anierh sighed. They were becoming *so* tiresome.

"I did nothing that you have not done in your own time," tr'Anierh said. "I was informed of certain—shall we say, disaffected?—personnel aboard those ships who were about to embark, in a concerted manner, on courses of action that would have been detrimental to the good order of our Empire as it stands at present, and to Fleet actions to be taken in the future. I therefore instructed those ships' commanders to withdraw before they reached station at Augo, and to return to intermediary bases where the personnel in question could be removed and questioned regarding their actions."

The others looked at him. Urellh was going quite pale with his rage. Tr'Kiell, for his part, was looking very much out of countenance.

"Those ships would have turned the tide at Augo!" Urellh shouted. "Their removal from the battle, your unilateral action—"

"It is treason," said tr'Kiell, "of the blackest kind."

"So was what those personnel would have done to the Empire *after* Augo," tr'Anierh said, "but let us leave that issue to one side for the moment. As well as the question of 'unilateral' action, which both of you have employed in the past. Sometimes," tr'Anierh added, "together."

They stared at him. "No matter," he said. "That particular blow against me has missed, and those involved are in no condition to strike another. The ships in question, having been cleansed—"

"You mean purged!"

"Tr'Kiell, I will not play semantics games all afternoon— we have too much to do. The ships are now back on active duty. And indeed we see that it was something of a blessing that they were not at Augo. Had they been, they would have been destroyed, or otherwise lost to us. Now we still have those ships in reserve, and they will be where they need to be in thirty-six hours. So our interests have been served. As have yours, because once again, one or the other of you has learned that we work best in concert."

The other two said nothing.

"There have also been certain unfriendly moves made against Senators affiliated with me," tr'Anierh said. "I think we have had enough of those, or I will have to start trumping up charges against some of *your* more egregious creatures. And trust me when I say that I know those charges will stick. But I would prefer not to have to waste my time right now, or yours, with such inconsequential matters. The rebels are coming. We have two worlds to protect, a number of threatened subject systems to consolidate, and numerous other tasks to perform that are associated with the maintenance of Empire. So I suggest we get on with them."

Silently Urellh and tr'Kiell sat down, and took the suggestion.

On *Bloodwing*, Ael went trudging down the corridor toward the ship's little sickbay, desperately tired. *We have won,* she kept saying to herself. *We have won. But this is not the final victory.* Nonetheless, now there was nothing to stop the inward plunge toward ch'Rihan and ch'Havran. *And very soon will come what I've been waiting for all this time,* Ael thought as she came up to tr'Hrienteh's door. *Soon, one way or the other, it will all be over, and I can rest.*

She touched the door signal. There were, of course, still many other matters of concern. The news that had come to them from the Federation agent on ch'Rihan regarding the disposition of those missing ships was good, but not entirely as good as it could have been. *Jim was right, as it turns out, but for the wrong reasons. Disaffection, as a blanket term, can mean all kinds of things. It need not be permanent.* And what tr'Tyrava had suggested to her was that those missing ships were not permanently out of play. They had simply been recalled, and once they were purged of politically "incorrect" staff, they would be sent out again. *We will see them at ch'Rihan yet,* Ael thought. *And as for our little Senator . . .*

The door opened. Tr'Hrienteh stood there, looking a little surprised. "My sorrow to keep you waiting, *khre'Riov*," she said. "I was calibrating some equipment."

"That's fortunate, for it's equipment I have come to see you about," Ael said. "You said you had some new biofeed-back gadgetry from McCoy?"

"Indeed I have, *khre'Riov*," tr'Hrienteh said. "Come in, sit down. I will set it up for you."

Ael came in willingly enough, and sat on the low bench near the left-side wall. As usual, the place was cramped and crowded with stacked-up medical equipment and supplies. This was no open, spacious sickbay like McCoy's, but a room hardly much bigger than some minor officer's quarters. Ael leaned against the wall, glancing up at the medication cabinets set overhead, and then at the sleek-looking little contraption that tr'Hrienteh brought over and set down on the bench beside her. The surgeon turned again and came back with some wrist-straps and wireless transpacks. "What manner of device is this?" Ael said, with a yawn.

"Oh, a clever thing that reroutes neural transmission in the brain," said tr'Hrienteh. "Another of their medical wonders of which they take so little note. It makes the alpha states much more accessible." Tr'Hrienteh touched the transpacks awake and fastened first one wristband, then the other, onto Ael's wrists. Again she turned and came back with soft round pads for Ael's forehead. Ael held her arms out, looking at them with interest.

"So nothing needs be done now except for you to relax," tr'Hrienteh said. "Just lean back and rest yourself."

Ael was more than glad enough to do that. "I cannot believe," she said, "how long it has been since I could do just this." She closed her eyes, not minding the hard surface against which she leaned, so long as there was, just for the moment, truly some rest. "Soon enough there will be—"

And then the voice froze in her throat. *Everything* froze.

She tried to open her eyes, and could not. She tried to move her arms, and could not. She was in the dark, all alone—and a pressure, a weight, began to come down around her mind.

Disbelief. Sheer disbelief descended upon her, as relentlessly as the darkness that also began to press down on her, as relentlessly as the pain that began to grow. Disbelief raged in her, and shock, and pure fury.

Not again.

Not again!

The voice she began to hear seemed to come from right inside her bones. *Now, traitress,* it said, *you have only one way to live through this. You must tell me who the Federation agent on ch'Rihan is. You must tell me all the details of the proposed attack. You must tell me everything.* And the pain began to grow more terrible.

The disbelief that had briefly defended her was now fading, and with it, its ability to stave off the pain. It was, as she remembered, very like hooks, tearing, worrying at her mind till the thoughts began to tatter away like rags. *You cannot resist,* came the voice. It seemed to fill the whole world, just as the pain seemed to do. *There is nothing you can do. Speak, tell me what I need to know, and live; live the poor short wretched life that is all that will be left to you. Or try to keep your silence.* The pain scaled up again.

Tr'Hrienteh, Ael thought, desperate, hoping still that this was some kind of bizarre delusion, some side effect of McCoy's machine. But moment by moment, as the pain grew, she knew better. This was no delusion, and the machine had nothing to do with McCoy. *Tr'Hrienteh! My friend! My friend of how many years?* All those years together on *Bloodwing,* all this time since *Bloodwing* had gone free of the fleet. *Why?* she thought. *Why!?*

Tell me what I want to know! the voice cried. The pain pressed down harder and harder from outside. It was like fire, now, akin to the one radiation burn Ael got all those years ago: a terrible thing, which always seemed as if it could get no worse, and yet got worse with every breath. *Tell me!* the voice cried.

Ael could not move, or breathe, or see, as that ruthless force tore at her mind. But she was not unarmed. Rage, that she had in plenty. And countering the rage, she also had the memory of standing on a plain of dark-crusted volcanic stone that stretched straight away from her to an unseen sky—the symbol of a defense, a barrier. She had been walking on that barely-solidified lava for some time now. Often enough, when she first began, it had cracked beneath her, but of late she had become more skilled in walking over the crust and not breaking through. *Tell me!* that voice shouted at her now, and the pain scaled up. But Ael, in the darkness, began to find the way through to asserting her own defense.

It was as Spock had said; practice made it easier. She stood in the darkness, and saw the lava, black, streaked with sullen red, spreading away all around her. Under that crust, the pain moved, but she did not have to let it through. It could not come through, not without her leave. And she did not give it leave.

It subsided, then surged again, trying to break through the crust. Ael thought of a cold wind blowing across that crust, a freezing wind from some planet's pole, freezing the molten fire down to darkness again. *Now, my Element,* she thought, *now I call on You. Come to my aid!* All around Ael, the lava began to darken. She caught, for the first time, a scrap of sound outside her prison—the sound of a device's controls being used, settings being altered. The pain scaled up again, trying once again to break through the crust, glowing solid red cracks spidering out, but once again, the wind came down from away behind Ael's back, and blew the lava dark. Once again it crusted over, and she began to walk slowly across it to a faint, faint glow on the horizon.

Tr'Hrienteh! Ael cried. *How can you be doing this?*

She sensed some agitation in the other's mind. *Feedback from my own condition?* she thought. Perhaps. If the operator of a mindsifter could hear the victim think, there was surely no reason the effect couldn't go the other way. Either way, it was a moment before an answer came back. *You cannot resist!* tr'Hrienteh said, but the tone was less certain. *The pain will only increase!*

It tried to increase again, and once again Ael called the wind from behind her, and the lava once more went dark. Over that crust she once again began slowly to advance. She was sure now that away at the edge of things, she saw light that was not the red sullen light of the magma-rage buried under the crust. Toward that faint chilly radiance she walked. *I was your friend,* she said. *We were good comrades for many years. How could you betray me so?*

I was your friend, the answer came back, furious. The pain scaled up once more. *And I was your* son's *friend.*

Ael started.

No, tr'Hrienteh said, *you never did notice, did you? You were too busy with your eternal plotting, with your vain dreams of freedom, to notice what was going on under your very nose. Tafv forbade me any role in the rising against you. He knew too well our old friendship, and did not want to wound me further by involving me in what was going to happen. I begged him, I pleaded with him, for I wanted to be with him, to protect him. I knew what you would do to him. And you did it. That day, the day you walked into MakKhoi's damned sickbay to see him, while he was yet alive, and then came out and left him behind you, dead, that day was the day I turned. That day I contacted Grand Fleet. Since then—*

She broke off briefly, wrestling with her own emotion. *You will never know from me the damage I have done you and your cursed Kirk. You would have gone to your death anyway. Now, at least, I will have the pleasure of sending you into the dark myself, and the rebellion assembled around you will fail. It will fail here and now, before it ever comes near the Hearthworlds. That will be some small repayment for the lost life of the one who would have been my lifemate—except for you. Now tell me what I want to know, before I kill you!*

The pain came swelling up through that dark surface with more strength than ever. Cracks ran swiftly everywhere, crevasses opened and the heat blasted up from them in fury. Ael held still, put her arms out in front of her, and called on the wind, called her Element by its name. The rumble in the ground and the rage of the pain slowly began to die away, leeching out of her consciousness. Things went dark again. *And now,* Ael said to the silence, *now,* and she threw her arms open.

Her eyes flew open, and saw light. Tr'Hrienteh staggered back from her, struck, bleeding from a head wound; she had been standing too close, and the powerpack from one of the straps had caught her near the eye. Ael tore the straps off her wrists, and the electrodes off her head, and went for tr'Hrienteh.

It was not going to be easy work, in so confined a space. And worse, the other was a student of the same arts that Ael knew. Tr'Hrienteh was strong, and fast. They had worked out too many times together at "laughing murder" for it to be otherwise. But Ael had to put those memories far from her now—forget the laughter, and concentrate on the murder. It was a grief to her.

But so was the memory of her son, and so was this new treachery, reborn from that one. *Will it never be done?* she thought, and she leapt at tr'Hrienteh, striking at her. Tr'Hrienteh blocked the blows expertly. Ael struck again, and again. They crashed into the cupboards in the little room. Ael was thrown back hard against the single pallet where patients were brought to lie. As tr'Hrienteh came at her again, Ael seized her upper arms, grappled with her, threw her across the room and up against the wall. Then she spun, using the pallet for leverage, and sank one boot into tr'Hrienteh's midriff on the lower right side, trying to strike straight through to the wall behind. She saw tr'Hrienteh's furious face suffuse with dark green. She heard the ribs by the heart crack, and then the spine.

For a long moment, tr'Hrienteh did not move. She just hung there, looking shocked. Then she slumped over sideways, half-propped against the diagnostic pallet.

Staggering, weaving, Ael pulled herself upright to brace herself against the wall, gasping. *This comes of too much trust,* she thought. *And of my own folly. But also, of theirs.* She looked over at tr'Hrienteh. *She, and those with whom she was working—they genuinely thought that if you strike off the* neirrh*'s head, the body will lie quiet afterward. They truly do not understand what has been happening to them— what is* about *to happen.*

And perhaps that is for the best.

Ael slapped the door-opener and staggered out into the hall. About halfway up the corridor, she had a sudden cold thought. Back to the sickbay she went at speed, never giving a second thought or look to the cooling body leaning against the pallet. Ael went to one of the equipment cupboards near the back of the room, touched in the combination to it, and got out tr'Hrienteh's disruptor. Ael unlocked it, armed it, and walked out the door again, more steadily this time, with the disruptor at the ready. *Who knows? My "old friend" may have other old friends aboard who are doing something similar on my bridge.*

But when she got there, and the lift doors opened, no one but her normal staff looked at her, and the Sword rested undisturbed across her seat. Aidoann looked at Ael, her expression one of utter consternation. "*Khre'Riov,*" she said, "what in Fire's name has come to you? You look ghastly."

"Fire's name indeed," Ael said softly. "Do not be concerned, Aidoann. I have simply been plugging a leak. Get me *Enterprise.* Now."

Kirk was sitting in his quarters, at his desk, staring at a dark screen.

It went well. It really did *go well, even though all hell broke loose at the end. So why do I feel so terrible?*

It was a foolish question; he knew perfectly well what was going on. He was deep in shock over Danilov's death, not least because of their friendship. But the timing was cruelly unfortunate. Dan had been the one man he could have known was absolutely both trustworthy enough to carry home the message that most desperately needed to get there, and influential enough to make sure that it reached the necessary destination. Now, before the other Federation ships left the area, he was going to have to think of something else to do, and fast.

The mental image of the terrible thing that was making its

way stealthily toward Earth's sun had been obsessing Jim through every minute that something more immediate hadn't. Now that Augo was over, it was starting to get in the way of eating and drinking and thinking and sleeping— which was completely understandable, but was also making it impossible for him to pay as much attention as necessary to the ten thousand other things he had to be taking care of right now.

He put his head down on his arms and tried to think. *I need another courier,* he thought, and laughed a small hopeless laugh under his breath. *Someone who has easy access to the highest ranks of Starfleet Command, and absolute credibility with them.*

The communicator beeped.

Wearily he reached out and punched it. "Kirk here."

"Captain," Ael said. *"We have a problem."*

"Really?"

She sounded rather surprised at the flatness of his tone. *"Or rather, we have had one, but it is solved."*

"Oh? What?"

"I have found out how Grand Fleet has been anticipating our moves so neatly."

He straightened up. "How?"

"We have had a Grand Fleet agent on my ship for quite a while now. But no more."

"Who was it?"

"Tr'Hrienteh."

He stood up in shock.

And I thought I *sounded upset.*

"Ael!"

"She will send them no more messages," Ael said. *"I am in the process of going through her computer storage right now. She seems to have thought that there was an adequate erase-lock on her files, but she was a doctor, not a computer programmer."*

"How long will it take you to go through her data?"

"Some time, I think. It is encrypted—"

"I'll have Spock give you a hand."

"I would very much appreciate that." She was controlling her voice very tightly.

"Ael," he said, "I'm so sorry."

"Yes," she said, and the weariness showed through. *"So am I. And, Jim, I sorrow for your loss too. Ddani'lov did not trust me, I know, but I also know that he was your friend and wished you well."*

"Yes," Jim said. "Yes, he did." He let out another of those long sighs that seemed to keep escaping him at the moment. "Ael, while we're talking—I want to conference with Veilt and his fellow Clan-Chief as soon as I can."

"Thala," Ael said. *"I will arrange it, if you like."*

"Thanks. The gist of it is this, though. We should go straight in, and immediately. You should call in all your remaining forces to meet us. I don't think that Grand Fleet now has enough ships close to ch'Rihan and ch'Havran to stop us. They've miscalculated, I think, and we should press the advantage before they think we'll dare to."

"I agree," Ael said. *"Spock and I will carefully check tr'Hrienteh's data to see if there is evidence to support your theory."*

"And if there's not?"

"Later for that," Ael said. *"But you are having one of your hunches, I think."*

"Don't know if I put much trust in those today," Jim said.

"I do," Ael said, *"so be still. Also, Captain—just before I went down to see tr'Hrienteh for the last time, I received a message from K's't'lk begging me to come to see her and Scotty as soon as I might. They knew you were busy with other things, so perhaps they have not messaged you as yet, or you simply have not seen it. But I think we must talk with them as soon as may be."*

"All right," Jim said, leaning on the desk again. "You sort out Veilt and Thala. I'll set up something with Scotty and K's't'lk. Call me when you're ready."

"I will."

There was a short pause. Then Ael sighed. *"We are both a little bruised right now, are we not?"* she said.

"Bloodied," Jim said, "but unbowed."

"There is the Kirk I know," Ael said. *"I will talk to you shortly. Out."*

Jim stretched, and glanced around his quarters. *A shower would be good, but it can wait for the moment.* He reached into the closet and pulled out a clean uniform tunic, stripped out of the old one, put the new one on, and headed out of his quarters and down the hall.

Another courier, he thought, trying to pick up where he'd left off. *Someone who has access to the upper levels at Fleet. But also somebody who can walk into the office of the President of the Federation and make himself or herself or itself heard. Someone I know to be absolutely trustworthy, and who the President will also know to be so. Somebody who—*

Right there in the middle of the corridor, he stopped. A crewman who was walking close behind him almost bumped into him.

Very quietly, and pretty vehemently, Jim began to swear, and to laugh.

"Uh, sorry, Captain!"

"Don't worry about it, Ensign Li," he said, and waved Kathy Li past him. "It wasn't you. Go on."

She hurried past him, blushing. Jim, though, stood there and shook his head at himself, then headed on down the corridor.

I can't believe it.

I can not *believe it! It's been under my nose for days. But all this damn admiral business kept me from seeing it.*

At Spock's door, he hit the buzzer.

"Enter," said the voice from inside.

Jim went in, glanced around as the door closed behind him. Spock was sitting in meditative mode at his desk, gazing at the screen, but otherwise looking surprisingly unoccupied. He started to rise; Jim gestured him back into the seat.

"Mr. Spock," Jim said, and came over to the desk, glancing at the screen. It was showing a view of ch'Rihan and ch'Havran.

"Captain?" Spock said, looking slightly bemused.

"I was just talking to Ael," he said. "She's found a leak aboard her ship."

"It would not surprise me," Spock said. "The strains of the recent combat on any vessel of *Bloodwing*'s age—"

Jim started to laugh again, and then stopped himself. "Not that kind of leak."

Spock's eyes widened. "You mean the 'mole' she has long suspected?"

Jim nodded. "Tr'Hrienteh."

That took even Spock by surprise. "She must be profoundly affected," he said after a moment.

"That'd be a fair bet," Jim said. "She's going through the surgeon's computer files at the moment. Apparently they're encoded. She could use your help."

"I will go immediately," Spock said.

"One thing before you go," Jim said. "And depending on the schedules of those ships out there, you may want to do it first."

Spock looked at him inquisitively.

"Mr. Spock," Jim said, "I want you to send a message to Sarek."

Spock put his eyebrows up. "I have been composing one. As a matter of course, I send such communications to my father whenever we . . ." He trailed off.

"Get into yet another life-and-death situation," Jim said. "Of course you would, Spock. It's entirely logical."

Spock gave him a quizzical look. "In fact," Jim said, "were I *ever* so paranoid about communications coming out of this ship, I would nonetheless assume that you would send such a message, and so no one else will be surprised when you do."

Spock was looking more mystified by the moment. "That seems an accurate assessment of the circumstances. But I fail to see—"

"So did I," Jim said, "and now I feel like an idiot. You, of course, won't be able to fall afoul of any emotion so sheerly messy. Lucky you. Tell me something, though. Do I correctly remember you telling me that you and your father have studied cryptography together?"

"It would be more accurate to say that I studied cryptography with him," Spock said. "Though he would describe his interest as merely that of what an Earth-human would call a hobbyist, his talent is considerable."

"So you would have no problem in composing what seemed a perfectly normal message to Sarek," Jim said, "and concealing other data in it."

Spock's eyebrows went up again. "Either as straightforward code, or as digitized data, the idea presents no difficulty."

"That's what I thought," Jim said. "So you're going to conceal information about the incoming nova bomb inside that message to your father, and you're also going to conceal in it my request that he take that information to the President of the Federation without delay."

Spock nodded. "The suggestion has great merit. I am absolutely at your disposal, Captain."

"And you're sure," Jim said, "that you can encode, or encapsulate, that message in such a way that no one but your father can get at it?"

Jim could have sworn that he saw the slightest smile cross his first officer's face, but it was gone again so quickly that he had to admit that it might have been a trick of the light. "Of that, Captain, I am quite certain," Spock said. "When you have composed your message, inform me and I will import it and encrypt it."

"Good," Jim said. He let out a long breath. "It's not a perfect solution, but it'll mean, at least, that the information about the nova bomb gets back to Earth and into the hands of the one human there who knows for sure that I haven't gone insane."

Spock nodded. "Captain, I regret not having thought of this myself, but then I was uncertain for whom outside of Starfleet you might have intended the message."

Jim made a face. "I *hate* sealed orders. Spock, when you have your own command, *never* let anybody stick you with sealed orders. When you think of all the trouble they've caused us, especially with the Romulans . . ."

"Should I ever acquire a command of my own," Spock said, "the exigencies of command structure itself suggest that I am as likely to get 'stuck' as you are, Jim." He gave his captain a look that even for Spock was fairly wry. "But I will bear that in mind."

"Good," Jim said, and suddenly felt as if a great weight had been lifted from him. "Meanwhile, have you heard anything from Scotty about how they're coming with fixing the antiseeding technique?"

"I have just received messages from him and from K's't'lk both," Spock said. "But the matters you have brought me are, relatively speaking, rather more urgent. I will deal with them instead."

"Thanks, Spock. I'll talk to you later." He went out.

SEVENTEEN

Jim and Ael walked slowly into engineering an hour or so later, deep in discussion of tr'Hrienteh's computers. "Everything," Ael said. "Every private communication on my ship for the past year may have been compromised. It is going to be very difficult to tell for sure."

"If anyone can find out," Jim said, "Spock can. Leave it with him." He shook his head. "When will Veilt and Thala be ready for us?"

"Within the hour. But, Captain, with or without the data from tr'Hrienteh's computer, they agree with you: we should set out immediately for ch'Rihan. The government there is apparently in considerable disarray, the uprisings have spread to ch'Rihan from ch'Havran, and there will be no better time for us to strike—for good or ill."

"Let's hope for good," Jim said. "Scotty?"

Scotty and K's't'lk were leaning over a tablescreen about two meters wide, arguing over some schematics. Jim peered down at the most complex of the schematics, then shook his head. It looked to him as much like an unusually involved board game as anything else. "Captain," Scotty said, and turned right back to K's't'lk. "Lass, you're missing the point. The problem the last time was just a function of the power. *This* solves that problem once and for all."

K's't'lk was chiming in an agitated way, and sounding

very out of tune. "I promised the captain there would be no creative physics!"

Scotty acquired a calculating expression. "Aye. But there's nothin' creative about de Sitter space. It's just *there*— we've known about it for centuries now. Infinitely massful, and infinitely hot, at near big-bang heat indeed. Too useful not to use, if only you can get at it by conventional means. Now if you stuck a wormhole into de Sitter space—"

K's't'lk jangled, incredulous. "One which had exactly the right mass-conduction characteristics to suit our needs? If you plan to just reach out into space and find one lying there waiting, then Sc'tty, you'll be tempting Dr. McCoy to come down and put you on such a course of psychotropics—"

"Nobody does that kind of thing anymore," said McCoy from behind Kirk and Ael. "Teaching the brain to readjust its own chemistry works so much better."

"Doctor, please," Scotty said, and turned back to K's't'lk. "Lassie, it wasn't a natural wormhole I had in mind. I'd thought of constructing a tailored one."

"No one's been able to get one to last more than a billionth of a second in the laboratory," K's't'lk said, dubious. "Without blowing up the laboratory, anyway."

"Serve them right for conducting those experiments in ground-bound facilities, then. Not that there hasn't been positive technological fallout from that kind of thing. Don't forget, Cochrane got his first ideas about warp induction from that wee accident at the Brookhaven collider, just before the war."

Spock appeared behind them. "Well," Jim said, "how about it?"

Spock leaned over the schematic, examining it. One eyebrow started to go up. "I read the abstract you attached to your message, Mr. Scott," Spock said, not looking up. "If you are discussing the construction of tailored microwormholes—especially in the light of the early Brookhaven experiments—then a billionth of a second might indeed be all that would be required to produce the desired result. Very considerable amounts of energy could be released by even so short an access to de Sitter space."

He straightened up and folded his arms, considering. "The difficulty would be a matter of precision: keeping the wormhole open for exactly the right time necessary to conduct the necessary amount of energy into the target, as well as in making sure it can be shut down while conducting such a flow. The wormhole experiments of recent years have all been attempts to connect into much more innocuous alternate universes, where the 'differential of dynamic' and the overall balance of energy states has been roughly equal. Such as that of our own universe with the one where our own 'dark' counterparts exist."

"Aye," Scotty said, looking glum. "Pumping unlimited amounts of energy into our universe. We're playing with fire."

"Every engineer plays constantly with the Elements," Ael said, "or so tr'Keirianh tells me. I see little chance of our doing so safely. Therefore we must needs nerve ourselves to the dangers, it would seem."

Scotty shook his head. "We could upset the local spatial ecology somethin' fierce. Control—"

"It is an issue," Spock said, "but I think not insurmountable. And the solution you are suggesting is an elegant one. Any nova bomb ignition starts out by instituting a collapse sequence. The insertion of the correct amount of energy would abort the sequence, canceling it out both by means of sine flux inversion and carbon-carbon cycle denaturation. I shall apply myself to the necessary mathematics and provide you with findings at the earliest opportunity."

Mr. Scott still looked dubious. "Scotty," Jim said, "we're running out of time. That thing's getting closer and closer to Earth. No one knows where it is, and if it's got one of those new cloaks on it—which I'm betting it does—no one's going to. I've sent messages back to Starfleet about it in every way I can think of that's safe—" He glanced at Spock, who nodded slightly. "But if I'm getting this right, and you think this resonance-wormhole-whatever technique can be used to keep that nova bomb from getting into the sun, or can disrupt its effects when it does get in, then it's worth doing. And doing right away."

"Captain," Scotty said, upset, "remember what happened to 553 Trianguli!"

"Something a whole lot worse is going to happen to Sol, and Sol III, if you don't give whatever you're planning a try!" Jim said. "I know this sounds terrible, but the sun collapsing is just slightly preferable to the sun blowing up. At least there's a chance to save some lives. But, frankly, neither option is acceptable to me. So do whatever you have to do, build whatever you have to build, and do it now!"

Scotty sighed and nodded. "You give me the numbers," Scotty said to Spock, "and I'll build what you describe."

Jim nodded and turned to McCoy. "Bones, this meeting— I think it would be smart if we brought Gurrhim with us. Can he travel?"

McCoy rolled his eyes. "More like, can he be *stopped* from traveling," he said. "Ever since he saw *Kaveth* arrive, he's been itching to get over there. Apparently they're some kind of relatives of his. He's fit enough now. I'd have discharged him already, if it weren't for the security situation. But I take it, after what happened with tr'Hrienteh, that the lockdown doesn't pertain anymore?"

Jim thought about that. "Probably not. If necessary, Bones, we can smuggle him down to the transporter room and make sure that our meeting on *Kaveth* doesn't happen anywhere public. But let me think about it for a little. I'll get back to you. Anything else here that needs my attention?"

"No, Captain," Scotty said. "We'll call you when we've got our prototype built from Mr. Spock's figures."

Jim nodded, and he and Ael headed toward the door. "Och!" Scotty said then. "Captain?"

Jim looked over his shoulder.

"I forgot. That other question you messaged me about this morning?" Scotty grinned. "Aye, we can do it. Gurrhim's wee widget suggested a method. I'll have more data for you later."

Jim started to grin; it felt strange, after the pain of the hours before. "All *right,* Scotty. You may have just won us this war. Get on it."

Kaveth was another ship in the mold of *Tyrava,* but bigger. Ael heard with amusement the sound Kirk made when he got his first clear sight of it after the battle. The ship's designers had gone, not for three outer hulls, but five; they were set far back along the bullet-shaped main body, producing altogether a sleek and deadly look. This probably should have been no surprise, for Kaveth-Clan was famous for the artistic sensibilities of its children, and for their gifts in design, whether in something so prosaic as a box for starchroot bread or as purposefully elegant as designer clothing or weaponry. In the ancient days when the Kavethssu first took flight, the saying was that they might chop you to bits, but they would do it with style. When they were done with you, you would be fit at the very least for an alien "craft butcher's" front window, or for an art gallery, if nothing further.

When the party coming in from *Enterprise* and *Bloodwing* appeared on *Kaveth*'s main transport pad, Ael made sure she was standing in such a way as to see Kirk's expression without seeming to have oriented herself so. Sure enough, his face was worth seeing. As he turned slowly around him, looking up and up, and his jaw slowly dropped,

Ael became sure that the captain had never beamed into a rain forest before—at least, not one that was *inside*. Kaveth-Clan had originally lived in the south-tropical continent of ch'Havran before the Empire relocated them half a century ago to distant outworlds like Mirhassa and Ssuvat, in an attempt to isolate what was seen as a dangerous desire to uphold the right of self-expression in the face of power. When the Kavethssu were stripped of their possessions and forcibly exported to those worlds, the Empire never suspected under how many cloaks and tunics were concealed the most delicate and best-loved of the Hearthworlds' plants. Now the massive boles of *tafa* trees, gracefully braiding their way upward in metallic-corded green-blue cables an arm thick, and the huge golden downhanging trumpet-flowers of *firjill,* surrounded the pad half a *stai* deep on every side.

"Eden," Jim said softly. "Tell me there are no snakes."

"What would a snake be?" Ael said, though she knew.

"Here?" Jim said. "Superfluous."

That whole large space was empty. They stood there, and after a moment Ael saw coming toward them a shape she had not seen for many years, since her younger days in Fleet. Thala tr'Kaveth was one of those astonishing women who simply did not change with age: raven-haired, tall, and slimmer than any woman had any right to be past her twelfth decade and her sixth child. The joke in the old days had been that her immediate family was a clan all to itself; and indeed the Kavethssu had a reputation for being willingly fertile, almost aggressively so. The joke among the Outworlds had always been that, were the Kavethssu Imperial, there would have been no need for armaments with which to conquer an empire; they would simply have overrun it by sheer numbers.

Now the Clan-mistress of *Kaveth* came toward them and greeted them all with warmth. Ael's hand she took and held to her cheek in a surprisingly open gesture of affection. "Instructress," she said—for Ael had been one of Thala's teachers at the Fleet during Ael's brief flirtation with the academic life there, many years ago—"I fear I have run away from school a little farther than previously."

Ael laughed. The others, who knew the story, smiled; Ael turned to Kirk, introducing him to her erstwhile pupil. "Thala was given to me to tutor in piloting, long ago," she said. "I fear my teaching methods weren't to her liking. She left Fleet shortly thereafter to become a farmer."

"It was not your fault," Thala said, laughing, and led them all off to one side toward a space among the trees in which a huge greenstone conference table was somewhat incongruously set. "Or, well, not entirely. When the government decided to uproot our whole clan and relocate it to some barren planet I'd never heard of, out at the back end of nowhere, it seemed a good time to take my leave of ch'Rihan before I became too much like the people who could do such a thing."

They all sat down. Kirk was still looking around him in astonishment—not just at the forest. "Thala," Jim said, "I'm sorry. The question has been burning me up. *How have you people built these ships?* We always thought the colony worlds were poor."

Thala smiled, as at a clever youngster. And Veilt smiled, and Ael smiled, and seeing Jim's face, she saw that he understood he had finally asked the right question.

"So did the Empire," Thala said, "since they beggared us. Who would we be to disabuse them of the notion? We were willing to live in peaceful lawfulness under their reign, but we had to speak our minds; that's our nature. When they decided that speaking one's mind was treason, at that point we let them send us far away from their notice, as they thought. It left us freer to speak, and to practice the peculiar form of criminality they had forced upon us. The forest, there—" She looked all around her at the green-and-gold trees surrounding them. "They never knew that we managed to bring the best of it away from ch'Havran with us. All they saw were poor people flocking onto the transports; destitute folk, with muddy plants in buckets. Do you know *tivish,* Captain?"

Jim shook his head, but McCoy looked up. "Jim," he said, "you remember the scarf wrapped around that bottle I brought Spock? That was *tivish.* It's a plant-based fiber, like silk, only much, much more so. The best *tivish* is so fine, you can have it in your hands and hardly know when you're feeling it."

"It is fabulously difficult to correctly process," Thala said, "and as a result, fabulously expensive. For the better half of the last half century, we have exported *tivish* to the Hearthworlds, albeit somewhat erroneously labeled. Our customers have always thought it came from south-continent ch'Havran."

"Elements forbid we should start some piffling quarrel about a matter of labeling," Gurrhim said, and coughed.

"And all we poor Kavethssu have gone about in rags and tags these many years, like subsistence farmers, growing the wretched groundroot," Thala said. "While quietly exporting the best possible hydroponically produced counterfeit Havrannssu *tivish* all about the Empire, and far beyond—and, from the profits, building ships."

She looked around her with utmost satisfaction. Ael saw Jim bow his head in what she thought was proper amazement at such determination. Then he looked up. "There would have been other sources for your income, of course."

"Ah, always. But no more illegal than absolutely necessary. Pirates and subversives the Empire might have made of us, but criminals? The Elements would never approve." Then Thala grinned. "Actually, perhaps we erred ever so slightly on the side of criminality. We *did* buy some banks."

Ael saw Jim settle back in his seat with a smile that said he entirely understood. "Every revolution," he said, "needs a friendly bank."

"How pleasant it is to do business with a thoughtful ally," Thala said. "So now you understand the context. We are happy to leave this corrupt Empire if we must. But far more would we prefer to take it back, and someday replant all this under the open sky where it belongs. Augo has gone some way toward that, but not yet far enough. There's yet much work to do, and little time."

"But matters are moving in a direction we would desire," Veilt said. "Through Kavethssu agents working on ch'Rihan and ch'Havran, much fresh intelligence has not come to us, and it is accurate. The agents' stake is in preserving their home, which they know is about to be involved in the Battle of Eisn. Public unrest is growing."

The hair rose on the back of Ael's neck as she suddenly heard her homeworlds, her home star, being for the first time given a name that turned them into a battle, an engagement. A matter of history—and possibly one of tragedy. ". . . has no idea what to do," Thala was saying. "The Defense Forces are torn. They little like to be sent against their own people. Some of the most enthusiastic of them have suffered at the hands of those they command. Numerous members of the forces have gone over to the insurgency and have brought much useful Intelligence and technology with them."

"That would be the best kind of news," Kirk said. "Thala, Veilt—*how many ships?*"

The urgency in his voice sounded the way a touched wound might sound if it had suddenly acquired the power of speech.

"That we know of," Thala said, "forty-nine."

Jim sat very still. "Forty-nine *capital* vessels?"

"No," Veilt said. "Twenty capitals, and twenty-nine lesser vessels of *Warbird*- or *Reha*-class."

"That we know of," Kirk said quietly.

"It seems very few," Veilt said, "I know. But by both acci-dent and design, we have made Grand Fleet empty its purse with some speed. Granted, they brought much more force to Augo than we had expected. But they hoped to strike a crushing blow there—and found their error when it was they who turned out to be tied to the anvil, not we."

Kirk sat there looking at his hands, folded on the table. "All right," he said. "Let's consider how these new numbers affect our tactics. I trust you've had time to look over the previous version of our battle plan?"

Thala nodded. "I have consulted with Veilt. Our major concern, as you might imagine, is the number of feet on the ground that we can contribute to this effort. Obviously, when we fight in defense of *Kaveth,* every able member of our population stands to arms. But for a battle outside our walls, even this one, we must necessarily be more sparing. We cannot leave our children's home defenseless, especially when it can most logically be expected to suffer attack during the time a significant portion of our forces are groundside." She sat back in her chair, and something in the change of light and shadow across her face suddenly showed Ael how unnerved Thala was by the prospect that lay before them all.

"Of our combined populations," Veilt said, "we can offer you two hundred and eighty thousand ground troops. This is ten percent over the numbers we originally discussed with you, Captain, when you first floated your master battle plan. But I still fear it may not be enough."

Kirk looked a little abstracted. Ael recognized the look of a commander rearranging a strategy on the fly. Then his eyes snapped back into the now. "I would have agreed with you previously," he said. "Since this is the one battle we can't afford to lose, it's also one to which I've always preferred to bring overwhelming force, along the lines of five-to-one odds. Today's numbers take us to about three-to-one, since even though they've been calling in everything they can, the Hearthworlds still have too little in the way of ground forces, and those ground forces have too little in the way of experience."

"It's as I told you, Captain," Ael said. "Rebellion has routinely been handled by Grand Fleet, not by putting boots on the ground."

"And the government has thereby created its own tactical vacuum," Jim said. "They've always expected the Federation and the Klingons to be locked in a permanent strategic stand-off, too preoccupied with each other to come this far into the Empire. And as our Intelligence now confirms, it's never seriously occurred to either Grand Fleet or the government that a local insurgency would ever gain enough momentum to become a serious threat. Or else anyone who suggested such a thing was either laughed out of the room, or silenced for talking treason." His smile went grim. "There's no question that whatever battle plan they've managed to cobble together will start to break down in earnest when their C&C starts trying to handle troops who not only have never taken seriously the possibility that the Hearthworlds might be invaded, but have never *trained* as if they might be. That'll be a good start for us. But to make our numbers count as if they were actually a five-to-one advantage, we are going to have to break that command-and-control *much* more seriously, and much more quickly."

His expression was acquiring a sly look, like that of a conjuror with a *smeerp* up his sleeve. Ael sat back and watched the others' faces as they watched Kirk. Thala, in particular, was favoring the captain with an expression suggesting that she thought she might be dealing with a madman.

"What did you have in mind, Captain?" Gurrhim said. "Forgive me if this has been discussed before, but I have been busy with other matters."

"Like healing a big hole in your chest," Kirk said. "Last I saw, that was acceptable as an excuse for missing a staff meeting or two." That smile got even more sly as it was mirrored by Gurrhim. Ael saw how much these two men had come to like each other, and was glad of it, as it would prove useful.

"Let's backtrack a little," said Kirk. "To reduce ch'Rihan—really our main goal, because ch'Havran will quickly follow—we have two primary objectives before us. First, we must take Ra'tleihfi, not just because of its symbolic value as the heart of the Empire. The command structures centered there have never been decentralized, again due to the inability to conceive of a direct attack on these two planets—and also, if I understand Ael correctly, due to the culture of distrust in both the government and the Fleet. Neither has ever been happy about the prospect of allowing your subordinates to get too far out of their sight, where they'll have leisure to plot."

"True enough," Gurrhim said. "Captain, the doctor gave me many things to read while I was lying on my back the first few days aboard, and while I was reading I found that we have a saying in common. 'Keep your friends close, and your enemies closer.'"

Kirk nodded. "So that concentration of resources and personnel will have to be disrupted or destroyed as quickly as possible. And our second task will be to capture and occupy all major centers of government in the city—meaning, most specifically, the Senate and the other buildings and facilities of the Tricameron, and the facilities associated with the Praetorate. The Praetors, also, must be neutralized—most particularly the Three."

"It is a very bland word, 'neutralized,'" Thala said.

Kirk had the grace to look embarrassed. "Yes. Sometimes the jargon creeps up on you when you're not looking. Thala, I would prefer not to kill those who don't need killing. But circumstance sometimes overrules our best intentions. To keep the civilian casualties to a minimum, the Praetorate has to be incapacitated and its members confined or eliminated as quickly as possible. They can't under any circumstances be allowed to escape. The emergence of a government in exile around which a counterinsurgency could crystallize would be disastrous for everybody. The Three, in particular, can't be allowed to escape—and when you look at the detailed battle plan, which I'll be revising again shortly, you'll see that a fair amount of materiel and personnel are devoted to this objective."

"The strategy as a whole, and the intention of taking the Three out of the equation, is well-intentioned," Veilt said, glancing down at the table, under the surface of which the many pages and interlocking structures of the battle plan were glowing. "But, as usual, physical reality intrudes. With all the best will in the world, when a culture has transporter technology, it can be very hard to prevent escapes."

Kirk's smile now became positively unsettling. "Well," he said, "we're just going to have to render transporter traffic impossible."

The others all stared at him, and so did Ael. "Captain, what in the worlds are you talking about?"

Jim looked a little sour, though amused. "Transporters break every chance they get anyway. You'd think it wouldn't take all that much to make them useless on *purpose*. Fortunately, Mr. Scott has been working on a protocol that will, for a limited area anyway, make transporter usage impossible. It's based on a union of one aspect of the new hexicyclic technology that you passed to us, sir," he said to Gurrhim, "and on some of the research that Scotty and K's't'lk have been doing on rendering the Sunseed technology unusable. I won't bother you with the technical details at the moment, but with the kind of mobile power that *Tyrava* and *Kaveth* make available to us, it will be possible to interdict transporter usage for fairly extended periods within a limited volume of space—specifically, over and around Ra'tleihfi.

Anywhere that beaming will still work will be too far away to be of any use against our operations on and in the city."

"But surely an effect like that would have to act against both sides," Thala said.

"You're right," Kirk said. "Here, though, we play to our strengths, and use *Tyrava* and *Kaveth* in their modes as hypertroop carriers. By the time our opponents figure out what's been done to them, our ground forces will already have been put in place by the large-class people-mover shuttles you're already carrying as part of your recolonization materiel. When everyone's in position, we then close down transporter use for the duration of the push into the city. If the government troops are going to fight with us, they're going to have to do it on our terms, not theirs. Timing is going to matter a lot, but assuming that we manage that correctly, they won't be able to stop us from taking the city."

Ael shook her head. "But this changes everything. If the attack on the city is now going to be terrain-oriented, rather than assuming large-scale troop emplacements via transporter . . ." She gave Kirk an annoyed look. "A pity you had not mentioned this possibility to me earlier! There would have been more time to develop this set of strategies."

"Since I didn't know myself that it was going to become possible until yesterday about this time, when Scotty told me," Kirk said, "I would ask you to hold me blameless, just this once."

She raised her eyebrows, then nodded acquiescence. "So after all our planning for direct injection into the city, now we must after all advance across terrain. And that leaves us only one option. We will have to go in through the Pass, past the Firefalls."

"But not until we've first suckered as many of their troops away from ch'Rihan as possible," Kirk said. "My intention is to turn this exercise into a logistical nightmare for them. We are going to strand as many of them as we can on ch'Havran, by doing everything possible to give them the impression that that's where we're going. That will be your opportunity," he said, looking over at Gurrhim, "to stop being dead. When you turn up on a broadcast, alive and breathing, and announce that you're heading for ch'Havran to take your planet back, everyone's going to find that completely believable, especially if we plant other information on ch'Rihan to confirm it at the highest levels. It'll then seem far too plausible to waste time on groundless suspicions that it's all a ploy. After all, it makes perfect sense for the insurgency to try to consolidate ch'Havran first. It's always been the more reluctant of the Hearthworlds to be subjected to the Imperial yoke, going right back to that old suspicion that the territorial settlement lotteries were rigged."

Ael smiled. "You are truly beginning to understand us."

"Only beginning?" Kirk said. "We'll discuss that later. At any rate, we'll be acting in every way we can as if ch'Havran was where all our landings-in-force will be. They'll think we intend to go there and consolidate our power before moving on ch'Rihan. But they'll have it exactly backward. Once they've swallowed the bait and committed large troop movements to ch'Havran, we do the switch and head for ch'Rihan instead. That's the point at which we interdict transport, and start large-scale jamming. They'll be doing the same, of course. It's going to be interesting to see whose jamming wins. It's possible theirs may. But we have other communications options to exploit that they won't expect. And after that, things will start to get interesting."

Kirk sat back in his seat, studying the table. "What if they do not swallow the bait, Captain?" Veilt said.

"Then we go ahead with the assault on Ra'tleihfi regardless, on a slightly different timetable, and using the transporter interdiction tool in different ways. But I firmly believe that they'll swallow it, because Ael has been kind enough to show me the most recent war-gaming scenarios that have been leaked to her from the Grand Fleet's War College. We're going to seem to be doing exactly what the very, very few tacticians to model this situation have said an insurgency would do. Not for the same reasons, of course, but every strategist is always happiest to see the enemy doing what he *believes* he should. It usually makes him so happy that when reality starts doing something else entirely, as we will, he disbelieves it for just long enough to render him vulnerable, and for us to do all the damage we need to." He let out a breath. "This will also be the time to take the Neutral Zone's surveillance satellites down—again, on both sides. Starfleet won't be able to see what's happening, which has its advantages at the moment. But neither will Grand Fleet. If we can also plant with them the idea that the Federation *itself* has taken those satellites down . . ."

"Before, they might not have credited that," Ael said. "But now the presence of Starfleet vessels at Augo will render them all the more likely to believe there will be a Federation strike force associated with our attack. Their worst fears will seem to be coming true all at once."

"The constructive bluff," Jim said, glancing at Ael. "Very useful in poker, as you'll find out someday when we get around to playing a real game."

"That was not real?" Ael said, ever so demurely.

Jim gave her a look.

Thala looked down at the battle plan and nodded slowly. "There is a great deal here to digest. Many more layers of detail. But the main structure of the plan seems sound. Now all we must do is attack, and find out how sound it really is."

They looked at one another.

"If our schedule continues to go to plan," Veilt said, "we will arrive at ch'Rihan in two days. We will need to be alert for the next day to make sure that we are not caught by surprise by some last-minute attempt to forestall our arrival in Eisn's system."

"But I think we need not fear that now," Ael said. She had been turning this issue over in her mind for some time. "I think the Three will be saying, 'If the traitress is so willing to come here, let her come. After all the trouble she's caused us, easier now to deal with her on our own doorstep than to chase her all over space. If she dies spectacularly within easy view of the Hearthworlds, that will suit us. If she falls into our hands, the whole reason for the insurrection falls apart, and that too suits.'" She gave Veilt and Thala an angry smile. "And in that concept lies a hidden strength for our side that cannot be counted in numbers of troops. If my last day's experience is anything to go by, neither the government nor Fleet understand at all that what is happening now, would have happened sooner or later whether I or the Sword were involved or not. And that fact, perhaps, will be worth more to us than twice or three times our numbers when we assemble outside the city."

"Always assuming," Kirk said, "that the people rise."

Ael shook her head. "No. If they merely fail to rise *against* us, that will be more than sufficient. The government, you understand, expects them to rise in *its* defense. I think the Three will find that they have grossly miscalculated."

"That the event must prove," Thala said, and rose. So did all the others. "Meantime, we remain here twelve more hours to allow the last of our shipborne assets to join us. Then— onward to ch'Rihan."

Arrhae woke up the next morning with the strangely disconnected feeling that had hung over every morning since her meeting with tr'Anierh. She lay there, staring at her ceiling, and thought: *I am still alive. It is a wonder.*

She sat up and looked out the window. It was very early. Arrhae was almost getting used to these dawn awakenings now—a harking-back to her days as *hru'hfe*, when her duties would have meant she needed to be up so early to supervise the household staff. Now, though, she knew the source of such early wakefulness. *Stress,* she thought, *nothing but the sheer stress of it all—the fear of the ringing commlink, of the sound of weapons blasting in the front door. I am not built for this kind of thing.*

But then she laughed out loud at herself, and stretched, looking out the window once more. *If I'm not, letting the Federation send me here was a poor career choice.* She threw the silks aside and got up, looking out at the weather. It was cloudy at the moment, but it was the kind of light cloud that suggested it would burn off when the sun had been up awhile.

Arrhae went into the 'fresher and took care of her morning routine, then headed out of her chamber into her little media room again. Since she started getting up so early again, Mahan had changed the household routine a little, and now always left a hot pitcher of morningdraft on the sideboard near the viewer, along with some plates of wafers and burnt bread and other light morning foods.

Arrhae brought the viewer up and flicked through various of the news channels, initially not much noticing what they were showing. It had been three days ago, that meeting with tr'Anierh, and once she had gotten inside her own door and shut it behind her, she had become most uncertain of what effect she might have had on him. All the rest of that day, and all that night, Arrhae had either paced the house like a trapped beast, or sat or lain awake in the dark or near-dark, certain that at any moment the people would arrive who would take her away to death or worse. But it did not happen. The next day Arrhae had spent in front of the viewer, waiting to see what result might come from the battle she knew was even then taking place at Augo. But no news came at all.

That, more than anything, started to calm her somewhat.

Had there been a great victory, even a moderate one, it would have been all over every channel. But the news channels remained, for all that day, as relatively uncommunicative as they had been for weeks, talking about "disturbances" or "isolated incidents" here and there in the Hearthworlds as if such things had happened forever and were of no particular import. That night Arrhae actually slept for a few hours, and woke up in the dark of dawn feeling merely anxious, not utterly terrified as she had been the day before.

That second evening, though, was when the news had begun to change. It seemed like a relatively minor business, at first. The government was announcing "security alerts" in all the major cities, a "civilian readiness exercise." "Readiness" seemed to mean that people were expected to be ready to lock their doors and stay inside when they were told to. They were also to make sure they had several weeks' worth of food and water laid by, and additionally had to see to it that whatever legal weapons they might possess were ready for use in what was being referred to as "a mass call-up of civilian defense assets." *And what about the illegal weapons?* Arrhae had thought with some amusement when House Khellian's version of this notification arrived. *Should we get those ready too?*

But these announcements told Arrhae what she needed to know, and grim though they might have seemed on the surface, they nonetheless lifted a great weight from her heart. The battle at Augo had happened, and it had gone well for the Free Rihannsu. *And now they're coming here. But the government doesn't know how to say, doesn't* dare *say, "invasion"—because then there would be too many questions. How is this happening; why is this the first we've heard of it; why haven't you protected us better?* And when people first heard that word used openly, something dangerous might happen: the unexpected.

So it was that Arrhae was one of very few people in the

city who knew that they were all about to be caught in the middle of a major military engagement, and somehow, on her own account, anyway, Arrhae found it hard to be afraid. *Is it because I've been seeing this coming for so long? Or because I've become Rihannha enough to* want *it to be happening, at whatever price?* For even before things had started happening in the Hearthworlds and the Empire this last year, Arrhae had sensed a long slow undercurrent building, a murmuring among ordinary people who kept hearing and sharing stories about things that had happened to friends of friends, to distant relatives—stories of heartless or cruel or stupid actions by the government or its agents. There had always been stories like that, sure enough, but over the past year they had seemed to gain momentum and weight, becoming an everyday matter, rather than something sporadic. Then slowly the small cruelties and little oppressions from above seemed to grow in number, to get closer. They became commonplace. But people were not taking them for granted. The murmuring grew quieter, but there was a lot more of it. Not that she heard it herself. Now that she was a Senator, Arrhae had noticed with some discomfort that even her own staff watched what they said in her hearing, or occasionally looked afraid at the thought of what they might have said in front of her once. Mahan, however, had privately confirmed her suspicions. The Rihannsu of ch'Rihan, at least those he knew, were becoming restive, frightened, and angry.

And it is not a good idea to frighten my people, Arrhae thought.

She sat in her chair for a while and drank her hot draft, flicking from channel to channel. She was almost amused to see that, despite all the alerts, the information about increased food supplies being made available and link-words for householders to call for advice, there was still not the slightest sense of what all the readiness was supposed to be *about.* The newsreaders speculated about the announcements in a manner that managed to be both tense and casual, as if this were something that happened every day—or as if they had been told to make it seem so. It could not have been easy work, and Arrhae felt sorry for them. *But my part is harder. I must sit here knowing at least some of the truth, and wondering what to do about it that will not put myself and the household in danger.* And then there was the Old Lord to think about, too, up there in the mountains, chivvying the construction workers who were working on the old shieling-house. At least the Old Lord was far enough away from civilization that he was unlikely to come to grief due to any civil unrest. But nonetheless, when the planet came under attack, his safety had to be thought of. And who was seeing about *his* food? And were his weapons in proper condition, and did he have enough clothing?

Arrhae smiled at herself, then. *I am a* hru'hfe *to the bone,* she thought. She changed channels one more time and found herself listening to an intent discussion of yet another food-availability announcement, one that spent entirely too much time concentrating on groundroot. Something about the tone of it, or perhaps just any Rihannha's usual reaction to the wretched root, especially when it might be all you had to eat for a while, made Arrhae start to frown. *I want to do something. I am not going to just sit here anymore.*

The thought decided her. Arrhae went back to her chambers and got dressed in the most casual clothes she could find—an old soft tunic and long skirt, and some comfortable softboots well worn in by what now must be years of wear. Then she went out into the front hall and fished her oldest morning-cloak out of the closet nearest the door.

Sure enough, Mahan was in the hall within a matter of seconds. "Mistress," he said, "where are you going? Was there a call from the Senate?" And then he blinked, and saw how she was dressed.

"Elements be thanked, no," Arrhae said. "They're not in

session today. But, Mahan, I can't bear it. I'm going to market."

"Mistress, no! You are a Senator, you are a—"

"—woman who's tired of skulking in here like I expect something terrible to happen, Mahan!" Arrhae settled the cloak around her shoulders. "Get me my shopping basket."

"But mistress!"

She gave him a look.

He sagged a little. "You can't go out like that, mistress!"

She allowed herself just a small smile. "Better. How would you have me go out, then?"

"Not in that cloak! You used to wear that when you were a, I mean, when you—"

"Mahan! I'm going to the market, not the Praetorate. Now go get that basket."

He opened his mouth to say something, but Arrhae simply looked at him. After a moment, Mahan went off, and Arrhae sighed. Mahan was feeling the stress as much as she was, if not more. She knew he suspected what her fears were, though he never said as much.

He came back with the shopping basket, a still-handsome thing woven of old weathered *tafa* withies and lined with felted fiber. The fiber was new. "You've been taking care of this for me, I see."

"Hifae spilled ale in it last week," Mahan muttered.

"Oh, well," Arrhae said. "That's what the lining's for, to catch things like that. Now, Mahan, the list."

The list of things they had to have on hand to fulfill the requirements of the "readiness exercise" had been their chief subject of conversation for the past day or so, and had also become a sort of code for all the things they were both worrying about but couldn't discuss in front of the household staff. "How much of it do we have now?" Arrhae said.

Mahan produced a much-folded scrap of writing plastic and handed it to her. Arrhae ran down it. "Root, quatchmilk, *hiuthe* juice . . . Are you sure about the brickbread? I hate that stuff, but are you sure there's enough?"

"More than enough, mistress."

"All right." She looked down the list. There were only six or seven things left to be purchased. "I can handle this."

"And you'll have them send anything not fit for you to be seen carrying?"

"Mahan . . . !"

He stopped then, and gave her a look. "Mistress, the House has its reputation to think of."

She smiled at him. "All right, I'll try not to carry home anything that would reflect badly on you. Digging equipment . . . livestock . . ."

"Mistress!"

Arrhae grinned. "I'm sorry, old friend. You make me tease you so. I'll be back shortly."

She glanced at the front door, and then in a spirit of complete rebellion, went out the back way, via the little door that was meant for the staff and delivery people. It gave onto a small landing pad, the part of the garden that was given over to kitchen herbs and soft fruit, and the wall that separated the hinder part of the House's grounds from the little private alleyway leading to the public road into town.

It was a pleasant walk, one she hadn't done in— As she shut the door in the back wall behind her, Arrhae shook her head and tried to work out when she had last had leisure for this stroll. Early in the morning, before the day's heat settled in, when there was still dew on the leaves of the trees that overhung the walls on either side of the alleyway, it had always been enjoyable to set out for the town market with the basket over her arm, and for just a little while to dawdle along listening to the birds and insects and thinking of other birds and insects far away.

There was more than dew in the air this morning; the rain was beginning. It wasn't heavy, and Arrhae pulled the cloak's cowl up and walked quietly down the alley to the road, and then down the road to market.

The stalls were put up each morning by smallholders who flew their produce and other wares down from the mountains very early, stayed until about midday, and then flew home again. They did a circuit of provincial markets that way, each one on a couple of different days each week. Some townsfolk did prefer to shop with the bigger retailers in town, but when Arrhae had been working in household management, she had quickly discovered that it was better to deal directly with a small producer than with a big company. The markups were smaller and the prices and quality of the goods were better, without forcing bulk-buying on you unless you really wanted it. She came around the last curve of the road into the town's main plaza and saw the stalls and stands laid out there, all in the same positions they occupied every week: and a sudden, completely irrational feeling of peace and happiness descended on her. *Order,* she thought, *is a lovely thing. For as long as it lasts.*

She went over to the soft fruit stall to get the quatchmilk, which was very sour and worked well as a preservative or a flavoring. As she was turning away from that stall and looking at her list again, a man went by in front of her, also cloaked, like any other householder come in early to do his own shopping. His cowl was up; no surprise, in this weather. But under it, as he passed, she caught sight of a face she thought she knew. She hunted the memory, caught it.

"Why, Ffairrl!" she said, "fair morning to you!"

He looked at her with complete surprise, and for a moment, from the look on his face, she thought maybe he hadn't recognized her either.

"Deihu," he said very quietly, with an expression both of shock and relief. "Whatever brings you here so early in the morning?"

"Believe it or not, the wretched root, mostly," she said.

"There was none in the market yesterday when my people came down."

"There's a great pile of it over there," Ffairrl said, "but it's been going fast."

"Where, exactly?"

"Come this way," Ffairl said. As they threaded their way among the market stalls, he said, more softly still, "I had been racking my brains to think of a way to reach you, noble *deihu*. I had hoped House Khellian's *hru'hfe* might turn up here today, or perhaps your worthy door-opener."

"I think you've found House Khellian's *hru'hfe*, whether either of us likes to admit it or not," she said under her breath, a little wry. "And, for pity's sake, *deihu* I may be, but you may leave the nobility out of it and be thanked! Arrhae, let it be."

Slowly he nodded as they made their way toward the vegetable stand. "But your cleverness astounds me," Ffairrl said. "The last thing the ones watching you would have expected would be that you would come *here*."

"Their expectations," Arrhae said, "are not entirely what they should be, Ffairrl. On that I think we can agree." She nodded to the stallholder, a woman she didn't recall having seen before, and started picking through the heap of groundroot piled up on the stall's table.

Ffairrl smiled. "They have seen you going about in your silks and riding in your patron's car, and now all believe that you have decided the fine life suits you too well for you ever to look into a cookpot or touch a cleaning-rag again."

She would have been annoyed, except that what he said obscurely pleased her. "That's well enough, then," she said, starting to turn the groundroot over. "*Au*, look at these, will you? The genetic manipulation's taken all the life out of them. They may crop like crazy, but they taste of nothing, and to look at them, you'd swear they're made of plastic. Have these things ever been in dirt?"

He chuckled, and said nothing while Arrhae turned over another few roots, looking for several of a decent size. Finally satisfied, she handed over the House's debit token and let the stallholder register it, then put the root into the basket with the milk and juice and walked on.

"I want to thank you," she said as they got out of anyone's earshot and made for the far side of the market plaza, "for the word you spoke to me the other day. It seems to have left me safe enough."

"After what you did," Ffairrl said, "yes. And not just you."

She darted him a sidewise look from under her cowl.

"There has of course been no news of a certain engagement," Ffairrl said. "But ten ships that might have been there were called away at the last moment by your patron. And their nonappearance would seem to have been the event that decided that engagement's outcome."

Arrhae busied herself with rearranging her basket's contents as they walked. "So," she said softly. "So all this 'readiness' *is* in aid of those who will be here shortly."

Ffairrl nodded. "If you do not have a plan for late tomorrow night and early the morning after, you should make one. It will not be safe in the city. Not at all. And when things become . . . unsettled . . . there will be too many opportunities for those who wish your patron ill to swoop down on you and carry you off to somewhere private."

That was a thought that had occurred to Arrhae more than once. "Well, I had considered the mountains," she said. "Someone needs to go up there and look after that good old man."

"I honor that thought," Ffairrl said, "but you might bring him into danger if you went there. One of your other staff might be better suited, one who would not attract so much attention."

"Mahan?"

"Yes. Indeed, no one would be surprised if all your household staff relocated there, as various other Houses have very, very quietly begun to do. Oh, your people might be watched at first, but probably not for long, especially when matters begin to become more interesting in Ra'tleihfi and its environs. And even less so should you somehow become separated from them when you were all in transit."

Alarm shot through Arrhae. "Separated exactly *how*, Ffairrl?"

"Well," he said, "truly, how can one predict such things? You might always be kidnapped by someone from one of the intelligence services. And once that had happened, none of the *other* Intelligence services would bother to look for you. Especially in the middle of an invasion."

She looked at him. Ffairrl merely smiled.

" 'Kidnapped,' " she said.

"But not a moment before you had had ample time to communicate some useful information to those who would be most concerned about your disappearance," said Ffairrl.

"And once I had made such communications, and become separated from my people?"

"There are quite a few of us who are preparing to make ourselves useful," Ffairrl said. "There is about to be a large gathering of us up near the Pass above Ra'tleihfi, to assist what is about to happen."

And once again Arrhae found herself faced with the choice. Trust this man? Or not? But so far he could have killed her any number of times, by action or inaction, and he had not.

"What information would you be speaking of?" Arrhae said.

Ffairrl peered into her shopping basket. "Is that a *hurvat* on that root?" he said, and reached out from under his cloak to pick the vegetable up.

Arrhae peered at it too. Of much of ch'Rihan's insect life, the *hurvat* was one of her least favorites. It could bore through a root in a matter of minutes, spoiling the whole thing with a corrosive acid. "No," she said after a moment, "I think it's just a spot."

"I think you are right." But she saw the place where his thumb pressed down on the root, and near the large spot they had both "mistaken" for an insect, there was now also a much smaller one. She put the root back into the basket, spot down, and shrugged.

"At any rate," Ffairrl said, "I'm glad to have crossed your path, Arrhae. If you think well enough of that root to make soup of it after you've peeled it, doubtless you'll find a way to let me know. Say, before midnight."

"Doubtless," Arrhae said. "I'll give it careful thought."

"Then fair morning to you, Arrhae."

"Fair morning to you, Ffairrl."

As he was turning, she said, "Ffairrl—"

He looked at her from under the cowl.

"Why?" she said again.

"Because," Ffairrl said, "there are many, many things worth saving on this planet—especially its only other Yankees fan."

Arrhae's mouth dropped right open—but he had already turned and was ambling away.

Quietly she turned and went to finish her shopping, and to otherwise get ready for what was to come.

EIGHTEEN

IN THAT SMALL shielded room on ch'Rihan, three men met for what each of them suspected might be the last time.

"Ten hours," Urellh was saying. He was past his rages, now. Even he was too worn out to indulge himself. "They will be here in ten hours."

"And our weapon," said Armh'n softly, "will be passing through Earth's orbit in thirteen. Should they acquire any kind of victory, they had best enjoy it, for it will be short-lived in the extreme."

"I am still not entirely convinced," tr'Anierh said, "of the effectiveness of this maneuver. I have had a chance to look at some alternate Intelligence—"

"Dubious at best," Urellh said.

"It was accurate enough," tr'Anierh said, "regarding the documentation that your agents aboard those ten ships were carrying." He looked from Armh'n to Urellh.

Both of them looked at each other with the kind of expression one might have otherwise expected to see on a small child caught stealing sweets: as if the matter were hardly worth the mentioning. "If some members of my staff got carried away . . ." Urellh said, waving one hand.

"Exceeded their authority somewhat," Armh'n said.

"Surely we have more important things to think about right now. The fate of the Empire . . ."

Tr'Anierh glanced down at the data display he had

brought with him. He had suspected that this was the excuse he was going to be offered. He was willing enough to let the other Two of the Three think he was accepting it, for the moment. "What is the most recent data on the number of their ships?" he asked.

"Thirty-four of capital size or equivalent," said Urellh, "plus or minus five. Many smaller vessels that are of much less threat. And two huge ships that appear to have been built with looted colonial resources. These are the chief threat in terms of sheer force. But far worse, in their way—"

"*Enterprise.*"

"And *Bloodwing.*"

Tr'Anierh sat back in his chair and frowned. "It would have saved so much trouble if our agent aboard *Bloodwing* had succeeded. The results would have been disproportionately useful. But as usual, an emplaced agent who has a vengeance-agenda may misfire at a critical moment. Never mind. The risk was worthwhile, and the woman provided us with a great deal of useful information over time." He shrugged. "We will put up a memorial to her heroism when we have leisure. Right now, there are these thirty-four ships to deal with, and the two large ones, which are far more of a threat—apparently most extravagantly armed."

"Someone's head," Urellh said under his breath, "is going to take leave of his or her shoulders when we discover who failed to get us timely intelligence of those ships' existence."

"There will be time to worry about that later. Those vessels made very short work of ours at Augo. Possibly they did more damage than all the other ships there combined. They must be our primary targets."

"And just what are we supposed to attack them with?" Urellh said, waving his arms in the air. "Good intentions? We have nothing suitable on-planet for dealing with such things. Look at the size of them; think what their warp engines must be like, how much power they must develop!

There must be some small *worlds* that have less power available to them!"

"Analyses of the recordings brought back from the engagement have revealed some promising weaknesses," said tr'Anierh. "The ships are using hexicyclic screens of a new type, and their weapons are similarly derived. Some of the Home Fleet ships and all of the defense satellites have weapons that can be tuned to go straight through those shields. The main question is where to best target the vessels. The Fleet tacticians are looking at the issue."

"That's some small help," Urellh said. "But I think you are missing a point here. That cursed woman is more dangerous than any ship, no matter how large. If we could find a certain way to get rid of her during the attack, that would go a long way to ending the problem. No matter their size, the only reason those ships are here is something to do with *her.* Unfortunately she'll probably stay hidden away, on *Enterprise* for all we know, or possibly on one of those giant vessels. She'd never be so lost to folly as to actually show herself in-system in *Bloodwing* itself." He was pacing and fretting again now. "And there's still too much uncertainty regarding what her other plans might be. Damned two-faced traitress, she wouldn't even tell her closest friend more than a word here or there about what she had in mind."

"In that she merely proves herself the careful commander we unfortunately already know her to be," Armh'n said, sitting down on one of the benches by the window and looking out over the city. It was night, near midnight in Ra'tleihfi's time zone. Light gleamed in the rain-wet streets below, and the shine of buildings and passing ground traffic, though there was less than usual of that due to the continuing security alerts. "And friend or no friend, the spy was her medical officer, after all. Did you seriously expect her to waste her time discussing invasion strategy and tactics with the ship's healer?"

Urellh glowered at Armh'n. "Fortunately for us," tr'Anierh said, "I have some intelligence regarding the invading fleet's intentions that you may find both interesting and useful. Our sources tell us that they are intending for ch'Havran. And they have brought Gurrhim with them."

The other two stared at him, open-mouthed.

"Impossible!" Urellh said. "Our spy reported that he had been killed! She reported it from *Bloodwing* itself! I heard the message from Kirk's own vessel, his own comm officer's voice."

"Apparently," tr'Anierh said, "the detestable traitress already harbored some suspicions that there was an active agent aboard her ship. The report was disinformation. They saved the man's life and brought him back here with them to be their tool on ch'Havran. Probably they've promised him that he'll be some kind of puppet governor afterward."

"I would be suspicious," Armh'n said, "that this report might not itself be disinformation. Has there been anything that could be construed as more concrete proof? Imagery, eyewitness reports?"

Tr'Anierh's eyes narrowed just briefly in annoyance. These men had come to assume that almost everything they heard was a lie. Themselves unwilling to waste the truth on anyone, it seemed to them that any other sensible person must therefore be as great a liar as they. "Not as yet," he said. "We will have to monitor that situation. If they truly have him, they will doubtless try to display him to the Havrannssu population via video or some similar method. We must prevent that. Otherwise the deluded idiots over there will flock to whatever force arrives to claim it supports his cause. And if he himself really is alive, and should make planetfall there, especially anywhere near his old power base, the place is all too ripe for him to consolidate power and come after us at his leisure. So we must keep the invading fleet, large or small, away from ch'Havran at all costs—keep them out of transporter range, at the very least, and deny them any other manner of landing."

"There is another matter about those large ships that requires our attention," Armh'n said. "One of the ingathering Grand Fleet vessels made planetfall at Kavethti to reprovision on its way in—and found the place a desert. The whole population was gone."

"Klingons, perhaps," Urellh said.

Armh'n shook his head. "There were no signs of combat. The cities were simply abandoned wholesale, and not in a hurry; residences were empty of possessions, industries had been stripped of all but the biggest equipment. If the missing Kavethssu should be *in* one of those ships . . ."

The three of them looked at one another in considerable concern. "There could be thousands of them," tr'Anierh said.

"Tens of thousands," said Armh'n.

"Or more," said Urellh.

"We cannot let them get near either ch'Rihan *or* ch'Havran," said Armh'n. "Ships we could have handled. But that many troops? Never."

"Ch'Rihan is more easily defended," Urellh said. "There are plenty of troops here, and using the orbital mass-transport facilities at Grand Fleet headquarters, we can put them anywhere on the planet we require within a single rotation period. If we need extra warm bodies to throw at the invaders while we deal with their ships, the civilian population can be mobilized. But as regards the Havrannssu, their mobilization had better start now—both as defense and preventive measure, should rumors of Gurrhim's status start to spread. Send as many army units over as possible and round up the city populations, issue them weapons, prepare them to resist the landings."

"They will not be willing," Armh'n said.

"They will be willing enough with the ground forces' disruptors pointed at their heads, and their children in safekeeping to guarantee their enthusiasm," said Urellh. "So let us get that matter in train. There then remains only the question of what to do with that wretched woman when we do get our hands on her at last."

"Kill her and be done," tr'Anierh said.

"Certainly that's too easy a fate for her now," said Armh'n. "For look how far she's come. Even if we recover the Sword now, and put it back where it belongs, everyone who looks at it is going to immediately think, 'Once upon a time someone stole that, and then returned with it to the very heart of the Empire, trying to make it all her own. Someone could do that again.' We need to make certain that any image of the Sword has that woman's shed blood associated with it. Her death must be public, prolonged, excruciating, and shameful. And with that in mind, our fleet's main priority must be to take whatever ship she's in, extract her from it, and get her offside somewhere until we can deal with the invading vessels. Once she's known to be in chains in Ra'tleihfi, the rebels on both worlds will realize that the only way to buy their own lives back from us is to repulse the invaders. Without her, Kirk and *Enterprise* will depart. Without her, the crews of the rebel ships will have nothing left to follow. They—"

Urellh's communicator went off in his pocket.

He frowned furiously, and tr'Anierh began to suspect that he had been too quick to judge the other's inability to work himself into one more rage. Urellh pulled the communicator out of his pocket, keyed it awake.

"Have I not told you *never* to—" he said to the air, but then he broke off. "They have *what?*"

The other two looked at him curiously.

"That cannot be the case. It is probably another software failure like that little one we had last—"

He broke off again. Tr'Anierh and Armh'n looked at each other with surprise as they saw sweat start to pop out on Urellh's forehead.

"How long until they are operational again?"

A silence.

"Well, what about the satellites on the other side? We should still be able to—"

He held still, looking out through the window at the night. "That's very interesting," Urellh said, quite low. "Yes. Yes, well, see what else you can— All right, go on. I am done."

Urellh slowly put away the communicator and just looked sightlessly out into the night for some moments. Then he turned to Armh'n and tr'Anierh.

"The monitoring satellites in the Outmarches have ceased to answer," he said.

Tr'Anierh looked at Urellh and started feeling something like panic crawling at the bottom of his gut. It made no sense. The news that there were about to be enemy ships, *alien* ships, in Eisn homespace tomorrow, should theoretically have affected him far more direly. But those satellites had always been a promise of a kind of security—a physical reaffirmation that, even at their least understandable, other species could be dealt with to a certain extent, successfully held at arm's length. Now even that old certainty was starting to crumble.

"Good Elements all about us," Armh'n said, getting up from his bench. "Who has done such a thing? The Federation? The Klingons?"

Tr'Anierh shook his head, starting to go colder still. "The Klingons would seem the more likely culprits. Why would the *Federation* be involved? They *insisted* on those satellites, they were an integral part of the treaty, so long ago. They would hardly—"

"I would tend to agree with you," Urellh said, deadly quiet, "since apparently the satellites on the Federation side have gone silent as well."

The three of them stared at each other. Tr'Anierh's mouth was going dry.

"Klingons," he said. "And to think we had such plans of playing them off against the Federation. *Now* we see what their intentions are. They will let these damned rebels reduce what's left of Grand Fleet to scrap, and when that's done, they will descend on us right here in our own homespace and take the Empire for their own."

But Armh'n was shaking his head. "No," he said. "Don't you see it? *The Federation satellites are gone too.* Don't you realize what this means?"

The other two looked at him, uncomprehending. "Have you already forgotten the Starfleet vessels at Augo?" Armh'n cried. "They've destroyed the satellites *themselves,* to make sure neither we nor anyone in the nonmilitary parts of the Federation is able to tell what's going on in this part of space—and now they're on their way here! The task force they sent to Augo was simply there to test our ability to defend ourselves against an incursion by enemy forces. They found that ability poor. Now, with oversight from their soft-minded civilian populations cut off, with no way for evidence of what's about to happen to reach the Federation worlds, Starfleet is coming here in force to deal with us once and for all. Perhaps with the Klingons as well. And perhaps . . ." He trailed off. "Perhaps this is because they have found out about the device."

"They have not," tr'Anierh said. "If they had, they would right now be spending every available resource to destroy it, and they have not. Our own spies in Starfleet have told us so. It remains hidden, as it must until it is activated just before its strike. You must keep your nerve, Armh'n. This is ill news, but hardly the worst."

There was silence in the room for a few minutes as each man contemplated his own vision of what "the worst" looked like. "This is all moons'-shine until we have better data that is not three-quarters subjective evaluation," tr'Anierh said. "Meantime, Grand Fleet is mobilized. The admirals will be meeting with us in the morning. The defense satellites are primed and fully manned. There is nothing we can do now, except wait our time."

"And consider our options for leaving here when the enemy—"

"*No,*" tr'Anierh said. "That is something I will not do. Nor, by the way, will *you* be permitted to do."

Tr'Anierh saw the looks of shock, of anger, on the others' faces, and had a brief moment of wicked pleasure as he watched those faces work and change. "After the business at Augo," he said, "I thought perhaps I had been paying too little attention, not only to my own security, but to the question of our joint accountability. So I asked some of my own staff to 'exceed their instructions' and 'get carried away' regarding the way the control codes are handled for the final activation of the nova bomb." He smiled. "You will find that they can no longer be independently activated. All three controls must be activated within a second of one another, all three must be no more than two arms' length from one another, and all three must be activated from within ten miles of the city limits of Ra'tleihfi."

The other Two of the Three stared at him, aghast. "If you had been a little less intent on saving your own skins at the expense of mine," tr'Anierh said, "and a little more intent on saving this Empire rather than abandoning it until it was bombed into a shape you better liked, who knows, you might have anticipated and prevented this. But now the culpability, if nothing else, will be a little more evenly distributed. Now you will be more intent on the preservation of the heart of the Empire than you have been, if you are at all concerned about the 'last great blow' truly striking home. And if in the process you have been paid in your own coin for your duplicity . . ." Tr'Anierh shrugged. "I, too, get carried away sometimes. But it will not be happening to me this time—or not me alone. Should it finally happen, believe me, you two will be carried away along with me, one way or another."

Neither Urellh nor Armh'n had a word to say. "So," tr'Anierh said. "Let us consider how and where best to meet the attack."

Through the long night of inner Rihannsu space the armada made its way, slowly growing as it went. It had met no resistance since Augo, and that worried Jim.

It also worried him that he had an armada, though theoretically it should have been a delight. And indeed, at this point, the night before their engagement, *everything* was worrying him. To be one of the movers of so massive a chunk of history would possibly be more enjoyable after the fact—if he survived it, and if he didn't screw up. But the night before the engagement, as Jim studied the battle plan, and revised it and revised it again, there seemed to be so many ways to screw up that he found himself increasingly willing to be relegated to footnote status.

Jim sat at his desk and paged back and forth through the display on a padd, revising, adding a thought here, changing a troop disposition there, consolidating a couple of movements in another spot. *There should have been another attack,* he kept thinking, as he corrected and altered and shifted minor puzzle-pieces around in his master plan. *This would have been a great time to hit us, just to keep us off balance, to give us something extra to think about. Why haven't they even sent some light craft out this way, some skirmishers?*

He rested his chin on one hand, studying the screen. *Do they really just not have the equipment to spare? Or are they suckering us again somehow?* The paranoia was biting him hard, now. *All these people on all these ships . . .* some *of them have to be Rihannsu agents. After all, if, on as little a ship as Ael's, the crewman who was almost her best friend could be an agent, a person well known, absolutely trusted . . .*

He sighed and put the thought aside one more time. There were many more things to deal with. Jim told the padd to send the latest copy of the plan over to *Kaveth* and *Tyrava* and *Bloodwing,* and then pushed back and stared at his desk, the viewer, the padd. He hardly saw them. What he was seeing was the space around Eisn. The positions of the twin worlds this time of year in relationship to the other uninhabited planets in the system, the orbit of Grand Fleet's headquarters around ch'Rihan, the defense satellites, the ships that would be awaiting them, their dispositions . . .

He closed his eyes and rubbed his face wearily.

The comm beeped. Jim reached out and hit the button. "Kirk here."

"Jim," McCoy's voice said. *"I have a message for you from* Tyrava.*"*

"What?"

"Veilt says, 'Tell your vhai'd *Captain to stop obsessing and leave us be for the night!' "*

Jim sighed. "It's all very well for him—"

"Yes," McCoy said, *"it is. And he's right. So shut up and let it lie for a while. Come on down to rec and I'll give you some of Old Doc McCoy's Overwork Remedy."*

"I don't feel like drinking, Bones."

"Of course you don't. But it was a kick in the pants I had in mind. Just get down here before I send security for you."

There was no arguing with McCoy in this mode. "Ten minutes," he said. "Out." He got up.

His door buzzed. "Come," he said.

Spock was standing there. "Captain," he said.

Jim grinned ruefully. "The doctor—"

"—is, as the idiom would have it, 'throwing his weight around,' yes," Spock said. "We can do little but comply at such times." He looked at the captain's padd. "Before he spoke to me, I was about to contact you about your last draft of the plan."

"Was there something missing?"

"Captain," Spock said, "reading it, I was reminded of the ancient Vulcan proverb about the masterpiece. It says that a minimum of two entities are required to create one: one to hold the brush, and the other to hit the first on the head with a hammer when it's finished, because the holder of the brush so rarely can tell that it is long since time to stop."

Jim's grin widened. "You two are ganging up on me again. All right. But before you ask," he said, only losing a little of the grin, "the answer to the question you haven't asked is: Scared. Scared to death."

Spock tilted his head a little to one side. "If you are planning to become a telepath, Captain, there may have to be changes in our watch-standing schedules. It can be most disconcerting hearing another being think on a regular basis."

Now Jim's grin went wry. "Have you been to see Scotty and K's't'lk yet?"

"I have."

"And how are they doing?" Jim went over to the closet to get out one more uniform tunic. It was astonishing the kind of sweat you could work up with nothing but a padd and a stylus.

"As regards the transporter interdiction," Spock said, "very well indeed. Mr. Scott's staff have installed his equipment on both of the Great Ships, and Mr. Scott has tested the field-generation system out to about fourteen thousand kilometers. It does not focus particularly well, but it does not need to. Even a small transporter malfunction is sufficient to render those working with a transporter most unwilling to use it until the malfunction vanishes."

Jim pulled the new tunic on. "Good. How about the jamming?"

"The modalities the Free Rihannsu forces were using at Artaleirh should serve us again," Spock said. "I have been working with some of the technical staff on *Tyrava* to improve the volume of space that can be affected. While it is possible that the ch'Rihan-based Rihannsu will have jamming of their own that will be as effective, we have been equipping every party of the mobile forces with at least one of the low-tech comm pods you set Mr. Scott to construct."

"Just hope they don't figure out in time how to jam them too."

"Captain, as technologically advanced a people as the Rihannsu are not only unlikely to immediately recognize the technology we will be using, but unlikely to be able to come up with a quick answer to the problem. Their sciences have been deeply affected by their mindset, and by and large they have been increasingly directed, not toward exploration or analysis of the new, but management and control of situations already extant."

"All right," Kirk said. He headed for the door, taking a deep breath and almost wishing he didn't have to ask the question the answer to which was going to scare him the most. "And about the nova bomb?"

Spock shook his head. "I have heard nothing from my father as yet," he said as they left Jim's quarters, "but then I would not expect to. The return message would have to come directly, rather than by boosted relay as it went out, and there would be a considerable delay. We can only hope that Sarek has been able to reach the President in time."

Jim sighed. "And then he'll do . . . what?" He shook his head. "You can't destroy what you can't see. And they won't uncloak that thing until the last minute, I'm sure of it."

Spock nodded. "However, as regards getting that news to Earth, Mr. Scott and K's't'lk have begun testing the new settings for the resonance inducer, but with an additional purpose in mind, not just the disruption of a star's seeding or of the detonation of the nova bomb, though they are still concentrating on that as well. They feel that they may be able to use the equivalence-induction technique on a star to transmit a message directly to Earth's solar system, via the sun itself."

Jim raised his eyebrows at that as they paused outside the turbolift's doors. "Do they seriously think they might get some results with that?"

"They do," Spock said. "The main difficulty is that there are no suitable stars along our present course on which they might safely test the technique."

Jim shook his head again. "We're getting short of time, Mr. Spock. Assuming we would have time to divert long enough for a test—which I'm not sure we would—what's the nearest star that would be suitable?"

"Eisn," Spock said.

Kirk groaned softly. "That wouldn't be optimal."

"No," Spock said. "I would say not."

The lift's doors opened; they got in. "Main recreation," Spock said, and the lift doors closed.

They rode in silence for a few moments. "Spock," Jim said, "you'll be pleased to hear that I'm learning something from this experience."

"What are you learning, Captain?"

"That I may be an admiral, but I still don't feel like one."

Spock put up one eyebrow. "I gather that you find this an inopportune time to have come to that particular conclusion."

"You have no idea." Jim rubbed his eyes.

"Captain," Spock said, "I have the fullest confidence in your ability for this task."

"Yes, I'm sure you do," Jim said, "and the problem is, *so does everybody else but me!*"

Spock looked at him, and the expression was serious, but not somber. "Jim," he said after a moment, "that uncertainty is a weapon in your hand. You will use it, I am sure, as effectively as the others with which chance and the moment have provided you. And all of us, who are equally part of that weapon, will do what we must to fulfill the mission that Starfleet has assigned you. On that you can depend."

Jim swallowed. "Thank you, Mr. Spock," he said. "And don't tell me that thanks aren't logical!"

The lift doors opened. "The thought had not occurred to me, Captain," Spock said.

Together they headed down the hall to main recreation. Once again, as they headed in, the place was quiet, but because of the rearrangement of some of the more critical shift rotations to take the battle scheduling into account, a lot of people seemed to have opted for an early evening. Across the room, though, over by the poker table, various crew were lounging and talking quietly. Ael was there along with McCoy and Chekov and Sulu and a few others.

As Jim and Spock approached, Ael put aside the padd she had been reading and stood up to greet them. "Captain," she said, "if your presence here means you are done with that for the moment—" She threw a sideways glance at the padd, then back at Jim.

Jim grinned and sat down. "Mr. Spock was threatening to hit me with a hammer."

"Captain," Spock said, "I was merely repeating an adage. Such behavior in actual practice would seriously contravene—"

Ael and Jim began to laugh together. "And as for you," Jim said. "Anything to add?"

She shook her head. "Without further data," she said, "further planning is idle. But now that you are finished, and I have finished looking over your plans as Veilt and Thala have, I can retire. In six hours, it will all begin, and begin to end." She leaned back and stretched, looking around her. "I have enjoyed my last night here."

"I wouldn't start calling it *that*," McCoy said.

She laughed gently at him. "Shall I try to hide the possibilities from myself, or you, McCoy? I think not. It may be my last night on *Bloodwing,* as well, if the Elements so please, but there I must be. I must be seen to lead the battle group into the system, from my own ship's bridge. After that, when it comes time to take our battle to the planet—there, too, I must be. My credibility is about to become as much a part of our battle array as anything with a warp drive attached."

"Well," Jim said, "once the transporters go down for everything in the neighborhood of the Hearthworlds, those of us who're going planetside with the troops will all need to be on *Tyrava,* but you've got the timings for that. Once Grand Fleet HQ has been dealt with, and we achieve local-space superiority, we're going to have to get our boots down on the ground along with everyone else."

Ael passed a hand over her eyes. "That remains my last nightmare, Captain. I cannot get over the fear that we will at some point find ourselves halfway over Mount Eilariv and unable to get in touch with our people because of the planet-based jamming."

Jim looked up and saw Scotty coming across the room toward them, with K's't'lk in tow. "As it happens, for a change, I think I have a straightforward answer for one of your problems." He looked up at Scotty. "Have you got our widgets, Scotty?"

"Aye," Scotty said, and pulled something out of a little case he was carrying. "It'll piggyback onto a communicator. You'll just need to stretch the usual slipcase a little."

Jim took what Scotty handed him: a small, silvery-cased device that looked to Jim like a communicator, though rather slimmer.

"This is it?" he said, turning it over in his hands.

"Aye," Scotty said.

Kirk flipped it open. The controls inside were minimal, and again rather like a communicator's. "I thought it'd be bigger."

Scotty shook his head. "Not at all," he said, and handed a similar device to Ael.

She studied the sleek little thing. "Another communicator?"

"Not the usual kind," Scotty said. "'Tis a radio."

Ael looked bemused. "A what?"

"Here," Jim said, "let me show you the wavelengths." He reached over to the poker table, brought up its undersurface gaming screens, hit the control that linked them out into the ship's main computers via the games computer's interface, and called up a diagram of the electromagnetic spectrum.

He pointed. "Right there," Jim said.

Ael stared. "But why ever would anyone use *that* range for communications?" she said, bewildered. "That whole part of the spectrum is endlessly vulnerable to every kind of jamming and natural interference. Even the sun can render it useless in active times!"

"Over long distances, of course it can," Jim said. "But over the short haul, when you have line of sight, it works pretty well. Add a ship in orbit that's able to act as a relay and overcome the line-of-sight problem in difficult terrain, and you have a perfectly workable solution when everyone around you is jamming more technologically advanced comms."

Ael looked over the little object and shook her head. "Tr'Keirianh will be completely fascinated. I pray these work as well as you say they will."

"We're betting they will," Jim said. "The basic concept goes back to a battle on Earth a few centuries ago when a technologically advanced power—for that time, anyway—went up against an opponent that was less well provided with the newest equipment. The vessel had long range propellant-based weapons that shot solid projectiles, and the computers that worked out the firing ranges and elevations for the weapons were calibrated for the most modern weapons that might be brought against them. The vessel's opponents, however, only had small flying craft called Fairey Swordfish, which dated back easily two decades, and had long since been left behind by faster and more advanced craft."

Ael's eyebrows went up. "You are about to tell me," she said, "that the firing solutions of the higher-tech vessels could not cope with the—Swordfish?" She smiled at the name.

"They shot the hell out of the battleships," Jim said. "It was a fluke, yes, but it worked. There have been times since when it's proven smart to look back for one's tech instead of forward."

Ael looked thoughtful. "So all our people who go dirtside are going to be equipped with these," Jim said, "and *Tyrava* and *Kaveth* have been fabricating them to Scotty's specs at considerable speed. Every assault group will be equipped with these—at least one to every fifty people, and sometimes more. So the assault on Ra'tleihfi won't have a chance to get too much out of hand."

Ael shivered. "Just the words trouble me, now that they are so close to being made real."

"It's the kind of commander who wouldn't be troubled by them," McCoy said, "who'd be giving *me* cause for concern."

"I agree," Jim said. "And though I understand your discomfort, this *is* what you came to do. Time to do it. Meanwhile, I'm going to turn in shortly." Jim glanced at McCoy. "Bones, just this once I want one of your mildest sedatives."

The doors to the corridor opened. "I'll get you that presently." McCoy got up and headed over that way.

"We're at a little less than T minus ten hours," Jim said to Ael. "I'll be up in six hours. At that point, as per the plan, we'll send out the smallships and cruisers that will be acting as skirmishers. They'll test the system's outer defenses and get firsthand Intelligence as to the disposition of Grand Fleet's big ships. Once we're sure where they are, we start messing with their minds." And at that point he grinned rather ferally. "Not that they won't have been well messed with already. There's nothing so effective against an opponent as rendering him uncertain of the effectiveness of his carefully crafted battle plan at the last minute. And there's some more of that still to come."

He glanced across the room. Gurrhim was heading toward them, progressing steadily, though still with the general air of a man who was somewhat sore in various parts of his person. "Captain," he said.

"Sir," Jim said, and stood up. "How are you feeling?"

"I have been better," Gurrhim said, looking around at them all, "but considering that without the good doctor I would simply be feeling dead, I will not complain."

"See that," McCoy said, ambling along behind Gurrhim, "an appreciative patient. There had to be one or two of them left in the galaxy."

Jim raised his eyebrows, but refused to rise to the bait. "So now's your time to take center stage," he said to Gurrhim. "Did the recording of your speech go all right?"

"It did," Gurrhim said, "for all that I am no great speech-maker."

Ael looked up at him and laughed. "Disinformation is in your blood, you noble fraud. How many times have I heard you on the floor of the Senate, bending them all to your will?"

"If anyone was swayed at such times," said Gurrhim, "it was not by my rhetoric or my sentiments, but by my stock portfolio. After all, when you have no choice but to buy your food from a certain stallholder, you listen to his maunderings and nod respectfully until you've agreed at a price and can walk off with a full basket." His grin wasn't nearly as sour as it might have been. "But the story will be far different now. All I now have to sell the government is quatchmilk; and just hearing my voice will be to them as if they were drinking it by the tankardful."

He eased himself down into one of the neighboring

chairs. "Now, however," Gurrhim said, "the point is to have them hear me. I left Lieutenant Commander Uhura completing the preparation of the raw video. She told me it would be ready to transmit about the time I arrived down here. So are you sure you can get the message to my Havrannsu through the jamming, Captain? For apparently it has already begun."

"We'll get it through," Jim said. "Scotty?"

"Aye," Scotty said, "we will. Jamming's only effective up to a certain point. If you're willing to punch enough power into a given signal, over limited distances, the jamming fails. And *Tyrava* has power to spare—more than our laddies down below are expecting, I'm thinking. We're going to feed the gentleman's video into a narrow-band hyperhet blast that'll go through any kind of jamming they've got like a hot wire through ice." He glanced down at K's't'lk. "And once that's taken care of, we can test a duplicate transmission through the resonance inducer at short range."

"Scotty!" Jim said. "The last time you did that you—"

"It's not going to be *that* kind of test, Captain!" K's't'lk said. "This is a wholly different effect. We're just going to get the star to 'exhale' a tachyon burst encoded with a copy of the transmission. If we can get Eisn to do that, then once we've set up the equivalency resonance with the sun, we can hook an entirely different message to it. Such as one keyed to destroy the nova bomb before it gets into the sun—"

Jim was starting to get nervous. "It sounds nice, but are you absolutely sure that there wouldn't be any untoward effects on Eisn?"

Scotty and K's't'lk looked at each other. "Well . . ."

Ael saw the look. "Not with *my* star, you do not! I have no desire to save my worlds from the Praetorate only to set them on fire!"

Jim wholeheartedly agreed. "Belay it, you two. We have enough problems right now. K's't'lk, have you got your ship ready?"

"Of course, Captain. I had her beamed over to *Tyrava* this morning. When the troop carriers go out and we go with them, she'll serve as admiral's gig for the engagement. She's better equipped for this kind of work than any of *Enterprise*'s shuttles would be."

"Very well." Jim got up; the rest rose with him. "Ladies and gentlemen, let's go to our rest. Sleep well—and wake up sharp."

The *Enterprise* crew and Gurrhim said their good nights and headed off. Only Jim and Ael were left, looking out those great windows.

"We have come a very long way," Ael said quietly. "And there is no refusing the rest of the course laid out for us—the course we laid out ourselves."

Jim shook his head. After a moment he said, "There was an old story on Earth about how someone went out in the dark and heard a great voice calling from the sea, 'The hour is come, but not the man.' " He looked out at the dark. "I guess we all come up against that sooner or later. The fear that we'll be insufficient to the moment, somehow, and betray the future."

Ael nodded. "I have no fear of that in your regard. You have kept faith when many another would have turned and gone his own way."

"And so have you," Jim said. "You've been serving this particular dream for a long, long while. So, let's get some rest. And in the morning, let's go make the future happen."

She bowed her head to him. "A fair night to you," Ael said, and left.

A few minutes after the doors shut on her, Jim went as well, leaving behind him a room full of nothing but silence and darkness, and the light of the stars pouring past *Enterprise* as she plunged toward her next battlefield.

NINETEEN

SIX HOURS LATER Ael was standing behind her command chair, intently studying the viewscreen on *Bloodwing*'s bridge.

Gurrhim stood there in front of the cameras with that blunt, bluff farmer's look that anyone who had seen him on a news channel in recent years would well have recognized; and he stood there in the robes of a Praetor. *Elements only know where he got those,* Ael thought. *Then again, it is not beyond belief that someone on* Enterprise *manufactured them for him. Certainly he had little but a hospital robe on him when he came.*

"*You see me standing here,*" he said, "*despite having been told that I was dead. I have no regret in telling you that the reports were premature.*" He smiled slightly. "*The Elements have plainly purposed otherwise for me. And in me now, you see the truth of the old saying that chief among all Elements is the element of surprise.*"

Ael had to smile. It was just like him to trot out these hoary old proverbs even at such a time, and the chuckle that went around the bridge told her that her crew was amused as well. *But see how sly the old creature is,* she thought. *No generated hologram version, no fake Gurrhim, would come out with such old-fashioned saws at a time like this, but the genuine article could not be prevented.*

"*Now I come to tell you,*" Gurrhim said, "*that those who

lied to you about my death have been caught in one lie too many. I have come to cast that lie back in their teeth—and I come with friends. One of them I suspect you will know. I will not say her name now. I am as conservative about such things as many of you. But there can come a time when a burned name can be rewritten and spoken again."

He looked into the recording device, intent. *"The government of our worlds, which is our right, has been wrested from our hands. Once upon a time, all the voices in our world had a right to speak. Perhaps for convenience's sake, they did it through representatives—but now those representatives have less voice than ever they had. The people of our outerworlds are disenfranchised. The people of our innerworlds are learning the taste of tyranny. They feed it to us in small doses, spoon by spoon, thinking we will get used to the flavor, like children being coaxed to eat something that will be good for them. But in no way is what has been happening in our worlds good for us! It is time to turn our faces away from the spoon, and push away the plate, and overset the table, and get up and walk away. When governments murder those who speak the truth, it is time to get new governments."*

He paused for breath. It seemed that this still sometimes came hard to him. *"At any rate, I am done being 'dead' now; so there is work to be done. To landholders of mine, and cousins and more distant relatives of our House, I say, now is the time to stand to arms. Await my coming. The government, hearing this, be assured, will cast me as a traitor. They will cast those among you who rise up to support me as traitors too. They will seek to raise up your neighbors against you, and sow dissension in your ranks. You must allow them to do no such thing! If they set you to killing one another, they have already won. To those uncertain of my motivations, or my desires, I say, wait. Close your doors and do nothing. Free Rihannsu must not make war upon one another, for it is what*

*the corrupt ones most desire. To my sons and daughters, I
say, this is the time that we have long expected. You know
what action to take. Prepare to receive many guests. To all
you minions and secret spies of the corrupt Tricameron,
lying in secret among us these many years, foisted upon us in
order to keep us subject, I say to you, make your farewells.
Countrymen, here are their names."*

Ael glanced around her. "Elements about us, who knew
what weapon those young men from *Gorget* brought us?"
She shook her head as the recitation of names Gurrhim had
begun went on and on. "How long has he been carrying that
list in his brain? And what kind of uproar will break out
now?"

Aidoann shook her head. "*Khre'Riov,* whatever the Praetorate and the Senate think in terms of our plans—whether
they think that the invasion is going to happen on ch'Havran
or not—they are going to have a busy day ahead of them. At
least their poor tools on ch'Havran will." She, too, shook her
head in admiration. "If they thought there was civil unrest
there before . . ."

Ael shook her head. "I see house-burnings, and all manner of trouble. And see again the old sly-boots' cleverness.
How he gives even those who are uncertain of him evidence
of the spies they have long suspected live among them. They
will love him for that." She straightened up. "Well, we will
see what happens now. What is our position?"

"We are one tenth of a light-year from Eisn," Aidoann
said. "We will be at the rendezvous point noted in the plan as
five-d in approximately three minutes."

"And that is well," Ael said. "Engine status?" It was more
than the engine she was inquiring about.

"*Khre'Riov,*" tr'Keirianh said from his station, "we're
ready."

"And the singularity?"

"Functioning quite normally, *khre'Riov.*"

"Pray it continues to do so," Ael said. "This would not be the time for a malfunction."

"We're agreed," tr'Keirianh said.

"And the weapons?"

"The augmentations seem to be in perfect order, *khre'Riov*," tr'Keirianh said. "All we need now is something to shoot at."

Ael smiled slightly and looked at the screen. "Show me tactical," she said to Aidoann.

The screen showed her a two-dimensional representation of the armada. Only the largest ships, and *Kaveth* and *Tyrava*, showed as actual shapes; *Enterprise* and *Bloodwing* and anything smaller than they showed merely as a spark of light, in the scale that was needed to express all the vessels that were there. *Enterprise* and *Bloodwing* were near the forefront, and a great curve of other vessels, such as those captured from Grand Fleet at Artaleirh and renamed, hung back just behind them. The whole array of vessels went to define the rest of a rough half-sphere, and the array was pointed roughly at Eisn in the distance, the tiniest possible golden globe. At such a distance, the planets were not visible. But Ael, knowing from what point she looked down on the solar system, knew exactly where they were. *Soon now,* she thought. *Very soon.*

"Dropping out of warp now, *khre'Riov,* as per schedule," Aidoann said.

Ael merely nodded. Though she had had much to do with the making of this plan, she would now have but little room for the spur-of-the-moment action that so routinely characterized engagements in her world. This game was being played on a different level. In some ways, it was much like Mr. Spock's chess—but in others, it was less a game than a dance. *I step here, you step there, or if you step that way, then I step another;* all planned, everything anticipated. The rigor of the structure would have seemed stifling, except that it was better, in this situation at least, to be stifled than dead. Dead folk could not complete the job they had come all this way to do.

Though their shields were up, Ael leaned on the back of her seat and felt decidedly exposed. Out of the corner of her eye, she caught the look that Aidoann was throwing at her. "I know," Ael said, "I know we're well outside what they will have assumed is our best scan range. Nonetheless . . ."

That was when the fire lanced out from space all around them, and the ships started to appear.

The initial fire splashed off their shields, due to the attackers' distance. Ael swallowed and stood up straight. "Khiy," she said, "fire and evasive at will, according to four-n. Mind our neighbors in the pattern!"

"Ie, khre'Riov—"

"They've decided not to let us in close," Kirk said from *Enterprise* as *Bloodwing*'s disruptors lanced out. Ael could just hear him grinning. *"All right, we can throw away everything from four-a through four-m."*

"Why?" Ael said. "What would have been your preference?"

"The closer to the planet, the better," Jim said. *"Any limitation of the enemy's maneuverability is to be welcomed. But if they want to have it out here, we're ready for that too. We expect more cloaked incoming, though."*

"We will be ready," Ael said.

Khiy threw the ship into evasive along the lines that had been laid down for it in the master attack plan. In this early part of the engagement, the ships would be moving largely in unison, while their commanders took a little time to grasp the numbers of the enemy and their disposition. *"Well,"* came Jim's voice over the comms, *"they're closer than I thought. Maybe we can throw out everything through four-p . . ."*

"It was only to be expected," Ael said, "that they might have acquired some data about our scan range. Tr'Hrienteh might not have gotten it from me, but she had access to ship's computers—it's information she could have easily picked up just from ship's comms in the last week or so. Well, we have a few surprises of our own."

Things were starting to happen more quickly. Ael saw three Grand Fleet cruisers diving toward her. "Khiy," she said, "this would be a good time to avoid them."

But he was already swerving away, angling upward and outward within the pattern laid out for them, and streaking briefly back toward the great ships. It was the strategy that she and Jim had agreed upon. "If you're going to be an idiot," he'd said, "and insist on riding out front, make sure you're covered. Don't be shy about letting the big gunnery handle your troubles." But she'd noticed that *Enterprise,* too, had been "riding out front," and she thought she had shown great control in not calling Kirk on it.

The pursuit dropped away behind them, but kept on firing. "They are none too eager to get near *Tyrava*," Ael said, and smiled. "Khiy, bring us round back of them; we will have another crack at those miscreants."

"Little time for that, right now, *khre'Riov*," Khiy said. The supercruiser was coming up behind them. Ael looked at it, concerned, thinking that its commander might have tractor beams on his or her mind. At the same time, she was tempted to laugh. How unlike this was from her usual fights. How strange, hardly to even notice the name of the ship as you shoot at it. *The world is not what it used to be.*

Khiy swung the ship back toward *Tyrava*. The cruiser was following her with some purpose, heading straight toward the great ship, and Ael grew uncomfortable. *There is something unwise about this,* she thought. "Khiy! Veer off!"

"*Ael,*" a voice came. It was Kirk, micromanaging his battle plan again. "*Where're you going?*"

"I am not sure at the moment," Ael said, "but I have the feeling that this is the wrong place for me to be."

Kirk said a word. It was not one she had ever heard from him previously; the translator refused to render it. *"Ael,"* Kirk said, *"I thought we've had this discussion enough times. There's very little room in this operation for spontaneity."*

And Khiy abruptly threw the ship to starboard. Not even *Bloodwing's* gravitational dampers could cope with the sudden move, and Ael had to grab the seat in front of her to stay upright, and with the other hand brace the Sword to keep it from falling off the seat's arms. Behind them, where they had been, a ferocious beam of blue-white fire ravened out from the cruiser and hit *Tyrava's* shields.

It pierced them. The beam lanced through, scoring the hull. A puff of air and fire washed out from the contact point.

"We are not the only ones with new technology!" Ael said. "Or with the wit to use it! Captain?"

"I saw it," Kirk said. *"Mr. Spock—"*

"Scanning," Spock said. After a second he said, *"They have augmented disruptors, similar to those we saw at Augo, but using a slightly different instrumentation of the hexicyclic waveform—"*

"Fine," Kirk said, *"but can we do anything about it?"*

"I can design a shield retune," Spock said, *"but it will take a few moments. Meantime, I would suggest that this implies six-b, a concerted attack on the great ships—"*

"I'd say you'd be right," Kirk said. *"All ships, six-b and six-b-1. Go, go, go!"*

New sets of vectors leapt onto Ael's viewscreen, as onto everyone else's viewscreens or tanks. She doubted, though, that her helmsman needed them; Khiy was already arcing away along a new course. Hard behind them came the pursuers—three cruisers, four corvettes. A significant portion of the attacking force was coming after *Bloodwing.* "Captain," Ael said conversationally, as Khiy went into evasive maneuvers again, "I begin to think you might have had a point about the wisdom of running out front."

"Don't make me be right," Kirk said. *"I hate being right."*

"Since when?" came another voice. It was McCoy; he had apparently decided to ride this particular engagement out in the bridge.

"This is no time to quibble, Bones," Kirk said. *"Everybody, six-c! Those cruisers—"*

Twenty of the available Free Rihannsu vessels, the biggest ones with the heaviest weapons, doubled back on their own courses and went after the cruisers that were chasing *Bloodwing*. This, too, was an exigency they had been prepared for. As Khiy's evasive maneuvers became more energetic, Ael finally yielded to the necessities of the moment, plucked the Sword off the arms of her command seat, and sat down in it, hard, just as the ship shook with incoming disruptor fire. She leaned on the sheathed Sword, staring at the screen. "There, Khiy," she said. "And there!"

But there was no point in telling Khiy what to do anymore. Sulu had, indeed, corrupted him too thoroughly; he had made of an excellent navigator and helmsman a superb one. *He would have come to this pitch eventually,* Ael told herself. *It was simply having someone else to encourage him.*

And Khiy was throwing *Bloodwing* around as enthusiastically as Sulu ever had done with *Enterprise*. Ael simply concentrated, for the moment, on not falling out of her chair. "Tactical," she said to Aidoann, and the screen shifted to that display so that she could see what the other vessels were doing, but there was almost too much going on for her to take in. One thing she noticed with relief—*Tyrava*'s screen had sealed over again, and two of the ships that had made similar holes and similar damage on the other side of *Tyrava*'s vast bulk now blew up, one after another, as the gunnery of first *Tyrava* and then *Kaveth* hit them.

"I have the retune," Spock said over on *Enterprise*. *"It may take some few moments for* Tyrava *and* Kaveth *to implement it."*

That was when the second wave of cruisers decloaked. They came full tilt at the great ships, and shortly after came a third wave, also decloaked and firing. All of them had the same augmented disruptor beams; all of them swarmed around the great ships like biting insects about cattle. Beams sliced out from the two great ships' projectors in all directions, but here, if anywhere, lay their weakness; they were not as agile as the smaller ships that plagued them. *"This is six-d-1,"* Kirk said from *Enterprise.* *"Go, go, go!"*

The ten largest Free Rihannsu vessels that had been acquired at Artaleirh and Augo, and ten of the smaller ones, now curved up and out to attack the attacking cruisers. *"Mr. Spock,"* Kirk said, *"what about that retune?"*

"Implementing now, Captain," Spock said. *"The routine has been disseminated to the cruisers. However—"* And Ael saw two brief flowers of fire, one after another, as two of the craft captured at Artaleirh were simply vaporized in the unforgiving lines of fire that lanced out from the attacking cruisers. Ael watched, and went hot with rage, and ached to throw *Bloodwing* at those ships and exact revenge, but the ship was too small. She could not compete with such weaponry, not even with her augmentations.

One more Free Rihannsu vessel vanished in fire as she watched; and a fourth one took a massive hit on its screens from one of those new, hot, blue-white beams. Ael sucked in her breath. But it did not explode.

"They have the retune," she said. "Khiy—"

"We have it as well, *khre'Riov,*" he said. "We're ready."

"Good. Then bring us where we can shoot one of those—"

Khiy flung *Bloodwing* at one of the cruisers. Her own disruptors raged out. A tattoo of fire ran all of them down the cruiser's hull. At first it seemed to have no effect, and then one beam pierced a shield that wavered. Seconds later, all the shields on that side of the cruiser failed. Khiy fired again. The cruiser blew.

Bloodwing shot through the glowing plasma as it self-annihilated, and out the far side—straight into the jaws of another cruiser. But Khiy was on it. Once more the disruptors lanced out, struck shield, struck through it. One of the cruiser's nacelles cracked away; the cruiser spun off out of control.

"Retune propagation is complete," Spock said.

"Six-g, six-h!" Kirk's voice said.

Once again, the Free Rihannsu vessels shifted configuration, making the half-bowl again—a little more compact, this time, to allow for the vessels that had been lost. Six cruisers were lost to their own complement; but easily fifteen of the Grand Fleet vessels had gone down under the guns of *Tyrava* and *Kaveth* and the other smaller ships. Though the great ships had suffered some damage from the cruisers, they had proven more than deadly enough in return. Ael sat there with the Sword across her knees, and considered that this was going to be one of those battles—or at least, skirmishes—that was won, not strictly by superior tactics, but by sheer brute firepower. *One begins to understand,* she thought, *why the Federation has always been sniffing about our doorstep in search of technology. When it makes this kind of difference in large engagements . . .* She looked thoughtfully at *Enterprise,* barely more than a tiny white spark in the display, some hundreds of thousands of kilometers away.

And now *Enterprise* had her own problems. There were several cruisers after her now, and she was corkscrewing away. "Khiy," Ael said, "do you keep your eyes open to see if there's a chance to do the captain a favor."

As she spoke, one of the three cruisers following *Enterprise* suddenly blew up as Sulu spun the ship a hundred eighty degrees in yaw and fired with forward phasers at something that a moment before had had only much weaker rear phaser banks to deal with. "And that is a trick that Mr. Sulu has taught me," Khiy said. "Would you like to see me do it, *khre'Riov?*"

"Not right this minute!" Ael said. "I should think you would have enough to do with *them* at the moment."

Bloodwing's disruptors lanced out again, and again; and another ship blew up. "Aidoann," Ael said, "what does that make our numbers now?"

"We are down to thirty vessels of cruiser size or larger, *khre'Riov,* but they are down to twenty. No, make that eighteen." She was peering down her own scanner, shaking her head. "Things are moving so quickly . . ."

We are so used to hunting on our own, Ael thought, *hunting in a pack is a new, strange thing to us. Well, if this works correctly, we will not have to do it much more often.*

"Three more vessels uncloaking, *khre'Riov,*" Aidoann said. And there was an urgency in her voice. "They're large."

"Define large," Ael said—and then she stopped. It was unnecessary. Whatever size they were, they were large enough to show as visible shapes on a screen that also contained *Kaveth* and *Tyrava.*

"They're like the supercapital vessels," Aidoann said, "But ten percent larger! Coming at us now."

"Those were not in the plan, Jim," Ael said, with some alarm, as the shapes began to grow on her viewscreen. "They cannot have any more supercapitals left."

"They can if we didn't know they had them," Kirk said. *"Mr. Sulu, let's see what they're made of!"*

"Kirk," Ael cried, *"now* who is being unnecessarily spontaneous?!"

"Whatever you say, Captain," Sulu said. But he sounded dubious. *"But they look a bit big for us."*

"They are *a bit big for you,"* came Veilt's voice from *Tyrava.* *"And there are some odd readings coming from those. I strongly suggest that both of you—"*

And from the attacking supercapitals came something like a globe of fire. It reminded Ael of nothing so much as the matter-dissolution weapon that her people had used years ago. "Khiy!" Ael said.

"Mr. Sulu!" Kirk said at the same moment.

"Yes, *khre'Riov!*" Khiy said, already flinging *Bloodwing* away. But that furious ball of force was still coming at them, expanding, and—Ael blinked. It could not actually be *following* them as they turned.

"I very much dislike that, Captain, whatever it may be!" Ael said.

"A programmable plasma," she heard Spock say. *"It shares some of the characteristics of the old molecular-disruptor weapon mounted on early birds-of-prey, but it would appear to have been upgraded somewhat."*

"Too much so for *me!*" Ael said, watching it match them arc for arc and keep on closing. "Khiy, get ready to go to warp."

"Ready, *khre'Riov,*" he said.

"Go!"

Bloodwing leapt away from the other vessels, curving up and away from Eisn. That ball of force followed. "Shield status?" Ael said to Aidoann as the thing got closer.

"They are at full, *khre'Riov,* but that thing is radiating such power that it will go right through them."

"If Spock is right about that thing's antecedents," Ael said, "we may be able to outrun it, as we've done with its predecessors. Khiy, make all haste! Tr'Keirianh?"

"I hear you," was all her master engineer said. It was going to have to be good enough.

Bloodwing ran, and the forceball ran behind her. Ael gazed at it on the viewscreen, its view now showing space behind them, the engagement continuing in the distance. Was it attenuating? Ael shook her head, watching it come closer.

"Warp three," Khiy said. "Warp four." He looked up at the screen, unbelieving. "*Khre'Riov*, that can't be *accelerating!*"

"It should not have been able to turn, either!" Ael said. "Just *go*, Khiy!"

He threw the ship into another of those turns that made *Bloodwing*'s bones groan with the stress of it, and still the forceball followed them, growing closer. But it was beginning to thin. "Yes," Ael said. "Go, just *go!*"

"Warp five."

It was not easy for a ship of *Bloodwing*'s class to accelerate so quickly. *But she is in a class by herself*, Ael thought, gripping the arms of her seat, bracing the Sword. *Go, cousin. Think what you bear, and save us one more time!*

Khiy swerved again, and once more the forceball followed them. But it was growing fainter, even as it accelerated one more time. Ael saw it coming faster and faster, and shook her head, hit the all-call button. "Brace, my children, brace, collision imminent! Collision—"

The thing struck them as tr'Keiriahn coaxed one last burst of acceleration out of the warp engines. Everything shook as if some huge fist had struck *Bloodwing* a great blow; the bridge went dark. Ael took that last long gasp of air that becomes second nature for one who routinely is in situations where the next gasp may be of vacuum. But though things stayed dark for some seconds, the hull did not crack, nor did the engines give out. A moment later the lights flickered back on again.

Aidoann was on the floor; she let out a little gasp, a little moan, as the lights came on. Ael left the Sword on the center seat and went to her, letting out that breath. She had thought often enough before that she saw her death coming, but this time it had just been a touch too close. She bent over Aidoann, helped her up. "Cousin, come on," Ael said. "Can you get up?"

"The count," Aidoann said faintly, and got to her knees.

"*Khre'Riov,* just help me sit for a moment, I have to get the count of ships."

"You will do no such thing," Ael said. "You will take yourself down to sickbay and tr'—" Then Ael stopped, and breathed out, and shook her head. Old reflex had asserted itself; it was hard to avoid. For so long, there had been that friendly face sitting in the cramped little space, always with a kind word or bandage, or at least a kind word when the bandages were few.

Ael helped Aidoann up to her seat. "Hvaid," she said, turning to the weapons officer, "you had some training with—with our healer." Already Ael was finding herself having trouble saying the name. *Maybe I now better understand those who have trouble saying mine, if they see my actions as anything like as treacherous as hers.* "Go you down to sickbay and run the basic diagnostic program on Aidoann. I would not like to think that she was concussed and still trying to stand up. Go now!" she said, as the two of them started to protest that they were needed here. "We have a lull for the moment. I will pull together the damage reports and do whatever's necessary up here for the next little time. Go now, while these few quiet moments last."

She turned to Khiy. "We have been run a good way off from the others. That may have been someone's intent, or an accident. No matter. Get us back to the armada. And be careful how you go."

The remaining Grand Fleet vessels were fleeing. Kirk stood in front of *Enterprise*'s tank and watched them go. *"They're falling back closer to ch'Rihan,"* Veilt said from *Tyrava. "I would be careful how we follow them, Captain. If we go straight in, or straight toward Grand Fleet headquarters, we will doubtless run into an ambush. And unfortunately, we have no way to break this new cloak. Such is a matter of long study, not something to be done in an hour."*

"Normally I would agree with you," Kirk said, "but when you have all *your* best people, and Ael's engineer tr'Keirianh, *and* Spock and Scotty and K's't'lk all in one place, I expect better results than usual. So let's jump down to . . ." Jim paused, picking up his padd, starting to page through it, and then tossing it aside; he already knew what he would have been looking for. "Seven-l. That section suggests that at this point, any forces we can successfully scan are probably the visible component of a trap for us—unless they are moving at considerable speed between ch'Rihan and ch'Havran, in which case they are the result of our 'Hail Mary' play."

Jim could just hear Veilt putting up his eyebrows. *"Captain, forgive me, but just who is 'Mary' and why would it be hailing on him?"*

"Um, let's just say that it's a slang phrase, and leave it at that. At any rate, three-k through -l suggest that this is the point in our choreography for a long elliptical insertion toward ch'Havran, one from which we can quickly break off toward Grand Fleet HQ. Let's pass all the ships the necessary ephemerides corrected for our present location, and get ready to start our fall into the system."

"Captain?"

"Ael," he said, relieved. She would have been the next topic of discussion. "Where are you? Is *Bloodwing* all right?"

"Well above the ecliptic," Ael said, *"and while we have some damage, we can function. But I desire no more violent maneuvers for a while. Aidoann is hurt, and so are a number of my other people, shaken about when that last plasma disruptor hit us."*

"I've been meaning to ask you about that. Looks like Grand Fleet has a few tricks up its sleeve that your sources didn't know about."

He heard Ael let out a breath. *"Our thoughts march together, Captain,"* she said. *"That was a very interesting weapon. I covet it, rather, as it suggests they have solved the problem of the old matter-disruptor's worst weakness. For all its effectiveness against the enemy, the technology had an unfortunate tendency to—I believe in your idiom the phrase would be, 'hot run in the tube.' Lack of maintenance, or lack of staff trained in proper maintenance of the weapon and its delivery system, meant that over time we lost nearly as many of our own ships to it as did the aliens we used it to attack. The technology was abandoned for a while. But if someone in Grand Fleet has hit on the idea of using newer technologies to update the older system, making the disruption plasma programmable as Spock was suggesting—"*

"*There's no reason it couldn't be done,*" Jim heard tr'Keirianh say from his position. "*In fact, if you attached a singularity to one of those old systems—*"

"*Tr'Keirianh,*" Ael said, "*you and your singularities! Tell me this is not something you're seriously considering.*"

"*Well,* khre'Riov, *it had occurred to me that—*"

What usually occurred to Jim when he heard his own chief engineer start a sentence that way was that it was better to steer the conversation in some other direction, quickly. "Uh, forgive me, Tr'Keirianh," he said, "but, Ael, is your shielding sufficient for the moment? We've got work to do."

"*We have some protection,*" Ael said, "*but not nearly enough to suit me. Certainly I do not desire to have that thing fired at me again, at anything like such close range! And I suspect you share this desire.*"

"I think you may have something there," Jim said. "All right, time to get cracking again." He paused and looked into the tank. "I expect Grand Fleet to be well protected, probably by ships with that weapon," Jim said. "Probably it's carrying some itself, now. So we have two choices."

"*What, Captain,*" Ael said, with just the slightest smile in her voice, "*you mean you're not going to direct us to the page for eight-a, 'sudden discovery of unknown super-weapon?'*"

"As a matter of fact—" Kirk said.

Ael cleared her throat. *"Were your gift for extrapolation not likely to keep the souls of many of us inside our skins today, I would swear you do it merely to annoy."*

"Ahem," Kirk said, and grinned. "The question now becomes, to what targets will the people commanding Grand Fleet commit the vessels carrying those weapons, if in fact Fleet headquarters itself isn't adequately protected? I think they'll be concentrating on *Kaveth* and *Tyrava*. They'll have had some time to prepare their strategies for such ships, but not very much. And under the circumstances, to make sure that they don't have enough time to move any useful materiel up to Grand Fleet or down from it, I think we had better get *Tyrava* down in there in a hurry and start interdicting transporter function."

"It is a little earlier than we have thought to be doing that," Ael said.

"Yes, well," Jim said, "I know you'd just love to flaunt *Bloodwing* in their faces some more and fight her all over the system, but if you were wise, you'd get your butt off that ship, send her out of harm's way, and put yourself somewhere well defended enough that we can ensure that at the end of this exercise, you're still alive." He was taking care to sound wry about it. This was no time to allow Ael to get into one of her aggressive lone-wolf moods. "And since Mr. Spock is looking at me, with *that* expression, and his eyebrows up, I can only suggest that you would be about to have some company in the form of *me*. I think it's become time to transfer the flag to *Tyrava*, at least for the moment, where K's't'lk's gig will be ready to take us where we need to be when the troops go down. Which reminds me; do you have body armor that you wear in battle situations, or something similar? If you don't, we can run something like that up for you."

"I am a naval officer," Ael said. *"Even on ceremonial*

occasions, we never wear armor. But I agree. If we are going down onto a 'dirt' battlefield, probably some minimal amount of protection is best."

"Listen to her," Jim said to Spock, slightly amused. "We'll take care of it. Meanwhile, we still have Grand Fleet HQ to think about." He looked at his tank.

Ael said, *"On the off chance that Grand Fleet or ch'Rihan has managed to install planet-based weapons of the kind we saw at Artaleirh—not that I think they have, but much can be done when one is terrified and has a few days' space—I would prefer to attack Grand Fleet when it is on the side of ch'Rihan, away from ch'Havran. Better to be caught between one set of such weapons rather than two."*

"Agreed," Kirk said. There was a moment of silence while he ran the planet positions forward in his tank. "We'll have a time slot suiting that description in one hour and forty-eight minutes," he said. "That window of opportunity will last approximately—"

"Fifty-six minutes, your time," Ael said. *"I know Grand Fleet's ephemera all too well. I will bring* Bloodwing *over, and we will grapple her to* Tyrava's *hull."*

"Ael, why grapple outside?" Veilt said. *"We have several holds big enough to take* Bloodwing.*"*

"Veilt," Ael said, *"you know I take that very kindly. But with all the respect due to your great experience, I would rather resist that suggestion. We will grapple to you. If there should later be need or desire, we can then let go quickly. But I would be glad if you would offer my people sanctuary until* Bloodwing *is ready to fly free again."*

"Let it be as you say," Veilt said. *"But you should get over here now. And,* Enterprise, *we would be pleased to offer you the same refuge if you like."*

Jim thought for a moment, then let out a breath. "With respect, Veilt, thank you, but no. There are certain—" He paused. "—legal niceties."

*"Such as the fact that being taken inboard by another
vessel can, in the case of an unfriendly court-martial, be
seen as a willing act of surrender,"* Veilt said. *"I take your
point. Nonetheless, Captain, in case of emergency, we have
room to take all your crew."*

"I'll keep that in mind," Jim said. "Meanwhile, let's move
on Grand Fleet HQ. Damage and readiness reports, all
vessels."

The next few moments became a hubbub of voices and
various electronic beeps and hoots as people reported in by
voice or simply signaled by a beep or two that they were
ready. "This is section seven-k," Kirk said. "Ladies and gentlemen, stay sharp and watch out for one another. I expect
Grand Fleet to have another of those plasma balls. I don't
want anyone getting personal with it. At the same time,
our job is to protect *Kaveth* and *Tyrava* until they can get
close enough to Grand Fleet to do what needs doing. Any
questions?"

There were none. "Then let's do it," Kirk said. "Seven-k.
Go, go, go!"

The ships began to move in a smooth synchronized curve,
outward and downward into the system, toward the plane
of the ecliptic. Slowly Eisn grew in the viewer, and slowly
the little sparks of light of ch'Rihan and ch'Havran, locked
in their eternal dance, began to swell on the viewscreen. In
her bridge, Ael stood up with the Sword in her hands,
watching them grow. Her hands were sweating, and in them
the Sword slipped, and was cold. *At last,* she thought. *At
last.*

"Khiy," Ael said. "It's time. Take the ship around the back
of *Tyrava.* Find a good flat spot to lock down. There are
plenty of grapples back there, as we saw from their plans."

"Ie, khre'Riov."

As they slipped around the rear of *Tyrava,* the view of

Eisn was hidden from them. Minutes later, *Bloodwing* made herself fast to a grapple sequence toward the back of *Tyrava*'s huge bulk. The whole ship clattered and rumbled with the sound of the grapples linking through the matching mating clamps on *Bloodwing*'s belly. Most larger Rihannsu ships had such, but for the sheer size of the surroundings, this was more like landing at a spaceport than anything else. Ael looked out over the huge expanse of the hull and prayed that it would stay sound, as *Tyrava*'s shields came to life again overhead.

Ael picked up the Sword and slapped the comms button on her chair. "All-call," she said, and the ship came alive with her voice. "Move out, my children. For the moment, we abandon ship. Once in *Tyrava,* go where your hosts direct you." She glanced around her bridge, let out the usual unhappy breath at leaving it, and waved Khiy to the lift. "Time to go."

They headed out. Together she and Khiy made their way down through the cramped corridors to the belly of the ship and the underside exit bay. Just being there again was odd. The last time they had used the airlock when grappling to another structure was when they had still been in Grand Fleet. *It seems a lifetime ago.*

Inside the bulk of the main mating clamp, they found the farside airlock already undogged for them. It was very strange to open their side of it and smell a strange ship's air flowing into *Bloodwing*. But there was little time to waste savoring the strangeness. Ael waved her crew on down the broad access ladder. One of the last to go down was Aidoann, moving like someone with a very sore head, Hvaid helping her.

Last of all Ael followed her crew down into the strange, slightly heavier gravity of *Tyrava*, then pulled from one of her pockets something she had not used since Fleet HQ—the electronic key that would open her ship to them again. The inner hatch shut down, and chirped its reassurance that it was locked.

At the bottom of the ladder they found themselves in yet another of *Tyrava*'s tremendous corridors. Crewfolk were running down toward a marshaling area at one end, all armed, some armored. They were getting ready to go downplanet when this phase of the attack was through. One crewman came hastening over to Ael. "Madam," he said, "Veilt asks me to bring you down to the launch bay. Kirk and his first officer and the Hamalki are there. They are getting ready to go downplanet."

"Lead on," Ael said, and they all trotted down the corridor in the crewman's wake. *Tyrava*'s own attack klaxons were sounding, and everywhere, in every direction, crewfolk ran by their hundreds, eventually their thousands. Being here was like being in a city that was about to be bombed.

Ael put that simile far away from her for the moment, as they came into another marshaling area. At the far side of it, K's't'lk's little gig was sitting. Kirk stood by it, along with Spock. The golden latticework of the thing intrigued Ael, but she had no time to spare for admiring its beauty. She hurried over to Kirk, who glanced at her, and the Sword.

"It goes where I go, for the time being," Ael said, "and probably for some time after that. Where are we wanted? The bridge?"

"No need for that, it seems," Kirk said. "Believe it or not, they've got a 'spare bridge' right over here." He waved off to one side. There, off to the right of the force-fielded hangar door through which K's't'lk had brought her ship, was an area with not only a huge viewscreen but a tank as well, and a number of chairs.

Ael privately doubted that any of them were going to be sitting very much. On that huge screen, the dive in toward Eisn could be seen more and more closely. The sun grew larger. "Captain," Ael said, "*Enterprise*—"

"Mr. Sulu has the conn," Kirk said. "He knows the battle plan as well as I do." He looked at Ael. "Ready to go?"

She nodded. "When it's time—"

On the screen, Eisn grew larger. The planets were now clearly visible—two half crescents against the night—as *Tyrava* and her cohorts swept into the system. They were no more than a hundred million kilometers from the planets, and there was no resistance—here, at least.

Kirk studied the screen. "A little quiet out there," he said.

Ael simply nodded. She held on to the Sword, saying nothing, and watched the sun grow.

They swept past Eisn. Ahead of them, as they dropped into the plane of the ecliptic, Grand Fleet Headquarters could be seen off to one side of ch'Rihan. Ael swallowed hard. She did not know which of the two she had more desire to see; the planet, or the thing she was about to destroy. But it was ch'Rihan that drew her eye. Those continents, those seas . . .

And then the light and the fire came boiling up from Grand Fleet. "Here we go," Kirk said. "Spock, that shield retune—will it hold?"

Next to him, Spock stood quite still and watched that bloom of deadly fire come toward them. "The odds are overwhelmingly in our favor, Captain."

"How overwhelmingly?" Kirk said.

"There is," Spock said, "of course, always a possibility— a probability I should actually say, a very small one."

"*How* small?" Kirk said.

"Oh, certainly no more than—" Spock looked thoughtful. "—approximately zero point zero zero zero zero zero one percent."

Kirk folded his arms and looked at the viewscreen. "Oh, well, if *that's* all—"

And the ball of fire struck *Tyrava,* which shuddered in all her bones. The whole ship jumped, the shields, seen on the viewscreen, whited out, and the lights flickered.

Ael swallowed. Seeing the lights flicker was never a good thing on a ship as huge and complex as *Tyrava*. But then they came back up again, and the screen as slowly came up out of the white blindness that the energy weapon had imposed upon it. "As I said," Spock said, very calmly, "only a hundred thousandth of a percent."

Kirk looked at him. "Mr. Spock, sometimes I suspect you of pulling my leg on purpose. But certainly you'd never do such a thing at a time like this."

Spock managed to look delicately offended. "Certainly not, Captain."

They stood there and watched *Tyrava* dive closer to Grand Fleet, with *Kaveth* coming up next to her now. They watched another of those blooms of guided plasma leap up at them from one of the ships riding guard over Grand Fleet HQ, and another one from another ship, and a third from the Fleet facility itself. They watched that weapon fire at them again, and at *Kaveth*, and at them both at once—not just once but a number of times. And it did no harm. Oh, the ship shook, things fell down, and people clutched at one another. Ael very carefully put the Sword down on the chair again, and braced herself against the back of it, as she had done many times before on *Bloodwing*.

"*Transporter interdiction is in place,*" Veilt's voice said. "*Ten seconds to optimum range . . .*"

Kirk looked at Ael. "How many people in HQ," he said, "when it's battle-staffed?"

She looked at the screen. "Between fifteen hundred and two thousand. Many of them are good people, who genuinely enlisted to do their worlds' service." She let out a breath. "Unquestioning service."

And once again her eyes strayed to ch'Rihan, off to the left of Grand Fleet HQ as they approached, and now rapidly swelling into something that took up almost all that side of the screen. Jointly, *Tyrava* and *Kaveth* fired down at the mas-

sive space station. The weapons fire from Grand Fleet HQ
had stopped a few moments before: now all its power was
being diverted to its shields. For a long time, as *Kaveth* and
Tyrava swept around the great space station in concert, that
shield resisted, always stubbornly reinforced where it was
beginning to waver. The two great ships fired on, while
around them raged a small cloud of Grand Fleet vessels of
every shape and size, firing wildly at the interlopers, trying
to overload the two ships' shields by sheer amount of
pumped-in energy rather than the power of any one weapon.
But finally one spot on that blue-burning shield around the
station started to burn less brightly blue under *Kaveth*'s concentrated fire, and less brightly still, and finally trembled
down into darkness. *Tyrava* came sweeping around and
brought her own beams to bear on the spot where *Kaveth* had
been firing. The beams burst through and struck the station.

Ael wished she could turn away and avoid the sight of
what was happening, but she did not have that right. She
stood still, and watched as the joint beams from the two great
ships started to carve the station open like a piece of fruit.
She watched it spill silvery air and fire and exploding plasma
out into the cold starry night. And then the beams hit the
matter-antimatter core at the station's heart, and it blew.

Kaveth and *Tyrava* peeled hastily away. As they did, the
defense satellites in high orbit lashed out at them with beams
like Grand Fleet's, but smaller. The great ships' shields flickered under the assault, but did not go down. The remaining
Grand Fleet cruisers, homeless now, also threw themselves at
Tyrava and *Kaveth,* and one by one, those that did not flee
were destroyed.

Kirk looked over at Spock and K's't'lk. "It's time," he
said. "Veilt?"

"*We are done,*" Veilt said. "*We have achieved local space
superiority. All remaining Free Rihannsu vessels, take high
guard. This is situation nine-b: physical interdict, double*

planet englobe, no vessel from planetside on either world to be allowed to leave the immediate neighborhood. Ready landing parties, launch. All remaining landing parties to their staging areas."

On the screen, Ael could see the troop carriers beginning to fall away from *Tyrava,* one after another, a seemingly endless series of them. They were huge. Every one of them carried three times the complement of *Enterprise,* which in turn had four times the complement of *Bloodwing.* They launched, and launched, and launched. *And how many of them will come back?* she thought sadly. You could never reasonably hope that all of them would make it home when you were engaged in combat on this scale.

Kirk turned toward Ael, gathering her and Spock and K's't'lk in with a look. "Let's get down there," he said.

The invasion of ch'Rihan began.

TWENTY

THOUGH THE INVASION might only be beginning, the War of the Free Rihannsu was already over—not that most of them knew it. Once Grand Fleet Headquarters was gone, and most of Grand Fleet itself had been destroyed, the Empire's ability to project power was effectively finished. Now what power it had left was confined to the two worlds where it had active ground troops.

On the planet that was actually less important in the conflict, except as a snare, the Empire's raw numbers were good enough to give the invading task a run for its money, but the way in which those numbers had been emplaced was dire, and Jim could only shake his head at the folly of a government that so thoroughly ignored its own experts. Hastily convoked to rubber-stamp the Three's decision, the Senate had ordered the Imperial Groundforce Command to send nearly two-thirds of their available forces, a total of a hundred fifty thousand troops, to ch'Havran. Again on the Three's instructions, the Upper Generals had been required—over their most strenuous protests—to scatter those Imperial troops all over the planet by their thousands and tens of thousands. This was what Jim had desperately hoped they would do, but would not have dared to count on. Fortunately, the paranoia of the Three, assisted by the fact that Gurrhim had major family enclaves in several large cities, made them try to protect *all* of these against an incursion by the traitor.

In so doing, they doomed their troops. The Three had misread not only Gurrhim's supposed intentions—which Jim had been counting on—but the temper of the Havrannssu as well. Led by Gurrhim's family and adherents, they did what no one had really expected, not even Ael or Gurrhim: they rose. In cities of a hundred thousand or more, when there were suddenly ten thousand Imperial troops quartered on them, the already angry and frightened populace started to come to the conclusion that one man may indeed be able to shoot ten people, but only if all the bystanders stand still and let him. And the Imperial Ground Forces themselves, willing enough to fight against evil alien invaders, or the traitress whom their government hated, became much more conflicted when faced with the prospect of having to shoot fellow Rihannsu or Havrannssu. In tandem with the uprisings— *surprisingly well-coordinated,* Jim thought, *but then they're a* tidy *people*—came mass troop defections, along with the informal execution of many officers whose orders the troops no longer saw any point in obeying, on either moral or practical grounds. It would take many weeks before the unrest on ch'Havran died down, or was quelled.

What remained to be settled was just who would be quelling it.

The situation on ch'Rihan was more complex, but in a way, not as serious. Initial scans from *Tyrava* as K's't'lk was getting ready to shuttle them down were more promising than Jim had hoped. Most of the Imperial Ground Force troops remaining on the planet had been concentrated around Ra'tleihfi, and their disposition provided no insurmountable obstacles to an invading commander. But Jim noted what he had expected—a significant concentration of troops in the Valley of the Firefalls, the most straightforward route into the city, and one that an invading force would need to secure to prevent further flanking attacks by a determined defender.

K's't'lk's little ship fell down from *Tyrava* toward ch'Ri-han at great speed, and Jim and Ael and Spock braced themselves in the seats that K's't'lk had had the ship grow for them. She was nested in a spiky, glassy contraption up at the front that was almost certainly a control console, not that Jim could either see any controls or how she was operating them. The fore end of the ship appeared from inside to be not so much transparent as simply missing, which was a good trick, since the ship had been seemingly opaque and completely portless when they boarded her. Through the transparency, the planet appeared to be diving straight at them at a truly unnerving velocity. "Uh, T'l," Jim said, "perhaps a little braking?"

"I thought you were in a hurry, Captain," K's't'lk chimed.

"Yes, but I don't know if I meant *this* much of a hurry!"

"Nearly there," K's't'lk said. So they were; they shot through several levels of cloud toward the pass west of the city, and came out in hazy sunlight, plunging toward the mountainous terrain like a falling star. The terrain grew, spread from side to side of the view, became all the view there was. And then, nearly at the foot of one mountain, they simply stopped in midair, with no jerk, no slightest jar or feeling of deceleration of any kind.

A moment later they were on the ground, tilted slightly downward. "Sorry about the tilt," K's't'lk said, "it's steep here. Screens are up. Phaser rifles are in the clips by the door. Make sure your armor's active before you step through the outer shield."

Part of the side of the ship unwove itself. Cautiously Jim stepped out, followed by Ael and Spock, and got his first up-close sight of the battlefield.

Taking it all in required a few moments—not surprising, for what Jim was looking at was partly obscured by the fume and smoke of the Firefalls themselves, not two miles away, and the carnage that had already begun to impose itself on an

already wild and inhospitable landscape. Jim and the others
were standing just upslope from nearly the highest point of
the old road that runs down from the Mehleifhi Highlands
down into the plain where Ra'tleihfi sits by its river. Scattered along the lower reaches of the pass below them were
perhaps fifty thousand Imperial Ground Force troops—very
confused, very frightened, and very outnumbered. The view
down the long, curving pass was largely hidden by dust and
smoke and blowing fumes from the Falls. Through this pall,
the fire of disruptors and phasers stitched an uneasy, sporadic
ground-based lightning. All the slope down from the mountain was afire with burning vegetation and crashed ships,
large and small—all the detritus of war, swiftly creating itself. It was the kind of warfare that naval officers were usually spared seeing, and it was no easier to bear, for Jim, than
watching the Fleet action had been.

They watched *Tyrava*'s and *Kaveth*'s ground forces
rolling down that valley both on foot and in mechanized
floating armor. Their passage was hardly uncontested; in
some places there was fierce fighting. Phasers, disruptors,
various kinds of explosives were in play—almost everything
but nuclears, since both sides had plans for this land that did
not involve making large portions of it uninhabitable. The
lower part of the pass appeared to have been mined—both
sides were avoiding it—but the upper part of the pass was
quiet and clear. As Jim looked up that way, he saw a number
of lightly armed Romulans who had been standing and
watching K's't'lk's ship come down. Now, seeing its occu-
pants standing outside it, a number of these people put their
weapons down and started to walk slowly down toward Jim
and the others, their hands out to either side to show that they
were empty.

Inside the ship's extended shield, the landing party lifted
their weapons, watching the strangers come. And as they got
closer, the foremost of the people approaching, a young

woman, suddenly struck Jim as being familiar. He gazed at her as she got closer—a woman in some kind of booted overall, soot-stained, with dark hair bound back tightly. And then he knew her face, even though it took him a moment because she had been dressed so very differently the last time he saw her.

She came up just outside of the shield and stopped. "Captain Kirk," she said. "Commander—"

"Arrhae!" Ael said. "Elements, woman—are all the Senators finding such rough housing and handling as you seem to have found?"

Arrhae shook her head. "I don't think so. But as for you, you're very welcome. There are many people here who have been waiting for you. They knew you'd come here first."

"After all, this was your family's land, once," said the man who was standing just behind Arrhae. "Before they took it from you. And, anyway, you've been saying all this while that you intended to retire here and become a hermit."

Ael's jaw dropped. Then she closed her mouth again. "Now by my Element, how came you to know that?"

"Commander," the man said, "not all the information that was leaked from *Bloodwing* fell into unfriendly hands. Some of it came to those who were intent on helping you. As we've been doing now." He looked around. "This place would have been fairly strongly held, except that a great many of us . . . interfered."

"Well, I thank you, and you will tell me more of this later, I hope," Ael said, "but first, how stands the city?"

Arrhae shook her head. "Yesterday much of the civilian population began to flee, despite the government's orders that they should stay where they were. Word got out somehow, you see, that the Senators were evacuating." She smiled gently. "And when the world's rulers leave in such a hurry, why should the ruled remain? Some did stay in place, true, but despite the government's increasingly noisy calls that they should take arms and go out and defend their city, they have not been moving." She shook her head and smiled. "Indeed, the question is how much government there is around here at the moment. The Senators, as I say, have withdrawn wholesale to their country estates all over the planet. They will not fight. And the Praetorate is fled. After all, they could look up and see what everyone else could." She glanced up through the clouds at the disastrous and expanding cloud slowly moving across the sky, getting ready to set at the moment, like a gigantic furry star. "They saw the defense satellites taken down, and Grand Fleet Headquarters fall. I think they know quite well that their power is done."

"And the Three?" Ael said.

Arrhae shook her head. "No one knows where they are, Commander General."

"But the odds would seem good," said the man standing next to Arrhae, "that they are somewhere on the planet. There has been a tremendous amount of confusion since transport became nonfunctional in this part of space." He smiled slightly. "So unless they've managed to find a craft fast enough to get them through the cordon that is being thrown around even as we speak—" He looked at Kirk. "—and that seems unlikely, then they are still here somewhere. I doubt that it will take too long to find them, either. Doubtless some forward-looking citizen will turn them in."

"It would seem," K's't'lk said, cocking various eyes up at Kirk, "that your plan is working."

Kirk looked down into the valley, where the phaser and disruptor fire was slowly growing more distant from the position where they stood. "It looks that way at the moment," he said. "But I'm not willing to get too excited about it all just yet. There's still the city to deal with. And after that, one thing that right now is feeling a lot more important to me moment by moment."

"Yes," Arrhae said. "The nova bomb."

"It seems like news is traveling faster than usual around here," Jim said. "Well, we need to find the Three just as fast as we can. But we can't get started on that until someone makes it publicly plain to both these planets that things are going to be run a little differently now."

"The Senate, then," Ael said. "The only other piece of equipment I need is in K's't'lk's ship."

"Let's go, then," Jim said. And he smiled, though it had a grim edge to it at the moment, and his fears for Earth were growing with every second. "Nine-j."

"You and your lists," Ael said, turning back toward the ship.

"They've worked, haven't they?" Jim said.

"That will be proven when we strike the last item out. *Deihu,* will you ride with us? The Senate will need to be recalled when things grow quiet again, and your advice will be uniquely valuable."

"My pleasure, Commander-General," Arrhae said. "But Ffairrl comes with me."

"Very well," Jim said. "T'l, kill that shield, let them in, and let's get out of here."

The city had a strangely empty feel, though it was hardly as if all the people had left. Some Rihannsu could be seen looking down from nearby office and government buildings at the strange little ship that landed on the plaza outside the Senate, and at the group that came out of it and paused to look down the great empty avenue reaching away from it. The sound of sporadic disruptor fire could be heard at the edges of the city, but there was none here.

One last figure climbed out of the ship: Ael, with the Sword in her hands. There she stood for a moment, looking around her, and actually shivered. "I did not think I would live to see this," she said. "On my Element's name, I did not."

Spock got his tricorder out. Jim pulled out his communicator. "Scotty?"

Nothing happened. Jim sighed. "I keep forgetting," he said, and pulled out the little radio instead. "Scotty?"

"Aye, Captain."

"Lock onto Spock's tricorder signal. We're going to need systemwide video for this. Replace the jamming signal with it."

"Aye, Captain," Scotty said again.

They walked away from the ship, toward the doors of the Senate. Slowly Jim became aware of people standing at the edges of the plaza, watching them as they made their way across it to the doors. Some of those people started to follow them. "Captain," Spock said softly, glancing at them.

"We're carrying a bud-off of my ship's shields with us, Captain," K's't'lk said. "I've got range enough to carry it as far as the Senate building. But once we get inside, the structure is going to interfere."

"Good enough," Kirk said.

They came to the doors, and here, on the very threshold of the place, Jim saw Ael hesitate. Behind them, the crowd of Rihannsu who had been following now started to gather and grow, but they didn't press forward. They waited. The high air was beginning to be full of Free Rihannsu ships patrolling, but all those people's attention was on the woman standing before the closed doors.

"Some of the marks are still here from where I landed *Bloodwing*," Ael said in a small voice. "They have not even finished the repairs."

"There'll be plenty of time to set your house in order later," Jim said. "But first you have to get *in* there."

Then Kirk's radio crackled again. "So much for the historic moment," he said. "Kirk here."

"Captain, you'd better hear this!" Uhura said. *"Local broadcast, low power, I'll patch you in."*

They heard the voice, then—dry, even, almost mild—and Kirk saw Arrhae go pale. *"—a matter of honor,"* it was saying. *"And those who have struck at our heart, will now find that we strike at theirs. Those who have fouled the Hearthworlds of the Rihannsu Star Empire will now find their own hearth going cold. Invaders, aliens, enjoy the light of our sun briefly, while you may still enjoy anything, for the light of your own star will shortly be gone. Enjoy what the traitress's empty promises have bought you: Your own destruction."*

"Scotty, the jamming!"

"Seems not to have affected whatever signaling modality they were usin', Captain. If they're sendin' some signal to activate the nova bomb, we can't stop it!"

Jim swore. "Beam us up!"

"We'd have to raise the interdict to do that. And if we do that, those devils will use the moment to get away!"

Kirk turned to K's't'lk. "I take back everything I said about your brakes. How fast can you get us back to *Enterprise?"*

"Come find out!" she said, and turned and ran back toward her ship, all those legs glittering.

Kirk ran after her. Spock glanced around, thrust his tricorder into Arrhae's hands, and went after Kirk. And it was only as Kirk was climbing back into the ship that he turned for a split second, remembering, to look at Ael, standing there all alone.

She stared back and then gestured at him furiously: *go!*

It was only a matter of a few seconds to get out of the atmosphere. Horrified as he was, Jim was still surprised that he wasn't able to feel even the slightest flush of heat as they plunged up through the air. "How can this ship *stand* that?"

"J'm, I do a lot of work in stellar mechanics," K's't'lk said as they flashed toward the tiny shape in orbit that swiftly resolved itself into *Enterprise.* "For that kind of thing you need a ship that can work in the corona, or even deeper. How's a little friction going to bother me?" Her legs danced in and out among the controls as she lined her little ship up with the hangar bay. "Sc'tty?"

"I'm on my way down," Scotty answered. He sounded out of breath. *"Captain—you know what we're going to have to do."*

"What?" Then Jim swallowed. "You mean, with the probe—" His mouth went completely dry. "Scotty, *you haven't finished testing it yet!"*

"We're about to finish that right now, I think," K's't'lk said.

"No," Jim whispered.

K's't'lk shot in through the hangar doors. "Force field only, Sc'tty, he'll be going right out again."

The force field came open in the gap between the hangar bay's physical doors, and the area began to pressurize. "Come on, hurry," K's't'lk said, climbing out of her seat. "Hurry!"

The pressure came up and the door of her craft opened. They all piled out. The corridor doors opened, and Scotty burst in through them, pushing before him an antigrav sled with a long, sleek torp casing loaded on it.

"You said it yourself, Captain," Scotty said between gasps as he came up beside K's't'lk's ship. The ship abruptly extruded a long set of thin spidery legs from inside, lifted the torp casing carefully, and pulled it into the body of the vessel; the door knitted itself closed again. "It's aye better to have the sun collapse than 'tis to have it explode. And besides, this'll probably work."

Jim started to turn to Spock for an estimate, and then thought better of it. K's't'lk laid a claw on the side of her little ship, and held still for a moment. "Done," she said then. "Let's get out of here and let him go."

"Mr. Scott!" Uhura's voice thundered in the air. *"We're getting video!"*

Scotty and K's't'lk stared at each other. "Record it!"

They both ran for the door, Spock close behind them, Kirk bringing up the rear. Behind them all the doors sealed: they ran for the turbolift.

"We will have to recalculate for Eisn's present condition," Spock was saying, and somehow managed to say it almost conversationally, even when on the run.

They all piled into the lift together. "But what about Eisn?" Jim was about to say, and then stopped himself. *An eye for an eye,* he thought. Then he felt ashamed of the thought—but not nearly as much as he might have.

And besides, if it works—

It had better. Because if it doesn't, we're all going to be sitting in the dark.

All of them burst onto the bridge together. Spock went straight to his station and started working over it. Scotty did the same, with K's't'lk leaning up next to it, her own claws working over the controls to one side. Jim could do nothing but look in horror at the viewscreen, which was showing an image of Earth's sun, getting closer and closer and almost completely obscuring the field of view.

"Processing the image," Spock said. "Uhura's recording shows me a reverse angle, Captain. Our message was received. I judge that there are nearly four hundred Starfleet vessels englobed around the sun."

"Oh, thank God."

"But they cannot see the probe!" Scotty said. "And by the time they do, it'll be too late. The thing will only uncloak to transport."

The sun grew to fill the whole field of view. Jim could see the sunspots, the swirl of the rice-grain structures of the surface, every one of them a cell of burning plasma big enough to lose a starship in. "Uhura," Scotty said, "split the screen, give us a view of Eisn."

The screen split, Eisn on the right, Sol on the left. Jim looked at them and thought, *How alike they are.* Eisn was a little more golden—a younger star, perhaps? Or maybe the difference was just in stellar class. But it was minor. *They're so alike. We're so alike. Why must our differences make our peoples so intent on each other's destruction that one side can seriously want to put the other's star out?* "Impose tactical," Jim said to Sulu.

Gridwork laid itself over the Eisn view. They could see K's't'lk's ship shooting inward on the lowest warp possible. "Is that safe?" Jim asked.

"No," K's't'lk said, "but it's safer than what's *about* to happen."

Jim sat down to hide the fact that he had begun to shake. The physical reaction to the day's events was beginning to set in, and there was absolutely nothing he could do about it. He was out of adrenaline. He hit the button on his chair. "Sickbay!"

"On my way up, Jim," McCoy said.

"Jim!" Ael's voice said from the planet's surface. *"Are they so lost to sense or propriety that they are* broadcasting *their crime?"*

Jim didn't have time to answer her. "'Tis sheer hubris, lass," Scotty said, laughing one furious laugh while working feverishly over his console. "They've given us the last thing we needed, the one thing: a timing. We've a chance now at an equivalence. And if we can get an equivalence, then— K's't'lk!"

"Settings are in. Mr. Spock?"

"Working," Spock said. "Approximately thirty seconds." His hands danced over the controls of the science station.

Jim sat there and gripped the arms of the command chair.

"Where are they getting their image from?" he said, as McCoy came in.

"The probe's spun off a secondary module," Scotty said. "Imagery only. They meant to watch this happen, and us to see it. They've *always* meant us to." His tone of voice was deadlier than any curse. To K's't'lk, he asked, "Where's your ship?"

"In the corona," she said. "Waiting for injection. He'll go straight in, dissolve himself, and turn the torp loose."

Coming up next to Jim, McCoy lifted a hypo, checked the contents, and shoved it up against his arm.

"What is that?" Jim said, not looking away from the screen.

McCoy had his eyes on it too. "Hope," he said.

They could see the Starfleet vessels in the distance, like little stars, growing, but they could do nothing. The probe was too fast. A phaser bolt came from somewhere, and another one, but there was no effect—they were all misses. Jim sat watching, his fists clenched in fury and dread. More phaser fire whited out the display again and again, but always the view of the sun came back, growing larger and larger.

The sweat had broken out all over Jim, but Mr. Scott was suddenly all cold precision, and the Scots accent had gone completely out of his voice. "Locked in," he said. "Waiting for the settings now. Spock—"

"Momentarily," Spock said, his hands working furiously over his console. "The sensor data are not real time. I am being forced to approximate."

Jim knew how his first officer hated that, but just this once he restrained himself from teasing him about it.

K's't'lk shook herself all over, one terrible jangling chime. "Transporter signal! The probe's in." She slapped a control on Scotty's board. "My ship's in the sun."

Jim watched her and Scotty as K's't'lk reared up on some

of her legs, leaning over Scotty's shoulder to look at the image of Sol, already beginning to deviate from its normal spectrography. The spectrum and the lines of it changed color; the light caught in her eyes and the delicate spines of the glassy fur on her back as she arched her forward eyes at the display in utter concentration. "Mr. Spock!" she said.

"Now," Spock said, and touched a control on his console, and straightened up.

The graphs and readouts above Scotty's station started to bounce around. "The probe's controls are online," Scotty said. "Adjusting for congruence."

"It's got to be a third or so higher, Sc'tty," K's't'lk said. "A little higher yet." Three of her spare legs were tapping at the controls of the station next to Scotty's, making adjustments to the probe on which they were all working. "This ought to do it."

"K's't'lk, I advise you to decrease the wormhole aperture," Spock said, suddenly sounding alarmed. "That much energy released so quickly could completely derange the star."

"Too little is going to leave Earth, or ch'Rihan, or both, with nothing but a brown dwarf, Mr. Spock!" K's't'lk jangled. "Not much improvement on a nova!"

"Not like that," Scotty said suddenly. "Spock, K's't'lk—like this."

They both turned to watch an adjustment he was making. Jim sat holding his breath, not missing the irony that, after everything that had happened, everything he'd seen them through, this was all that was left to him at the end. *They also serve . . .*

He saw Spock and K's't'lk both sag, not in satisfaction, but as if realizing there was nothing further that could be done. "That's it," Scotty said. "There's no more time."

They all turned to the viewscreen. Jim's hair stood on end as he saw Sol's corona began to flicker, shiver—

—and start to fail, dying back toward the star, going faint, going out.

Jim had seen this before. He swallowed.

"Enterprise!" came a cry over comms.

Jim started. It was tr'Keirianh. *"I have your settings,"* tr'Keirianh said. *"Not point six on the entasis level, Mr. Scott! Point eight! Point eight!"*

"What?"

"Point eight!"

"But it makes no sense, it—"

Scotty froze. Then he reached down a hand, hesitant. The hand hovered.

On the front screen, both Sol and Eisn began to darken.

Scotty swallowed, and made a single change to his console. Then he closed his eyes.

Jim stared at the screen. Sol was still darkening, visibly, as if someone was turning down a dimmer—

—and then the dimming stopped. At the same time, Eisn darkened too.

The silence on the bridge was total. "Oh, my God, *no!*" Uhura said softly.

"Congruence," K's't'lk said, just three notes' worth of wind chime, and held her breath.

Both stars shivered, and their surfaces began to boil with sunspots. Scotty opened his eyes again, stared at the screen. "Sweet heaven," he whispered.

And some thousands of light-years away, Earth's sun began to sing.

On the screens they could see what could also be seen by the closest Starfleet vessels, and what the population of the Earth would see in eight minutes or so, as the surface of the sun began to flare and shudder. They saw a sight like something out of old folktales or miracle stories, the sun dancing in the sky, shivering with light, vibrating like a struck gong—a thing out of an old miracle, a reenactment of stories of the ancient past in many species, when beings on many planets worshipped their stars, and the stars (so the stories said) took notice.

The shivering propagated through space, and into subspace, each of them in its own way resounding, the emptiness proving more vocal than anyone had ever dreamed. When the shockwaves and radiation fronts that were moving through normal space struck the worlds in orbit around each of those stars, their upper atmospheres flared into light, auroral discharges more profligate than had ever been seen, as if Earth in her system, and ch'Rihan and ch'Havran in theirs, were trying to grow coronae of their own. Light flared like doomsday on the three worlds' nightsides, and turned their daysides' upper atmospheres pearly blue or pearly green. And from the tops of those atmospheres to their depths, in all the places where the air was dense enough to conduct sound, the song was heard.

Some said it was like an earthquake, but buildings did not fall. Some said it was like thunder, but no lightning struck, and thunder quickly ceases where this did not. In Ra'tleihfi and every open place across the northern continent, and in every other place on ch'Rihan or ch'Havran that was turned toward Eisn; on Earth, from the North Pole down through the eastern hemisphere, from Japan to the South Pacific and into the Antarctic Circle; every being that stood out under either trembling sun heard that rumble, that inexpressible basso shivering, that single note of astonishment, in the flesh, in the bones, in the cavity of the chest, as if it were singing *them*. The single note, the stars' breath, went on and on in a phrase that seemed likely never to end. Every seismograph on all three planets had a sudden and enthusiastic fit as it was drowned in an ocean of signal of which it could make no sense. Unshielded satellites shivered apart, not having been built to deal with an influx of shock or radiation like this.

No eye could have seen the tiny streak of light that was the pressure-crumpled shape of a probe as it was spat out of Sol's chromosphere and then lashed and further fried by the corona, now stimulated well past the usual million degrees. But the instruments saw it, and tracked the probe, or what was left of it, away from the star. Moments later a starship's phaser found it and blew it to hell.

On *Enterprise*'s bridge, though, it was some moments before anything but a stricken silence reigned. And then it was broken by just one voice.

"They didn't blow up!" Scotty whispered.

"They weren't *supposed* to blow up," K's't'lk said. She managed to sound both scandalized and immensely relieved.

McCoy shook his head. "Were they supposed to *sound* like that?" he said.

K's't'lk managed to look uncertain. "I don't know. It wasn't in the equations. But I wouldn't have missed it for any world you can imagine."

Jim stood up. He still felt shaky, but that would pass. "Mr. Spock?"

Spock straightened up from his viewer. "Captain, I would quote you very high probabilities that Earth has not been destroyed. I think there may well have been some damage, possibly even some loss of life on orbital installations that were not able to cope with the effect—but far, far less than would have happened otherwise."

"Tr'Keirianh," Scotty said, "you're the hero of the day."

"*Not I,*" tr'Keirianh said. "*I merely know my homestar a little better than you. But we will have time to argue the point. Who is the hero—the one who forges the sword, or the one who swings it?*"

"Now there's a question," Jim said, "and it reminds me of another one. Uhura, get me Ael." He turned to K's't'lk. "Meanwhile, T'l, congratulations. But I'm sorry about your ship."

She laughed. "It's all right, J'm! I'll knit another."

"Ael is on for you, Captain," Uhura said.

"*Jim*," came her voice, very softly, "*what* was *that?*"

He told her.

Down there before the doors of the Senate, Ael was now standing in front of a crowd that had grown into the thousands. They had been uneasy at first, muttering; the mutter had grown to a slow, low roar, but she had stood her ground. She had been about to speak to them when a voice much greater than hers had made itself heard.

After it ceased speaking, none of them had been able to manage anything but silence. Now, however, she looked out over the gathered people, and caught the eyes of the foremost.

"Rihannsu, hear me," Ael said. "You heard from their own lips what those who ruled you were doing in your name. Why should it have surprised you? A long time ago they took your *mnhei'sahe*, and your very lives, to do with as they pleased. They took your worlds. They took your suns. And at last they took you to war against those who meant you no ill. But now they have paid the price for that.

"And now Eisn itself has spoken against them. Nor will it need to do so again, for an equivalency has been forged between our star and Sol. Who tries to seed Earth's star, seeds ours at the same time."

The crowd became silent. "Now we will take back what was taken from us," Ael said. "It will require some time. Let the Senate be recalled. Let the Praetorate, as many of them as can prove they had no connection to the vile crime committed today, return as well. Let the Tricameron sit tomorrow, and declare the hostilities done. And when they come here, this will return to its rightful place." She hefted the Sword.

The nearest of the crowd actually backed away a little, as if they were afraid the Sword might leap out of her hands and do something unexpected. And then, gradually, the movement transmitted itself back to the rest of the crowd. Slowly they began to move away. The rearmost of them turned and began to leave.

Ael watched them disperse. Beside her, Arrhae watched them go as well, and lowered Spock's tricorder. She glanced over at Ael. "Commander-General, are you all right?"

Ael looked at her in surprise, and then laughed. "I was just lost in contemplation of my own folly. For somehow I was expecting something else. Do not ask me what!" She rubbed her eyes, which suddenly felt impossibly grainy. "But now . . ."

She let the hand fall, and laughed again. "Now my work is done," Ael said. "Or very nearly so. Shortly, tomorrow morning perhaps, I will no longer have a job. And it feels very strange! For I have only had this one job, all my life, it seems."

Arrhae reached out and took Ael's little radio from her. "*Enterprise?*" she said. "I think perhaps you might send a shuttlecraft for the commander. She will need a ride back to *Bloodwing,* or wherever she wishes to go."

"*On its way,*" Uhura said.

Ael let out a breath as Arrhae handed her back the communicator. "Where else would I wish to go?" she said.

Arrhae quirked an eyebrow at Ffairrl, and said nothing, as Ael looked out across the plaza and down the great avenue, silent again under the sun.

TWENTY-ONE

AT NOON THE NEXT DAY, the plaza was full. The next morning, when *Bloodwing* landed there again—quite cautiously, off to one side in a space pointedly prepared for it, and in company with one of *Enterprise*'s shuttlecraft—the whole place was simply packed full of people.

Kirk and Spock and Scotty and McCoy got out, as did Uhura and Chekov and Sulu, all in dress uniforms. K's't'lk followed them, ununiformed as usual. The group looked around at the crowd, who eyed them with curiosity, but not nearly as much as Jim had been expecting.

"What's our percentage of the gate?" McCoy muttered.

"Shush, Bones," Kirk said under his breath.

They walked toward the doors of the Senate; the crowd parted for them. As it did, one of the side hatches of *Bloodwing* opened, and Ael's crew came out, one by one, all in Grand Fleet uniform. They formed up into a double corridor between *Bloodwing* and the doors.

Then Ael came out, also in Grand Fleet uniform, but without the marks of rank, and in her hands she held the Sword. At the bottom of the ramp she paused for a moment, looking around. Then she walked briskly down between her people, who saluted with fists to chests in the old way as she passed.

At the doors, Ael and the group from the *Enterprise* met. Jim smiled at Ael. She smiled back, though a little somberly. "I think they are ready for us," she said.

"Then let's go in."

Ael went to the doors. Slowly they swung open.

There, in its many concentric rings, the Senate sat. Every Senatorial seat was full. But missing were the seats held by almost all the Praetors. Of the twelve, only Gurrhim tr'Siedhri stood in his place, rising as all the others did as the Sword reentered the chamber. Gathered all around the rings of Senatorial seating were a great crowd of noble House Rihannsu, politicians of every stripe, and members of families influential in business and public life. These stood silently and watched, and all their eyes were on what Ael carried.

Behind her, walking up slowly into the center of that great gathering, Jim saw something most unusual start to happen. He motioned with his hand to his people, and all of them stood still where they were. All around the circle, the Senators and all the rest who stood there to watch were beginning to drop to their knees as Ael passed. Jim had never seen such a gesture from Rihannsu before. It seemed illegal, somehow.

Ael walked up to the dais where the Chair still sat, unhurt. She held the Sword up in front of her, and for the space of several breaths it was the focus of every eye in that place. The sunlight that fell through the piercing of the dome onto the Sword seemed to illuminate everything else but the curve of that black sheath. Ael looked at it with a terrible, edged satisfaction, and slowly put the Sword back down across the arms of the Empty Chair.

Then she stood away, and turned.

The people on their knees did not get up.

"It is done," Ael said. "It is over."

Many eyes looked up at her from all over the room, but no one moved.

Ael began to look disturbed. "What are you waiting for?"

Gurrhim rose. "I believe they look for some word as to what part you will take in the remaking of the Empire."

Ael's eyes widened. "We have many things of more im-

port than that to consider at the moment. There are two
planets' worth of battle damage to repair, thousands and
thousands of Rihannsu dislocated in the uprisings who must
be housed. Fires to put out, roads and public works to re-
build—"

"And a people to be led," Gurrhim said.

Ael stared at him. "Ah, no. Gurrhim, are you mad? The
doctor's medications have unseated your wits at last. Your
children will be furious with me."

"His children," one of Gurrhim's sons said, coming up beside his father, "are in complete agreement with their father.
And enough of talking around your name as if you weren't
here, no matter how many times it might have been written
or burned. T'Rllallieu, enough of your prevaricating! You
have done your part so far. Now you must do the rest of it!"

There was a mutter of agreement from around the floor.
Ael looked from face to face of those nearest her, and in all
cases looked away again hastily—the expression of a woman
who does not like what she sees, and seeks a better answer
elsewhere. "Doubtless I will take some small part—"

"You will *not!*"

Quite a few people looked around in shock as the
youngest of all the Senators got up off her knees and came
out of the crowd to stand there looking at Ael. And then she
turned to the rest of them.

"Will you let her off so easily?" Arrhae cried. "She has
risked everything, again and again, for your sakes. She
deserves better at our hands! She has given us back our
mnhei'sahe, she has taken back the sun for us to live under
again, and driven off the shadow that has spread over us all
this while, sapping our strength, killing our pride. She has
brought her fate upon herself, and are we mad to let her escape it?"

The rest of the crowd was starting to get up off its knees
now. The closest of them started to move in toward Ael a lit-

tle. She moved just slightly, once, like a woman who felt she
wanted to run, but she held her ground.

"We are an Empire," Arrhae said. "Perhaps it is time now
we had an Empress."

There was silence at first. Then a very subdued mutter.
Then the mutter grew to a grumble, and the grumble to a
roar. "The Empress!"

It was a word Jim had never heard before in Rihannsu,
and he glanced to one side and saw McCoy say it once,
softly, under his breath, trying it out: *"Llei'hmnë."*

Ael looked horrified beyond belief. "This is nothing but a
road to tragedy. You are dooming yourselves! We are never
best led when only one leads."

"But never before did so many *choose* to be led!" Arrhae
said. "You are no Ruling Queen. Nor will be! We know you
too well. Her way was to order others where she herself
would not go. That's not what you have done."

"It is the sheerest folly!" Ael said. "No possible good can
come of such power concentrated in only one pair of
hands!"

"It would never be such," Gurrhim said, "and you know
it. We would look to see the legislative powers restored to
their old puissance. If they had an Empress looking over
their shoulders to make sure their jobs were being done correctly, then such would be all to the good. And as for the rule
of the many, too much we've seen of late how those many
may pull in three or twelve different directions, each serving
his own interests at the expense of the others' and those they
represent. Perhaps the little Senator here is right. Perhaps it
is time that we went down a new road."

"The Empress!" some of the people in that vast hall began
to shout again. "The Empress!"

Once more the scattered shout turned into a roar. Ael
looked helplessly over at Jim. He returned the look.

"This can only be an error!" Ael cried over the noise.

"The blood of your brothers is on my hands today. To make such a decision now—"

"It *must* be made now," Gurrhim said. "You know what danger it brings our people not to be ruled. For the moment, an Empress is what we need. You proved yourself apt enough to war. Are you afraid of failing to manage the peace?"

Jim thought he could see the answer to that behind her eyes, and he entirely understood it.

After a moment, she held up one hand. The shouting dropped off to silence; this too seemed to unnerve her. "We will hear what the captain says," said Ael.

"Me?" Jim took a few steps forward, looking around. "I don't think *they* need to hear me. Sounds like *they* know what they want. *You,* though—" He walked up to her. "You've known for a long time what you wanted. Your people, free to make their own choices, rather than being dragged into them. Now it sounds like they're making a choice. You've devoted your whole life to bringing about this set of circumstances, in which they could choose their own road. Now—" He smiled. "—suddenly you're going to part company with them again? I don't think so."

She was standing close enough to him now that she could be heard even when she spoke very softly. "Jim," she said, "you are serving me very ill, after all my good usage of you in the past."

Suddenly someone else was standing beside Jim. "Oh, you think so, do you?" McCoy said, speaking as quietly as Ael had. "Well, you'd better just be quiet now and take your medicine, because you've brought this on yourself. Admit it: you didn't think it through, did you? Oh, you saw *this* moment, all right! You saw the Sword back on its chair again, and all the rotten politicians and plotters and schemers chucked out on their kiesters, and then you had some hazy image of how it would be afterward—good politicians somehow magically rushing into the vacuum left by the old ones."

McCoy snorted. "Wishful thinking of the first order, Commander. You'd never fight a battle that way. Whatever made you think you'd be allowed to just fade away afterward?"

Jim, looking sideways, thought that it was a good thing his back and McCoy's were presently turned to the great assembly gathered before the Chair; that way none of them could see the sarcastic look McCoy had fixed on Ael. She looked from him to Kirk. "I would have thought that was what happened to old soldiers in your world," Ael said, sounding a little forlorn. "And what in your world or mine is a 'kiester'?"

"We'll discuss that another time," Jim said. "Meanwhile, *think*, Ael. Stay in office long enough to get things stable, and then bow out if you have to. But things are very broken loose right now, and they *need* you. More to the point, Starfleet needs you. *You,* sitting here, are the only one who can ensure that they'll leave you alone until you can put things back together again. And the Klingons will, too. You can always abdicate later."

She shook her head, more in indecision, Jim thought, than negation. " 'Office!' You heard them—you heard what they want to call me! I will *not*—"

"Ael," Jim said. "Remember the Fizzbin tournament?"
She blinked at him.

"Change the rules," Jim said. "If you're the first Empress of the Rihannsu, you get to change the rules. In fact, you get to *invent* them. Invent a new game!"

He watched the thoughts moving around behind her eyes—or at least he tried to. It was always a chancy business, trying to anticipate what Ael was thinking. Perhaps aware of his attempt to assess her thought, she bowed her head.

Then she looked up. "All of you," she said to those who were still on their knees, "stand up. I will not be one of these bow-and-scrape rulers who judge their own power by how much they can see of their subjects' backs."

The shouting started again, especially among Ael's crew, and in many cases, the shouting was composed as much of laughter as of praise.

"I will not sit in that chair," Ael said. "Someone fetch me another, and put it to one side. In that I will sit."

She sounded fretful, like someone being held to a bargain they never intended to keep. "Captain?" Spock said.

Jim glanced at him. "Would you excuse me for a moment?" Spock said.

"Huh? Sure, Spock, go ahead."

Jim watched with some amusement as the Senators on that side of the chamber rustled about a little, as Gurrhim went down among them and then went out of the room. A minute or so he came back with a chair not too dissimilar from the one across which the Sword lay.

McCoy let out an annoyed breath. "I thought I told you *no lifting.*"

Gurrhim chuckled and ignored him, putting the chair down by the Empty one. Ael turned and was about to sit down in it, when a voice said, "One moment, madam." Spock's voice.

Everyone turned to look. Then suddenly there was a great pushing back out of his way among those who were gathered nearer the doors, and many of the Senators craned their necks to see what was coming—and stepped back when they saw.

Through the middle of the Senate came Spock, holding something dark in his hands. The whole room rose as they saw it and recognized it as what it was: another S'harien, his family's heirloom, cousin to the Sword itself. Spock stopped in front of Ael as she stood in front of her own chair, and held the sheathed sword up.

Around them on the Senate floor, dead silence reigned. In a single swift and economical gesture, Spock unsheathed the S'harien. In all that sudden quiet, the sound echoed fiercely, and the light from the piercing in the roof glinted blindingly on the steel. In Spock's hands, the sword looked most improbably deadly.

Then he sheathed it again. "Madam," Spock said, "it is better that these two should be together. Let one be for the past, if you will, and the other for the future. The one may rest, and the other may be used."

A hiss and whisper of wonder went up among the people all around, then a patter of applause that grew slowly to a thunder, and then a roar of approval and cheering. Spock held the sword out.

Very slowly, Ael took it. She hesitated, as if calculating something; then she bowed her head to Spock, and sat down.

In the continuing roar, the rest of the attending *Enterprise* crew walked up to the throne—for so it was now—to greet her. Jim came up first, and reached out to take her hand.

"Not here," Ael said under her breath, giving him a look. "Are you still unclear what that means among my people?"

Jim grinned, dropped his hand, and sketched her half a bow. "Congratulations," he said, "Empress."

She bridled, though she tried to conceal it somewhat. "This is all your fault," Ael said under her breath.

"Guilty as charged," Jim said.

"I am going to see to it that you are duly punished by Starfleet," she said. "With something more onerous than admiralty, if such exists. If I must suffer, by my Element but I shall see to it that you do too."

Jim's grin got broader. "And our relations were getting off to such a good start. We're fighting already."

"You two cut it out," McCoy said from behind Jim, "or I'll separate you."

They both turned an amused look on the doctor. He gave them an innocent look. "You hesitated a little there," Jim said, glancing at Spock, who had stepped back.

"I was making a new rule," Ael said. "How much an Empress bows to diplomatic representatives."

Jim nodded in approval. "You've got a lot of that ahead of you today. Is this about right?" And he tried the bow again.

Ael tilted her head to one side. "A little insolent. But I am in a forgiving mood."

"Then we'll head out for the moment," Jim said, "and let you get on with it." He smiled at her, and turned away.

"Twenty hundred," he heard McCoy say to her behind his back. "Be there or be square."

The Empress of the Rihannsu nodded to him, smiled demurely, and beckoned forward the next group of those who waited to greet her.

The *Enterprise* crew all walked out together. "Spock," Jim said quietly, "do you think your father's going to approve?"

"He approved some months ago," Spock said, "when I first suggested the possibility."

Jim gave Spock an astonished look. "Some *months* ago?" He shook his head. "How could you possibly have known?"

They made their way out into the plaza. "Some threads of history," Spock said, "can seem surprisingly predictable when one examines them from a sufficient distance to perceive gross detail in the pattern. Perhaps I should simply say that our people are closely enough related that we have some patterns in common, and I saw a very Vulcan thing happening here: the best person for a job finding themselves thrust into it."

Jim nodded as they got into the shuttlecraft. "And your father concurred."

"Some time ago, as I said. In any case, that gesture will say more to the reconstituted Empire, and to the people of these worlds, about the intentions of the Federation toward them, than any number of treaties could."

Sulu buttoned up the shuttlecraft as everyone got settled.

"And now," Jim said, "we watch this whole part of space re-make its alliances and shape itself into something new."

"We can only hope," Spock said, "that the new shape becomes superior to the old."

"Or remains that way," McCoy said.

"Ever the cynic, Bones," Jim said as the shuttlecraft lifted off.

"Time passes, gentlemen," McCoy said, "and everything changes in time. But for the moment, we're off to a good start. Let's enjoy it while we can."

Jim nodded and leaned back, and the shuttlecraft leapt through the atmosphere toward the airlessness of space, with Eisn shining golden on her hull.

That night there was a celebration aboard *Enterprise,* as usual. Jim was at the heart of it, but he was hardly the guest of honor. That privilege was being reserved for another. At any rate, there were many other guests to see to—visitors from *Tyrava* and *Kaveth* and the rest of the Free Rihannsu fleet, curious Senators, various other prominent Rihannsu.

The guest of honor was late, but that hardly bothered Jim, considering that tardiness is royalty's prerogative across the known universe. When she finally showed up, the crew welcomed her with cheers, and then got on with their usual business of eating and drinking and engaging with their guests.

Jim watched with interest as she paused, not far from the door, and went down on one knee. It took him a moment to see what was transpiring—the crowd near the frontmost buffet table was in the way—but some of his crew were standing further from the table than they would normally have needed to. When the press of people parted, Jim saw Ael deep in conversation with what some people might have taken for some kind of igneous outcropping, but was actually Lieutenant Naraht.

He smiled to himself as he saw her lay a hand on that

bright stony hide, saw the Horta shuffle and wriggle under the touch with a touch of uncertainty, a wriggle that was in a way charmingly like a puppy's. He didn't quite understand what special thing there seemed to be between Ael and Naraht, but it struck him at the moment as just another manifestation of what *Enterprise* seemed to bring out in people—the ability of the wildly diverse to come together and make of its multiple selves far more than could have been reasonably expected. *But maybe that's the secret,* he thought. *We* expect *more . . .*

After a little, Ael stood and moved on through the crowd. Jim bowed to her as she approached.

Once again she eyed him and then laughed. "Still a little too insolent," Ael said.

"I've got some ale over here," Jim said, "and we can work on it."

He led her over to where McCoy and Spock were sitting. McCoy held out a cup to Ael. She sat down beside him, had a long drink of it, and then leaned back in the chair, glancing around at the three of them. "We have caught them," Ael said.

"Who?" Jim said. "The Three?"

"They were betrayed," Ael said. "Is it not apt? But those whom they had paid for a clandestine escape actually delivered them into our hands this afternoon." She let out a long breath. "At any rate, we may now lift jamming and transporter interdiction in the system. There is much to do, and we need everything running again."

"I'll tell Scotty," Jim said. "Or maybe you've already passed the word to *Tyrava.*"

She waved a hand. "Someone will coordinate it," she said. "I am told that wise empresses do not micromanage their staff."

Jim chuckled.

"So what will you do with them?" McCoy said.

"First," Ael said, "ask them a great many questions. Who

knows, perhaps I may even find out where my poor exiled niece has gone."

" 'First,' " Jim said. "And after that?"

Ael sighed. "I much fear that I must have them converted to the Empire's permanent custody."

"Sounds like a long time in stir," McCoy muttered.

"Eternity," Ael said, "or thereabouts."

McCoy stiffened, looking at her.

"Come, Doctor," Ael said. "You see the situation as clearly as I do. Mercy is wasted on such. Letting them live would be seen as proof positive of my weakness. I can afford no such misconceptions among my enemies right now. They are in disorder, but given a whisper of reason, they would begin to draw together again. I intend to give them no such cause. If I must seem ruthless now, it will be in service of many decades, perhaps even centuries of peace later, for millions, perhaps billions of my people. I will not risk so fair a chance for the life of men who have had their chance, and squandered it."

"It must be nice," McCoy murmured, "to be so certain."

Ael simply looked at him; then glanced away. "It would be, I am sure. But here we run aground on the rocks of cultural differences, Doctor. Those men would have murdered your homeworld. I think we would probably be well rid of them. Yet as of this morning I also have in hand a communiqué from the President of the Federation, requesting that they be extradited." She sighed. "So that may yet sway me. Either way, they are safely disposed for the moment."

She held out the ale cup for a refill. "After all," she said to Jim, "you were chaffing me with it the other day. Am I afraid to lose the peace? Of course I am. Only a madwoman would not be. So I will walk warily for a while. Besides, for the time being, we are much dependent on others for our security, and I would dislike to alienate those who have so far been such good friends."

Jim leaned back, nodding. "We'll be guarding your borders for some time," Jim said. "Until Grand Fleet is rebuilt, and your new HQ is established."

"It will be a joint headquarters," Ael said, "split between the Two Worlds, and no longer sited in space. Space-based facilities we will have as before, but I will no longer allow administration to be based above the world and looking down. It needs its feet, as your people would say, firmly on the ground, in order to keep in touch with those it serves. There, Starfleet's model will serve us well." She looked at Jim thoughtfully. "Though some careful thought will have to be given to find ways to keep the new Grand Fleet from distrusting and ostracizing its more, shall we say, proactive commanders?"

They both smiled. "As for the borders," Ael said, "yes, I accept that assistance with thanks. But not for too long. Otherwise my people will start to become restive."

"The Klingons will soon enough be along to test your border," Jim said. "When that happens, call. We'll find a way, I think, to be in the neighborhood. After all—" And he didn't care if he looked and sounded a little bitter. "—we got what we paid for."

"The price," Ael said quietly. "Yes. It is on my mind as well. Not only others' lives, but the price we have paid in our own experience, our own pain. Still, would you have it any other way? Would you willingly serve a less trying master than you do?"

Jim thought about that. "Maybe not."

"And so it has been for me," Ael said. "Even though I am in worse position now than ever I was, for now I serve the Elements Themselves. Oh, do not give me that look," she said. "This is not . . . what do you call it? A religious matter. But when you rule so many people, the sense of the Elements' continued attention becomes rather surprising. No matter. I will cope."

"Speaking of which," McCoy said, "I meant to congratulate you. What a whopper you told those people yesterday."

She looked at him innocently. "Why, whatever do you mean?"

"About Sol and Eisn being in permanent equivalence."

Ael smiled very slowly. "There are, I think," she said, "good lies and bad lies. Would you agree?"

McCoy raised an eyebrow.

"That, I think," said the Empress of the Rihannsu, "will be a good one. Let them think no threat between our peoples of that kind is possible. You, of course," she said to Jim, "will help Scotty and K's't'lk finish their work in taking the Sunseed technology permanently off the gaming table." She cast an amused eye at the poker table off behind them. "So the trouble that brought us together at the beginning will be solved at last."

Jim nodded.

"Meanwhile," Ael said, "Mr. Spock, I cannot thank you enough for the great gift you have given me in your sword. Or rather, that you have given my people. It was a gesture that is already being deeply discussed."

Spock bowed his head to her.

"And I bet I know in what context," McCoy said. "Reunification."

Ael's eyes went distant and thoughtful. "There's a dream worth dreaming," she said, very softly, as if afraid someone might overhear her and take offense. "But I much doubt it can come in my time. Right now my people are bruised and battered enough. Such an idea must wait a time when the Rihannsu truly feel themselves strong again—strong enough that such a move could not possibly be seen as weakness. No, that's a matter for a century hence. *You* may see it." The look she threw at Spock was challenging. "But you will not have the handicaps under which I must labor, these decades coming."

Spock said nothing, only looked thoughtful himself. Ael shook her head. " 'Someday' must take care of itself," she said. "Just at this moment, the thorny 'now' will be more than enough trouble to keep me very busy."

They all glanced up as several people approached. It was Arrhae and Ffairrl, and Aidoann with them. "Here then," Ael said, "comes the Empress's Lamp, as the office will be called. The Senator will serve as an adviser, and an aide in, shall we say, alien matters."

Terise Haleakala-LoBrutto smiled. "Captain," "Arrhae" said, "we didn't have a lot of time for this earlier. Perhaps I may make known to you 'Ffairrl'—by his right name, Ron Ruis. He was my steward on *Gorget,* and a lot more, it turns out."

"When I left," Ruis said, "my rank was lieutenant commander. Elements only know what it is now." And Jim's eyes went wide, for the man's accent suddenly was pure Bronx.

"But Terise wasn't the only Earth-originated agent on ch'Rihan," Ruis said. "Some of us have been there a long, long time. Some of us have made strange friends along the way, or were placed with them to begin with." He glanced across the room at Gurrhim. "And more than one of us have wound up working both sides of the street. It seems," he said, looking at Terise with amusement, "to be an occupational hazard."

"I'll be staying on, Captain," Terise said, "and under cover. I think I can do my best work here, in the Senate, helping it find its feet. The local government has apparently already vouched for me with Starfleet." She looked slyly at Ael, and grinned.

"Indeed," Ael said, looking up with an expression in which amusement was well mixed with annoyance, "I have no intention of letting this young woman go anywhere. She was instrumental in dooming me to my present position. I shall make sure she stays within arm's reach to suffer as I suffer. And so may her associate," Ael said, glancing over at Ffairrl, "to whom I wish all luck in assisting in her political career, which is likely to become lively, as the rest of the Senate try to come at me through her." She waved a hand. "Off with you now, my children. They are eating your share of the dainties over there."

Arrhae and Ffairrl bowed and went off, but Aidoann stayed, and Ael reached her up a cup of ale. "Aidoann will remain with me too, for a while," Ael said. "I will be needing a steady second-in-command. The rest of the crew—oh, they will still be with me from time to time: but they have their own homes to find, or found, now, and their own lives to pursue."

"In an Empire at peace," Jim said.

Ael drank, looked over the cup at him, and finally set it aside. "I can give you no assurances in that regard, Captain," Ael said. "I will control my people as best I can. But the Klingon situation will remain volatile. That grudge is an old one now, and the Klingons have done nothing to try to mend it. It will take many years to teach my folk not to hate them, if indeed it can be done at all. And until that day comes, if it ever does, we will attack them when we may come at them, take back from them what they have taken from us, and defend what is ours from them when they try to take it."

"Surely that won't be anytime soon," McCoy said. "There are too many imponderables floating around, and they prefer an easy game to a hard one."

"True, but their memories can be short when their own Imperial policy is served. If they would leave us alone, we would be glad enough to do the same for them. What odds would you give on that happening?"

McCoy recognized the smile. He had seen it over a hand of cards not too long ago. "Probably about the same as for a busted flush," he said. "But then the Chancellor will be realizing, now, that the flush on the other side all of a sudden is royal."

Ael knew the hand of which he spoke as well as he did, and bowed her head to him. "I am assuming they will be too Klingon to admit being frightened of us for the moment. And as memories fade and the sound of boasting grows louder, even the memory of *Tyrava,* like death's shadow at the battle of Artaleirh, will begin to slip. We will have to remind them. Fortunately we now have the resources to create many more like *Tyrava.* As I gather the Empire back together, it is possible that there will be worlds that want no more of any empire, for good or ill; worlds that want to go their own way, or peoples whose planets have suffered so in this conflict that they desire new ones. Such peoples we must see safely on their way. It means a new fleet of generation ships, though at least this time the populations who leave us will not be lifetimes about it."

"Khre—" Aidoann stopped, then, and laughed. "Madam." She made a slight face at the word, and perhaps only McCoy fully understood how strange the word sounded that no one on ch'Rihan or ch'Havran had previously used of one of their own species: the address-form of *Llei'hmnë,* "Empress." "Madam, there are those who will see your letting such people go as a lesser weakness of the same kind as letting the Three live would be."

Ael stretched her arms out before her, let them fall again. "They'll soon enough learn I am not weak in the ways they think. Oh, I will not be cruel. When there are people who need killing, I will not hold my hand. But as for staying in the Empire-to-be, or leaving it, that decision all but the innermost coreworlds must make for themselves. Eventually, even those. Forcing the Outworlds to participate in Empire without consulting them, or hearing their voices raised in protest, was the seed of this problem. I will not compound the error. Our behavior toward them will give them the data they need to decide whether to go or stay. But I have a number of years of bad habits to train our people out of. Or to attempt to." Ael briefly looked grim. "Even I have only so many years to me. Some day, by knife or disruptor or disease or just time's long malady, some day I will fall; after that, the peoples of the Empire will do as they will, and those who survive me will discover, only then, how well or ill I did my job."

The assembled group glanced at one another. "Morbid," McCoy said after a few seconds.

"Ah, McCoy," Ael said genially, "in your job you see as much death from day to day as any of us. Possibly, in the long run, more. You surely would have to agree that ignoring mortality is the best way to invite it. I am merely turning my eye toward necessary precautions. It's good to have a plan, and to strike the last item off the list."

She smiled at Jim, and stood. "Aidoann," she said, "go you and tell the escort I am ready." Aidoann smiled at them and went.

Jim and McCoy and Spock stood to see Ael off. "I cannot stay any longer," Ael said. "Already they await me, down-planet. Until we all meet again, whenever it may be, I bid you go with the Elements."

Spock bowed his head slightly, then glanced up again, and Jim could make nothing of the look that passed between them. But McCoy's eyes went wry, and he reached under his tunic and pulled something out. It was a card. He held it up between him and Ael for a moment, letting her see it.

It was a woman, royally robed, big-bellied with child, sitting on a wide and splendid throne that at first glance seemed built of dark stone, but stars and the endless night of space were buried in that stone, intractably fiery and reaching back through unplumbed darkness to unlikely depths. The dark-haired woman was crowned with those stars, some of them tangled in her hair like fireflies on a summer night. The woman gazed into the distance, holding a scepter that blazed at its end with one star shining paramount beyond all the others. Water flowed behind the woman's throne, on the card; the wind blew through the trees in the near distance, and at the feet of the great snowcapped mountain behind her, fire ran down half-seen hills. The word IMPERATRIX was written on the bottom of the card.

Ael took the card and looked at it closely, then glanced up at McCoy. "I did not see this card in play the other night," she said.

McCoy smiled gently. "It was in play," he said. "Without a doubt. Take it as a keepsake."

Ael took the card and tucked it away. She gave to Spock and McCoy the same small bow she had given to Jim the day before, then turned to him.

"Perhaps you will see me to the door?"

He nodded. They walked together through the revelers, human and alien and Rihannsu together, and Ael nodded and smiled at all who greeted her until the two of them came out past the crowd.

"And one last thing," she said to Jim as they came to the doors. "It must be handled now, for I fear that this is as private as we will ever have a chance to be again."

Uh-oh, Jim thought.

She paused a little way from the door. "Enough dealing with superficialities. Let us finally, now that we have the leisure, to say a word about what has not as yet been said openly between us."

Uh-oh! Jim thought again.

"Loyalty," Ael said quietly, "honor, and friendship—these are the banners we have been holding up between us, we two, for quite some time now. But they are not why we are here. Not *just* those. Are they?"

She moved a little toward him.

Jim stood his ground. "No, I would say not."

She moved a touch closer. "I am glad to see you ac-knowledge it."

And then she reached into a pouch at her belt and handed him something. It was a little green-metal cube, about the size of a small apple, and except for its shape, rather like what Gurrhim had brought aboard *Enterprise* with him.

"This is what Starfleet sent you for, the President tells me," she said. "This is what brought you all this way. Tech-nology. You would have stolen it if you had to. Loyalty, to your orders, yes, that would have bound you to the theft. Oh, you would have asked first! And then done your best to steal better technology than what we gave you, fearing, perhaps correctly, that we would give you less effective material, and keep the best for ourselves."

She gave him an ironic look. "But so far you have held your hand, not just to keep from interfering with the achieve-ment of my goals, I think. So it is my pleasure to give you freely what even the President of the Federation is not sure I will give you. The thing you need, the thing you came for—and the reason I am now Empress of the Rihannsu."

She smiled. "Is there anything else you need?"

All Jim could do was shake his head. "*Damn* you, woman!" he said, but very quietly.

Ael smiled.

Then Jim reached down. "Was there anything else I needed, did you ask?"

And he took her hand, and touched it in a specific way.

Ael's eyes widened.

"Also, one last thing. I didn't dare ask McCoy," Jim said. "You'll have to tell me if I pronounce it correctly."

Jim leaned close to her, and spoke a word.

She did not look away.

"Yes," Ael said. "Yes, that would be about right."

And then she freed her hand, and reached up to take his face between her hands, and drew him close.

A moment later she let him go. "Is that how it is done?" she said.

Jim couldn't say a word.

"I go," Ael said. "Call on me when you need help from this side of the Outmarches. But bear in mind that things will change here, and may do so unexpectedly. When they do, I will react as I must. It has even occurred to me that, if matters do not go as I plan, you should not be surprised if, for some while, I and all my people might close our borders, and vanish, to put our house in order. At that time, the less Federation presence there is in our systems, the better."

Jim nodded.

"It will not last forever," Ael said. "Nothing does. But after such a withdrawal, or absence, when we appear again, possibly you should not be surprised if we do not look, or act, as we do now. There is always the possibility—"

"That something will go wrong?"

"That something will go as the Elements please," Ael said, "and not as we plan. They will have Their way. Perhaps our plans will coincide with Theirs. If not—" She shrugged, and turned again, heading for the door, and the Imperial escort waiting outside.

"But who knows?" Ael said, as the door opened, and she stepped through it. "In the name of peace, just to reassure other species, you understand, who can say? We might even start calling ourselves 'Romulans.'"

EPILOGUE

THE SEQUELAE of the Romulan Civil War (as it eventually became known in the Federation) naturally lasted for many months. The war's repercussions traveled as if on slow-moving wavefronts all across and through that part of the galaxy; political and trade alliances among worlds shifted to accommodate it, and here and there, in the spaces on either side of the Neutral Zone, planetary governments fell or were radically changed. Inevitably, on both sides of the Zone, historians started their work, sifting through all the available data to support their own theories of what had been going on, and why, and how. A few of them actually got close to the truth.

As is so often the case, those closest to it had least to say in public on the subject. In some cases this was because they were bound by the exigencies of circumstance, or service-based oaths of confidentiality. In others because the events they had striven to bring about were best served by their silence. In a few cases, it was a combination of the first two, as well as just being too damn busy.

James Kirk would have fallen into the last category. What with one thing and another, it was almost two months before he and *Enterprise* made their way back into Earth orbit for a long-scheduled, much-needed dry-dock period. Jim's time off, as was so often the case, was much delayed by the business of getting his ship and people settled in. He had two appointments that were the first things he'd wanted to handle on returning, which turned out—after a most exhaustive debriefing at Starfleet Command—to be the last.

The first of these was in an office in Paris, as evening fell, and outside the office window the lights began to race up and down the Eiffel Tower. Jim stood there in his dress uniform, chafing in it somewhat as always, and received from the President the Federation "Medal of Peace" decorations for Spock, McCoy, Scotty, and himself—the decorations that none of them would ever be able to wear in public, because no part of the reason they'd been awarded could ever be revealed.

And having done so, Jim was able to sit down with the President and give him a piece of his mind. It took quite a while, and the President sat there and took it like the seasoned campaigner he was, watching Jim thoughtfully over one of the pair of glasses of brandy he'd poured. At the end of it, when Jim had run down—it took him nearly an hour—the President refilled Jim's glass.

"Every word you've said is true," the President said. "No one should ever have to be in the kind of position in which I put you. But I won't say I'm sorry, because I saw what needed to be done, and you were the only man to make it happen. I have only one question to ask you. Will it have been worth it?"

"I'm not sure yet," Jim said. "But in the long run, I think so."

The President nodded. "Thank you," he said, and raised his glass.

Jim hesitated, then lifted his glass and touched it to the President's.

They stayed there talking until quite late—one of those long discussions that reminded Jim, as he left, that the loneliness of command comes in many different forms and qualities. But the late night led in turn to a late morning, so that he was delayed in checking out of his Paris hotel, missed his originally scheduled beam-up time, and had to call *Enterprise* for another. As a result, it was half-past predawn twilight before he materialized on a stony hillside in the middle of what had once been the Sespe Condor Preserve in the wilds of central California.

The gully wound down and away through the hilly ground as it had when he was last here—a lifetime ago, it seemed. Everything was utterly still except for the thin trickling sound of the little creek that ran down through the gully, off to his right. A thick mist lay in the gully, hiding the water from sight; the top layer of the mist shifted slightly in the light of a setting moon just barely past its full.

Carefully—for the footing was uncertain in this twilit mist—Jim started to walk up the length of the gully, paralleling the creek as he headed for its source. Sometimes the mist hid the smaller watercourses that fed into this one, little stony runoffs that were live only in the rainy season, so that he stepped down onto the tumbled stones about twice as far as he thought he was going to have to; once he almost twisted his ankle in one of these. But he just smiled to himself in the predawn light, and kept on going.

The damp smell of wild olive and scrub oak around him, of sage and piñon, seemed to get stronger as the sky lightened. Jim reached the place where the rough path by the live streambed had been blocked by a fall of rocks from the steeper bank on the right. He crossed the creek, missing his footing once, splashing into the water and cussing absentmindedly at the cold of it. But just a little way beyond him, farther up the hill, was the place he had been heading for, the last thing he needed to do.

The old wild olive tree was deeply rooted in the steep hillside, just above the source of the spring that fed the creek. More bears had been at it since Jim had been here last: deep splintery clawmarks zigzagged the largest trunk where it reached out over the downfalling water. Jim paused, sniffing at a faint charred smell that hung in the damp air. Some of the tree's upper branches were missing, others broken over sideways, still others scorched. The tree had been hit by lightning again since he'd been here last.

One branch, though, much slenderer than the main trunk, had not been touched. Its leaves were sparse, and unlike the last time, there were no olives; this was the wrong season. But the pennon hung where he had left it. The red polymer of the pennon was unfaded, the glyphs on it still in clear contrast, getting clearer by the moment as the dawn grew slowly nearer.

Jim glanced around to find the best way up, over a few newly fallen boulders, and scrambled up onto the olive's main trunk. Carefully he stepped out toward the branch where the pennon hung. The branch hadn't yet broadened out enough for the polymer strips holding it in place to sink much into the branch's rough bark, but olives are slow growers.

He pulled out his phaser and took careful aim. The first shot severed the nearer of the two strips, so that the pennon slumped down, hanging by just the remaining strip with the other top corner folded over the first couple of glyphs. But Jim didn't need to see them to know what they said. If his memory had needed any refreshing, the memory of the pennon's twin—now hanging as a standard outside the Senate on ch'Rihan, bearing glyphs as tall as a man—would have been more than adequate to the task.

But only one such standard was needed. That name would now be remembered and spoken again in the world that had given it birth, and in many others. Or at least the first three words of it would be.

Very quietly, Jim spoke the fourth word of it, the name not written on either pennant. One time for each of the Elements he spoke it, as was appropriate, and then one last time for the Archelement that encompassed them all, that It might know the soul that owned that name to be home again at last. And with the fifth repetition he fired once more, severing the second fastening. The pennon fluttered down toward the water.

His final phaser blast reduced it to its component atoms well before it hit the stream. At first the thought of that name vanishing in fire one more time had troubled him, but she'd told him not to be concerned. *As you see,* he could still hear her saying, *I have come through the Fire and out the other side. From that Element, at least, I've nothing further to fear. The rest of my life's problems, now that my name is written again where it is, will be made of Earth and Water and Air. That's the destiny I've wrought for myself. Now, set me free of Earth—* She'd smiled at the pun. *—and get back to finding your own.*

Jim stood there for a moment, looking up into the swiftly lightening sky. The stars were fading, but still he waited.

And somewhere down the watercourse, a California jay suddenly spoke up, making a noise like an extremely rusty hinge. Then it made it again, much louder.

Jim let out a breath of amusement at himself. *Hanging around here like someone waiting for a sign,* he thought, *while there are things to do. Destinies to find.*

He put the phaser away and pulled out his communicator, flipped it open.

"Enterprise, *Commander Uhura.*"

"I'm done here," Jim said. "Any time you're ready."

"*Yes, sir. Transporter room, one to beam up.*"

The captain of the Starship *Enterprise* vanished in dazzle. A few moments later, the rising sun cresting the hillside above the gully struck through where he had been, throwing the olive's shadow stark against the slope.

Only a few breaths after that, silent, riding the wavecrest of morning, the condor planed by over the stream—its wings bloodied by the new morning's light—banked sideways, briefly silhouetted against the setting moon, and was gone.

ABOUT THE
AUTHOR

Diane Duane has been making her living writing fantasy and science fiction for more than a quarter century, and has written for *Star Trek* in more media than anyone else alive. Born in Manhattan, a descendant of the first Mayor of New York City after the Revolutionary War, she initially trained and worked as a psychiatric nurse; then, after the publication of her first book in 1979, spent some years living and writing on both coasts of the United States before relocating to County Wicklow in Ireland, where she settled down with her husband, the Belfast-born novelist and screenwriter Peter Morwood. Her work includes more than forty novels—a number of which have spent time on the *New York Times* best-seller list—and much television work, including story-editing stints on the DiC animated series *Dinosaucers* and the BBC educational series *Science Challenge,* a cowriter credit on the first-season *Star Trek: The Next Generation* episode "Where No One Has Gone Before," and (most recently) another on the Sci-Fi Channel miniseries *Dark Kingdom: The Dragon King,* written in collaboration with her husband. When not writing, she conducts an active online life based around her weblog (http://www.dianeduane.com/outofambit), her popular "Young Wizards" novel series (http://www.youngwizards.com), and her European recipe collection (http://www.europeancuisines.com), while also stargazing, cooking, attempting to keep the cats from eating all the herbs in the garden, and trying to figure out how to make more spare time.